THE MAGIC SEEKER

A FAIRY TALE WITH BENEFITS

The
MAGIC
SEEKER

JANE BUEHLER

Published by Emily Jane Buehler
PO Box 1285, Hillsborough, NC 27278 USA
https://janebuehler.com

Publisher's Note: This is a work of fiction. Names, characters, businesses, places, events, locales, and incidents are either the products of the author's imagination or used in a fictitious manner. Any resemblance to actual persons, living or dead, or actual events is purely coincidental.

The Magic Seeker (Sylvania Book 6) / Emily Jane Buehler
ISBN (print): 978-1-957350-16-5
ISBN (ebook): 978-1-957350-17-2

Library of Congress Control Number: 2025917156

To all of us who don't know where we fit in

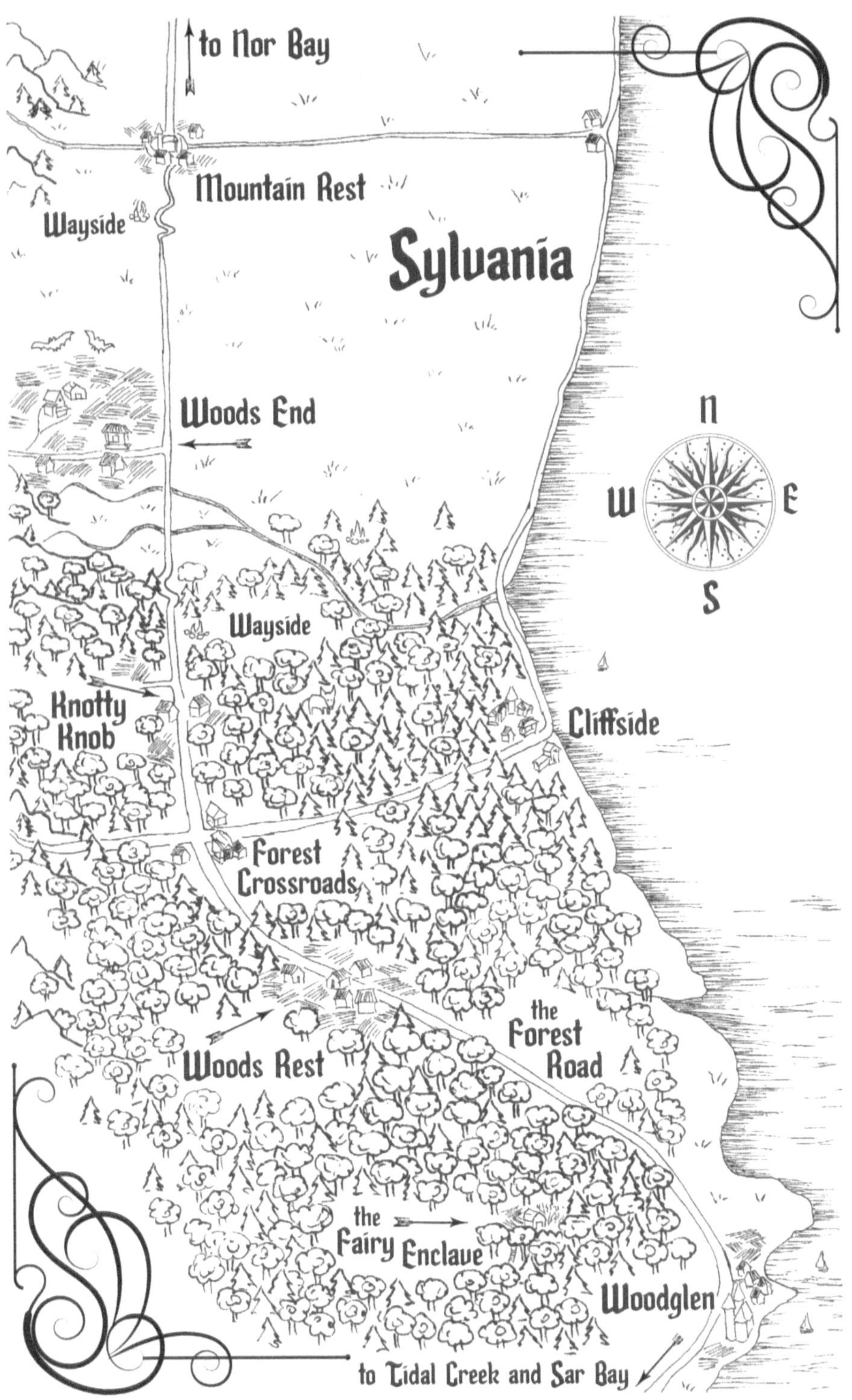

to Nor Bay
Mountain Rest
Wayside
Sylvania
Woods End
N
W   E
S
Wayside
Knotty Knob
Cliffside
Forest Crossroads
the Forest Road
Woods Rest
the Fairy Enclave
Woodglen
to Tidal Creek and Sar Bay

Chapter 1

SNOWDROP LEANED HER BROOM AGAINST the rocky wall of the underground passage. She cupped her hands together and gently enclosed the crane fly flittering along the rock. The fragile insect must've slipped into the caverns by mistake.

"There's no mates for you in here, little one." It bounced against her fingers. She didn't dare adjust her hands for fear of hurting its long, delicate legs.

She turned toward the mouth of the passage and walked carefully along with her arms out in front. Only dimly glowing lamps powered by sun magic lit the space. And if she tripped, she might hurt the crane fly.

She could try to reach the insect with her own magic—the tiniest bit, communicating her desire to help it. If she could calm it, it might ride in her hands without the needless fluttering, risking damage to its wings. Could she use magic properly this time? Slowly, she sent peaceful thoughts out into the air and toward the crane fly.

But something dark stirred in the back of her mind.

She closed her mind off, wiped it blank, stared at the rocks around her as she walked, all to ground herself in the mundane setting. The darkness inside her mind faded.

Snowdrop sighed—she'd known it would happen. Why had she even tried? The very thought of using magic could bring on the dark feeling she dreaded—menacing, dangerous. If she continued trying to reach the crane fly, she risked killing it in her attempt to communicate with it. Because her magic always came out wrong.

She passed through the barrier marking the edge of the caverns—not a solid barrier but a magical one that appeared solid to humans. As a fairy, she could see it but she could walk right through.

The caverns weren't exactly secret anymore, not since Queen Oleander had been overthrown. But after a human had wandered in and gotten lost, the fairies had decided to maintain the illusions at the entrances. To a human—without magic—the outer entrance resembled any old rock. And even if someone did get through and came down the steps, they'd find a short passage ending at a rock wall. They'd even feel the solid rock if they touched it. They'd need a fairy to teach them how to pass through it.

Besides, it wasn't like the humans had any right to come wandering through the fairy caverns. The fairies didn't barge into human homes, walking around gawking at things. But the fairies could now visit the human villages and occasionally traded for the strange tools the humans made. And a few fairies had gone to live in Woodglen and Woods Rest, the two nearest villages. That had happened only after Oleander was deposed. Oleander had forbidden the fairies from leaving the caverns, much less venturing into a human village.

Oleander. Also known as Mother.

The passage sloped upward and a warm breeze touched Snowdrop's face. She hadn't been outside in a few days. She'd forgotten the season. Shade and sunlight dappled the steps ahead. She squinted as she reached the bottom of the steps and the daylight brightened. The breeze brushed down on her, sifting through her ashy white hair. She climbed into scattered patches of morning sunshine, breathing deeply the forest scents of grass and earth and decaying leaves. Oak trees surrounded the exit. The season was still summer, but barely—the smattering of brown and orange among all the green overhead hinted at the coming change.

She opened her hands and the crane fly bobbed out, adjusting to the breeze. "It's still warm out," she told it. "There's time to find a mate and lay your eggs before fall."

It hovered over her hands. Maybe it would land and rest a moment. But a breeze caught it and it cartwheeled away until it disappeared against the craggy branches and the bright blue sky beyond the trees. Snowdrop exhaled, wishing the little insect well.

She paused a moment. Even without anyone nearby, the forest made more sounds than the caverns—leaves rustling, morning birdcalls, the harsh caw of a crow somewhere in the oak branches, the drone of insects. The early sunlight fell softly in broken patches that shifted with the stirring leaves. The damp ground beneath her bare feet was cool, but sunlight warmed half of her left foot as if inviting her to step forward into its full glow. Her long bangs blew across her cheek and into her eyes. When she tucked them back, her rough fingertips scratched against her skin.

She could live out here. Most of the fairies had homes in the trees and used their rooms in the caverns only when the cold of winter drove them inside. Some didn't even return for the winter. After being kept underground by Oleander for so many seasons, they never wanted to go back inside.

But Snowdrop couldn't live out here. The fairies didn't want *her* living among them. For one thing, she couldn't manage any of the tasks the fairies needed help with. Gardening, crafting, foraging . . . they wove their magic into everything they did, either to get it done faster or to make a better result. That was why she swept the caverns. Cleaning was about the only task she could do.

But also, she didn't want to make everyone uncomfortable. Even the sight of her frightened the others—she could tell by the way they shied away from her or flinched if she lifted her hands. They were scared of her magic. Not the normal fairy magic, the kind she couldn't perform.

The magic she *could* do was what scared them.

Snowdrop turned back to the steps. The chill of the rock hit her soles and whispered around her bare ankles and calves below her cut-off trousers. Living alone in the caverns all summer wasn't so bad. She stayed in the rooms she'd shared with Oleander and her servants. She had more space than anyone.

But before she descended, she gazed around at the trees one more time. Nature always brought comfort. She was content with her life in the caverns. She didn't expect more. Yet seeing the sky and trees and feeling the wind and sunlight made her feel . . . like she had a friend? She had to remember to come up here more often, even if only for a moment.

A tiny brown wren swooped across the clearing and landed on the nearest trunk—its little claws gripped the bark, holding on sideways as its tail flicked up for balance. It looked at her. It opened its beak and let out a volley of chirps.

Snowdrop sighed. "Hello, Marshmallow." She didn't need to understand whatever the wren was trying to tell her. Only Dustan would send a bird to find her, and Marshmallow was his most eager messenger.

Marshmallow darted off the tree toward her but veered sideways—as if he thought better of landing on her. He perched on a low branch. His beady eyes stayed on her as his head twitched this way and that. Her brother must want something.

"Fine. Let's go." She started along the path out of the copse and toward the gardens, and the bird swooped by. As she cleared the trees, the sunlight slanting in warmed her. The packed dirt was cold from the night but that wouldn't last on such a clear day. Marshmallow flitted along on her right, one tree to the next, occasionally rooting around in his downy feathers with his beak before fluffing himself up and taking off. She let her senses reach out to him, only listening, and a vague sense of pride came to her—the silly bird was glad she was following so he could impress his favorite fairy.

She stopped herself from trying to learn more. If only she could use her magic! Communicating with animals would be so . . . so . . . It would be so *fun*.

Snowdrop walked around the gardens. Tangles of dried-up vines filled this side of the empty garden, with the last few summer squashes and cucumbers clinging to them. A few blossoms dotted the thick green stalks amid the browning leaves, but the first frost would come before they produced fruit. She passed the garden supply sheds, one with tools and one with seeds and the long third one with the transparent roof where the garden crew sprouted seedlings. This late in the summer it housed sacks of potatoes for planting next spring and the baby strawberry plants that would soon go in the ground. Beyond was the open pavilion where the crews bundled garlic and packed root vegetables for storage, and where they would sit around laughing when they took a break from the work.

A distant hammer blow rang out behind her. North of the gardens was a rocky courtyard where the fairies had a forge. The absence of trees and plants made the walled-in courtyard a safe place to use fire. This past summer, two new wielders of fire magic had been found. Only a few fairies possessed fire magic: the skill of turning dragon fire into the powder that would keep a fire burning hot with no fuel. The two had been working with their dragons in the forge all summer. And since one of them was a child, her mother was there as well, practicing her blacksmithing.

The trail wound south past one of the orchards. Voices called through the apple-heavy trees. The low sun pierced through the leaves as Snowdrop located the workers on the far side. Some were up in the trees and others held baskets on the ground. She ducked her head and her bangs slid forward to hide her face as she kept walking into the shade of the trees.

"Good morning, Snowdrop."

Snowdrop startled and looked up. She blinked as her sight adjusted to the shade. Holly stood at the edge of the trees with a full basket in his arms. The older fairy led one of the garden crews, consisting mostly of younger fairies who now clustered behind him. A few were her age—they all stared at her and in back, one leaned in to whisper to the fairy beside her.

"Good morning," Snowdrop whispered. She cleared her throat as her hands curled around the hem of her tunic. Words bubbled up—to tell them she'd been sweeping the caverns, that she did contribute, she wasn't just dallying in the forest while they worked. But no one was accusing her of anything. Should she ask about the harvest? Would that sound normal?

"Here." Holly balanced his basket on his knee and handed her an apple from the top. "Fresh off the tree. It's a plentiful harvest."

"Thank you." She tried to smile at him—at all of them—but the smile stretched unnaturally across her face. She nodded a few times and started walking again. Marshmallow chirped from a branch and darted after her, and the whispers of the fairies followed her.

The apple filled her hand, a rosy red fading to light green. Her belly rumbled and a flat taste leaked onto her tongue. She'd forgotten to eat that morning. And she hadn't eaten much yesterday, come to think of it. To partake in the fairies' community meals, she had to leave the caverns. She tried to arrive late to avoid the worst of the crowd, but sometimes she was too late and other times she simply forgot.

She took a bite of crisp, cool apple, sweet and fresh like being out under the stars. For some reason, her chest tightened and she needed a few deep breaths to loosen it back to normal. She continued walking on, eating the apple.

At the south end of the gardens, the path wound into real forest. She walked past rope ladders and under treehouses the fairies had built. Unlike the caverns, the forest was filled with murmuring voices. When she reached the clearing where the fairies held dances and other gatherings, she couldn't help gazing in. Children ran laughing across the grass, and a couple lounged on a blanket in the sun.

Even when Oleander had had everyone trapped in the caverns, the fairies had made friends, fallen into lust or love, and sometimes had children. Oleander couldn't stop them from living their lives any more than she could stop the cycle of the seasons. Even Oleander's four sons had managed to build lives and have adventures. Only Snowdrop had been stuck, forever by Oleander's side.

Marshmallow dove past Snowdrop's face with a chirp. She had drifted to a halt while watching the children.

"I'm coming," she told the bird. "Hang on." At the edge of the clearing were the remains of the morning's breakfast. Val was just clearing the dishes. Snowdrop took the last bite of her apple and tossed the core into the bin of scraps for the compost pile. Val looked up.

"I could take the dishes," Snowdrop said.

Val smiled gently. She was small and quiet, just like her name plant, Lily of the Valley. "Thank you, Snowdrop. But you washed them all yesterday. I can do it."

Snowdrop nodded and smiled back. Her smile felt natural this time. If it weren't for her past, she and Val probably would have been friends.

She followed Marshmallow away from the clearing and onto a side path to the tree where her brother and his mate lived. The ladder was down. Marshmallow clung to the trunk as Snowdrop climbed, hopping along and chirping as if she needed encouragement. As she neared the top, he launched himself upward and disappeared, trilling like mad. By the time her view cleared the wooden patio floor, Dustan was waiting outside the cottage to give her a hand off the ladder.

Dustan was the youngest of her four older brothers and had always been her favorite. Mostly because he was the least awful . . . although she couldn't truly call him awful anymore. Since he'd fallen in love with Rose, he'd become a lot more caring. She eyed his dark messy hair.

"What are you doing awake this early?" she asked.

"Rose got me up."

"Why don't you ever comb your hair?"

"Rose likes it messy."

"Stars, you're hopeless," she said, but she smiled a little.

He ran a hand over his head, making the peaks of hair worse. "Thanks for coming."

"Is something wrong?"

"Didn't Marshmallow sing? Marshmallow was supposed to sing cheerful songs to let you know it wasn't an emergency."

"Oh, that's what the chirping was about. I thought he was trying to show off."

The wren swooped out the open cottage door and landed on Dustan's shoulder. Dustan usually gave the birds seeds after they helped him, but Rose must've done it because Marshmallow wiped his beak a few times on Dustan's shirt, pecked him once (lovingly, of course), and flew away.

"So nothing's wrong?" Snowdrop asked again.

"Um, no. No, I— I don't think so."

"You're not convincing me."

"Come on in and I'll explain," Dustan said. "Have you eaten?"

"Holly gave me an apple."

Dustan crossed to the cottage door and disappeared inside. Snowdrop followed slowly, scanning the leafy branches and the shady patio. A pair of chairs against the cottage wall faced outward so one could sit outside and gaze into the trees, and a rumpled blanket rested on one seat as if someone had recently stood and left it behind. A low railing marked the edge of the wooden terrace.

Living here in the forest must be nice. Rose and Dustan had hinted many times that she could live out here. They would help her clean up one of the old treehouses or build a new one if needed—she knew they would.

But what right did she have to live out here like any other fairy? As if she could leave behind the caverns and everything she'd done there. Everything she'd been a party to. Nothing she could do would ever make up for the harm she'd helped Oleander cause.

And even if the other fairies said it wasn't her fault, no one really wanted her here.

Light filtered in the treehouse windows as she entered. They were open to the summer air. Like most fairy abodes, this one had only the barest of furnishings: a solid wooden table at which Dustan now sat, a shelf with pottery bowls, the woodstove for heat in the cooler seasons, a woven rug on the floorboards.

Rose came out of the back room carrying a bowl. She'd changed since the first time Snowdrop had seen her, when she'd come to the caverns to rescue the half-human children Oleander had used as servants. Rose had the same bright green eyes and chin-length dark hair. But while she'd projected confidence that first time, now she was imbued with it and completely at home in the forest. Maybe falling in love with a fairy prince and being chosen as the fairy queen had given her unlimited confidence.

Rose beamed at Snowdrop. "Come in. Here, this is for you." She set the bowl on the table. It contained yogurt covered with blueberries and golden bits of something crunchy looking. Oats?

Snowdrop took the seat near the bowl and Rose sat beside Dustan, who reached for her hand as if he couldn't be beside her without touching her. Snowdrop resisted rolling her eyes. She didn't want to be cynical about how sappy the two of them were, when she truly was happy her favorite brother had found someone—even if that someone was half human.

"Are you going to watch me eat?" Snowdrop asked, picking up the spoon. She scooped yogurt onto it with a berry and some of the oat clusters. She peered at the odd food.

"The humans call it granola," Dustan offered. "It's delicious."

"Because it's made with an excess of honey?" Humans had terrible eating habits.

"Just a little," Rose offered. "Besides, the oats are healthy."

"Did you call me here to feed me?"

Rose bit her lip and folded her hands in her lap, leaving Dustan's hand empty on the table. She looked at him. He cleared his throat but stared at the bowl of yogurt.

Snowdrop ate the bite on her spoon. Tangy yogurt, sweet berry, and wow, the granola was tasty. She crunched through it. "Did you make the granola?" she asked Rose.

"What? Oh, no. It's from the village baker in Woodglen."

Snowdrop narrowed her eyes as she scooped another bite. "What's with you two? Have I been banished? What don't you want to tell me?"

"Of course you're not banished," Dustan said, not picking up on her sarcasm. He faltered again. He looked at Rose with big eyes, and Rose caved like a house built of sticks. She turned to Snowdrop, the smitten-with-Dustan light lingering in her eyes.

Ugh, the two of them!

"We're worried about you," she said. "All summer you've stayed in the caverns. We barely see you."

"You know you don't have to clean down there," Dustan added, but Rose took his hand and squeezed, and he hushed.

"It's wonderful you contribute that way," Rose said. "We just want you to be happy. But it seems lonely for you to be down there all the time."

"I am happy," Snowdrop said automatically. "Not everyone needs . . ." She gestured around at the cottage. A loving home. Friends, partners, family. She couldn't quite meet Rose's gaze.

Dustan cleared his throat again. "Snowdrop," he said gently, and the unexpected tone made her throat tighten. "What our mother did to you wasn't right. She kept you isolated."

"And who let her do that?"

Dustan ignored her jab. "She should've let you learn to use your magic with the other children. You should've been allowed to make friends—"

"No one wanted to be friends with me. No one *wants* to be friends with me."

"They would if they knew you. No one blames you for the things Oleander did."

She shifted in her seat. He didn't know that. "But they fear me."

Her brother didn't argue. Fairies as a rule were bad liars. Although some of them had sneaky ways of getting around the truth.

"You could learn to use magic," Rose said. "I learned to see through illusions, and Rowan learned to use his fire magic this summer. You don't need to start as a child."

Hope prickled inside her, but Rose was wrong—she could never learn. "I don't need magic. Humans get by without it."

Dustan leaned in. "But learning magic might make you feel more connected here."

"You don't understand," Snowdrop said. "I've tried. And I can't."

An awkward silence followed.

"We need help with something," Rose said.

Snowdrop looked up. "Help?"

Now Rose was making a pleading face and her hands lay flat on the table. Dustan reached for one and it trembled as he took it. Snowdrop narrowed her eyes. Half fairies weren't so bad at lying. But Rose was awful at it. What was she nervous about?

"Yes," Rose said. "We need help and we thought of you."

Snowdrop sighed. "What do you want me to do?"

Rose straightened. "The Council of Villages is having their first official meeting. It's in Mountain Rest to the north. Representatives are gathering from all the villages across Sylvania. Guests are even coming from Norland and Merlandia."

"You don't want me to go, surely?" Having her represent the fairies at such a meeting would be ridiculous.

"Not alone. Larkspur is going as our representative, and we'd like you to travel with her as an assistant."

"Larkspur?" Larkspur was one of the fairy elders. Snowdrop had encountered her a few times—most notably when Oleander's child servants had become sick. Larkspur and her friend Thistle, the fairies' best healer, had come to take the children away, one by one as they succumbed. Remembering those times still brought on a mess of emotions—the ache and the guilt and the anger.

"Dustan was going to go," Rose continued. "But something has come up and he needs to travel to Tidal Creek, in the opposite direction."

Dustan's fingers on the table curled into a fist, and he pulled his hand holding Rose's hand toward him. This "something" was the thing causing their nervousness.

"What has come up?" Snowdrop asked quietly.

Rose again turned to Dustan and this time she nudged his arm.

He reluctantly sat up. "The village elders in Tidal Creek sent a message. Odd things have happened in the past moon and they can't figure out why. Things like animals disappearing and crops dying. They asked if the fairies could send someone to investigate."

"But why you?" she asked. Dustan was skilled with magic, but many of the fairies could use their skills to investigate—questioning the local creatures about anything they had seen and identifying signs of illness among the plants.

"Some travelers passed through the town who weren't merchants or researchers or the like. The men wouldn't give any details about themselves. And the problems started shortly after. Ever since, the townspeople have spotted figures in the swamps who disappear into the mist when the townspeople call out. They think it might involve rogue fairies."

"You know a few fairies left this enclave when Oleander lost power," Rose added.

"The bad ones," Snowdrop muttered.

Rose deflated. Snowdrop couldn't understand how she always saw the best in people. Even Rose had to admit some of the fairies had done terrible things to gain Oleander's favor. "We hoped the ones who left would find somewhere to live and not cause trouble," Rose said. "But if they are interfering with humans, it's our responsibility to stop them."

"I still don't see why it has to be Dustan, though."

Rose looked to Dustan and when he didn't speak, she continued. "We think it might be your oldest brothers causing the trouble."

Snowdrop shuddered. Aside from Oleander, her twin brothers Beech and Sycamore were the meanest fairies she knew. The one silver lining was they were both terribly unskilled at using magic.

"But what harm can they do?" she asked. "Those two couldn't convince a mouse to do anything for them, much less a herd of livestock."

"There are tools more powerful than magic," Dustan said. When Snowdrop shook her head, he added, "Human inventions."

Dread crept up her spine. The humans invented all kinds of things using wood and metal and fire. Some of the inventions were useful, like clever garden implements beyond the simple tools the fairies used. But others were awful, like their guns, which existed only to kill other living things, or the glass chambers they used to imprison other creatures. If her brothers had turned to human inventions, they might be even worse now than they'd been in the past.

"So Dustan has to deal with our horrible family," Snowdrop said. "But what makes you think Larkspur will travel with me?"

"She asked for you," Dustan said.

"She did? Me?"

"Aye. She, um, she offered to give you magic lessons."

Snowdrop sat up, her eyes wide, and her next breath was filled with hope. Larkspur was one of the oldest and most skilled fairies. If anyone could help Snowdrop learn, it would be her. Maybe she'd have ideas on how to stop the dark magic from rising the way it did each time she tried.

"Why would Larkspur ask for me, though? Why would she offer to teach me?"

"You'll have to ask her." Dustan's shoulders relaxed, projecting the calm confidence he lived with that things would always go his way. And they did go his way. But Rose's fingers tapped on the table and her eyes darted between her mate and Snowdrop.

"What aren't you telling me?" Snowdrop asked.

"Nothing," Dustan said, but he winced. "We simply want you to travel with Larkspur as a companion and assistant, and she'll help you with your magic. And you'll see the continent and get out of those caverns for a bit."

Snowdrop turned to Rose. She lifted her brow and waited.

"You'd be traveling with humans," Rose said. "Not many, but Larkspur arranged to ride with the representatives from Woods Rest."

"I don't mind humans," Snowdrop said, and Dustan snorted. "What?"

"You're somewhat critical of humans," he said.

"I am not. It's their stupid behaviors I criticize. And how they put sugary syrups on everything they eat and how they talk loudly all the time."

"Well regardless, you'd be traveling with them. You'd have to be polite."

"I'll be polite."

"So you'll go?" Rose asked, and her big green eyes were wide. She gripped Dustan's hand on the table and bit her lip again.

"Fine," Snowdrop said.

Rose beamed even brighter than before as Dustan pushed out his chair and stood. "Wonderful. Pack your things and I'll take you to Woods Rest on Redbud. We can be there by nightfall."

"What, today?"

"The traveling party leaves tomorrow morning," Dustan said, as if packing up and leaving home for a moon or two were no big deal. Maybe it wasn't for him, but other than a few visits to Woodglen, she'd never been outside the fairy enclave.

"But don't you have to go to Tidal Creek?"

"I'm waiting for Larch. I promised Rose I wouldn't try to deal with them on my own. So I have the time to bring you to Woods Rest." Dustan came to take her hands. "Snowdrop," he said, and he used the gentle voice again. He was probably using some kind of magic on her, to calm her. Maybe he'd made a potion and put it in the granola. "Give it a chance. Try going somewhere new, try learning magic again. Larkspur will watch out for you. The humans will be friendly. You deserve to be happy, too."

She nodded. But he was wrong. She didn't deserve any such thing.

Chapter 2

⋇

AFTER LEAVING DUSTAN AND ROSE, Snowdrop crossed the fairies' clearing to reach the closest entrance to the caverns. Val and her cart of dishes were gone. On this side of the central fields, a work crew knelt in the dirt, transplanting seedlings. She kept her face down and circled around the gardeners. Maybe this whole "travel with Larkspur" thing *was* a ruse to get rid of her for a while. To give the fairies a break from seeing her lurking in the shadows. She wouldn't put it past her brother.

But if Larkspur had asked for her . . . ?

Maybe Larkspur truly wanted to help with her magic. Maybe she felt sorry that Snowdrop was still an outcast even now that Oleander was locked away.

Or maybe Larkspur wanted to atone for the way she'd misled Snowdrop about the sick children—making Snowdrop think they had died. Anger flared hot and sharp in her chest. She understood why the older fairies had deceived her. But thinking the children were dead had devastated her.

Snowdrop breathed in and out deeply to calm herself. That was the past. Maybe Larkspur really could help with her magic. She'd focus on that.

As she descended the steps into the familiar cool dimness of the caverns, she exhaled and her fists unclenched. Almost no one had been down here all summer. She could move through the passages without the constant tension of watching for others.

But soon she'd be traveling! She was tempted to go to the enclave's library to check the large map of the continent that hung on the wall but she had no time.

And besides, she had stared at that map so often she had it memorized: The forest to the north ended at a human town called Woods End (humans were so unimaginative!) and a grassland spread out toward the warmer northern region. What must that look like—all grass and no trees? She'd be able to see clear to the mountains, if the map didn't lie. And maybe the humans wouldn't be too annoying. They might not know anything about her past—that would certainly help them like her. She could start over.

She grabbed a satchel from a storage room and hurried to her chambers to pack her clothes, comb, and twig toothbrush. Her short-sleeved cream-colored tunic would be fine for today, but she stuffed her long-sleeved knitted sweater into the bag. She took a few stretchy bands to tie up her hair. One of the fairies had invented them last winter using thin knitted bands and elastic spider silk—and magic, of course.

As she finished packing, unease gnawed in her belly. She'd never left home for more than a day. She'd never slept anywhere but her pallet in Oleander's rooms—her rooms now. How did one even find a place to sleep in a human village?

Never mind—Larkspur would know what to do.

Should she take shoes? Like most fairies, she went around barefoot, but the humans might find the habit strange.

Well the humans could deal with it. If she needed to wear shoes for the meeting, Larkspur would know where to find a pair.

She glanced around the room. A few of Oleander's possessions remained on the shelves, dusty and dull. For all her dislike of humans, Oleander sure liked their pointless trinkets. Snowdrop didn't need anything else. She was done here.

Unless she wanted to visit Oleander before she left.

Her chest tightened at the thought—not with the nervous excitement of leaving the fairy enclave but with dread. She hated visiting Oleander. Dustan said she didn't have to, but if she didn't, no one would. And if she didn't go, Oleander might become angry.

Not that it mattered. Oleander couldn't hurt anyone anymore. But Snowdrop had lived most of her twenty-three winters avoiding making Oleander angry. She couldn't shake the habit. Once a moon, she forced herself to walk down the tunnel to the fairy prison. It had three small apartments and only Oleander lived there. She must be lonely.

But each visit was the same: Oleander whining about how the fairies kept her locked down there, blaming Rose (like Oleander's horrible behavior was Rose's fault), and wheedling Snowdrop to let her go. As if Snowdrop could! The fairy prison didn't work like the human version—it didn't have human locks and keys. Magic kept it shut and the only way for Oleander to get out was to become a better fairy.

But Oleander hadn't become better at all. Not only was she not sorry for the things she had done, but she also seemed to have no inkling of which actions had caused her to be locked in the prison in the first place. She'd harmed innocent people, fairies and humans. And children! But she recalled "the old days" with longing. After five minutes with her, Snowdrop would be irritated. She'd let her mother talk as long as she could stand to listen and then make an excuse to leave. And she would feel guilty the rest of the day: for leaving her mother, for the children, for everything.

She wouldn't visit. But how long would this trip take? She might be gone a whole moon. Oleander would be upset with her if she left without saying goodbye . . .

So what? What could Oleander do? She was contained in the fairy prison. She couldn't use her dreadful magic to hurt anyone anymore.

Snowdrop swung the satchel over her shoulder, closed the door to her chambers, and started along the passage. She had enough on her mind today without a visit to her mother. She'd visit when she returned.

She hurried through the passages to the northeast exit, the one that came out next to the barn. The sun was rapidly climbing the sky as she ascended, and the shade of the trees that surrounded the exit was shrinking. Behind the barn, a few goats grazed out in the pasture.

Inside the barn, the dark silhouettes of the horses were framed by the wide entrance at the far end, which opened onto the pasture. Clover was sweeping out one of the stalls. As Snowdrop entered, ey looked up, squinting into the sudden light streaming in the open door.

"It's Snowdrop," she said, and quickly added, "Dustan's meeting me here."

Clover's shoulders relaxed. "Are you riding today?"

"He's taking me to Woods Rest on Redbud."

Clover looked to the horses and a single breath passed in silence before her brother's horse, Redbud, snorted, rubbed noses with the others, and plodded into the barn toward Clover. Snowdrop watched as the short-haired fairy stroked Redbud's side with a callused hand. Clover was so lucky, getting to manage the stable. Maybe in a different life, Snowdrop could have been eir assistant.

Redbud was a beautiful dark brown horse with a chestnut mane. Snowdrop had always been jealous over her—why did her brothers get horses and all she ever got were ingredients for the tinctures Oleander wanted her to brew? When she'd asked, Oleander had said Snowdrop didn't *need* a horse because she never went anywhere, as if it were simply a fact and not Oleander's will keeping Snowdrop at home.

Oleander had used the brothers—Dustan, Larch, and the older twins, Beech and Sycamore—to bring her things from the human village or to travel across the country for ingredients, like the sweetly scented vanilla the sea merchants brought to Nor Bay or the cranberries that grew only in the colder climate to the south. Snowdrop would have loved to escape the caverns and travel on errands like that. Especially if she got to do it on a horse.

She hovered inside the door. Clover looked up. "You can come in if you want."

Snowdrop edged closer and reached her fingers out to Redbud. The horse rubbed her soft nose against them and Snowdrop stroked her forehead.

"She likes you," Clover said. Eir green eyes watched her and for once Snowdrop looked back. Only a pace separated them but Clover didn't twitch away from her.

"She said that?"

Clover nodded. "Your brother still rides bareback, if I remember."

"Yes."

"I'll leave you to wait for him. Let me know if you need anything." Ey patted Redbud one last time and stepped away, retrieving a bucket from the stall ey'd been sweeping and heading past the other horses into the sun. The horses lumbered after em. Ey hadn't even asked why Snowdrop was going to Woods Rest, as if it were a normal occurrence. Maybe the other fairies didn't notice her as much as she assumed.

Redbud snorted against Snowdrop's fingers. A moment later, Dustan entered the barn. His gaze darted over Snowdrop.

"Here," he said, lifting a bundle in his hands. "Fire powder in case you need it, but let the humans manage without it if you can. We still don't have a lot. Besides, humans take great pride in starting the campfire."

"Now who's being snotty about humans?"

"I'm making an observation. But about that . . ."

He hesitated, and Rose wasn't in the barn to help him out. Snowdrop dropped her chin and lifted her brow.

Dustan inhaled and made eye contact. "I know humans can have odd habits. But most of them are very nice. You could make new friends if you give them a chance."

Snowdrop squinted one eye. "Okay . . ."

Dustan sighed. "Sometimes you come across as very rude."

"Me? Rude?"

"You make sarcastic comments and I know you mean to tease, but to someone who doesn't know you, you sound condescending and cruel."

Snowdrop's mouth dropped open.

"I want people to know how kind you are, and I want you to try to be friendly on this trip."

Snowdrop stared and Dustan looked away. He patted Redbud's nose and she butted up against his hand.

Snowdrop shook her head, trying to clear her confusion. People thought she was rude? She never insulted people to their faces. But Dustan worried that people would find her disrespectful. She blinked a few times and shook her head again. "Okay," she managed to whisper.

"I brought the rest of the granola for you," Dustan said, changing the subject, to her relief. "Pack it up and we'll get going to Woods Rest."

She knelt on the dirt floor to open her pack and add the new items. "How big is Woods Rest?"

"Not big at all. We'll find Larkspur easily."

"Dustan," Snowdrop said as she stood, "the children are in Woods Rest. Not Elle, but the others Rose rescued."

"Aye, what of it?"

"I don't want to upset them."

"Why would you upset them?"

"If they see me. I took care of them for many winters. They might remember me. And their mother, Maryanne, she's the one who hates fairies, right?"

"I wouldn't say she *hates*—"

"I heard you and Rose talking about her."

Dustan paused. "Maryanne is not fond of fairies. But you're worrying for nothing. I can hide us if she's around."

Dustan was skilled at all types of magic. He probably couldn't make an entire horse with two riders invisible, but he could change his own appearance with no effort at all. And if he took her hand so they were touching, he could change hers as well.

Dustan stroked Redbud's back and vaulted himself on. He held an arm for Snowdrop, and she gripped it and pulled herself up behind him.

"You know," Snowdrop said as Redbud took a step, "I could ride Redbud myself. She wouldn't have to carry both of us."

"Do you think you could?"

Snowdrop shrugged. "The humans do it without magic."

"But they use other tricks to communicate with the horse. They tap the horse's sides with their knees, things like that. They have to practice."

"I could learn."

"Who would get her home?"

Snowdrop scoffed. "You know Redbud doesn't need a rider to get home."

"I know. I want to make sure you find Larkspur."

He'd just said she'd be easy to find. Snowdrop closed her eyes and exhaled. He was right—she didn't know how to communicate with a horse and riding off as if she did would be foolish. And besides, much as she'd love to ride Redbud alone, she was glad he'd be with her when she arrived in Woods Rest. Even if the village was small, she didn't know where anything was located, least of all Larkspur.

Redbud clopped past the other horses and out into the meadow. Clover waved from across the grass by the pump as water gushed into eir bucket. Insects droned in the hot sun and the goats looked up as they passed. The goats were wild. They came down from the mountains for the winter and often showed up at the fairy enclave if food became scarce. Sometimes a few of the lady goats stuck around after the spring, sleeping in the barnyard and snacking on the goat treats the fairies made in exchange for their milk.

The fields had different scents than the forest, sweet and damp and grassy. She inhaled deeply. A trodden path began under Redbud's hooves and broadened into a double track wide enough for a wagon. The track led into the forest. Redbud picked up speed and soon they were jostling along beneath the thick leaves.

The track took them to the forest road, as the humans called it, their wide passage through the forest from north to south. The same road continued all the way to Nor Bay and Sar Bay on the far tips of Sylvania. Redbud turned north toward Woods Rest.

"Hold on tight," Dustan said, and the moment Snowdrop curled her hands into his shirt, Redbud took off.

Wind rushed over Snowdrop and through her long hair, pushing back the bangs that usually framed her face. She closed her eyes and inhaled as the air surged past her. Redbud's hooves pounded on the dirt road, obliterating the rustling of leaves and birds.

Dustan tensed into a crouch in front of Snowdrop, holding them both on the rocking horse. He would let Redbud run as long as she wanted, Snowdrop knew. She clung tightly to her brother but turned her head and opened her eyes. The nearest trees flashed by.

She was leaving! She was going somewhere. She wanted to feel elated, momentous, but her insides were a stew of nerves and questions and uncertainty and doubt that she should be leaving home like this at all.

She'd seen the forest road before, and she had visited Woodglen a few times with Rose or Dustan. She knew what a human shop was and how humans lived in cottages on the ground and had bakeries where they bought bread if they didn't want to make their own, and pubs where they gathered to drink ale and socialize, the same way the fairies gathered in the clearing. She knew humans segregated themselves into small families and came together only for occasions.

But she'd never spent any time among them. She'd never slept in one of their buildings or eaten in a bakery. Getting on Redbud and riding away from her whole life was strange.

At last Redbud slowed to a canter and Dustan settled on her back. Snowdrop loosened her grip. They rode in silence for a while.

"I didn't say goodbye to Oleander," Snowdrop said at last.

"Good."

"You don't think it was wrong?"

"You shouldn't visit her at all. She wouldn't visit you if you were the one in prison."

"You don't think she cares about us?"

Dustan paused. "I don't know what goes on in her head. But she certainly never acted like she cared."

Snowdrop didn't reply. Her feelings toward their mother were so confusing.

"Look at what she did, Snowdrop," Dustan said, as if he knew she was swimming in doubt and saw a chance to convince her. "Not only to the fairies, keeping them trapped in the caverns for so many seasons. She brainwashed all the fairies into thinking humans were a threat to us. She used the humans' children as servants. She convinced us all that humans had the brains of a sheep and wouldn't miss a child. When I refused to seduce Rose, she locked me in a cage."

"I know."

"Human mothers are different than fairies—they keep their children close for many winters, until they're adults and even longer sometimes. They never stop caring about them. Taking a child away is about the worst thing you can do to them."

"But did Oleander know that?"

"I don't know. But I doubt she cared enough to find out. She was wrong to take the children, regardless."

Snowdrop couldn't argue. Oleander had hurt so many people. And if she never acknowledged it, the fairy prison would never let her out. Why couldn't Oleander just admit she'd been wrong and try to change? Did any chance exist that Oleander might become a better fairy?

"How is Jane?" Snowdrop asked at last. "I heard hammering at the forge this morning."

"They're well. Rowan is already able to make fire powder, and Elle is learning fast."

That was lucky. The fairies had almost run out of fire powder because no one had been able to make it for so long. Only it turned out there *had* been a fire magic user among them—Rowan, her brother Larch's best friend. As children, Larch had sabotaged Rowan's attempt to leave the caverns to go with his dragon and learn to use his magic.

Then last spring, a dragon had appeared in Woods Rest, called there by a half-human, half-fairy child named Elle who possessed fire magic. Quite ironically, Snowdrop thought, Larch had sired Elle by seducing Elle's mother, Jane. He'd stolen Elle to be one of Oleander's servants. But when Oleander was overthrown, Elle was rescued and returned to her mother. Who then fell in love with Rowan and convinced him it wasn't too late for him to learn to use his magic, too. All summer, Elle, Jane, and Rowan had been camped out at the forge along with their two dragons.

Snowdrop knew all this only from talking to Dustan and Rose. She never went near the forge because she feared Elle would remember her. She had cared for the child for a turn of the seasons before Rose rescued her. And if Elle remembered her, seeing her again might upset the child.

Elle's presence at the enclave was another reason she had stayed out of sight in the caverns when the other fairies moved out into the forest homes in the spring. Jane would never bring her child back underground, so if Snowdrop stayed down there, Jane and Elle would never have to see her. Jane didn't know who she was, but Rowan certainly did. Things were better this way.

"And Jane?" Snowdrop asked again. "Is she learning?"

"She'll be a fine blacksmith with more practice. She made Rose a flower."

"She made a flower?"

"Out of iron."

"Why?"

"It's pretty, I guess? Who knows. As long as she's happy."

"You think she's happy?"

"She's got Rowan tumbling her every night. What do you think?"

Snowdrop cringed behind her brother. As if tumbling were the secret to happiness. And why was he talking about Jane's personal life that way? "How would you know what they're doing?"

Dustan laughed. "She comes for tea with Rose sometimes. They talk about all kinds of things when they think I'm sleeping."

"When you're lazing about in bed, pretending to sleep."

"Waiting for my love to come wake me up, so I can pull her—"

"Ugh, stop!" Snowdrop frowned at the back of Dustan's head. Why did fairies think sex was the answer to everything? She'd tried it a few times when she'd first reached the age for it and didn't see the allure. "I'm glad Jane has Rowan," she conceded. "After how Larch used her, she deserved to find someone nice. Where is Larch, by the way?"

"He went on a merchant ship to the eastern islands as an ambassador. At least that's what we told him. Mostly Rose didn't want him around this summer while Jane is nearby. But he's on his way back now that we have to investigate this situation in Tidal Creek."

Larch was like a cross between her other brothers, Snowdrop figured. Sometimes he'd been kind, but he'd wanted so badly to impress his older brothers that he'd usually gone along with whatever scheme they were involved in.

Beech and Sycamore were the worst. They were many winters older than Larch and a pair of morons. Neither one of them could use magic well. Like Snowdrop, they hadn't learned with the other children, but they probably could have. Oleander had let them do as they pleased. And all they'd wanted to do was drink elderberry wine and inhale moonflower dust and tumble anyone who'd have them. They never worked at anything or put effort into anything unless Oleander ordered them to.

After Oleander's fall from power, the twins had disappeared. Without Oleander supporting them, they weren't as much of a threat. But if they ever returned to the fairy enclave, they'd probably end up in the prison beside her. Whatever long-ago fairy had created the magic permeating the prison had done a miraculous job. When someone was inside it, the magic knew when to let them go. It knew when they had paid the price or changed inside, when they were truly sorry and had changed enough to live a better life.

"You're quiet," Dustan said.

"Do you want me to talk all the way to Woods Rest?"

"I just want to know you're all right back there."

"I'm fine." The nervous knot in her stomach persisted, but nothing Dustan said was going to make it go away.

"I should've said this to you a long time ago," Dustan said, and Snowdrop stilled. He took a deep breath. "It was wrong how we left you with Oleander. She let the four of us have freedoms you never did. And I don't think she would have let us run around the way we did without you there to occupy her. All her attention was on you and we were glad of it because we didn't want to deal with her. But it wasn't fair to you."

Snowdrop's throat tightened for the second time that day. Inside, the familiar resentment simmered hotter. But Dustan couldn't undo the past any more than she could. And at least he recognized the part he'd played.

"I'm sorry, Snowdrop." He half-turned on Redbud's back until he could look Snowdrop in the face. "I'm very sorry. And if I can do anything to make up for it, I hope you'll ask."

Tears pricked her eyes. "You've been kind to me," she said. "You and Rose both."

"You deserve more than your brother and his mate being kind to you," he said. But she wasn't sure she did.

He faced the road and they continued in silence. Noontime

passed and they stopped for a rest and the lunch Dustan had packed and then resumed their journey. Late afternoon came before they left the thick woods and trotted out into a wide meadow—not as sprawling as the ones at Woodglen because here trees lined the edges of the fields. Recently shorn sheep rested in the shade under an elm alongside the road, behind a wooden fence.

A few minutes later, they ambled past a cottage. It resembled the ones she'd seen in Woodglen, with a thatched roof and a garden beside it. But the detritus of human life littered the yard—a wheelbarrow parked on the side, a leaky-looking barrel in front of the window, a pair of shoes in front of the door, and a lone sweet potato on the front stones as if it had fallen from someone's load and no one had bothered to pick it up.

"Humans are so sloppy," Snowdrop murmured to herself.

"Be nice," Dustan replied.

Right. No more sneering at the humans. She had to remember.

They passed another cottage, and a cluster of taller buildings appeared ahead that must be the center of the village. People moved about in the open square and a hammer clanged on iron. Snowdrop shrank behind Dustan.

"Give me your hand," he said, reaching out to his side.

She put her fingers in his and the tingle of his magic raced up her arm and over her head.

"What did you do?"

"Made your hair purple and gave you tusks."

"Dustan!" She tried to pull her hand away but he held on. Everyone would stare!

But her brother laughed. "I'm teasing. I made your hair even longer and whiter and aged your face. No one will recognize you."

She exhaled. "Thank you."

"You know, you don't look much like the Snowdrop of last summer anyway. Not with your long hair and the light color."

She didn't reply. Her mother had created a dye to color Snowdrop's hair the stark brown most of the fairies had. She didn't need

another reason to stand out, her mother had said. So when Oleander was locked in the fairy prison, Snowdrop's hair had shifted to
its natural color. She could make the dye herself—it didn't involve
magic, just a color made from nuts that appeared brown even to
other fairies. But she didn't bother. And she'd let it grow long, not
even trying to hide the pale tresses. Everyone was already staring
and keeping out of her way, regardless.

Redbud stopped at the edge of the village square. Humans
swarmed everywhere—standing, walking, pushing a wheelbarrow,
or chatting with others. Voices drifted in the air and the scent of
baking bread made her mouth water. Buildings lined two sides of
the open space. They were shops, based on the humans coming
and going with baskets and bags. Across the way, a stone wall
with an iron gate enclosed a grassy area and flower garden. A large
stone building with a tower stood behind it.

Dustan gestured to their left, where a road veered off the square
between more shops. "Rose's friends live that way in a large stone
house."

Rose's friends . . . and Oleander's victims.

"Most humans can't afford to keep a horse," Dustan continued. "If we ride into the square, we'll draw their attention. But we
could dismount and walk in, if you want."

"No," Snowdrop replied quickly. "I can go on my own if you
tell me where." She scanned over the people in the square. Three
men sat on the porch of one building. Older folks were playing a
game with rolling balls on the far side. None of these people could
be Maryanne, the mother who lived in Woods Rest and the main
person she hoped to avoid. "I don't need to hide."

He squeezed her hand and let go, and his magic slid off her like
raindrops off a duck. He kept his arm out and she gripped it as she
climbed off Redbud. Her toes hit the road and she stretched her
feet, then her legs and back. Much as she loved horses, it was good
to be on her feet again.

Dustan pointed at the second building from the right, the one with the men on the porch. One of them stood and nodded at the others, spoke a few words, and stepped down. He ambled across the square and headed north on the forest road. The others said goodbyes as they stood and shook hands.

"That's the village pub," Dustan said. "Larkspur and the others are meeting there this evening. You can wait for her out front or inside."

"Do you know what it's like inside?"

"Remember the White Pony in Woodglen?"

"The place where Rose drank two mugs of ale and you had to carry her home?"

"Aye, that place. It's like that."

Snowdrop grimaced. It had been dark and full of people. And she hadn't much liked the taste of human ale. Which was how Rose ended up drinking two mugs of it.

"The pub owner's a good man. Well, I assume he's a good man. If he weren't, Larkspur wouldn't be tumbling him."

Snowdrop blushed. There he went again, talking about other people's business. "How do you know that?" she asked. "Does she come round for tea, too?"

"No, but Jane was here the first time Larkspur came to meet the Woods Rest elders and their village representatives. And she spotted Larkspur and the barkeep being, uh, friendly with each other. And then *Jane* came round for tea and told Rose. Because they're gossips."

"Maybe Larkspur and the barkeep are friends."

"He had her up against a wall with their hands in each other's clothes."

"Ugh, you're the gossip! What was Jane doing there?"

"Jane was cutting through an alley from the forges to the square and stumbled upon them by accident."

"Stars above." Snowdrop shook her head, wishing they could go back to the part about her waiting out front or inside. Was she the only one in the world not tumbling anyone? She always felt a little bit like a failure when she heard talk about such things. Because it was obviously so much fun—everyone said how amazing it felt, and had been saying so since she was a teen—but when she'd tried it, she hadn't felt much at all. Over the seasons, she'd kept thinking something would change, that she would learn how to do it better or find a better partner, or that she'd suddenly start to crave sex the way other fairies seemed to. But nothing changed. Why didn't sex work for her? All she could think was that something was wrong with her body and she had no idea how to fix it. Maybe that's why it bothered her to hear how everyone in the world aside from her was tumbling everyone else and loving it.

"And speaking of the lady Larkspur," Dustan said, "look who it is."

Larkspur was crossing the square toward them. Her familiar face and long gray braids pinned in a crown on her head calmed Snowdrop. She didn't exactly have a relationship with Larkspur but since her childhood, the older fairy had always been around. Watching. As if she'd been checking on her. Maybe she had been, but she'd never tried to take Snowdrop away from Oleander. Not the way she had taken the half-human children, pretending they had died to get them to safety. Why hadn't she taken Snowdrop?

Would she have wanted to go?

Larkspur wore a plain, woven dress and her feet were bare. "You're here," she said and a smile lit her face as she spotted Snowdrop behind the horse. "I'm glad you decided to come, Snowdrop."

"Thank you for inviting me."

"Dustan, you're well? Everything at home is fine?"

"Aye," he replied, "other than the possible sighting of my twin brothers in Tidal Creek."

Larkspur frowned.

"I'll head south as soon as Larch returns from his sea adventure to join me. I hope it's nothing. But I should get going so I'm not riding all night." He glanced down at Snowdrop. "Are you all set?"

She nodded but her throat closed so she didn't speak.

He held out his hand and squeezed hers once more. "Try to enjoy yourself."

With a goodbye to Larkspur, he turned Redbud and headed out the way they had come.

Larkspur was still smiling at her. "Go on over to the pub," she said. "I'm running to get my shawl before the sun sets and I'll be right back." And with that she bustled away, leaving Snowdrop standing alone.

Snowdrop swallowed. She checked behind her but Dustan was riding away fast, already past the cottages and leaving a haze of dust in his wake. And Larkspur had disappeared down a side street. She couldn't keep hiding here on the edge of the square like a fool. She headed slowly out into the open.

Shouts sounded and a herd of children swarmed into the square after a rolling ball. Snowdrop ducked her head and hurried forward as the children kicked the ball ahead of the group, until their voices veered away and they ran off. She neared the steps of the pub.

The front door pushed open.

"—having an ale!" called a voice inside.

A woman stepped out, peering backward over her shoulder. "You were having an ale last time, too!" she said sharply. "I don't know why I bother with you." But she paused in the doorway as if waiting to hear the reply.

"Because you like the way I hammer a tin cup on my anvil?"

"Are you calling me a tin cup?" the woman shouted, but her voice held a hint of amusement.

The voice inside laughed: "You keep comin' round, Maryanne."

Snowdrop froze. Maryanne. The mother of the rescued children. The one who hated fairies. Snowdrop stepped away as Maryanne turned. She couldn't hide herself.

But nothing would give her away as a fairy as long as she hid her green eyes. Maryanne would never know who she was.

Snowdrop turned and walked along the edge of the porch. She

didn't dare check if Maryanne had noticed her. She cleared the final building, rounded the corner, and sagged against the stone wall. She was out of sight.

A row of apple trees lined the square, giving her cover. A worn path led toward the back of the building between rocks and tufts of grass. But the village square was clearly in view behind her so she followed the path away. At the far end, she peeked around the corner.

An alley stretched along the back side of the shops. The buildings on the righthand side were low, like a row of stables or storage rooms, and a dank smell of ale and horses hung in the air. A stack of crates stood beside a door on her left, and a cat sat on the step watching her.

Snowdrop walked into the alley. There'd been a shop on the end of the row and then the pub, so the second door on her left should lead into the pub, shouldn't it? That door also had a stone step. A barrel stood by the step along with several empty crocks and a glass jug, the kind of things she'd expect outside a place where humans gathered to drink.

Did customers use this door? What if they didn't and Snowdrop got arrested for sneaking in? What if the back door opened into a private chamber, like the pub owner's bed chamber? A vision of Larkspur popped into her head. Was this the alley where Jane had seen Larkspur and the pub owner kissing? What if Larkspur had returned with her shawl, and she'd joined the pub owner in his bed for one last go before she left for—

"Hey, love, are ya going in?"

Snowdrop spun around. A man had come up behind her, human for sure. He had a dark tan like he worked in the sun all day but even darker as if he were a northerner, and he had none of the glow of fairy skin. His eyes were a warm brown like the smooth outside of a hazelnut shell. He took a step toward her and she stepped back. He was the same height as her but so broad in the shoulders he still seemed to crowd her.

"Didn't mean to startle ya," he said, lifting his hands slightly, palms down, but standing his ground.

The alley was empty behind him. They were all alone. What did he want?

Snowdrop swallowed and took another step back. Her heel hit the step. She wobbled and tipped backward, her arms flying up too late to balance her.

The man grabbed her arms, holding her up. "Steady, love. Don't want to fall and knock your head on the stone." He let her go as soon as she was upright and she rubbed the spot where he had held her. His shirt was untucked and he had dirt under his fingernails. And she still didn't know what he wanted.

"Thank you," Snowdrop whispered.

"It's no trouble."

"I'll, um, I'll be going," she said. As she stepped around him, he turned to watch her go but didn't try to stop her. She hurried away without glancing back.

Chapter 3

THE HUMAN HAD STARTLED HER, that was all. Maybe he hadn't meant any harm and was simply cutting through the alley. Maybe his endearments were how they talked in Woods Rest, familiar with complete strangers. And he hadn't made any move to stop her leaving.

Snowdrop leaned against the side of the building, mostly out of sight of both the alley and the square. She inhaled and held the breath as long as she could before letting it woosh out. All she had to do was wait until Larkspur returned. Once Larkspur was with her, the elder fairy would know how to handle the humans. Maybe she was already inside the pub.

Snowdrop crept to the front of the building and scanned the village square. Maryanne had disappeared and the front porch of the pub was empty. She could reach it in ten quick strides. Without stopping to think, she hurried over, opened the door, and slipped in.

The air cooled and a toasty smell like bread hit her, followed by the acrid smell of ale. The Woods Rest pub did resemble the White Pony, as Dustan had said. A bar ran along one side and tables filled the rest. Two older women sat together, one with short gray hair and the other with paler skin and blond spiraling curls over her shoulders. They held hands across the table and didn't look up. Down at the far end, a man hunched over the bar, leaning on his elbows with his hands around a mug, talking with the man standing behind the bar.

Was that the pub owner? Larkspur's lover?

Snowdrop hesitated inside the door. She could do this. She was going to be friendly and polite to everyone. A row of stools lined the bar so she went to one. The pub owner glanced up and came toward her, and the other man followed.

"What can I get you, dear?" the owner asked. Dear, love . . . it must be a human custom to use such terms. The skin by his eyes held creases from laughing, and he clutched a towel in his bony hands. Hands he'd had in Larkspur's—

Snowdrop shook her head. Why had Dustan told her all that? Now she couldn't stop thinking of it. Should she tell him she knew Larkspur?

"Is it okay if I wait for someone?" she asked instead.

"That's fine." He moved away and began stacking mugs on a shelf.

The other man leaned on the bar with one elbow, his mug in hand, facing her and eyeing her up and down. A lock of hair fell into his eyes. He pushed it back. "You're not from here." His eyes were watery and his ale-ridden breath hit her even two paces away. He sounded like the man who'd been calling after Maryanne.

"No." She faced the bar and her hands curled into fists. Where was Larkspur?

"So where you from?" he persisted, sliding closer.

Her face warmed. This was another reason she avoided people. Especially men. Sometimes when they talked to her she sensed their interest floating in the air but she couldn't describe anything concrete to tell them to stop doing. But she hated how that interest felt on her skin and swirling around her, and she never knew how to answer their questions.

"You don't have to say," he said and slurped his ale. "Your eyes give it away."

Snowdrop stared at her lap, hoping her bangs hid her face. But it was too late—he knew she was a fairy. Did he care? If Maryanne hated fairies and he was involved with her maybe he hated them too. Maybe he was up to—

"So what brings you here?"

Her heartbeat accelerated. "I'm waiting for my friend."

"You came all the way from the forest at Woodglen to meet a friend in the pub?"

"Yes. No." She looked up. "Why are you talking to me?"

He jerked back. "I'm being friendly. What's your problem?"

"I don't have a problem." Snowdrop said, flustered. "It just seems like if you're . . . 'hammering' Maryanne, you shouldn't be talking to me like this."

"Skies, I'm just talking. It didn't mean nothing." He shook his head, narrowing his eyes.

Heat flooded her face. She shouldn't have assumed. But she'd felt sure he was after something from her.

"What, you thought I was hitting on you?"

"No, I didn't mean—"

"Because I wasn't."

"Of course you weren't, Wells," said another voice. The man from the alley came up behind Wells and slapped a hand onto his shoulder. "It always means nothing after they reject ya."

"Sod off, Arley," Wells replied and pushed himself up from the bar.

Snowdrop tensed. Would he start a brawl?

Arley removed his hand from Wells's shoulder and backed away. Wells trudged past him toward the end of the room. "Don't bother with her," he muttered as he left.

"Kind of you to welcome her to town," Arley called after him, frowning.

Snowdrop slumped in her seat. So much for being polite—she'd completely bungled her first conversation with a human.

Arley turned to Snowdrop, lowering his voice. "Don't mind

him, love. He's an ass. He'd hit on a rock if he thought it might get him somewhere."

"So he *was* hitting on me?"

"'Course he was."

"But he said he wasn't."

"Only 'cause you shut him down. Believe me, if you'd been into him, he would'a gone out back with ya in a heartbeat."

Did *everyone* here use the back alley for trysts? Stars, she was never going out there again. "But what about Maryanne?"

Arley grinned. "Aw, don't worry about her. I don't think she minds as long as she gets what she needs, to put it politely."

That was the polite version?

"Look," Arley continued, "I'm sorry I startled you outside. You're here to meet Larkspur, aren't ya?"

"You know her?"

"We met because of the upcomin' meeting. She's a nice lady. Hey, you need a drink?"

"No, thank you." She faced the wall across the bar. Turning away was probably rude but she needed a moment to collect herself.

Arley hesitated. "All right. Let me know if ya need anything." He moved away. She stole a glance after him as he approached the table with the two women. They smiled and greeted him, and one placed a hand on his arm as he sat. He rubbed the back of his neck as she spoke, and his laughter rolled out in reply.

At least Arley had backed off. Hopefully Larkspur would get here soon so she could get away from all these humans. She'd been by herself for so long—she wasn't used to being surrounded by this many of anyone, much less humans.

The hairs on her neck prickled. The door opened and voices boomed in, and her heart sank as four more humans entered, all knocking into each other and laughing. If only she could use magic! She'd be able to disappear and wait for Larkspur in peace.

The group of people swarmed the bar like bees to their queen, clustering next to her as the pub owner headed over. Dirt and sweat filled the air with their noisy chatter as they ordered ales. Their clothes were muddy like Arley's. One of them glanced her way and she tucked her head down. She furtively scanned the space, hunting for an escape.

At the front of the pub in the corner opposite the door was a nook between the end of the bar and the front of the building. One tiny table squeezed into it. She slid off her stool silently as the pub owner passed out mugs of ale. She crept around the crowd toward the door. Which opened. A man with a white beard and a leather apron held the door as three people her age jostled in, all of them smudged black with coal dust.

Snowdrop dashed to the corner table before they blocked her way. The seats at the counter filled as the new group crowded in. It must be the end of the workday in Woods Rest. One of the young men peeked over and she dropped her gaze to her lap, her shoulders tight. She waited. He received his mug and moved off with his friends.

She unclenched her shoulders and settled in her chair. She had her back to a wall now and a view of the square out the front windows. Everyone else moved down the counter to fill the end of the room, and the noise dulled to a distant grumbling pierced by an occasional shout. From her low seat, she couldn't see Arley.

She picked at the hem of her satchel. Her belly rumbled. What in the stars was taking Larkspur so long? Was she tumbling someone else in this town, too?

Beside the table, a shelf was built into the wall below the window. Wooden boxes were stacked on it and they were labeled with words she didn't know: mancala, mills, backgammon, checkers . . .

Wait, she knew checkers. The fairies had a checkers board in one of the community supply sheds. The boxes were human games! She reached for the top box and slid it off the shelf. As it came, something slid across the top of the box, a flat square of wood with wooden pegs stuck into it. The wooden peg board slid off the box and fell to the floor with a thunk and the pegs splayed out in all directions. Snowdrop jerked too late to catch it, halfway standing as she did. She lost her grip on the mancala box. She fumbled a moment as the box tipped in her hand and watched in horror as it slipped out and hit the floor with a crash. The box burst open and dozens of stone marbles spewed over the floor, clattering on the floorboards and rolling across the room.

The pub went silent. She slowly peeked up. The row of faces at the bar stared at her, and more people stood up behind them, all of them gaping. So many faces—even more must've come in the back door. She could see Arley now that she was standing. Wells smirked at the far end of the room.

The door opened and everyone turned as three more people entered. And slipped on the marbles.

A warning cry sounded too late. The newcomers grabbed each other as they slipped and fell, banging into a table and knocking over a chair, landing in a heap. Snowdrop moved to help and her foot rolled out from under her. She landed on her elbow with a sting of pain. Voices buzzed in the room. The people on the floor untangled themselves, cursing. More people barreled in the door and a cry went up to stop them.

Snowdrop pushed herself up and winced from the lingering ache in her elbow. She crawled under the table to retrieve the mancala box. A wooden board had fallen out and she fit it back in. She picked up the nearest marbles, dropped them into the box, and scrabbled across the floor like a beetle, sweeping up marbles. Her face burned.

Someone moved beside her. Another hand picking up the pieces. Arley was on his knees on the floor.

"Kind of early in the evening to be spilling the marbles!" someone joked from the doorway. The people who'd come in hauled up the people on the floor. Thankfully none of them seemed injured.

Arley grinned up at them. "It's never too early to spill the marbles."

"Want a hand, Arley?"

"Naw, go on and get your ales." The newest patrons picked their way across the sea of marbles to the bar.

Arley didn't say anything to her. Stars above, this was embarrassing. All she'd had to do was go inside the pub and wait for Larkspur, and she'd managed to make a mess and get every human in Woods Rest staring at her. Hopefully she'd be on the road soon and she'd never need to see any of these people again, and especially not Arley. She'd embarrassed herself *twice* in front of him.

The door opened. Arley rose up on his knees with his arms out to block anyone else from stumbling on marbles.

Larkspur entered. She looked down at Arley, who grinned up at her as her brow wrinkled. She spotted Snowdrop and her face brightened.

"Oh good! You two have met."

Dread pooled in Snowdrop's chest. Hadn't Dustan said they were meeting their travel companions at the pub? And they'd be traveling with humans?

Arley lumbered to his feet and she scrambled up beside him, holding the half-filled game box. "We've met," he said, "but I didn't catch your name, love."

"This is Snowdrop," Larkspur said.

Snowdrop swallowed as she faced Arley. His eyes twinkled in the afternoon light through the open door. Did he never stop grinning? He must think her a complete fool after how she'd behaved.

"Arley Farnwell," he said, extending his hand. The dirt was gone from his fingernails. She carefully freed one hand and shook his. It was warm and callused.

Larkspur touched his arm, radiating admiration. "Arley will be driving us to Mountain Rest."

Chapter 4

❦ ✳ ❦

Driving them to Mountain Rest. Arley. Of course he would be. Snowdrop would never get away from him.

"Oh." She looked between Larkspur and Arley. He winked.

"And over here is Edna," Larkspur continued, indicating the table with the two women. They'd remained seated throughout her mishap with the marbles but now they watched her expectantly.

"Go on," Arley said, taking the game box from Snowdrop's hands. "I'll get the rest of the marbles."

She met his gaze once more before turning to follow Larkspur. They picked their way through the remaining marbles. People at the bar were talking again but a few still glanced her way.

The woman with the short gray hair stood to greet them. She was Edna, the Woods Rest representative to the Council of Villages meeting, and the pale woman with the long curls was her partner, Ruth. Arley, they adoringly explained, had volunteered to drive them to the meeting. He worked on someone's farm and didn't have land of his own so he was free to go on the trip, especially now that the summer crops were harvested.

Ruth and Edna rejoined their hands on the table as soon as the introductions were done. Ruth had come to the pub simply to spend more time with Edna before she left on the trip. Which was odd since they apparently lived together, but Dustan would behave the exact same way if Rose were to go on a trip without him.

Snowdrop's head was spinning from all the talking. The door opened and yet another group of people came in, all in boots and trousers with dirt on the knees. Several called hello to Arley down on the floor. He'd cleared the entryway and must be under the corner table—she could no longer see him. The newcomers lined the bar, ordering drinks.

Larkspur took Snowdrop's hand. "Let's step outside."

Snowdrop followed Larkspur to the door, keeping her eyes on the floor to avoid any last marbles. The open air of the outdoors was a relief as the noise of the chattering pubgoers dissipated into the early evening. The square was bustling with villagers but with Larkspur by her side, she no longer feared who she might encounter. Larkspur would know how to handle anything.

The sun was nearing the horizon and a chill crept through the air. Larkspur led her into the garden with the iron fence and to a bench in the late sun. "It's lovely out," she said, sitting.

"It was awfully loud in the pub." Snowdrop sank down beside her. "Is it always like that?"

"In the evenings. Not my favorite place to spend time, but it was convenient for today's meeting. We'll go to Edna's cottage for the night and that's much quieter."

"You don't need to return to the pub?" Maybe Dustan had been wrong about Larkspur and the pub owner. Or maybe they'd broken up already. Larkspur hadn't looked his way once when they'd been inside.

"I met with Edna before you arrived. We were waiting for you and Arley. He arranged the wagon and horses for tomorrow."

"We really leave tomorrow?" A thread of excitement curled up her spine. What new places would she see? Where would they be this time tomorrow?

"Yes. The council meeting's not for another half-moon or so but we all want to leave early in case anything goes wrong. And if we're early, we'll have time to sightsee. Mountain Rest is at a crossroads, with merchants coming through from all directions."

Snowdrop couldn't begin to picture it.

"How are things at home?" Larkspur asked.

"Okay."

"I haven't seen you since . . ."

"Since you came to tell me Anemone and the others were alive," Snowdrop finished. She fixed her gaze at the grass in front of her, clenching her jaw. She needed Larkspur's help. She didn't want to start an argument.

But she couldn't help her anger. She could still feel the anguish of learning each of the children had died—first Anemone, the oldest at eight winters, then Chrysanthemum, Alyssum . . .

Only they hadn't died. Larkspur, Thistle, and their friends had smuggled them out of the caverns and away from Oleander and kept them safe until Oleander was no longer a threat. Snowdrop was grateful the children had been rescued. But had the elders truly needed to mislead her into thinking they were dead? She never would have given away their secret to Oleander.

Larkspur had come to tell her the whole truth last summer, once Oleander was contained and the children were safe from her. Larkspur had apologized. They hadn't known if they could trust Snowdrop, she said, as she spent all her time with Oleander. Her mother. And Snowdrop understood—keeping the children safe had been their priority. But it still hurt to remember how awful it had been. And it hurt to be lumped together with Oleander when she'd never wanted to be her daughter and had tried not to be like her.

"I know I can't make up for hiding the truth from you," Larkspur said, "no matter how many times I apologize, but I'm sorry we put you through that. I wish we had known you better. I wish we had known we could trust you."

"How are they?" Snowdrop asked to change the subject. Anemone would be sixteen or seventeen winters. She'd arrived as a baby when Snowdrop was only eight so she'd been like a little sister. Snowdrop had loved to rock her to sleep. Oleander had chastised

Snowdrop, saying Anemone was different—she was half human, she couldn't use magic, and on and on, but Snowdrop loved her anyway.

Snowdrop was fifteen winters when Larkspur told her Anemone was sick, and later that she had died. And then Larkspur told Oleander . . . and Oleander didn't care. She waved her hand to dismiss Larkspur and went on with whatever she'd been doing, and she kept on stealing the humans' children even though bringing them to the caverns had led (as far as she knew) to Anemone's illness. That was the first time Snowdrop hated her mother.

"They're well," Larkspur said. "They've come out of hiding, as you know. Alyssum's mother turned out to be a friend of Rose's, one of the women who used to live here in Woods Rest. She lives in Woodglen and Alyssum's there with her."

"What about Anemone?"

"Her mother was also here—"

Snowdrop jerked up. Anemone was here?

"—but they live in Cliffside now. It's on the coast, east of here. Anemone's grandmother lives in a large house and they invited the rest of the children to live with them as they figure out their next steps."

"I'm glad they have a safe place," Snowdrop said.

"You know . . . you could reach out to Anemone. You could send a letter and offer to visit her."

At the suggestion, Snowdrop's pulse quickened. Anemone was grown, almost an adult. Would she even remember Snowdrop? Did the younger ones remember her? If they had blocked out all thoughts of their past and of living underground with Oleander, or if they had moved on, Snowdrop didn't want to remind them. She shook her head. Hopefully Larkspur would drop it.

"There's something else I wanted to ask you," Larkspur said.

She said it lightly but she couldn't hide her hesitancy. Snowdrop swallowed. Larkspur smiled at her, too brightly.

"While we're on the road," Larkspur ventured, "we could practice using magic. I could teach you. I used to teach the youngsters—it would be no trouble."

"I can't learn to do it."

"I'm sure you can."

Being able to use magic would change everything. She'd be able to help on one of the work crews at home—in the gardens or with the animals. And if fairies saw her helping, maybe they'd come to trust her. If they knew she could control her magic properly and wouldn't hurt anyone, they might not be scared of her.

"If you learned magic," Larkspur went on, "you could . . . be more comfortable in the world. You'd be able to hear the animals and you could hide yourself from humans—not that you need to hide from them. But I know sometimes they can be, ah, they can come on a little strong."

Snowdrop twisted her hands together in her lap. "You don't understand."

Larkspur studied her. "Do you think you're too old to learn?"

"No," she said. "It's not that. And I *want* to learn."

Larkspur squinted. "You're afraid to try."

Snowdrop nodded.

"Tell me why, Snowdrop. Maybe we can figure it out together."

She'd come here to learn. She wanted to tell Larkspur. But what if she told her and Larkspur recoiled in disgust? Still, if she was going to try to learn, she had to tell Larkspur what happened when she tried to use magic. It would be irresponsible not to warn her.

Larkspur patted her leg. "It's been a long day, especially for you with the ride from the forest. Why don't we get some rest and we can talk once we're on the road tomorrow?"

Snowdrop slumped against the bench. "Okay."

"You know," Larkspur said, "you don't always need to know how to do something from start to finish. Sometimes all you need to know is the next step. You take one step at a time and eventually you get somewhere. Just focus on the next step."

But if the next step failed, what then?

The sun had dipped behind the treetops. Only one villager crossed the square, and lights illuminated the windows of the nearby cottages. Light shone from the pub, where the door stood open to the cool evening air.

A person came around the corner of the buildings leading two horses. They stopped in front of the pub and shouted, and Arley's silhouette appeared in the doorway. The broad shoulders gave him away. He came out and took the lead ropes, and the other person went into the pub.

"Those must be our horses for tomorrow," Larkspur said, standing. "We have a wagon to carry us."

Snowdrop followed her back into the square. The horses matched, brown with white diamonds on their foreheads. She drifted toward them in spite of Arley standing nearby. They watched her approach and she held out her hands, and Arley gave them enough rope to reach her. They nuzzled her fingers and let her stroke their foreheads.

"You ride?" Arley asked.

"No. My brothers had horses, but I was never allowed to have one. I never learned."

"That's hardly fair."

One of the horses stuck its big nose into her hair and wuffled, and Snowdrop smiled and squirmed with how it tickled.

"We had an old draft horse on the farm," Arley went on, "but I learned to ride properly in the King's Guard."

"Lucky." Rose had talked about the King's Guard. When the old king had had her locked up in a tower in his castle, she'd been guarded constantly, and some of the guards had delivered her to the merman who'd dragged her out to sea. Eventually, most of the guards turned on the king. Rose hadn't mentioned the horses though.

"Lucky?" Arley said. "Ya wouldn't say that if you knew the King's Guard."

Larkspur had gone inside, leaving only Snowdrop and Arley in the square with the horses. The orange light of sunset beamed on the storefronts.

"Do you know their names?" she asked.

"Ah, I believe it's Lady and Bird," he replied, pointing at each horse.

Snowdrop cringed and Arley laughed.

"Do ya want to sit on her back while we wait?" he said, nodding at the horse she was patting, Lady.

"Could I?" she blurted out before she'd realized it. "I mean, do we . . . aren't we . . ."

"We're waitin' for Farmer Joe to return, and then we're takin' 'em over to the stable for the night. He's lendin' them for our trip. Go on."

Snowdrop smoothed her hand along Lady's shoulder. The horse was so tall. How would she get on? She looked to Arley for help.

"Here," he said, and he walked the horses in a loop until Lady was alongside the porch of the pub. Snowdrop climbed the steps and lowered her bag to the plank floor. She pushed herself onto the horse's back. Lady's powerful body was solid beneath her, like sitting on a rock except she shifted a little side to side. Snowdrop wove her fingers into the coarse mane. Lady stepped a few times and settled down.

Arley grinned up at her. "It suits you, bein' on a horse."

And she remembered how he'd noticed her in the alley and again in the pub—the uncomfortable feeling in the air. He was doing it again. She shifted her gaze to the horse's neck, her hands clenching in the long mane.

Arley looked away. "So, ah, I know fairies have their own ways of doin' things. With horses, I mean. If you wanted to ride like a human, you'd squeeze with your calves to tell her to walk. And of course, if you're standin' here, you want to avoid squeezing so you don't confuse her."

Snowdrop had to resist moving her calves. She wanted so badly to see if squeezing Lady would work.

Arley assumed she could communicate with Lady like any other fairy. Larkspur thought she could learn magic. She closed her eyes. Very slowly, she imagined the blank space all around her, just searching, not taking. If she could find any sense of the horse's mind, she could listen—she didn't need to do anything else.

And there it was, curling around her like the mist off a pond in the morning. The horse felt like trust. Lady wasn't sure why they were out of the barn this late in the day but she liked Arley. And she could tell Snowdrop liked her.

Snowdrop reached too hard and a dark thread of fear joined the others.

She gasped, opened her eyes, and cleared her mind. Lady stepped side to side. No magic here. None at all. Snowdrop let it all go before it went any further.

"You okay, love?" Arley asked. "Sorry, um, Snowdrop. Edna said I shouldn't use—"

Shouts erupted in the pub, and the horse stepped sideways into her companion, moving away from the noise. Arley's eyes widened. He clicked his tongue and tugged lightly on the leads, and the horses started away from the porch.

Something crashed inside and more voices shouted. Wells fell out the door holding a glass jug. He staggered to the edge of the porch and dropped it off, right in front of the horses. The jug hit the dirt, and Snowdrop winced but it didn't break. It spun on the ground. The cork popped out and a spray of liquid shot out, and the jug launched the opposite direction, careening right into Lady's hooves.

Lady reared up and screamed, and Snowdrop leaned against her neck and clung to her mane. Bird whinnied beside her, knocking

Arley back. Lady's lead rope swung from her head as her hooves hit the ground and she bolted.

Chapter 5

LADY RUSHED ACROSS THE VILLAGE square and onto the road. Snowdrop tightened her fists in the mane and clung with her knees, and she leaned forward because that's what Dustan had done that morning when he let Redbud run. The solid body bucked against her and could throw her to the ground in a moment. Dirt filled her nostrils along with a whiff of the bakery as they cleared another set of buildings and open road appeared ahead. Cottages flew past, a startled villager, and then only fields.

The ground raced beneath the thundering hooves, and her mind raced but found no solutions. The hard-packed dirt was dim purple in the coming twilight, hard to see. Her fingers ached from clenching. How long would Lady run? How long could she hang on?

Should she try to reach out with magic and calm Lady?

Her magic hadn't worked before, and they'd been standing still. Communicating would be even harder in this panicked state. She'd never manage it, not without letting loose those threads of darkness she'd felt earlier. She couldn't risk hurting Lady.

All around were fields. Snatches of hay and wheat scent wafted over her. Strands of hair clung across her face and stuck to her lips. Lady's neck was sweating.

Why hadn't she agreed to learn magic? This situation never would have happened if she'd been able to communicate with Lady from the start. All she had to do was tell Larkspur she wanted to learn. She should do it before something worse happened that she couldn't solve.

The beats of Lady's hooves drummed under her, but was Lady slowing? If she usually pulled a slow cart or plow, running with a rider might tire her. Snowdrop kept her tight hold even as her racing pulse began to calm. She wasn't going to fall. But she might have a long walk back to the village.

Far across the fields, the dark forest was silhouetted against a band of pale pink at the horizon. The light sky over the trees deepened to blue higher up. The first star was probably out but Snowdrop didn't dare look overhead.

The rhythm of Lady's hoofbeats echoed, but the echo began to have offbeats before turning into a separate set of beats behind them. A moment later, another horse appeared by her side. In the twilight, the white patch on the new horse's forehead shone—it was Bird. She kept pace with her sister, slowly moving ahead until Arley was riding beside Snowdrop. He'd come after them. Even after she hadn't been nice to him, he'd come to make sure they were all right.

Arley held Bird's lead and gently turned her head, and she nudged Lady off the dirt and onto the grass, where Lady slowed until she trotted alongside the field.

Arley leaned far out, reached across, and caught the lead rope dangling from Lady's head. Bird slowed and pulled Lady back. Together, the two horses slowed to a walk and after a moment they stopped.

In the sudden silence, the horses snuffled and touched noses. Lady's sides were heaving like a bellows. Snowdrop slowly sat up. Cool night air hit her front where Lady's warm body had been. All around were fields of grain hemmed in by the forest, and the clear dark dome overhead was twinkling with the earliest stars. She unclenched her fists from Lady's mane and breathed in and out once, twice, and her shoulders relaxed. Arley sat beside her, holding the two lead ropes. His face was in shadows and he wasn't smiling.

She held on to Lady's neck and slid down from the horse's back. As her left toes touched the ground, her knee buckled and she clutched the horse as her other leg came down. She hung on to avoid falling.

Hands gripped her arms and held her up. His fingers were rough. They must get calluses from working on the farm. He'd dismounted so quickly she hadn't heard him. She moved her legs and they worked properly this time.

"You got it?" Arley asked.

She nodded.

He let go and stepped back. "You did well hangin' on."

"But I couldn't stop her. I couldn't use magic to calm her."

He shook his head, squinting in confusion.

"Dustan would've been able to."

"When a horse is panicked like that, sometimes all you can do is hang on. I'm sure you tried your best."

"I didn't, though. I didn't try at all."

"Well in the moment, ya did what you could and hung on and—"

"I don't have any magic."

He stared. "I thought all the fairies could use magic."

"I can't." Her voice had dropped to a scraping whisper.

He didn't reply and when she stole a glance, he was frowning, his lips pursed tight and his brow furrowed. He caught her gaze and shrugged. "Humans ride without magic. You could learn that way."

"I couldn't learn to ride her. I couldn't even sit on her back without making a mess of it."

"Now that wasn't your fault," Arley said, and his voice hardened. "I don't know what that idiot Wells was up to—prob'ly thought it would be funny to shake up a jug of ale to see what happened. And it just about exploded on you. He's lucky I had to come after you. He better be gone when we get back."

He glowered at the ground, and Bird took a step away.

Snowdrop chewed on her lip. Arley thought she could learn to ride a horse? And Larkspur thought she could learn to use magic. Why did she feel sure she couldn't learn anything?

When Oleander had sent her brothers to the stables to see their new horses, she had tagged along after them. Four horses for the four brothers . . . But even if Oleander had brought a fifth horse, Snowdrop would have been too intimidated to ride it. Not Dustan. He marched right up and befriended Redbud, and soon all four boys were out riding and she couldn't even try to follow them.

"I won't be able to ride," she said.

"You don't think so?" Arley frowned. "I bet ya can. I'd bet coin on it."

She squinted. "You want me to make a bet that I can't learn to ride a horse? Why would I do that?"

"You'd win either way, the way I see it. If not the money, at least you'd learn to ride."

"I don't need human coins."

"We don't have to bet for money." He grinned.

She ignored his innuendo. "What would *I* get if I won?"

"Whatever you want, love."

"Don't call me that." She winced as she remembered she was supposed to be polite—had that been rude?

His grin faded. "Sorry, I forgot. Edna told me not to say it to you. My ma calls everyone 'love' and I picked up the habit but Edna said the fairies don't use the word that way."

So he hadn't meant anything by it, not if his mother said it too. "It's all right."

"If you won," he continued, "you could ask me to take you riding."

"But I'd already know how to ride! Besides, how is that not a prize for you, too?"

He winked at her. "It doesn't much matter what you pick," he said, "seeing as how I'm goin' to win."

He was taunting her. Something inside reared up, urging her to challenge him back. She wouldn't give him the satisfaction.

"In fact," he went on undeterred, "I bet I could ride better than you even if you *were* trained in magic."

Snowdrop's brow furrowed in confusion. "So we're betting that you can ride better than me? I thought we were betting I could learn?"

"We can bet on whatever you want." He crossed his arms and jutted out his chin. "I'd even bet on you being able to learn magic, no matter what ya say."

She frowned. "Larkspur thinks I can learn magic."

"So that's your plan? Ya trick me into a bet under false pretenses, and then let on that you will, in fact, be using magic?"

Stars, he tried her patience. She inhaled deeply to keep her voice calm. "I'm not tricking you into a bet."

"If you do, I'll allow it. It won't be cheatin' if you use magic. But I'll still win."

She shook her head slowly. Was she going to learn to use magic? She'd been skilled at using the spells she'd learned as a child before she realized the harm they were causing. Maybe she truly could master the usual kind of fairy magic—if she could find a way to stop herself from hurting anything.

The horses were quiet, standing patiently. An owl hooted in the dark across the field. Arley handed Lady's lead to Snowdrop. He circled Bird around on the road and Snowdrop copied him. They headed back toward the village with the horses clopping on either side. Overhead, several stars blinked in the blue-black sky.

"Don't ya want to know what prize I'll pick when I win?" Arley asked.

"No."

"It'll be a surprise then."

"Okay." Snowdrop waited. Arley wasn't going to be able to keep his mouth shut.

"Maybe I'd ask for a kiss."

She closed her eyes briefly and huffed out her nose. "You would not."

"No. But a man can dream."

"Stop flirting with me."

He watched her. "All right, lov— All right."

Another owl called and the light drained from the sky. By the time they reached the village, all the stars were shining.

Chapter 6

❖

SNOWDROP WOKE THE NEXT MORNING on the sofa in Ruth and Edna's cottage. She had a sofa in Oleander's chambers but not like this one. Oleander's sofa was stuffed so hard you could balance a mug of tea—or elderberry wine—on it. But this sofa was wide and soft, and Ruth had piled on blankets and pillows until Snowdrop was swimming in them.

She hadn't expected to sleep after the tumult of the previous day—first her unexpected meeting with Rose and Dustan, her sudden departure for Woods Rest, the stress of being in the pub, and the grand finale of Lady bolting as Snowdrop clung to her back. She'd expected to close her eyes and hear the pounding of Lady's hooves and see the ground racing by on the backs of her eyelids.

But once she'd reclined on the pillows and pulled up the blankets, she'd thought of Arley. She hadn't liked when he looked her over in the bar, but he wasn't so bad when he kept his distance. He was still annoying with his endless talking, but after that first time he had made an effort to stay out of her personal space. When he winked at her, the action wasn't threatening the way it might be with another man. His nut-brown eyes were always friendly. Even when she sounded rude, her tone didn't seem to affect Arley one way or another. She hadn't done so well at being polite, she now realized.

And so she'd drifted to sleep thinking of Arley. And here she was waking up and still thinking of him.

She pushed off the blankets, sat up, and shivered in the morning air. She pulled off her nightshirt and got on her top and calf-length trousers. The cottage was quiet but the sun was peeking above the trees outside. Hopefully the light would wake the others and they could be on their way before the village awoke. And she'd never again have to see Wells or any of those pub patrons who'd witnessed her humiliation last night. Of course she'd be stuck with Arley for the next quarter-moon, but once they reached Mountain Rest they'd be with so many people, it wouldn't matter.

She shivered again. The fire in the hearth had burned out during the night. She could try to light it or use Dustan's fire powder. But either way was a waste as they'd only be leaving.

Instead she rummaged to the bottom of her satchel and pulled out her knitted sweater. Rose had gotten it for her from a shop in Woodglen. Over the muted shades of tan and brown were stitched a clump of blooming snowdrops in stark white and vibrant green yarns. The green was much brighter than anything she'd seen before, but the humans did things like that. The fairies tended to use what they had nearby when making things—like onion skins for a dull green-yellow dye. Rose's friend who owned the yarn shop had made the deep green color with goldenrod and a blue dye from the indigo plant, which came all the way from Norland.

Snowdrop ran her fingers over the flowers before donning the sweater and settling back on the sofa to wait. She'd never seen a real snowdrop flower—they didn't grow in the forest. If they had, she might have been able to learn proper magic by now, because a fairy's name plant sometimes aided them in using certain types of magic. It differed for each fairy, but sometimes having your name plant could help you learn.

Soon the three older ladies were awake and Ruth made them all pancakes with late summer blackberries. Edna forbid Ruth from coming to the village square to see them off because apparently Ruth would start crying, and if that happened Edna would start crying. Snowdrop kept her mouth shut. She never wanted to be this codependent on anyone, but having watched her brother and his sweetheart over a turn of the seasons, she knew some people behaved this way. When the couple began their goodbyes, Larkspur and Snowdrop went outside to wait.

Finally Edna joined them and the three of them walked along the lane of cottages and into the town square. A wagon stood in front of the general store with Lady and Bird hitched to it. The fairies had a simple wooden cart for hauling things, but this wagon was much larger. It had swooping wooden hoops over it with a canvas cover rolled up on the sides. The back board hung down at an angle with a step on it, and at the other end, the driver's seat extended out with a storage space behind it.

Arley stood up behind the horses and dusted off his knees.

Polite, Snowdrop reminded herself. She was going to be friendly and make friends. She grimaced.

Arley walked around the horses, checking the harness. He wore a different shirt than he had yesterday, a strange one with thin, crisscrossing stripes going up and down, and side to side. It appeared deep blue at first but as they neared, the stripes showed as red, orange, and brown.

"What are you wearing?" Edna called as they crossed the square toward him, and he looked up.

He regarded his shirt. "Do ya like it?" he said, holding out his arms. "My ma sent it. Says they're all the rage up in Woods End since someone started weavin' 'em. They call it plaid though I've no idea why."

They stopped in front of him. Edna rubbed the hem of his shirt between her fingers. It hung untucked over his trousers. "That's some fine weaving," she said. "How's it feel?"

"Like a woma— Ah, like a baby's bottom, as they say."

Edna smirked at him.

"I don't wear it in the fields but seeing as how we're representing Woods Rest I thought I'd look my best."

"You look handsome," Larkspur said, stopping beside the wagon, and Arley actually blushed.

Larkspur hefted her bag over the edge of the wagon onto a bench along the front end, followed by Edna's and Snowdrop's bags. "I'll go get our lunches," she said and headed around the horses and up the steps of the store. Edna went after her. Snowdrop watched them go but stayed outside. She went forward to pat the horses.

"How'd ya sleep?" Arley asked.

"Fine."

"I couldn't sleep at all. I kept seeing Lady rearing up with you on her back, and that idiot Wells with his exploding jug of ale. And with the departure this morning . . . I always get the nerves when I have to travel."

"You do?" She'd been tense yesterday, but since she'd found Larkspur the feeling had faded.

"Every time. It was a drag in the King's Guard. You could never let on you were nervous in that crowd."

"Why?"

"It was a bunch of macho asses all feeding off each other. Being nervous meant you were scared which meant you weren't a *man . . .*" His voice had gone a notch louder.

Snowdrop frowned. Rose hadn't described the guards that way but maybe they'd been different around her. "Well the human king and his guards are gone."

"Right he is. Thank the skies."

Snowdrop worked her way around Bird's nose to Lady's and Arley followed. She kept going along the side of the horse and peered into the wagon. It had the wide driver's seat up at the front, with a cushion and a footrest. The back section had a cushioned bench at the front end, back-to-back with the driver's seat but separated by the storage, but the floor of the wagon was wide and open with a rug covering the boards, a pile of blankets in a corner, and a few pillows. A water barrel was fastened on the far corner with packages stacked beside it.

She peered up at the canvas. "It rolls down for shade?"

"Yeah, and to keep the rain off. It's heavy enough to be waterproof. And some people like to have a bit of a roof when they're sleeping."

"We're sleeping in there?"

"Depends how far we get each day. We might reach an inn. But if we need to we can. I'd sleep on the ground and leave the wagon for you ladies."

"You can sleep on the ground?" Humans were supposed to use giant beds and mattresses.

"I can sleep anywhere. I could sleep on the ground with horses tramping around me. I wouldn't expect you to do it, though."

"I could do it."

"Well," he said, "if you want to give the elders more room or to enjoy the night air, you can sleep outside too."

She narrowed her eyes.

He lifted his hands, palms out. "I'm not flirting! I'm just saying you can sleep where you want. I'm not saying you'll be sleeping with me."

"Okay."

"Although you could." He grinned.

She wanted to wipe the grin off his face but she grasped for a comeback. All her thoughts had fled.

Arley looked away as someone approached across the square and Snowdrop followed his gaze. A woman with long dark hair came their way slowly, her face turned down to watch the small child she held by one hand. Snowdrop's stomach plunged to the ground and her throat went dry. She dropped behind the wagon, down by the wheel.

Jane was supposed to be in the forest with the fairies, not here in Woods Rest! Snowdrop had heard her hammering at the forge yesterday morning! What was she doing here? After a whole long summer of avoiding her and her daughter, it figured she'd come walking up the moment Snowdrop let her guard down.

Arley was eyeing her, crouched on the ground.

Snowdrop shook her head rapidly, pleading with her eyes. Arley frowned. But he stepped toward her and turned away as the toddler's body and Jane's shoes came into view out the other side of the wagon. Jane's hands reached down and scooped Elle off the ground.

"Hi, Arley," Jane said in a gentle voice, and Elle's voice garbled a few words too.

"Hello, Jane. Miss Elle," Arley said. "I hear you're quite the master of fire these days."

"Sunshine says I'm real good," Elle blurted out, and Arley laughed.

"And where is Miss Sunshine?"

"She's sleeping."

"We left her outside the village," Jane said.

"Prob'ly best," Arley replied. "No need to scare our pants off again, swoopin' over the village on your dragon."

"How was your summer?" Jane asked.

"It's been fine. We got all the squashes and corn in at last. You lot back from the fairies for good?"

"Not yet. We came to get a few things for autumn. Warmer clothes and things."

"Can't you have one of the dragons breathe on ya?"

"They breathe fire, not heat!"

"I'm teasin' ya. How's the smithin' going?"

"I'm getting there. I'll be glad when we're back here and I can be a proper apprentice with Master Smith."

"You better than Rowan was at least?"

Jane laughed. "That's hardly a high bar."

Arley laughed too. "Tell him hello from me when you get back."

"I will."

Arley nudged Snowdrop with his foot. She scrambled under the wagon and he stepped in front of her as Jane walked by. Snowdrop peeked out between Arley's legs. Elle waved at Arley over Jane's shoulder as Jane climbed up the steps of the general store, and Jane turned her face to kiss the child's cheek before lowering her to the floor. Elle toddled forward and they spent several moments getting the door open with her "help" before walking into the store. The door swung closed at last.

Snowdrop sucked in rapid breaths, trying to stop her tears. One rolled down her cheek and she brushed it away before Arley saw. She'd known Oleander was wrong about the humans and their children. She'd known Oleander had hurt them. But she'd never seen one of the mothers interacting with her child like that. Jane's face plainly showed how much she loved her child. How could Oleander not have known? Or had she known and not cared?

Two sets of feet joined Arley's, dresses swishing about their legs. "Where's Snowdrop?" Larkspur asked.

"She's, ah, she's checkin' out the axles. She wondered how wagons work."

How wagons work? Did he think fairies were incompetent? Snowdrop took one last deep breath to settle herself and wiped her eyes again. She crawled out from under the wagon.

"Ready to go?" she asked, pushing herself to her feet. Larkspur was staring at her but Edna wandered to the back of the wagon as if getting down to examine the axles was normal. Snowdrop reached for the package in Larkspur's hands and placed it in the wagon. "We'd best get going before the sun's too high. We can make the shade of the forest before the road heats up so we won't have to unroll the wagon cover." She took Larkspur's elbow and hurried her to the back to join Edna, who'd grasped the side of the wagon and stepped up onto the back board. Edna climbed in and sat on the rug.

"Do we have everything we need?" Larkspur asked, scanning the storefronts. "I didn't get any hostess gifts."

"I'm sure we'll find something along the way," Snowdrop said. "Do you need a hand getting in?"

Arley was grinning at her from the front of the wagon. He sauntered toward them. "She's right. We could make the forest crossroads by nightfall if we get an early start."

"All right, child, we're going." Larkspur climbed in as Edna scooched herself back.

As Snowdrop moved to join them, Arley pulled up the wagon board, cutting her off.

"You wanted to ride up front for a while, right, lo— Snowdrop? So you could learn to drive the horses?"

Blast him, tempting her with horses! But he would let her drive Lady and Bird? She stepped back and he fastened the wagon board in place, grinning.

"Go on up," he said, walking her to the front, "and we'll be on our way before anyone else comes along who needs you to check the axles."

Snowdrop pulled herself up onto the driver's bench as Arley checked the horses one last time. Behind her, Larkspur and Edna sat on the rug like children having a tea party.

"There's a cushion on the seat," Arley told them as he climbed up beside her, but they waved him off.

"I'm going back to sleep as soon as we're out of town," Edna said. "Ruth had me up half the night, saying goodbye." She snickered.

Stars, who said things like that? But Arley snickered too and Larkspur laughed.

Arley took the reins and glanced her way. She lifted her eyebrows and held out a hand.

"Right out of the barn? Okay. Here ya go, lo—" He snapped his mouth shut.

Snowdrop took the reins, careful not to slap them against the horses' backs. The reins ran up to the horses' heads on the outside with a crisscross between their bodies.

"So, ah, you'll want to face your whole body forward. And you . . . you need to hold the reins a little different."

She had looped them around her hands several times, fearful she'd drop them. She looked at him.

Arley wiped his hands on his thighs. "I might need to touch your hands. Okay?"

Snowdrop swallowed. "Okay."

He reached over her arm and slid the loops of rein from her left hand, letting the leather strip fall straight. He took her hand and bent it, palm inward. "Keep your forearms out straight and bent at the elbow."

He wove the rein under her fingers, up the palm of her hand, around her thumb, and over the top. She tried to copy the weave on her right hand, and he leaned over to help. For a moment, his head was in front of her nose and his hair smelled nice.

"There ya go. Ya got that? You can hold them tight with your thumbs."

She straightened up and nodded.

"Hang on, ladies," Arley called over his shoulder. Snowdrop didn't dare look back. He faced her. "Now tap both horses with the reins."

She did it and the two horses started forward.

They started forward! She was driving a team of horses! They clopped across the square heading toward the bakery. Straight toward the big window display of loaves of bread and baskets of rolls.

Oh no. Where was the road?

"To the right, nice and easy," Arley said. "Pull gently with your right hand."

She slowly pulled on the rein and Lady's head turned, leading the team to the right. The road opened ahead, the same road she'd thundered down last evening. This time she was able to see the front of the general store in the side of her vision and the cottages that came into view behind it.

She flicked the reins a little harder and the horses began to trot.

"What do you think?" Arley asked.

"It's not hard."

"No."

"But I'm scared to look around."

"Smart of ya. You look off over the fields and next thing you know the horses are veerin' off the road. You want me to take over?"

"Don't you want to watch the scenery?"

He scoffed and reached for the reins. His fingers tangled with hers as he took them. "I can watch and drive at the same time."

He turned his face to wink at her and snapped the reins without looking where they were going. Lady and Bird jolted into a faster cadence, straight down the road. Snowdrop rolled her eyes at him and he smirked.

With Arley managing the horses, Snowdrop put her feet up and leaned back. The cover on the wagon extended out so they'd have shade, too, when the sun was high, although they should be in the forest by then. For now she was glad the heat of the sun shone on her face. She was used to the chill of the fairy caverns—the sunlight felt like a gift. They rumbled past cottages and on along the road.

"So is it the 'love' you don't like or is it any such endearment?" Arley asked. Of course. He wasn't going to drive to Mountain Rest without talking the whole way.

"It's not that I don't like the word. It just doesn't fit when you say it to me. I'm not your love. We don't even know each other."

"So if we *were* in love, you wouldn't mind?"

"It's kind of sappy too. My brother Dustan is always calling Rose 'my love' and I think I'd be embarrassed if I were her."

"But you wouldn't mind another nickname?"

Snowdrop narrowed her eyes. "Like what?"

"Oh, I don't know. How about peanut?"

"Pea-nut? What's a peanut? It sounds . . . small and hard."

"No, no," he said. "Well, okay yes, it is small and hard, but it's not a bad thing. Peanuts grow to the north. They're like a . . . like a lima bean but they grow in the dirt on a scrubby little plant."

"Oh, like a root nut."

"Root nut?" Arley lifted an eyebrow. "That the fairy word for it?"

"They have a light brown shell and they're shaped like bumpy slugs."

"Sounds right."

Snowdrop cringed. "They grow in the dirt and they're hard and shaped like slugs. Why would you call anyone that? Unless you hated them."

"It's not an insult. Peanuts are the best. They taste better than anything."

Snowdrop squinted up at him, shaking her head.

He blushed. "Not that you, oh, never mind peanut then."

She settled back.

"They do taste exceptional though. You can roast them to add crunch. But I like 'em boiled in salt water. They soak in the brine and ya get this weird salty-crunchy-squishy mix."

"You're really not selling it."

"We'll find you boiled peanuts when we get to Mountain Rest. You'll see."

They'd left the village behind. The woods loomed ahead where the road wound from the fields into the thick forest.

"So are you going to tell me why you were hiding back there?" Arley asked.

Snowdrop smoothed her hands over her thighs, watching her fingers. She'd temporarily forgotten her most recent embarrassment. She must have looked ridiculous, cowering under the wagon. She didn't want to talk about it with Arley though. She barely knew him.

"Surely you're not scared of Jane?" he went on. "She's the nicest lady in the village."

Snowdrop paused, thinking. Arley hadn't given her away back

at the store when she'd hidden from Jane. He'd helped shield her from view and had gotten the wagon moving to avoid another encounter. Maybe he wasn't the worst human to talk to.

"Although Jane's got quite the biceps," he rambled on, "now that she's been smithing all summer. She could prob'ly knock out a mule."

Besides, Snowdrop reasoned, Arley wasn't going to stop babbling until she told him why she'd hidden. "It was her daughter," Snowdrop mumbled.

"Elle? Yeah, I guess I can see how you'd be scared of *that* one—"

"She was taken by the fairies when she was a baby."

Arley frowned. "I heard that story. But Jane's okay about that. You know she's courting with Rowan, right? It was the fairies' old queen who took Elle away."

Snowdrop rubbed the hem of her tunic between her thumbs and forefingers. "But I was there."

Arley shook his head. "I don't understand what you're worried about."

He truly didn't know who she was? No wonder he'd been nice to her. She swallowed. "Queen Oleander is my mother. I was with her the whole time she was stealing the human children. I lived with Elle. I worried Elle might recognize me."

For once he was silent. The wagon rolled under the first branches and into the shade.

"Maryanne was in the pub yesterday, too," Snowdrop went on. "I thought if she realized I'm a fairy it might upset her. That's why I was hiding in the alley when we met."

He faced down the road. "It must have been hard to live with that queen."

"The children are the ones she hurt the most. And their mothers." Snowdrop slumped on the seat. "And I was there," she mumbled, "doing nothing to help."

At least he'd stop talking now. She scrunched lower and picked at a thread on her tunic. Behind her, Larkspur lay with her head on a pillow, watching the fall leaves pass overhead with Edna snoozing beside her.

"You did something today to help," Arley said. "And last night. You avoided them seein' you."

Snowdrop snorted. "That hardly makes up for the past."

"No. But you can't change the past. You did what you could today." He lifted a hand to scratch his neck. "Can't fairies use magic to disappear?"

He knew they could. She didn't bother to answer.

"You know if you learned to use magic, you could hide yourself even better the next time you see one of your mother's victims."

"I know."

"Are any of them in Knotty Knob?"

Was he honestly going to keep talking about this? "Um, I think just one."

"Where are the others?" He watched her as he drove but the horses headed straight along the road.

"Most of them are in Cliffside."

"We'll be passing the road to Cliffside soon."

"I know."

"So if you went back there and had Larkspur show you how to be invisible, you wouldn't have to worry about running into any of them."

"I *know how* to turn invisible. It's just that . . . I can't do it."

"You can't?"

She shook her head.

"I bet you can. You don't want to." He peered at her. "Why? What's wrong?"

She didn't want to talk about her abnormal magic, especially not with a human. She'd never spoken about it with anyone.

But maybe that had been a mistake. She'd have to tell Larkspur how her magic went awry, if she expected Larkspur to help her. Talking to Arley might even be easier than talking to Larkspur because he didn't know anything about magic and wouldn't understand how peculiar she was. She didn't know him, but he didn't seem dangerous. He seemed harmless and a little goofy.

Besides, he wasn't going to stop asking if she didn't answer. He was still watching her as the wagon rolled along without him steering. She might as well answer if it got him to stop questioning her. She sighed. "Do you know how magic works?"

"Not really."

"Fairies have magic inside them but nature helps them use it. Especially when they're first learning. Dustan can change his appearance in a snap but when he was a child and had never done it before, he might have stood in a patch of grass to practice turning himself green."

"Could he get stuck being green?" Arley asked, wincing.

"No. The change is an illusion—he's not really green. As soon as he stopped trying to make himself green, it would fade. But once you're skilled at it, you can keep it in place without thinking about it at all."

"Can he trick other fairies?"

"No. That kind of illusion works only against humans. Fairies can see through it. It's like we see both the real thing and the illusion on top of it."

"So why won't you learn to do it?"

"Usually fairies learn as children. But I didn't get to learn."

"That 'cause of your mother?"

Snowdrop steadied herself and forced her hands to flatten from the fists they'd curled into. "Aye. Oleander." She took a deep breath. "She kept me with her instead of letting me do anything with the other children, whether they were having magic lessons or other schooling or even playing." Arley listened quietly and she found herself adding, "Not that they wanted to play with me. They were scared of her and I was her daughter. Anything they said to me might get back to her—being who I was made them fear me."

"Sounds lonely."

She didn't reply.

"That still doesn't explain why you won't learn to use magic now though. Isn't Rowan learning to make fire this summer? And he's at least as old as you."

"He's learning fire magic. That's true. But it's different for me. I could learn except . . ." She paused and sat up straight. This was the hard part to explain. "Something goes wrong inside me when I try," she said slowly. Saying the words scared her but she also felt relief as they came out. Anyway, it was too late to stop. She'd have to trust that Arley wasn't going to flee when he learned. "Because I *did* learn to use magic but I learned from Oleander. And she uses it wrong. Normal magic works together with nature. Like using the color of the grass as inspiration to turn green, or reaching out with your mind to communicate with a bird and asking it to take a message for you. But when Oleander uses magic, she demands instead of asking and she sucks the life from things. She'd use a flower and it would shrivel, or she'd demand that birds stay in the trees over her head singing and they'd do it because she intimidated them. Once I saw her stand barefoot in a field at twilight and suck the energy from all the life around her so she could make a light glow in her hands. She left a ring of scorched hay and dead lightning bugs behind. She overpowered everything around her."

"And she taught you to do that?"

Snowdrop dropped her gaze. "I thought it was how everyone learned and I'd get better and stop hurting things. I thought I just wasn't good enough yet."

"What happened?"

She hated to remember this next part. "This one day . . ." She swallowed, bracing herself. Arley waited in silence.

"I'd only ever seen her work with plants. But this one day, she, um, she used a mouse. Instead of a plant. She sucked the life from it to make a spell that enabled her to move twice as fast as normal." Snowdrop's eyes filled with tears. "It was so little and it curled up in her hand and died. She didn't care. She knew she would kill it and she didn't care. That was when I realized how our magic worked and that it wasn't the same as what most fairies did. I wasn't going to get better with practice. I was doing something completely different and wrong." Tears slid down her cheeks.

"How old were you?"

"Ten winters."

He kept silent.

Snowdrop suppressed her emotions. "I told her I wouldn't use magic anymore. I thought she'd be mad but she didn't say anything. She already had me taking care of Anemone, so I stopped trying to learn magic and ended up being a nanny as she got more and more half-human children."

"But I still don't understand why you can't learn to use the other kind of magic—the kind that doesn't hurt anything."

"When I try, I can't do it without the bad kind interfering. Like if I touch a branch of forsythia flowers to help me amplify a sound—forsythia does that because of the V-shape of the flowers—at first I sense this joyful energy from the plant and I can picture how the magic will work. But then this dark feeling rises up and interferes. So I stop trying. I don't want to risk hurting anything again."

"Does Larkspur know that happens?"

"She knows I can do Oleander's kind of magic."

"You should tell her what happens. Maybe she'll have ideas of how to help."

If anyone would know, it would be Larkspur. She was one of the most skilled fairies when it came to magic.

"And then you'll be able to win our bet when we get back from this council meeting."

"I didn't take your bet!"

He winked at her. "I know, cabbage. But once you start learning magic, I bet you will."

"Cabbage? That's worse than peanut."

"I love cabbages."

"What do you like about cabbages?"

"They're reliable to grow, and they're easy to put up for the winter. I could eat cabbage pickled in salt all winter. Don't the fairies bottle foods to preserve them?"

"Yes. But why would you call *me* that? Why would 'cabbage' be a good nickname for *me*?"

He leaned in, and his eyes crinkled. "They've got layers."

Snowdrop pushed his shoulder away as he grinned.

"Go on," he said. "Climb back there and talk to Larkspur."

She wanted to. She wanted to learn to use magic, and Larkspur might be able to help. Larkspur had offered. And all she had to do was talk to her. Maybe Larkspur would change her mind about teaching Snowdrop when she knew what they were working with.

"Fine," she said, and Arley's grin lit up his face.

Chapter 7

꧂✳꧁

SNOWDROP STOOD UP BESIDE ARLEY on the driver's seat. He reined in the horses and their pace slowed.

"Want me to stop?" he asked.

"No. I can climb over." She carefully stepped into the storage area between two crates, then onto the bench seat behind that. Larkspur craned her neck and when she saw Snowdrop coming, she pushed herself up to a sitting position.

Snowdrop lowered herself into the shade beside Larkspur, careful not to bump Edna as she snored quietly.

"How was driving the horses?" Larkspur asked.

Snowdrop smiled. "It was fun. But I let Arley take over so I could watch the scenery. I've never traveled this far."

"I know. I've never been past Knotty Knob myself."

"I, um, I was thinking about your offer. To teach me magic?"

"I would be happy to."

"There's something you need to know." Snowdrop sat up straight and inhaled to steady herself. "I'm scared I could hurt someone if I try."

Larkspur pursed her lips. "Why do you think that?"

"You know Oleander's magic? The way she used other living things to power it?"

Larkspur nodded.

"You know she taught me to use magic that way. But I haven't done it since . . . since I was young and I learned how it worked.

I don't want to use that kind of magic ever again. But when I try to use magic the right way, I keep somehow . . . going off track. It starts okay but then it goes wrong."

Larkspur's brow furrowed. "Can you describe it more fully? What exactly happens?"

"When I try to use magic . . ." Snowdrop closed her eyes and imagined her recent attempts. "When I try to use magic, I can sense the living things around me. I reached out to Lady last night and I felt her trust. But then it goes wrong. The wrong kind of magic mixes with it. And I get scared and stop."

"When you say 'mixes with it,' what do you mean?"

The way she pictured it seemed silly but she didn't know how else to describe it. "This . . . this *darkness* comes in. With Lady, as I first reached out to her, the magic felt like mist off a pond as happiness swirled around me. But when the other kind of magic crept in, it felt like dark threads weaving through the mist. Upward from the ground."

"Huh." Larkspur thought quietly for a moment. "Oleander would touch the objects she was taking power from, right?"

"Yes."

Larkspur pressed a finger to her lips, thinking. "Would it help if you weren't touching anything living?"

Snowdrop shook her head. "I've tried. I've tried communicating with Dustan's birds or matching my hair to the color of a flower from a distance. It still feels like Oleander's kind of magic is creeping in—like the air is living. Like I'm somehow reaching through every tiny insect in a web of magic, and maybe nothing will happen but I'm not going to risk killing anything to find out."

"We could start slowly and carefully," Larkspur said. "We could try to find a way."

"But—"

"Have you ever hurt anything? You're always able to stop, right?"

"Yes."

"I think you're afraid of losing control but that won't necessarily happen. The fear of what might happen is making you panic, and that makes it all worse."

"I wish I could forget her magic and start over."

Larkspur smiled. "If only we could all start with a clean slate." She pushed herself up to her knees. "Let's sit on the seat up there. I have an idea."

"Now? We're starting now?" Snowdrop's chest tightened.

"You're panicking already. We'll do something easy—so easy you won't have anything to worry about. We won't even use magic—we'll practice sensing it in the air around us."

She had to trust Larkspur. Larkspur wouldn't risk harming their companions. Snowdrop followed her up to the seat. Arley glanced over as they sat, back-to-back with him. He didn't start talking but he met Snowdrop's glance with a calm smile.

They were deep in the forest. Brittle leaves swept along the road as the horses and wheels stirred them. Squirrels searched the ground or carried acorns up trees, and the birds were busy finding seeds. The sun had reached high overhead and its light danced in patches on the ground as more leaves drifted down.

Larkspur leaned out the side of the wagon and squinted up at the sun. "We could start with sunlight," she murmured, "but we'd need to be out of the forest." She turned to Snowdrop. "We can start by using the wind. You'd have a hard time damaging the wind."

Snowdrop didn't understand but she watched and waited.

"All I want you to do is connect with the wind. You don't need to do anything with it. Simply let it in and feel it around you. I'll do the exercise with you. Close your eyes and feel the wind on your face." Larkspur sat up straight and closed her own eyes. Her hands were flat on the seat beside her.

Snowdrop had never tried anything like this. What good would it do? Still, she copied Larkspur, sitting up with her hands beside her and closing her eyes. The clomping of the horses' hooves filled her ears, and the mild jolts of the wagon's movement bumped against her palms and her bottom. The scent of dying autumn leaves overpowered the other forest smells.

A breeze tickled her nose. It cooled her cheeks.

"You feel that?" Larkspur whispered.

"Yes." The breeze faded and returned, soughing around her until she shivered.

"Now imagine the wind is a living being, like Lady. Reach out the way you did last night, but do it with the wind."

Snowdrop took a deep breath and let it out slowly. She imagined the blank space all around her, the way she had last night. She couldn't hurt the wind.

The cool breeze ruffled her hair and she welcomed it. She shivered and the breeze warmed. It smoothed over her shoulders like a sweater, surrounding her. A warm force enveloping her. No darkness, no hint of Oleander's type of magic.

The wagon still jostled beneath her but the noise of travel quieted. The wind brought chirping birdsong and slowly creaking branches. The scent of the trees and a hint of ocean air, even though the ocean must be leagues away. The light against her eyelids flickered.

Snowdrop stayed motionless as the wind swept around her. Like a comforting blanket. Nothing dark appeared. She continued, resting in place.

A warm hand covered hers.

Snowdrop blinked open her eyes and the wind slipped off her shoulders and away. Her cheeks were wet and cold. Edna sat upright at the far end of the wagon bed, leaning against the water barrel and knitting with purple yarn. The horses clopped along the road. The trees were thinner and the sunlight bright around them.

"Are you all right?" Larkspur asked quietly.

"Aye." Snowdrop blinked again. They were in a different part of the forest entirely. How much time had passed with her eyes closed? Her stomach rumbled.

Larkspur removed her hand and didn't say anything about the strange magic lesson. Had it been magic? Snowdrop had felt different while sitting with her eyes closed. And she'd lost all track of time. But she hadn't *done* anything with the wind. She'd just kind of . . . let it be with her.

But nothing bad had happened. She didn't know what good the exercise would do her, but at least she hadn't felt the darkness creeping in.

Larkspur watched the trees pass and Edna focused on her knitting. Behind her, Arley drove in silence. She didn't need to say anything. She settled onto her seat and watched the road spool out behind the wagon.

A short while later they stopped to give the horses a rest and eat the sandwiches Larkspur had gotten at the general store that morning. After lunch, Larkspur rode up front with Arley. Edna showed Snowdrop the leagueposts along the forest road and explained how the numbers worked. After that, Snowdrop couldn't stop watching for the wooden posts, counting down the distance left to the crossroads. Soon she was twisted on her seat, peering ahead for the first sight of the outpost.

"There's nothing much there," Edna said, concerned.

"There's an inn, though, right? And a store?"

"But nothing else."

"I still want to see it."

"It's her first time traveling," Larkspur offered from the front.

"I see." Edna patted Snowdrop's knee. "It's always exciting your first time."

Arley choked back a laugh.

Snowdrop looked to him, but Edna continued, smiling slyly. "I remember my first time—how awkward I was! No idea what I was doing."

Arley stifled another laugh. Larkspur shook her head, and Snowdrop's face heated as she realized why he was laughing. Could he be any more childish? He was as bad as teen-aged fairies. If they weren't tumbling, they were talking about it or joking about it. Why was it such a big deal?

Another leaguepost appeared and she read the marker as they rolled past. They overtook a group traveling on foot and a moment later the trees opened into a wider dirt lane. A brightly painted sign on a post read Welcome to Forest Crossroads. The open area was smaller than a village square but had a wooden inn on the right and cottages on the left. The inn was freshly painted white and had a wide front porch with rocking chairs facing the road, and the cottages had thick glass windows and sturdy-looking shingle roofs.

Arley stopped the wagon in front of the inn. Beyond the inn, another road crossed theirs east to west. A small wooden sign decorated with painted flowers and with an arrow pointing east read The Inn at Cliffside. Beyond the crossroads was the general store, and beyond the store the trees closed in and the northern-heading road continued on under the branches.

Everyone clambered out and took a moment to stretch. Arley loped off and disappeared into the trees, and Snowdrop flushed and turned away when she realized she was watching as he went off to relieve himself. She hurried over to Lady and Bird. They stood patiently and nuzzled her hair when she neared.

When Larkspur went inside, Snowdrop followed. A staircase with a wooden railing climbed out of sight and the front entryway opened on the left into a dining room filled with tables and a large hearth. The innkeeper sat behind a wooden counter like in the pub but with fewer ale mugs on the shelf behind her. With the woven rugs on the floor and a few lanterns lit, the place felt cozy.

The inn had only one available room, so Larkspur took it for herself and Edna. She offered to share it with Snowdrop too, but if Snowdrop had to sleep on the floor, she might as well be in the wagon or on the ground outside. Or, the innkeeper offered, they could use the hayloft over the stable, although one other traveler already planned to sleep in the hayloft that night.

Larkspur paid for the room and the space for the horses and they returned outside. Arley was back from the trees and waiting by the horses, who nipped at his shirt as if they knew he was the one who'd get their dinner. Larkspur explained the sleeping arrangements.

"I'll go see the stable before I move the horses," Arley said. He addressed Snowdrop. "Want to check out this hayloft?"

She nodded and followed him around the building as the ladies unloaded their bags.

"We've a hayloft in the barn at home," he said over his shoulder. "It was, ah, a popular place among my brothers and me."

"Why?"

He gave her a pointed look.

She deflated. "Right. Tumbling."

"Although myself," he went on, as usual, "I like hay as much as the next person, but it always seemed a bit of a cliché to ask a girl to go romp with ya in the hay."

"Seems like a cliché to ask for a 'romp' in the first place," Snowdrop muttered and Arley laughed.

Down a wide path and around the back of the inn was a grassy yard with a pump in the middle. A woman filled a water gourd at the pump. As they approached, she looked up at Arley with wide green eyes.

Snowdrop went still and her heart dropped. Arley blocked the woman's view as he moved toward her. Snowdrop stepped backward and slipped into the cover of the inn. She leaned on the wall for support.

The woman had green eyes. She was a fairy. Or a half fairy. And if she was a half fairy, she might be . . .

"Good evening to ya," Arley called out, his voice clear from around the corner.

"Good evening," came the reply, and the voice was so familiar. The woman was Anemone.

Chapter 8

TEARS SPRANG INTO SNOWDROP'S EYES at the familiar sound of Anemone's voice. She hadn't seen Anemone or heard her speak in more than eight winters, but the moment the woman at the pump replied to Arley's greeting, Snowdrop was sure. She'd lived with Anemone in Oleander's chambers for seven full turns of the seasons before Larkspur had taken Anemone away.

When Snowdrop had learned Anemone was alive, she hadn't tried to see her. She'd been scared to try—would Anemone want to see her again? Would she want to be reminded of the horrible seasons she'd been trapped underground, serving Oleander?

And now here she was, right where they would be spending the night. What should she do? Anemone and Arley were making small talk around the corner—she'd missed what they said. Why was Anemone here? Was she traveling somewhere? What would Anemone think of Snowdrop now that she'd been free of Oleander for so long? By now she must have realized the magnitude of the wrong that had been done to her. Did she blame Snowdrop for her role in Oleander's schemes?

The voices stopped. A footstep crunched and Snowdrop shrank down against the wall, crouching on the sparse grass. She was too late to hide herself.

But Arley rounded the corner alone. He glanced down at her and exhaled. He took her arm and gently lifted her up to walk beside him, away from the back of the building.

"It's Anemone," Snowdrop whispered. "I know her."

"She introduced herself as Nem." He kept his voice low to match hers.

She blinked her eyes clear. "She was the first half-human child Oleander stole."

"I figured she might be by how you disappeared." His face was serious but his tone remained calm.

Snowdrop unclenched her hands. "Did she say why she's here?"

"She's travelin' north to visit someone."

"Who could she be visiting?" Snowdrop frowned. "She lived in hiding until a few moons ago."

"Maybe one of the other children?" He stepped away and rubbed the back of his neck. "I, uh, I offered she could ride with us. I'm sorry, Snowdrop. I didn't notice you were gone at first. It's only, the mail cart won't come through for another quarter-moon and I worry to think who might pick her up in the meantime. She'd be safer traveling with us."

Snowdrop fought off the rising panic. She had to get through this somehow. "It's okay. It's the right thing to do."

"We'd be sleeping with her anyway, unless you want me to leave the wagon outside and you could sleep in it. But . . ." He went silent.

Snowdrop guessed what he was thinking—he'd said it earlier that day. She couldn't change the past but she should do what she could to help others, today. She should face Anemone even if it scared her. "I shouldn't hide from her," she said. "But I don't know how to do this. I don't want to upset her."

"I don't think you can control who gets upset, love. But if you try to do what's right, it should work out. Don't ya think?"

"So do I walk up to her and apologize?"

He pressed his lips together and hummed. "Apologizing might make things about you. It seems better to focus on her. She's got a life. You don't know what she thinks about the past or even if she does. I don't know if you should be the one to bring it up. And besides, I'm not clear on what you're apologizing for. How long has it been since you've seen her?"

"Eight winters?"

"Well she hasn't seen you in eight winters, either. And she's grown up. She might remember things differently than you."

"What should I say?" Snowdrop asked.

"Maybe start with 'Hello' and see what happens? It might be more important to listen than to say things."

"That's something Larkspur would say."

"What can I say?" He grinned, and the familiar expression on his face calmed her nerves a smidge. He was about to say something arrogant that she'd roll her eyes at, at any other time. "I possess the wisdom of the elders."

She shook her head slowly. "I don't want to startle her."

"Why don't I go ahead and warn her you're here. If she runs screamin', you'll know she doesn't want to see ya."

Snowdrop laughed in spite of herself, and Arley smiled.

She followed him back toward the corner of the inn. Arley stepped out and, after scanning the yard, motioned her to follow. The stable yard was empty.

The stable was a long wooden building with large, shuttered windows along the side and a sloping roof. On one end, a large hanging door could slide open to allow wagons in. They crossed the grass to the smaller side door.

"Wait here," Arley said and he pulled open the door and disappeared into the dim interior. The weathered door swung shut behind him. Snowdrop leaned on the doorframe, near the crack where the door opened, and strained to hear.

"Hey, Nem, are you up there?" Arley called.

Anemone said something back, but Snowdrop couldn't make it out.

"One of my travel companions would like to meet ya." He

didn't call as loudly that time, but his voice still reached her clearly. Like he was making sure she could hear. A pause followed. "The thing is," Arley continued, "she says you've met before and she doesn't want to startle you. And if ya don't want to see her, she'd understand. Her name's Snowdrop."

Anemone gasped. "Where is she?"

"Just outside."

Snowdrop stepped back and held her breath, gripping the door-frame to stop her shaking. The door creaked open, and the grown-up Anemone faced her.

A moment passed in which they both stared, probably only a heartbeat, but it seemed to stretch on and on. Snowdrop swallowed, grasping for the words she'd planned to say. All that worry about what to say and now she couldn't say anything.

Anemone's lips parted and nothing came out. Anemone was older but her face was the same—deep green eyes, pert nose, un-smiling but she had always been a serious child. She wore her straight brown hair pulled back in a long braid. And she was so tall! Snowdrop remembered picking her up, carrying her on her hip, laying her to sleep on her pallet.

Snowdrop couldn't stop her tears. She swiped them away before they could fall. What was Anemone thinking and feeling? The other woman blinked a few times as if she, too, were fighting off tears.

"I, um, I didn't know . . ." Snowdrop tried. Was this a mistake? But Anemone wouldn't have come outside if she hadn't wanted to see Snowdrop. Arley had given her the option to say no.

Anemone took a small step forward. "I missed you so much," she whispered.

Snowdrop's tears welled over and she clamped her lips tight to stop her face from scrunching up.

"Trillium and Woodbine said you had to stay with Oleander," Anemone went on, "and that I couldn't contact you."

"It wouldn't have been safe," Snowdrop blurted out. "Not with Oleander . . ." She took a deep breath to steady herself. "I missed you too." She didn't say that she'd thought Anemone was dead. She didn't know what the fairies had told Anemone.

"I'm sorry we left you there with her," Anemone said. And this time she hiccupped at the end and her face crumpled as tears rolled down her cheeks.

Snowdrop stared for a heartbeat. And then she fell back into her role as if the past eight winters had never happened. She put her arms around Anemone and held her, telling her everything would be okay. She'd always struggled to say those words when Anemone was a child, managing only because they were vague enough not to be a complete lie. But this time, the words came right off her tongue. Everything would be okay.

When they'd both recovered, they walked to the bench beside the back door of the inn. Anemone wore a simple dress and her feet were bare. They sat facing the stable, and Anemone folded her hands in her lap, her demeanor steady, just as it had been as a child. Neither one of them had ever been talkative but Snowdrop was the older one here so maybe she should take the lead?

"Arley said you're traveling to visit someone?" she ventured. As she spoke his name, Arley slipped out the stable door and crossed the yard.

"Yes. You know what happened to us after . . . after . . . ?"

"I didn't know until two springs ago. Larkspur told me where you were. And she said you're in Cliffside now with your mother and grandmother."

Anemone smiled. "I wish you could meet them."

"You don't think they'd hate me? I was Oleander's— I don't know. I helped her."

"Did you? All I remember is you hiding us when she was angry or drunk."

"But I didn't stop her from keeping you."

"You were barely older than us."

"I got older, though. I should have done something."

Anemone blinked a few times before replying. "It's over. It's better to move on."

Her words were as Arley had said. Anemone didn't need Snowdrop dredging up the past to assuage her guilt if others had moved on.

A jangling sounded and Arley led the horses down the path into the yard, pulling the wagon. He turned them on the grass to park the wagon alongside the stable and began to unhitch them.

"How are the other children?" Snowdrop asked. "How is everyone?"

Anemone—or Nem as she was called—told Snowdrop all about Trillium and Woodbine, the other children they had rescued from Oleander, the refuge they'd built to house them all in the western woods, and the adventures she'd had that spring when the first of their mothers had been found. As she spoke, Arley led the horses into the stable.

Nem spoke with fondness of her new home in Cliffside, where she helped run the inn and had nature lessons from Woodbine. She was traveling only because one of the younger children had gone to live with family in Mountain Rest, and a letter had come in which he sounded homesick. Nem had offered to visit to see if she could help.

As the sun set, the waxing moon appeared high overhead and the last crickets of the season chirped from the tree line. The night air cooled and smoke from the cook fire drifted across the stable yard. Snowdrop and Nem went inside to find Larkspur. She and Edna had a table in the dining room, where the innkeeper had served them a mushroom and root stew she made special for her fairy guests, along with thick slices of a wheat and rye bread. She brought two more servings and left a covered dish for them to take out to Arley.

The travelers they'd passed on the road were at another table, plus a few other guests, and the dining room buzzed with chatter. Snowdrop had never been around this many humans without feeling anxious. Usually their loud talking made her jittery and she wanted to escape, but sitting in the dining room with the low conversations mixing all around was pleasant. A man lit a fire in the hearth as darkness set in. Finally the elder ladies said goodnight. Snowdrop took the covered dish of stew and Nem wrapped the remaining bread in a napkin to carry out to the stable.

The wagon stood silently in the dark. The stable's side door was propped open and golden lantern light shone out into the yard. Arley passed by the doorway, carrying hay for Lady and Bird.

"He's nice," Nem said as they neared the door.

"Hmm?"

"Your beau. He's nice."

"Oh!" Snowdrop's face heated. "He's not my beau. We're traveling together because of this council meeting."

Nem tilted her head, smiled, and shook it once. "Well, he's nice," she said again.

Snowdrop found herself not able to disagree.

"Are you tired?" Nem asked.

"I might sit out here for a little while."

"I'll take the food in." Nem reached for the dish. "I'm glad we'll get to spend time together tomorrow and all the way to Mountain Rest."

"Me too."

"Goodnight, Snowdrop." Nem lingered in the doorway, the side of her face illuminated in the golden light.

Snowdrop bit back sudden tears. "Goodnight."

Left alone, Snowdrop went to the back of the wagon where the board had been left down. She climbed in and lay back on the rug. Tears lingered in her eyes before a few rolled down the sides of her face.

Nem was fine—confident, well adjusted. In spite of being taken from her mother as a baby and used as a servant by Oleander, raised by an inept young Snowdrop, and kept underground for seven winters, she was okay. When Nem described her new home, she sounded content.

All these winters Snowdrop had carried so much guilt for her role in Oleander's schemes. Dustan and the other fairies said none of it was her fault, but she knew she could've done more. But all the guilt in the world wouldn't help anyone now. Did Larkspur wallow in guilt over lying to Snowdrop? No. She offered to help Snowdrop learn magic. And she volunteered to attend the humans' meeting, to build bridges between them and the fairies. As Nem had said, it was better to move on. She could support Nem on her visit to Mountain Rest. If she learned magic, she could use it to help the other children. What else could she do to make a difference now?

The moon crept farther along the sky and shone under the canvas cover and onto the wagon bed. All the stars had come out and the crickets were silent. The woods behind the stable yard rustled and a few bats swooped overhead, catching insects in the lights of the outpost.

The wagon jostled and someone sat beside Snowdrop's legs. She wiped the tracks of tears from her face. When the person didn't move, she slid herself over to the edge of the wagon bed. Arley lay back with an overly loud sigh. He'd lain as far away as he could, leaving a wide gap between them, but the faint heat of him reached her in the cool evening air.

"That seemed to go well," he said quietly.

"Yes."

He stayed quiet for a full ten beats. "The stars are nice out here away from village lights."

"Yes."

"Be better stars without the moon, though. That's an awfully bright moon for being only halfway full."

Snowdrop couldn't stop herself from smiling. He was messing with her. He was going to keep talking until she responded.

"I like the moon and stars together," she said, "even if you can see only a few stars because of the moonlight."

"Is that so?"

"Yes."

"I'm glad you've got the view then. We could roll down the sides of the wagon cover."

"No."

"Well," he said, apparently satisfied now that he'd gotten her to speak more than a single-word answer. He sat up. "The horses are bedded down and fed, and the elder ladies are bedded down and fed, and I'm fed, and Nem is on her way to sleep in the hayloft, so I was thinking of going to bed myself."

She shook her head against the floor of the wagon.

"Do you want me to leave the lantern burning in the stable?"

"No."

"Here." He got up on his knees and rummaged around above her head. A blanket thumped against her elbow. He stacked a few more beside it. "In case you get cold."

"Thank you."

Arley climbed out of the wagon. She turned her head to see him. He paused to stretch his arms upward and twisted his hips back and forth.

"I haven't done so little work in ages," he said. "Tomorrow, remind me to move a bit more 'stead of sitting like a lump on the driver's seat."

"Okay."

"Maybe you can drive and I'll jog alongside."

"Okay."

"Okay then." He walked along the wagon toward the stable door.

"Arley?"

"What's that?" He held the side of the wagon and gazed down at her.

She met his gaze a moment before she looked away. "Thank you."

Chapter 9

⁕

SNOWDROP WOKE TO THE SPLASHING of water. She snuggled under the heavy layer of blankets in the nippy morning darkness. The sun was barely up and not yet over the trees or the roof of the stable, but the stars had faded in the coming dawn. A faint golden light shone out the open stable door. A hint of cooking smoke reached her on the cold, damp air.

She rolled over but the splashing sound came again and she was too awake to go back to sleep. A plunking smack against water—what was that? And more splashing. She sat up on the creaking wagon boards and rubbed her eyes. A few birds flitted across the yard and a light winked on through the trees in the direction of the general store. She pulled the top blanket around her shoulders, saving her body's warmth before the morning air whisked it away.

The stable yard was barely lit by the dawn light. Arley stood at the pump with no shirt on.

Snowdrop's face heated and she crouched back into the wagon. If he saw her watching him, he'd surely tease her about it. But he faced away from her. She hooked her fingers over the side of the wagon and peeked out. He had his trousers and boots on at least. Water droplets glistened on the back of his neck in the faint morning light, and the surface of the water filling the trough rippled as the bucket bobbed on it.

He leaned forward to push the bucket under, filling it, and lifted it from the water with one muscular arm. He slowly poured the water over his head, running his free hand through his hair as the water cascaded down his neck and off his shoulders. Snowdrop pulled the blanket around herself more snugly. Wasn't Arley freezing out there half naked and dripping wet?

He dropped the bucket back into the trough and Snowdrop flinched as it smacked the water again. He reached for a towel that hung tucked into the side of his trousers, pulled it out, and used it to rub his neck and hair dry. He draped the towel around his neck and leaned forward to scoop water in his hands and splash it on his face, scrubbing and drying before tucking the towel onto the side of the trough.

He stepped away from the pump and stretched his left arm up and leaned his wide frame over to the right, stretching out his side. Snowdrop squinted. He switched sides, leaning the other way. Then he dropped toward the ground and began pushing his body up and down, his biceps bulging. Was he doing some kind of morning exercises? One of the fairies led a gathering in the clearing each morning, but her exercises were all gentle stretches and balance poses. They never looked like this. Maybe Arley had learned this routine in the King's Guard. He pushed himself onto his feet and began to alternate standing and crouching, holding his arms out for balance.

A window sash scraped open. The growing daylight illuminated the upper story of the inn and glinted on the glass windows as the middle window slid up. Edna pushed aside a thin curtain and leaned out. "You're putting on quite a show out there, Arley," she called into the quiet morning.

He turned his head up to her. "Oh, ya like what ya see?" He grinned and stood, flexing both biceps at once and turning his torso slowly back and forth. Edna swiped the back of her hand across her forehead and pretended to swoon out the window. Arley nabbed the towel off the edge of the trough and flung it over his shoulder. He caught the tail end and held it diagonally across his muscular back before rubbing it up and down, wiggling his

hips suggestively. Edna barked in laughter. When Arley started ro-
tating in a circle, Snowdrop dropped down into the wagon so he
wouldn't catch her watching.

Snowdrop frowned. With his broad shoulders and his trousers
tucked into the tops of his boots, he reminded her of the fairy
prince in one of the old story scrolls in the library—the one who
bested the cunning bear who'd kidnapped the neighboring court's
children. When he returned them home, he danced with one of the
princesses at the celebration in the moonlight, and they fell in love
and it ended with a happily ever after, like every other story in that
series. Always a romantic happily ever after between two fairies.

But Arley wasn't a fairy prince who danced in the moonlight.
He wasn't even a fairy. He was a human farmer who jabbered on
about nothing.

And even if he had been a romantic fairy prince, he was no longer interested in her. He had been when they first met, she was sure
of it, but his interest had gone. What if she hadn't gotten panicky
when he first approached her? What if she'd let him keep flirting?
What if she'd known how to flirt back?

What if Arley were her beau, as Nem had assumed? Would he
take her on one of the human "dates" the fairies had been going on
about all summer? Would it be romantic? Or would he make jokes
and tease her the way he usually did?

Or, would he take her hand and try to kiss her?

A sick twist tightened her guts at the thought. That was the
trouble with romance. She liked daydreaming about all of it—the
flirting, the touching, the kissing, the thrusting. She liked reading
it in the stories in the library. But the times it had happened in real
life had been so different from her imaginings. She had felt special
at first, glad to be noticed. But as the situation rolled onward she'd
felt lost. The romance turned to discomfort, and she felt helpless to
stop it. She had learned to avoid romance.

Edna was laughing nonstop now. Snowdrop couldn't hide in
the wagon forever—anyone would have been woken by all their

fussing. She sat up. Arley was facing her and wagging his bottom at Edna, with the towel pulled tight against it, in spite of his trousers being on. Snowdrop kept her gaze on his face so he wouldn't tease her for ogling his naked chest. His eyes crinkled and he winked at her and gave an extra waggle with his butt before straightening.

Nem came out the stable doorway and toward the wagon. "It *was* quite a show," she said dryly.

"I missed it."

"Don't you think he's handsome?" Nem sounded curious. Arley gave his hair another swipe with the towel.

"Sure," Snowdrop conceded. "But he's not . . . " She couldn't find a way to finish the sentence. "He seems to like flirting," she offered.

"Does he flirt with you?"

"He did but he stopped after I told him not to."

"Maybe he shows off when you're around because he wants to flirt with you."

Nem wasn't the type to tease. But she was wrong. Since Snowdrop had rejected his initial advances in Woods Rest, he had stopped flirting with her, at least seriously. In the beginning when he'd flirted for real, the actions had had that edge of menace—the way flirting always had with other men. Now when he flirted with her, she could tell he was only joking.

Snowdrop studied the wagon boards as the daylight brightened. The wood was worn smooth by use. Out in the yard, Arley had resumed his exercises.

"But aren't humans . . . naturally flirty?" Snowdrop asked Nem. "I've never known any humans. Except for Rose's friends, who we visit in Woodglen, and they're all women. But the human men I've seen on the streets always seem very forward."

Nem leaned on the side of the wagon. "I don't think they're all flirty or outgoing. It's the same as the fairies—the flirty ones are the loudest so you notice them most. My friend in Cliffside, Burne, the one who lived with us in the forest when we were hiding from Oleander, he's not a flirt. He's the opposite—like you."

Like her? What did that mean? What was the opposite of a flirt?

"What am I like?" Snowdrop asked.

"I don't mean it in a bad way. You were always quiet, though. You didn't seem interested in the fairies your age. I thought maybe you were quiet to avoid drawing Oleander's attention."

"You were right. But I think . . ."

Nem tilted her head and waited.

"I overheard Dustan and Rose once. They said I have 'intimacy issues.'"

Nem frowned.

"I think they might be right," she hurried on. "What they said made sense, anyway. That growing up with Oleander, and her lack of emotional connection, and me not connecting with other fairies, might've resulted in me being scared to get close to others."

"Well that might be true," Nem said. "But I don't think that's the only reason you don't like flirting. Burne's mother is the nicest woman you'd ever meet, and she was kind to him and took care of him. And Burne was surrounded by nice people growing up, all the way until he had to join the King's Guard, which was how he ended up hiding out in the forest with us. But he's still . . . reserved about things. It's how some people are."

"Does Burne date people?"

Nem smirked. "I don't think he ever did much. He didn't have any idea how it worked. No one tells the human children any-thing—not like Queen Delphinium's lessons in love and lust like we were taught."

Snowdrop bit her lip. She'd never had those lessons, although she'd heard of them. "When did you—"

"Trillium taught us when we were old enough."

"So how do humans learn about sex?"

"They kind of just bumble through it? The horny ones figure

out they want to tumble each other and the rest follow along, and some of them end up doing things they don't like, or they end up hurting each other because they want different things. They're very bad at communicating most of the time. You need to be straight-forward with them about what you want."

Snowdrop remembered telling Arley to stop flirting with her. She'd been clear about it, and he had complied.

But Wells had gotten upset with her. "This man in the pub in Woods Rest kept trying to talk to me," Snowdrop said, "like he was interested. But when I told him to stop, he insisted he hadn't been flirting with me."

"Some of them are like that. They take it personally when you're not interested in them. I guess they're embarrassed because they think you're insulting them somehow. And they try to pretend something is wrong with you for not wanting them."

"He did! He told Arley not to 'bother' with me, like something was wrong with me. But Arley ignored him."

"Good. Nothing's wrong with you. And to answer your first question, Burne did date and he's partnered now. And you'll never guess who it is."

"Of course not. I don't know any humans."

"It's a fairy!"

"He's with a fairy?" How could he be with a fairy? He hadn't ever come to the fairy's village in the woods, as far as she knew. And only a few of the fairies had left the woods to live in human villages.

"Remember that teen-aged fairy everyone complained about because he wouldn't do any work and he was always goofing off?"

Realization dawned as Snowdrop remembered hearing about which fairies had left the woods. "Wait, your friend Burne is with Grape Hyacinth?"

Nem grinned. "He goes by Gray now. He moved to Woodglen with his sister, and he and Burne met picking flowers in the woods or something ridiculous like that, and they fell in love."

"But he was . . . he was so experienced. The fairies he court-ed with used to whisper about him being the best lover they ever had."

"I guess? He was single when he met Burne. They live with us in my grandmother's house. They're completely besotted with each other. But it took Burne forever. He was so awkward at first that he could barely talk to Gray."

"And Grape— Gray, he was okay with someone like that?"
Nem nodded.

"Morning, ladies." Arley approached the wagon. He'd put his shirt on, finally, the one with the strange pattern of crossed stripes he called plaid. He grinned as he ambled past and entered the stable.

Nem lifted a hefty bag over the side of the wagon. "I've got sticky buns if you'd like one. They're a human thing—a bun with maple sugary goop and nuts on top. My mother makes them. Sometimes I scrape the topping off before I eat one."

Snowdrop pushed off the blanket from her shoulders. "Let me check with Larkspur. I think the innkeeper might be providing us with breakfast since we're traveling on 'official business' for this meeting. We could share whatever we get—I bet Arley and Edna will want the goopy sugar buns." She held back her thoughts about humans and their unhealthy sugary foods. She wasn't going to be rude and she'd probably love sticky buns too, if she'd grown up eating them. Besides, she wasn't about to insult anything Nem's mother did.

Snowdrop had slept in most of her clothes but she pulled the rest on as Arley and Nem brought the horses out of the stable and began hitching them to the wagon. Nem's gossip circled in her mind. Grape Hyacinth had been the biggest flirt in the caverns back when they were teens—he was about her age. He'd never given her any attention but that was to be expected. No one had wanted to upset Oleander or her sons, and being involved with Oleander's daughter was a risky thing to do.

Only two fairies had ever bothered with her, and long ago she had realized it hadn't had anything to do with her—they hadn't particularly liked spending time with her or found her attractive. They had gotten involved with her for the thrill of doing something dangerous, of being with someone dangerous and not getting caught. But they'd gotten over the thrill and moved on, and she hadn't liked being with either one of them much anyway.

But in spite of how experienced he'd been, Grape Hyacinth had met someone inexperienced, someone like her, and had wanted to be with him. Exclusively. Even though that someone was awkward and shy. Like her—but human!

Snowdrop climbed out of the wagon and folded the blankets one by one. Arley glanced up from the other end where he had Lady and Bird standing in position as he hitched them to the wagon. "Good morning, sunshine!" he called.

Snowdrop closed her eyes and shook her head before walking up the wagon path.

Chapter 10

SNOWDROP WALKED UP THE PATH to the front of the inn. A lantern burned on a post by the road although the sun was bright enough now that the light barely showed. To her right, a voice sounded. A cart full of baskets and crates was parked at the general store and a few people milled nearby, unloading the goods and carrying them in through the propped-open door. The dust of the roadway lingered in the air, mixing with the cold, damp smell of morning in the forest.

The sun might be up, but the crossroads was enclosed with trees, leaving the ground and buildings crisscrossed in shadow. One oblong patch of pinkish sunlight stretched across the center of the crossroads from the eastern road, the one to Cliffside.

Edna rocked in a creaky chair on the inn's porch and greeted Snowdrop as she rounded the corner. "They've packed us hard rolls," she said indicating a parcel on her lap, "and boiled eggs and some other things for breakfast, if you'd like any."

"I can wait until we're on the way." Snowdrop climbed the steps. The inn door was half open and warm air wafted out. "Arley is hitching the horses. And Nem has something called 'sticky buns' to share."

Edna perked up, her eyes alight. "Sticky buns! I love sticky buns!"

Stars above, they were just buns with maple sugar. But Snowdrop's sarcastic response faded and she didn't say it. Edna could enjoy them all she wanted. Maybe they had some special meaning in the human community.

"Where's Larkspur?" Snowdrop asked instead.

Edna lifted her chin to point across the road. Larkspur stood on the roadway heading west. That direction was overgrown with vines crawling across the ground and branches hanging down as if not many travelers passed through. Larkspur stood motionless, her head cocked to one side.

"What's she doing?"

Edna shrugged. "She's been over there ten minutes."

"Where does that road go?"

"Straight into the mountains. But it's a long way through and the road gets rocky. Anyone wanting to cross usually goes up to Mountain Rest."

Larkspur shifted, facing back toward the inn. She frowned as she crossed the road but as she reached them, her expression smoothed over.

Snowdrop wasn't fooled. "What's going on?"

Larkspur smiled. "Nothing. I was listening to the morning news to see if anything was amiss in the forest."

Edna leaned toward Snowdrop. "By 'listening' she means listening to all the birds and critters gossiping." As if Snowdrop didn't know how magic worked! But Edna was too earnest to be annoyed at. Larkspur sat in a rocker but kept watching the trees across the road.

Nem joined them with her packet of sticky buns. Edna moaned dramatically as she took one and had a bite, and even Larkspur tried one of the dripping, oozing buns. When Snowdrop shook her head, Nem deftly peeled the top crust off a bun and handed the gooey layer to Edna, who moaned again, clutching part of a bun in each hand.

Nem grinned at Snowdrop as she passed across the plain, doughy bun bottom. Snowdrop sniffed it and nibbled the edge. The bun was yeasty and fancier than the fairies' usual bread, even without the topping. Her next bite had a drip of the topping and the sweetness exploded in her mouth. Skies above, it was a hundred times sweeter than the granola had been. As soon as she swallowed, she was tempted to ask for more.

Soon Lady and Bird clopped out from the wagon path beside the inn. The ladies climbed into the back and passed around the innkeeper's boiled eggs and apples as well as a hard cheese, not anything like the cheeses the fairies made. No one wanted the hard rolls after the sweet buns, so Larkspur packed them away.

Standing beside them, Arley snarfed down his food, eating the whole apple, core and all. He wiped his fingers clean and climbed up to the driver's seat.

"Had to eat fast in the King's Guard," he said, winking at her. "One of the many pointless rules."

"Did you want a sticky bun, Arley?" Nem asked.

"Ah, no thanks, love, although they look delicious." He clicked his tongue and the wagon jerked forward. The horses jogged north across the east–west road and when Snowdrop looked east the morning sun blinded her. The forest closed in around them and they left the crossroads behind.

The moment they finished eating, Larkspur turned to Snowdrop and her stomach sank.

"Are you ready for today's lesson?" Larkspur asked.

Couldn't they roll along a few minutes before she had to try? Weren't fairies supposed to wait fifteen minutes after eating before using magic, or was that a myth?

But the lesson yesterday had gone well—whatever that exercise had been about. Maybe it would be okay today, too.

"Snowdrop's getting magic lessons," Edna said to Nem as she pulled her knitting out of her bag, and Snowdrop's stomach lurched again.

"Nothing bad," Snowdrop said quickly. Nem was unflappable but her eyes had widened a smidge and her lips had parted. "Not like, you know. Not like *her*. Larkspur's trying to teach me to use it the way most fairies do. Simple things like changing my appearance."

Nem closed her mouth, nodding.

"Tell me if you want us to stop," Snowdrop added.

Larkspur watched them. "Yesterday Snowdrop and I did an exercise to connect to the wind," Larkspur told Nem. "The wind is a force of nature even though it's not a living thing. We can use such forces as inspiration for our magic." She turned to Snowdrop. "I was thinking today you could use the sky as inspiration to make your hair appear blue."

Snowdrop peered up at the canvas. She scooched to the side of the wagon bed and leaned out. The wagon rolled between tall trees on both sides, but overhead a strip of sky showed. The sunlight had brightened into the full light of day as they had eaten breakfast and now the sky was a clear and vibrant blue. Falling leaves blew across the view as the branches rustled, as if the wind were encouraging her to try.

"What do you think?" Larkspur asked. "You can't hurt the sky."

Snowdrop's palms were sweaty and her insides were tied in knots but she nodded. She wiped her hands on her trousers and sat up straight with her back against the side of the wagon. The sky beamed down at her. She closed her eyes and tried to settle herself, listening to the wagon creaking and the horses' hooves on the road. She breathed in the damp autumn air. The wagon bumped beneath her and the barest breeze blew across her face.

She opened her eyes and took in the blue sky. She couldn't feel anything about it or sense herself touching it, not like the wind. She shook her head.

"Imagine that color on you," Larkspur said quietly. "Maybe swirling down through the air like the falling leaves."

A leaf drifted by across the brilliant blue backdrop and Snowdrop imagined the blue trailing after it, floating down from the sky. Back and forth it went, floating nearer and nearer, moving ever closer. More leaves joined it, strange leaves all with a point at one end. They swirled together as more and more leaves joined in a spiral heading toward her.

Was she doing this right? It didn't feel the way it had yesterday. But she didn't seem to be hurting anything.

Don't panic, she told herself. She closed her eyes and imagined the leaves carrying the blue of the sky onto her hair.

Something wooshed by her face and Edna shrieked. Snowdrop's eyes flew open.

The spiral of leaves unwound as it descended and shot across the wagon. Only they weren't leaves. They were swifts, a whole flock of them blasting across the wagon bed. Nem ducked and Edna pulled her sweater over her hair. Up front, Arley spoke calming words to the horses as the birds darted over them and away. Larkspur followed the path of the flock into the trees.

Snowdrop clung to the side of the wagon. "Did I hurt them?" she whispered.

"No, they're fine."

"I thought they were leaves." Snowdrop's face burned. She wanted to pull her own sweater over her head like Edna had, to hide in shame. "Why did they do that?"

"They thought you were asking them to join us."

"I'm sorry." She peeked forward but Arley was focused on the horses, who had resumed their even gait.

"No need to apologize," Larkspur said. "It was your first try. And nothing got hurt."

"I can't imagine ever doing it right."

"You will. It takes time to learn." She sighed. "If only we had snowdrops. Having your name plant might make everything easier."

Snowdrop sagged against the side of the wagon. "It figures I got stuck named after a flower that doesn't even grow here."

Larkspur frowned. "Who told you that?"

"I . . ." Snowdrop had no answer. "No one told me. Everyone knows that."

"It's not true."

"Yes it is. Isn't it? Snowdrops grow in the eastern islands."

"It's not true, Snowdrop. They bloom all across our continent too. They bloom early in the spring with the crocuses."

"But I've never seen one."

Larkspur sighed again. "They used to grow throughout the forest." She lowered her voice. "Your mother destroyed the ones near the enclave."

"Oleander destroyed them? Why would she do that?"

Larkspur's eyes were sad. "I don't know."

Snowdrop kept her face toward the forest. Her fingernails dug into the side of the wagon. Some fairies were unlucky to receive a name from a plant that didn't grow nearby. They might never see their name plant. And Oleander had such a name—oleanders grew on the warmer northern continent. Oleander had often spoken resentfully about her name.

But if snowdrops actually did grow in central Sylvania, in the forest where she'd been born, why would Oleander have destroyed them?

Snowdrop took a deep breath and let it out, swallowing. "Larkspur," she said, "you knew Oleander before she was the queen. Was she always . . . the way she is?"

Larkspur stared at the road stretching behind the wagon but her eyes lost their focus. "Oleander was awkward around others. But she didn't crave power when she was young. Our community failed her. If she had been happier, she might not have turned out the way she did."

"Why was she unhappy?"

"She had trouble making friends. She just wasn't . . . nice. She'd say hurtful things and not realize the hurt she caused. So her peers didn't seek out her company."

Snowdrop felt a pang of sympathy. "No one wanted me for a friend either."

"They were scared of Oleander, and you were stuck by her side."

"What happened as she grew older?" Snowdrop asked.

"You know how fairies are once they reach a certain age."

Snowdrop shook her head.

Edna looked up from her knitting. "I think she means they get horny."

Of course.

"Oleander saw all the others fooling around or pairing off, and she had no one. She must have craved a connection but she only grew more isolated. We didn't know it at the time, but she started visiting the human village and pretending to be human to meet men. It wasn't forbidden and plenty of fairies did it. But it was always done as a fling, and other fairies were careful to avoid pregnancy—because the fairies were a bit secretive and lived hidden in the forest. And everyone understood you wouldn't pair up with someone who lived in the village and had no magic."

"Fairies live in the village now," Edna said.

"True. But it wasn't done back then. So Oleander met someone—a human man—and she thought they were in love. She thought he would bond with her. But, to her beau, they were having fun and nothing more. When he ended it, she saw it as a betrayal."

"How do you know all this?" Snowdrop asked.

"She told Thistle."

"I can't imagine Oleander sharing something like that with anyone, even Thistle."

"No, she wouldn't. But after he ended it, she needed help. You see, she had stopped taking her bitter herbs. She thought she and the human were on their way to a life bond and she'd be able to leave the fairies and start a new life with him in Woodglen. And part of her plan worked. She got pregnant."

"What?"

"And when Thistle explained her options, she wanted to have the child."

"But who . . . ?"

"Your oldest brothers."

"Beech and Sycamore?" Snowdrop's face scrunched in confusion.

"Didn't you ever wonder why they're so bad at using magic?"

"I thought they were lazy. They spent all their time snorting moon dust and tumbling anyone they could instead of learning. But they can't use magic at all?"

"I don't think so."

"But what about the time they decorated the clearing for Oleander's celebration—remember, when they were teens and they made glowing lanterns float in the air and vines twine around the tree trunks in time with the music? They insisted they had done it for her."

"I think the times we saw them use magic, Oleander was doing it for them. Or she had created a potion for them to use with the magic imbued inside so anyone could use it, even a human."

"So they can't use magic at all . . ." Snowdrop shook her head slowly, thinking over all her memories of her oldest brothers.

"They can see through illusions the way other half fairy, half humans can. But I don't believe they can use magic. Oleander claims their father was a fairy from the north that she'd met outside our enclave, but I don't believe it. She couldn't admit to having consorted with humans when she wanted everyone to believe how awful they were."

Her two oldest brothers were half human! And Oleander had lied about it. Did her *brothers* know, or did they wonder why they couldn't use magic? An unusual sense of empathy for her least favorite brothers filled her. Failing repeatedly when trying to learn was hard—she should know. They'd think they were doing some-

     Jane Buehler

thing wrong when really the skill wasn't in their power—they'd never succeed no matter how hard they tried. That frustration would eat at them. No wonder they'd spent their time hallucinating on moonflower dust.

Oleander *would* keep something like that a secret. She hated the humans so much. She'd never admit to having a child with one.

Had all that hatred resulted from the betrayal of one human man? Or maybe it resulted from years of pent-up loneliness and sadness, and he provided a convenient target.

"Does Dustan know about our brothers?" Snowdrop asked. He was riding off to Tidal Creek right now, thinking he might find the twins.

"I told him my suspicions," Larkspur said. "I might be wrong but I don't think so."

Snowdrop stared at the floor of the wagon, trying to wrap her mind around this revelation.

Larkspur stretched. "Let's take a break from the lessons. We can try again later."

Edna settled back against the water barrel and her knitting needles flashed. After a sympathetic smile at Snowdrop, Nem unwrapped a bundle of fabric, took out a small, sharp knife, and began carving the handle of a wooden spoon. Larkspur leaned over a pamphlet with her lips moving silently as she read—it must be information about the upcoming meeting.

Snowdrop leaned against the side of the wagon and watched the trees move past. Some unease stirred inside her at everything Larkspur had said. She thought of her mother, leagues away, locked underground and now with no one to visit her. Her mother knew how the fairy prison worked. She could try to improve herself, to feel sorry for her actions. Why didn't she try to better herself? Did she, and she was unable to? How hardened must she be to not be able to find a path forward, to not be able to repent the slightest bit?

Up front, Arley reclined with his arms on the back of the driver's seat and his face tilted up to the sun, holding the reins loosely and not even watching the road, as near as she could tell. Snowdrop tilted her own face up and closed her eyes, soaking in the air as it warmed with the day.

They passed a few leagues in silence, the only sound the clopping of the horses' hooves echoing through the forest. Snowdrop pictured the map in the fairies' library. The next town along the forest road was Knotty Knob, just a few hours' drive. A day after that they'd reach the edge of the forest at Woods End, and their destination of Mountain Rest was another day's drive north of that. In Mountain Rest, another crossroad headed up over the mountains to the west, to the cities on the far side of the continent, and east to the coast of Sylvania.

One of the youngest half-fairy children whom Snowdrop had cared for lived with her mother in Knotty Knob. Nem wouldn't remember her—Nem had been gone many seasons before Oleander's final victims arrived. After the near run-ins with Maryanne and Jane in Woods Rest, hopefully they could pass through Knotty Knob without seeing anyone else from her past.

They ate a light lunch of bread smeared with sunflower seed butter and blackberry jam that the innkeeper had packed for them. Arley ate while driving so they could keep moving, hoping to be well past the village before the end of the day. Should she go sit with him on the driver's seat? He was up there alone, working while the rest of them talked and relaxed in back. And he'd said he wanted to get out and walk for exercise while she drove—had he meant it seriously?

But if she moved up front, he would tease her. She couldn't bring herself to do it.

The afternoon warmed as they neared Knotty Knob. The ground in the forest was rockier, as if a ridge of the mountains extended out this way, but it stayed flat so maybe the rocks were simply the bedrock beneath the forest and something had washed away the soil. The trees grew more stunted, with scraggly bushes filling the spaces between them, and the road was often in full sun. Nem and Snowdrop untied the canvas wagon cover and rolled it down a few hand's widths until it shaded the wagon bed. They could watch the passing scenery, but the cover blocked the sky.

As she settled back, Snowdrop glanced at Larkspur. She hadn't mentioned magic lessons again—maybe she'd had enough of Snowdrop being a disaster for one day. She had her eyes closed. No more lessons then. But Snowdrop could try to connect with the wind the way she had the previous day. That had worked and it wasn't dangerous. Snowdrop lifted her chin up and waited. Nothing brushed her cheeks. The air in the forest was still.

Larkspur's head tilted slightly. Was she doing it again—listening to the "news" of the forest through the chatter of the birds, chipmunks, and other forest residents?

Snowdrop closed her own eyes and leaned back against the sideboard. She tried to relax, opening herself up and letting the sounds and smells and feelings in. This was a one-way channel with everything coming to her—she wasn't trying to communicate back. She wouldn't cause any harm if she only listened.

She heard the usual forest sounds—the chirps and rustlings—but those were nothing special. A human could hear those sounds. She waited and tried to stay patient. If she tried too hard, she'd ruin her chances.

A thread of something new reached her, curling through the forest sounds. Birds finding seeds. A crow with a nut, holding it against a wide branch and pecking to crack it open. Mice hiding in the leaves, waiting for a safe moment to dart across the ground. Squirrels scrabbling over who could be on a certain tree, with one triumphing as the other pranced away.

A dissonance joined the rest of the emotions. The birds swooped in a flurry to the treetops. She sensed impatience from the squirrels on branches or now hiding on the back sides of tree trunks. They wanted to be on the ground gathering more nuts for the winter, but something unusual was down there.

A stronger presence bumped against her—agitated but not scared. She couldn't place it, though. A larger animal but not a horse or a deer. Her eyelids fluttered open and she met Larkspur's gaze.

Snowdrop startled and the tendrils of thoughts and feelings flinched away.

"It's a boar," Larkspur said quietly.

Snowdrop closed her eyes again.

"What else can you hear?" Larkspur asked.

"The birds and squirrels are agitated. Something unusual is in the forest."

"Aye, I heard that too."

"I've never seen a boar."

"They're stout and tough, with a thick hide. They can run fast when they need to. And they're some distance away. I don't think you could hurt one from here."

Should she try to communicate with the boar? Maybe she could do it without Oleander's type of magic interfering.

"In fact," Larkspur continued, "they're far enough away that most fairies wouldn't be able to hear them."

Not all fairies could reach animals over a distance? And she could?

Snowdrop licked her lips. She focused on the boar's presence in her mind, waiting to see if she could understand more of its thoughts. It was in a group. Buddies? She kept getting a feeling that made her think of her brothers when they were younger, as if the boar was palling around with its friends. The group was resting for the day, but the boar was now unsure if they should stay in this location.

"Can I have another sticky bun?" Edna's voice broke her focus.

For half a beat, Snowdrop imagined the sugary buns Edna and Larkspur had eaten that morning. She returned her focus to the boar, but its thought pattern had changed. The boar was questioning.

It was asking her about sticky buns.

Snowdrop froze. Up until now, she'd been only listening, but the boar was communicating directly with her.

She wouldn't hurt it. No hint of the other type of magic was around, and besides, the boar wasn't nearby.

She imagined a sticky bun, the topping flavored with maple sugar and pecans, the doughy bun beneath. The boar sent back a picture of a parsnip it had rooted up in the forest, and a pang of longing for a sticky bun followed, and Snowdrop grinned. It understood it couldn't have one. It started reminiscing about a loaf of bread it had once stolen from a human campsite it had come upon in the forest.

How should she respond? She could offer it a sticky bun but enticing the boar toward them might cause a problem. Instead, she tried to express sympathy.

The boar's thoughts jilted and fear swirled through her. Boars rose to their feet, bumping and jostling, and her boar was gone. Worry hung in the air as they moved chaotically until their focus narrowed onto a leader and they followed him into the forest on a familiar track. The chaos rearranged into a flow of bodies through the forest, crushing plants as they moved in a wide pack.

But the fear remained, and suddenly the familiar dark strands of magic were in her mind, reaching up for the boars, waiting to ensnare them when they were in range. The boars were heading this way. What had she done?

Snowdrop opened her eyes and cut off her connection to the animals, snuffing out the hint of darkness. She registered the wagon bed, the tranquil forest alongside them, and Edna and Nem watching her intently. No one was hurt—she had stopped in time.

"Arley!" Larkspur said. She scanned the forest. "Stop the horses."

Arley called out "Whoa!" and the wagon jerked to a halt.

"A herd of boars is about to cross the road and I don't know where. And I can't stop them."

Chapter 11

✻

THE BOARS WERE COMING TOWARD them. Snowdrop swallowed. Had she called them in this direction?

Arley stood. "Stay in the wagon." He leapt to the ground. "Which side of the road are they coming from?"

Larkspur pointed. Arley took the horses' lines near their heads and walked them around to place the wagon between them and the oncoming herd. He stayed out there, rubbing their foreheads. They stepped uneasily from side to side. Could they sense his nervousness? Or maybe they felt vibrations of the stampeding herd coming their way. The usual birdsong had stopped and the few squirrels she could see were darting up tree trunks.

"Anything you can do to calm the horses?" Arley called.

"I'll try," Larkspur said. "Hang on, everyone."

Nem had the oddest expression on her face, but it vanished as Edna hunched beside her. Nem offered a hand but Snowdrop shook her head and slid closer to Larkspur. Larkspur had her eyes closed as she focused on communicating with Lady and Bird.

A distant crashing came from the woods. As they watched, a wall of dust rose up, roiling through the forest toward them. The braying of panicked boars reached her before she could spot one. The first broke through the curtain of dust, then another, running straight for the wagon. Even from far away she could see they were giant, at least up to hip height, but low to the ground on stout legs, and they had large, pointed ears and round snouts. They appeared gray and brown but with the screen of haze, she couldn't tell their color.

Edna muttered a curse and the wagon wobbled with the movements of the horses. Could Arley keep them still? She put her arms around Larkspur and held on.

The front line of boars thundered out of the dust and to the edge of the forest, weaving around the trees and onto the road, and the ones coming at them veered to avoid a collision. They bumped the wagon and it jostled back and forth, jerking forward toward the horses. Dust rose and filled the air. Edna pulled her sweater over her face and huddled with Nem. Snowdrop turned her face into Larkspur's shoulder. The squealing was awful.

The boars wove around the wagon until one hit it with a hard jolt, causing the wagon to twist to the side and slide. With a mighty crack, the wagon bed tilted and threw them all sideways, falling down and against the opposite side of the wagon. Though Larkspur fell on top of her, Snowdrop held her steady. She checked and Edna and Nem were still together, their eyes open and both hanging on to the low side of the wagon. The crates had slid across the floor, and the wagon had shifted sideways. A horse whinnied.

The thundering of hooves lessened and the braying quieted. Several more coursed by but spaces opened between them. A few final animals ran from the forest and disappeared around the wagon, and the pounding dulled and faded.

Thick dust hung in the air. From outside, Arley spoke soothing words to the horses as the forest went silent. Larkspur was still lying on top of Snowdrop, and they dragged themselves apart. Edna pulled her sweater off her face and pushed herself upright.

"Is everyone all right?" Snowdrop asked. Her voice rasped from the dust she'd inhaled.

"I think so." Edna rolled her head back and forth. "Let's get down from here." She crawled along the slanting wagon bed to the back as Arley appeared alongside and lifted the crate out of her way. He frowned at the wheel but moved to open the back and help Edna out, followed by Nem. Snowdrop crawled after them and he gave her his arm to lean on. He was quiet and his face serious. Larkspur climbed out last and they stood in the dusty road.

The wagon had moved to the edge of the road and been knocked sideways into the ditch, angling it down on that side. Lady and Bird stood quietly. The nearby shrubs and thickets were flattened from the boars' hooves, except for the few bushes protected by the wagon. Even the tree trunks were nicked in places. Arley brushed the front of his plaid shirt and dust swooshed off.

Everyone was all right. She exhaled in relief—her magic hadn't hurt anyone. But her attempt at magic might have led to the wagon being damaged. She wrapped her arms around herself. She'd have to tell Larkspur what she had done.

"Believe it or not," Nem said, "that's the second boar stampede I've been caught in since the spring equinox."

Everyone regarded her. It wasn't like Nem to make a joke.

"Is it now?" Arley said.

"I was caught in one last spring when we first left the Haven."

"I never heard about that," Larkspur said, squinting.

"Burne and Gray were embarrassed about it so I never told anyone."

"So," Arley said, grinning, "which boar stampede was better?"

Nem answered with a straight face. "Last time we climbed a tree and the boys lost all their food and blankets plus all our coins. So maybe this one?"

Arley grinned wider as if he'd won the boar stampede contest. Stars, the things that made him happy.

"We've not lost our food and blankets," he said, "but we may have lost our wagon." He nodded toward the low side. "Let me have another look."

Snowdrop followed Arley around the side. The wheel had lodged in the ditch. A few of the spokes were broken and the wood of the outer rim had cracked in one place, although the iron band on the outside held it together.

"I don't want you all ridin' on that," Arley said. "It could crack further if we start rollin' it."

"How far are we from Knotty Knob?"

"Not far. We already passed the nearest leaguepost. Little more than half a league to go, I'd guess. I can take one of the horses and ride for help. Someone in Knotty Knob will have a wagon to come get the rest of ya."

"Or we could all walk," Snowdrop said. She didn't like the idea of standing around in the woods waiting for him to return. What if the stampede came back? Or something worse? What if her faulty magic was an animal magnet, and they were endangered all the way to Mountain Rest?

"What made them start running?" Edna asked as Arley shoved at the wheel and called to the horses to step forward.

Snowdrop opened her mouth but Larkspur answered first. "I thought I saw a figure running at them."

She snapped her mouth shut.

"A figure like a person figure?" Edna asked.

"The boars were resting but uneasy because something unusual was nearby in the forest," Larkspur said. "And quite suddenly a person ran at the herd with a stick held aloft and the boars panicked."

"Were they hunting?"

"I don't think so. A hunter would shoot one or two and leave the rest. This figure was chasing them."

"But why would anyone chase boars?"

"And who would be way out here?" Nem added.

No one had an answer.

The wagon jerked forward and righted itself as the wheel came out of the ditch. Arley straightened and called to the horses to stop. The wagon was somewhat level, but the side with the bad wheel sagged. Edna and Larkspur voted to walk, so Arley secured the horses' reins and went up front to lead them.

Snowdrop moved alongside Larkspur. "Are you sure it was that figure who startled the boars?" she asked quietly.

"I sensed nothing else amiss."

Snowdrop nodded, and if Larkspur wondered about her question, she didn't let on. Maybe the boar stampede hadn't been her fault.

In spite of the sparsity of the trees this far north, this last stretch of road was dappled with shade. It remained fairly flat despite the bare rock showing through the dead leaves and layers of moss. They walked in silence, the only sound the clopping hooves and an occasional burst of wind that ruffled the top of Arley's hair as he walked in front of the wagon.

They passed the half-league post, then the quarter-league post, and the trees broke, revealing a cultivated field. Rows of green chard filled the ground near the road, and something taller grew on the far side—maybe peppers and tomatoes. As they cleared the end of the trees and walked along the edge of the field, a voice called out a greeting.

A person waved from the far edge of the field, and others stood until half a dozen people gazed at them. Snowdrop and her companions reached a wagon path leading in to where the farmers had gathered. Arley walked over to speak with them. He returned with one of them driving a wagon. She introduced herself as Greta and offered them a ride to the village. Apparently Knotty Knob's representatives had recently left for the council meeting also. The village blacksmith could fix their wagon and do it quickly to get them on their way.

They climbed into Greta's wagon, leading Lady and Bird with the broken wagon behind them. A little while later, they rolled into a small village center. Trees surrounded the human shops: The one with barrels, sacks of grain, a straw hat, and so much more visible through the front windows must be a general store. The one with the door standing open revealed a bar inside, so that was the village pub. And one had a few empty tables out front and a pie on the sign—a bakery? A handful of cottages peeked out from the trees behind the shops.

"Most everyone is down in the lower acre harvesting the corn crop," Greta said, turning to face them, "but the smith should be in. He's had a pile of work keeping him busy. And the cafe should be open if you want to wait inside." She gestured to the shop with the pie sign.

Arley hopped off the back of the wagon and led the horses to the smithy while the rest of them thanked their driver and trooped across the empty square to wait in the cafe. The sun was high overhead, but the village was deserted.

Snowdrop pulled open the cafe door and a bell rang. The most delicious scent wafted over her. Like pecans and Norlian cacao and toasting bread all rolled together into one delightful aroma. "What is that smell?" she whispered, lifting her nose to inhale again.

"And can we afford it?" Edna added.

"It's Norlian coffee," Larkspur said, "and probably not."

A counter ran along the opposite wall and a few tables and chairs filled the rest of the room. Someone stepped out from a doorway. He'd finished making sandwiches for the workers in the field, he explained, but he could slap together a few more for the travelers.

Larkspur insisted on giving a few coins, and then she glanced at Snowdrop and asked the owner if they could see the coffee. It had come all the way from Norland and a cup of it cost more than Larkspur had. Almost no one could afford to drink it, the owner said, but everyone loved the way it made the cafe smell. He held open a burlap sack. Pea-sized, dark brown seeds filled it—beans, they were called. Snowdrop held back her hair, leaned forward, and inhaled. She could smell coffee for hours and never tire of it.

"It smells even better when you grind them up to make the drink," the owner said as he cinched up the top of the sack. He put it away before turning to their sandwiches: shredded kale leaves tossed in oil and piled on top of slabs of cheese on a dark brown bread. They took the second lunch to a table to eat.

They'd rested about an hour when the door's bell rang. Arley plopped down in a chair. "Is that sandwich for me?" He picked up half of the final sandwich, studying it before he took a bite. He must have shaken the dust of the road off his shirt because its colors were bright again.

"How's the wagon?" Edna asked.

"It's fixed," he said around a mouthful of kale before swallowing. "The smith fixed it right off so I waited. Soon as I finish eatin', we can be on our way."

Larkspur stood. "I'll resecure the items in the wagon," she said. "And I'll get us that berry pie on the counter to enjoy tonight." Edna and Nem stood as well and the three of them left the cafe. Snowdrop debated going but Arley would be alone. He picked up the second half of his sandwich.

"Did you notice the aroma when you came in the door?" Snowdrop asked.

"Yeah. Coffee."

"You knew?"

He nodded, munching through a bite of sandwich.

"It costs too much to drink," she said.

"It smells better than it tastes."

"You've had it?" How could it possibly not taste good, with that aroma?

"I had it once in the King's Guard. Trust me, the scent is the best part."

She frowned, and he grinned.

"Do ya want it to taste good, when you can't have any?"

"Someday I'll drink it."

"Can fairies make money with their magic?" he asked and took another bite.

"Sometimes? We can make magical things to sell to humans but that's not always smart. Mostly we sell them foods from the forest or herbal remedies—things they could find or make themselves, but that we're better at finding or making."

"What's wrong with selling magical things? What kind of things?"

"Things like sleeping potions—you wouldn't want it to end up with someone who'd misuse it. We don't exactly have rules against it, but most fairies wouldn't sell something like that to a human. Someone could end up sleeping forever if no one tried to wake them."

"What about your famous fairy love potions?" He said it with no change in his voice, but the corners of his eyes crinkled the slightest bit.

"Are you flirting again?"

"Maybe."

It didn't grate on her the way it had before. "What do you mean, 'famous'?"

"Your brother used one on Princess Rose. Everyone knows that story. Maybe you can make them, too. You could make a fortune selling those to humans. And come to think of it, how do I know you haven't slipped one into my tea? And then you blame me for flirting. What a swindler you are."

"You don't have any tea. And I can't make love potions. And even if I could, I would never use one."

"I know, piglet. I'm teasin' ya."

He finished his sandwich but leaned back in his chair instead of standing. He folded his hands across his belly. Maybe he needed a rest before they set off.

"Where did you try coffee?" she asked.

Something strange flashed across Arley's face—his forehead

wrinkled and his eyes dropped. He sat up and didn't speak right away. Was he . . . unhappy?

"In a village up north."

"Nor Bay?"

"Not that far. And Nor Bay's a city. Nah, this was a tiny village on the edge of the mountains. I don't even remember why we were there. Some lord hadn't paid enough taxes or some nonsense."

"You were there with the guards?"

"Yeah. And the village had a shop like this one but with a little elderly lady behind the counter." He wasn't smiling.

Dread crept into Snowdrop's chest. "What happened?" she whispered.

"There was six of us. And it smelled like it does here, and someone asked what she was baking that smelled so good and she told us the smell was coffee from Norland. And the thing was it tasted so bitter no one liked it, but one of the men started saying how hard it was to get and how they could sell it for a killing. So they demanded she give them the bag. And she tried to reason with them and they began smashing her teacups on the floor, and she gave in."

He examined his hands, picking at his thumbnail.

"Did they hurt her?"

He didn't answer for several heartbeats. "Wasn't just them, Snowdrop. It was me too. But no, we didn't hurt her after that." He wouldn't meet her eyes.

"Why did you do it?"

"That's what I was like back then."

She didn't believe him. How could he have been that awful, when he was so kind now?

"How old were you?"

"Twenty winters." He looked up at last. "Don't look so agonized, piglet. You haven't done anything wrong."

He stood before she could figure out how she should look, swept the crumbs from the sandwiches onto the tray, and carried it to the counter. He sauntered back toward her and held out a hand. "Come on, piglet," he said. "We've got leagues to go before bedtime."

"Don't call me piglet," she said, and took his hand.

Chapter 12

❧✳☙

OUTSIDE THE CAFE, THEIR THREE companions waited in the wagon. Nem yawned as they came out the door and Edna was already knitting. Snowdrop hesitated and then climbed onto the driver's seat beside Arley.

He uncharacteristically did not comment but only smiled and gathered up the reins. "You want to drive?"

She shook her head.

As Lady and Bird trotted out of the square and back onto the forest road, her company waved hello to a few farmers returning from the fields, one carrying piles of hard squashes in his wheelbarrow and another with a wagon full of tired workers. After passing a few scattered cottages, they were back in the forest but the trees were more open now. Roads branched off the main highway, and through the spindly maples and isolated sweetgum trees were wide fields. They rolled on and, as another leaguepost passed, pine trees filled in around the road, blocking the spaces between the hardwoods.

Arley stayed silent. What he'd said in the cafe—he'd done things in the past that he wished he hadn't, just like her. Did he still feel guilty? Did he feel like a bad person? Or had his attitude about being a better person in the present helped him?

Snowdrop itched to talk. Would it bother him if she asked more questions about his past? She glanced sideways at him. It wasn't like *he* worried about bothering *her* when he talked endlessly. Or if he did worry, he didn't pay any attention and went right on bothering her.

"What's up, sunshine?"

She'd been staring at him, frowning. She turned away.

"Out with it or I'll start guessing what's on your mind."

What she wanted to know was if he had truly been the awful person he'd described in the cafe. And had he started that way, or had being in the King's Guard made him that way?

"You're wonderin'," Arley said, "How I keep my figure—"

"Why did you join the King's Guard?"

He grinned at her interruption but it slipped away as he shrugged. "I wanted to prove something, I guess."

"To who?"

"My family."

"Your parents?" Humans kept ties to their parents, not like fairies.

"My older brothers."

"You have older brothers?"

"Two of 'em."

"I have four."

"I know about Dustan and I heard Larkspur mention the older two."

"Larch is the fourth. He's the one who seduced Jane and stole the baby."

Arley cringed. "Your brothers might actually be worse than mine."

"What are yours like?"

"They're loud and pushy and they always take charge of every-thing."

She waited.

"It was clear they would take over the farm when my pops got old. An' they were always sticking me with the jobs they didn't want and wouldn't listen to anything I suggested. I didn't want my whole life to be like that."

"They sound like asses," Snowdrop said.

Arley laughed. "They're not that bad, but they're . . . I don't know. Not very sensitive, I guess. I wouldn't want anyone I liked to date 'em."

Snowdrop squinted. "You mean you don't trust them to be nice on a date."

His eyes crinkled. "They'd be nice. I wouldn't trust them to keep being nice."

"You mean after they got what they wanted."

"That's right, sunshine. Anyway, I didn't want to stick around the farm to muck out the barn for them, and joining the King's Guard seemed glamorous, and neither one of them had done it."

"Did you like it? I mean at first."

"I did. I know it's awful but I liked being on top of the pile. The one bossing others around instead of being bossed. I got in with the right people and avoided the worst of the bullyin'."

Snowdrop remembered her childhood with her brothers. They'd ignored her more than anything. What if she'd had a chance to go somewhere else and be in charge of things? It might go to her head, too.

"How long were you in the guard?"

"Four winters. When the revolution came, I realized I couldn't fight for the king against his own people."

"Did you go home?"

He shook his head with his eyes on the road. "Nah. I didn't want to see them, not after everything. Would'a been another failure for my brothers to laugh at."

"You didn't fail!" How could he think that? She leaned in. "You didn't fight and you helped the people defeat a bad king."

"They'd find a way to tease me though." His shoulders slumped.

Snowdrop frowned but couldn't think how to reassure him. "So you've been farming ever since?"

"Yeah. I got the work in Woods Rest and stayed."

"Where is your family?"

"In Woods End."

She sat up straight, her hands in fists. "But we're going through there!"

"Yup."

"We'll be there tomorrow." She stared at him.

"I know, sunshine. It's my big homecoming." He saw her watching him and grinned but it wasn't as enthusiastic as usual.

"Do they know you're coming?"

He shrugged. "I sent a letter."

"Will you be glad to see your family?"

"Sure."

She waited but he didn't continue. "Even your brothers?"

"Rolf and Peter? I can stand 'em for two nights."

She chewed on her lip. Keeping him talking had never been this hard. "How big is Woods End?" she asked at last.

"It's barely there. Just a store and a smithy. No grange hall or anything."

"How many families live there?"

"There's about twenty-five farmsteads within a day's drive. My parents' place is close to the town so they often host gatherin's."

"What kind of gatherings?"

"Seasonal celebrations like for the harvest and solstice. Parties after a life bonding ceremony and after people pass on. That kind of thing."

"Are there dances?"

"There's usually dancin'. The fairies have dances, right?"

"Aye."

Her answer came out quietly and he perked up at last, considering her. "Ya don't sound fond of them."

"I never danced much. I just watched."

"That's no fun. Didn't ya want to dance?" He glanced to the road and back to her.

She stared at her lap, willing her face not to blush. "No one would dance with me. They were scared of my mother."

"Oy, that's rough," he said.

"But I'm not sure I'd like it much anyway. From the edges, it always looked like the dancers were throwing themselves around and grinding on each other while some music played."

Arley cringed. "That's not how human dances work."

"How do they work?" she asked, looking up.

"There's a pattern and ya follow the steps." He turned back to the road, adjusting the reins in his broad hands. "I'll show ya what I mean when we get to camp."

"You like to dance?"

"Sure."

"Have you danced since you left home?" she asked.

He tilted his head. "I used to go in Woodglen. Some of the guards would go each moon. I think they were hopin' to find sweethearts."

"Did they?"

"Some did. But not me." He glanced over and winked. "In case ya were wonderin'."

"No, I assumed *you* didn't."

Arley snorted out a laugh.

He didn't say anything else, so Snowdrop settled back on the seat. Remembering the dances she used to attend made her wince in embarrassment. Since Rose had become queen, Snowdrop had stopped attending dances—even though Rose invited her to every one.

But back when Oleander had been queen, she had insisted Snowdrop attend. Oleander had had a throne-like platform built for herself at one end of the clearing—it was gone now—and the fairies danced on the grass in front or mingled on the edges of the space. Except for Snowdrop.

No one wanted to dance with Oleander's daughter. And she didn't want to sit on an elevated platform with all the fairies eyeing her and shunning her. Once she realized no one was going to ask her to dance, she started escaping into the trees. She had to wait only until Oleander had had enough elderberry wine to stop noticing her and then she'd slip away and find a seat in the shadows where she could watch the dancing without anyone minding her.

And while she meant what she'd told Arley about the unappealing dancing, she *had* wanted to join in and to have someone choose her. But maybe she'd been better off with no one asking, given how the fairies danced like they were having sex with their clothes on.

But humans danced differently, according to Arley. What did he mean, he would show her? They didn't have any music out here, and the dances she'd seen required at least eight or ten dancers. Maybe he hadn't been serious.

Sunlight hit her face and she squinted as it flitted in and out through the tree branches. The wagon cover had blocked the sun at midday but now the sunlight shone in from the west. Snowdrop closed her eyes and savored the warmth on her skin fighting against the cool air of fall. Arley stayed silent. Behind her, Nem and Larkspur talked quietly.

As the sun got lower, Arley turned the wagon off the main road onto a side lane. A leaguepost at the split was marked with a 10.

"Are we making a turn?"

"No. This is a wayside."

"A way-what?" The lane curved to the right and a grassy area appeared.

"Out here where the distance between villages is greater, the forest road has waysides where ya can pull off to rest for the night."

"So the ten on that leaguepost means . . . ?"

"Ten leagues to Woods End."

A rough wooden table sat beside the lane under the trees. It had benches attached on either side. Nearby a ring of stones marked a firepit. Sawed-off sections of a large log stood or lay around the firepit for seats. Ahead the lane curved back to the left and rejoined the main road. Arley called to the horses to stop.

Everyone stood and stretched and climbed down from the wagon. The last of the sunlight glinted low in the trees. Snowdrop helped Arley unhitch the horses and lead them to a grassy spot while Edna and Larkspur laid out their supper on the table. Nem ventured into the woods to gather fallen branches for a campfire.

After Arley checked Lady's and Bird's hooves, he handed Snowdrop a brush with a handle and showed her how to comb it over their coats. He filled up their water bucket and opened one of the crates to get them grain. He took over the combing, moving twice as fast as Snowdrop to finish it. He handed her a different brush, this one full and soft, and as she brushed Bird, he retrieved a small handsaw from a toolbox at the foot of the wagon. Nem had returned dragging the remains of a small tree and he proceeded to reduce the trunk to logs.

Peeking over Bird's tall back, she watched him sawing away at the tree. He must be tired after everything that had happened that day but he didn't let it show. He stacked the logs by the firepit and returned to help her finish caring for the horses.

She had fire powder. She could save him the trouble of starting the fire. But she was supposed to let him show off his fire-making skills, Dustan had said.

"Supper's ready," Edna called and everyone gathered at the wayside table. They had a green salad of spinach Edna had gotten from a farmer outside the cafe in Knotty Knob, shredded into ribbons and topped with pecans, apple slices, fresh goat cheese, and a dressing made of oil and vinegar. They also had the berry pie. By the time they finished eating, Nem was slumping on her seat. She yawned.

"Everyone up for a bonfire?" Arley asked, interrupting all the follow-up yawns.

"Aren't you tired?" Edna said.

"We'll have a little one. Nem brought us all that wood."

"We can't possibly burn it all tonight," Larkspur said as they stood.

"We'll sit by a fire for a little bit and leave the rest of the wood for the next visitor," he said.

They gathered on the log seats around the firepit. Arley knelt in the center and stacked three of the smaller logs. He'd brought a box of supplies from the wagon. He opened it and took out a dried moss-like substance and arranged it under smaller twigs and dead leaves, which he placed one by one. Dustan was right—Arley was taking this fire very seriously.

He got out a piece of flint and a steel band—Snowdrop had seen this human tool in the fairies' supply shed—and he struck the steel against the flint and sparks cascaded onto the moss. A few stuck and held, and he leaned forward to blow on them. A flame caught and spread to the kindling. He poked a stick in and used the taper to spread the flame before sitting back on his heels as the fire crackled.

"Are you all goin' to sleep in the wagon tonight?" Arley asked. "We shouldn't have rain but you'd be up off the ground."

"I think four of us can fit if we squish," Larkspur replied.

"I'll sleep out here," Arley said.

An odd gnawing filled Snowdrop's chest. Disappointment? Annoyance that Larkspur had included her in the wagon?

"Won't you be uncomfortable?" Snowdrop asked.

"Nah, I told ya—I can sleep anywhere."

She frowned but he only grinned at her.

"Well now that's decided," Arley said, "I promised Snowdrop a dance lesson."

Her heartbeat sped up. He had remembered.

"If ya still want one," he added.

"Um, okay. But don't we need music?"

"Not for waltzin'."

Waltzing?

"We need a beat and I was goin' to ask everyone to help." He strode over to the wagon and rummaged in the storage area, coming out with a cooking pot and wooden spoon.

Edna pawed through her bag. She pulled out a tin whistle. "I thought I packed this."

"You play that?" Larkspur asked.

"I'm learning."

Arley gave the cookpot to Nem, who whacked it with a resounding clang. She rapped it more quietly.

"I need it like this," Arley said and tapped on his thigh, first a strong beat and then two little ones, all evenly spaced. "It might help to count: *one*-two-three, *one*-two-three."

Nem copied him and soon had it down. Edna's first blow into her whistle produced a shriek that startled birds out of a high tree across the road. At one time, Snowdrop might've felt annoyed at the disturbance, but Edna hadn't meant to do it. Edna softened her playing and added a few notes to the beat. Larkspur patted her knee in time. As music went, theirs was pretty awful, but with the fire lighting the undersides of the branches overhead and the first stars appearing, Snowdrop could almost pretend she was back in the fairy clearing—if the band had inhaled a whole lot of moonflower dust before they started playing.

Arley held out his hand. She swallowed and took it. He led her away from the noise to a flat place on the wayside lane. The cool air was welcome after the heat by the fire. He kept holding her hand.

"The humans have group dances too but a waltz takes only two people."

"Okay."

"And ya have one person lead and the other follow—do ya know about that?"

"I guess? I never understood it though. They're following the same beat and steps, aren't they?"

"Can I show ya?"

She nodded and he let go of her hand and placed his palm against her side. It was warm through the fabric of her tunic. She rested her left hand on his shoulder as she'd seen dancing couples do, and her right hand ended up held loosely in his. They were the same height so their faces were close. He checked their hands and she dropped her gaze before he turned to her. Her bangs fell, screening her face.

"Is this okay?"

She felt a little breathless so she nodded again. Arley had positioned them so she faced the main road. Behind her, the music had slowed to a cacophony of random beats and shrieks.

"Hey, musicians," Arley called, and the drumming picked back up. Nem called out a count of one-two-three and the beat sped up and evened out to its initial speed, with everyone somewhat in time.

"Can ya feel when my hand moves on your back?" He slid his hand farther around her body and stepped in a smidge closer. His hand tilted, turning her body.

"Yes."

"That's how ya know which way to turn. And here too"—he pushed lightly against her hand in his—"you can feel it." He pushed harder and she fell back a step but he kept her upright. The fire's reflection danced in his eyes.

"How do I know what to do with my feet?"

"I could tell ya to make a box or whatnot but I think it's easier to stumble through it. Start with your right foot going backward and listen to the music and see if you can feel what to do. I won't let you fall."

She watched their feet in the darkness as he pushed against her and she took a step back.

"Good. Keep alternatin', *right* left right, *left* right left. Maybe don't watch your feet."

She looked up—and back into his eyes. The eye gazing was too much, even with him smiling softly.

"How about closin' your eyes," he offered.

"But—"

"I won't let you fall. Being the person following is all about trustin' your partner and lettin' go of being in control."

She closed her eyes and hung onto him harder with her hands.

"Ready?" he asked. And he again gently pushed her backward. She stumbled back a step until he began to quietly chant left-right-lefts for her and she got on track. They swayed forward and back several times.

"That's good," Arley said. "Want to try movin'?"

She swallowed. "Okay."

"Keep your eyes closed and don't worry." And without breaking a step, his hand tugged on hers and they moved across the ground, moving and stopping in time with the music. His wide hand on her back turned her body and steadied her over and over. It felt . . . really nice.

He came to a stop. She opened her eyes and scanned around. They stood all the way out in the main road. The fire flickered a hundred paces away and the music was quieter.

"Wow," she panted. She beamed at Arley.

A smile slid across his face. "All right?"

"That was . . . good."

"All right. Now let's do it with your eyes open."

This time when he moved, she resisted. She didn't want to resist, exactly. But she thought she knew where to go and her mind tried to go that way and forgot to pay attention to what his hands were telling her.

She stepped into him and trod on his foot. "I'm sorry."

"It's harder, isn't it? You overthink instead of feelin' it."

Dancing was kind of like trying to use magic. She needed to relax and let go.

She took her position again and settled her gaze on his ear. She wouldn't try to see where they were going. She dipped her chin once and he moved again. This time she focused on the places where his hands connected to her body and followed as he moved her back and forth and then out and across the flat road, slowly turning in a circle. The music went on and Edna seemed to be making progress with her notes.

Out here was dark enough that stars shone. The air must be cool as night came on, but she was hot from moving and Arley was hotter than she was everywhere they touched. Even though his hands held her steady, he always left a space between them, but his heat reached her across it.

"This isn't how the fairies dance," she said, once she felt comfortable talking while continuing to move in time. "They hold each other much closer."

"Ya want me to hold ya closer?"

"No!"

He grinned and his eyes twinkled like the stars. He was teasing again.

"I like this way fine," she muttered.

"Me too, princess."

"Princess?"

"I suppose ya hate that one too?"

"I'm not a princess anymore."

"Maybe not that kind of princess. Sometimes humans use the word when it doesn't mean royalty."

"What does it mean when humans say it?"

He shrugged the shoulder her hand rested on. "Uh, it means you're special, untouchable, and maybe a little bit imposin' to all us common folk as want to be around you."

"Stop teasing."

"I'm not teasin'."

She shook her head and returned her gaze to his ear, and he didn't continue speaking. Beside his ear, his cheek was rough with stubble. He'd been clean-shaven that morning when he'd been washing up at the inn. Stars, was that only this morning? And how often did he have to shave?

And what a thing to wonder.

"I think you've got the hang of this, princess." He twirled her back toward the fireside.

"I like it."

"Yeah, me too, but I'm about to fall over from how tired I am. I might need to get to bed."

He slowed to a stop beside the fire, and Nem gave a final roll on her cookpot-drum—she somehow had two wooden spoons now— and Edna let out another whistle shriek, and the music stopped.

"That looked wonderful," Edna said. "Was it fun?"

Snowdrop watched Arley's face so close to her. "Yes." She slowly took her hands off him.

He blinked and stepped away. He scanned the ground by the fire where Larkspur had spread out a bedroll.

"Thanks for the music," Arley said, rubbing the back of his neck. "We'd better get some sleep."

Snowdrop kept watching him as the others stood and stretched. She watched until he glanced up at her so she could smile.

Chapter 13

THEY WERE ON THEIR WAY early the next morning. Snowdrop expected the trees to grow more and more sparse as they neared Woods End, where the forest gave way completely to grassy plains. Instead, the trunks grew wider and encroached on the road again—not with sprawling branches crisscrossing in diagonals overhead, but with limbs twisted across like awkward lovers holding hands, and with a lacy gray moss hanging off them. Arley said they were a kind of oak but they didn't look anything like the majestic oaks at home.

Larkspur suggested they take a day off from magic lessons after all that had happened the day before. Was Larkspur giving up on her? Did she think Snowdrop was hopeless? Snowdrop tamped down her disappointment as she climbed onto the seat beside Arley, who slumped forward holding the reins and barely smiled in greeting. Instead of lessons, Larkspur entertained Edna by creating illusions and convincing birds to alight on the edge of the wagon and take breadcrumbs from their hands.

For the first time since they'd left Woods Rest, the road climbed over gentle hills. The uphill stretch always went on longer than the downhill that followed, as if they were climbing up away from the level of the sea.

Even with Snowdrop beside him, Arley grew more and more silent as the morning passed. She didn't like how he stared ahead down the road, lost in thought. The silence and tension were so unlike him.

"Are you nervous?" Snowdrop finally asked.

He jerked his head toward her and blinked a few times. He shook his head. "Nah." But then he exhaled and relaxed. "Maybe a little."

"Because of your family?"

"Maybe? I know they'll be glad to see me. And my ma will have places ready for all of you to stay and she'll dote on everyone."

"Then what are you nervous about?"

"I've been away for a while."

A gnat landed on her arm and she waved it away and scratched her skin. "How long?"

"Five winters."

She waited.

He sighed. "I'm a different person than I was. An' I know they're gonna treat me like I'm fifteen winters old an' when they do, I want to let it slide right off. But I won't. I'll get upset and start whinin' like I'm fifteen. And they'll grin 'cause they'll know they got to me."

"Dustan says I whine," Snowdrop offered.

"You don't whine."

"I do sometimes," she admitted. "I don't mean to. It just happens. He says, 'Act like a grown-up if you want us to treat you like one,' but he fusses if I do anything on my own or if I talk to a stranger. I'm already nervous enough *without* him fussing. So *he's* what makes it harder to be a grown-up."

Arley ran a hand through his hair. "He let you go to Mountain Rest."

"Only because Larkspur's here to babysit."

"Maybe it'll be different when ya go back."

She resisted a sudden urge to poke him. "Maybe it will be for you, too."

He kept facing the road but his shoulders relaxed slightly. "My brothers will try to get a rise out of me."

"Like how?"

"I don't know. Sometimes they play stupid pranks. But other times they know exactly what'll hurt me most."

"Older brothers are the worst."

"Yeah." He paused and glanced at her. "They, uh, they might hit on ya. Like Wells was doin' back in Woods Rest. They're used to flirtin' with all the pretty girls."

"That'll be fun," Snowdrop said wryly. She let his comment on her appearance slide past.

"I can tell 'em to leave you alone but . . ."

She followed his thinking. "They'll turn it around as a way to pick on you?"

"Yeah."

"I can handle it," she said, sitting back. "I was on edge in Woods Rest so I got upset about Wells. I'd never been alone in a human village, and Maryanne appeared and that rattled me. Now that I've been out here a few days, things are less intimidating."

"That's good. You, uh, you might like my brothers. Girls always seem to." His shoulders stiffened again.

Snowdrop huffed. "A stranger flirting with me is the surest way to make me dislike them."

He smiled, caught himself, and stifled it. "Well let me apologize in advance if they annoy ya, or if ya witness me shoutin' at them or whinin' at my ma."

"Okay."

They stopped for lunch at a wayside, and shortly after, the road sloped steadily downward. It turned northeast for a ways until they came to a curve so sharp Arley had to slow the horses to navigate the wagon around it. And then they traveled back the other direction.

"The turns are to get us down the hill," Arley explained. "It'd be too steep for the wagon if the road barreled straight down."

                    Jane Buehler

They turned another sharp corner. Snowdrop sensed open space and bright sun through the trees on the downward side of the hill—more light and yellows between the trunks than when she scanned the trees on the uphill side. That bright openness grew as the road at last straightened and headed due north again. The trees remained thick around them, but ahead on the road they seemed to . . . vanish. She waited, staring ahead as Arley glanced over with a grin and called to the horses to go faster.

The light brightened and they rode out of the forest onto a stretch of road across a wide field with clear blue sky overhead. The trees lingered on the edges of the field and covered the hillsides behind it but ahead was only plains. Wind whistled across the earth and the grasses undulated in patches as the wind came and went, and a gust hit the wagon and brushed her hair into her eyes.

A sweet grassy smell graced the air. The landscape was open and free, with the wind blowing and the grasses swaying. Lady and Bird tossed their heads as they stepped along. They'd probably never seen plains either. Maybe they wondered if they were going to have to plow all of this. She squinted in the brightness of the endless sun and smiled.

Arley slowed the horses for a narrow wooden bridge over a creek and the wheels rumbled as they crossed. All along the creek bed, scraggly bushes with tiny green leaves hid the water, but the bushes revealed how the creek squiggled across the land. A group of animals—like forest deer but with straight antlers—grazed far off the road on the right, and on the other side, a house was tucked under the trees at the bottom of the hill. A minute later they passed a dusty drive that must lead to it.

The wind was getting nippy, actually, with its unceasing gusts. Snowdrop pulled her sweater tight around her. In back, Edna dug in her bag and came out with a knitted hat, and Larkspur wrapped a scarf around her neck. Behind them, back down the road, a vast hillside covered in green leaves speckled with fall color rose up. They had come down that hillside—they had been up so high!

"Has none of ya ever been this far north?" Arley asked over the wind, and everyone said no.

"I can't understand how the trees stop so abruptly," Edna said. "Shouldn't they peter out more slowly?"

"The birds are completely different outside the woods," Larkspur said. "I hadn't expected that."

"Can you talk to them?" Edna asked.

"I can hear them. I'm not sure any of them have communicated with a fairy before."

"It'll be another half league to Woods End," Arley told them. "My parents' place is not far beyond the town on the western road."

Another creek passed under the wagon, again lined with bushes. The tree-covered hillside to the left ended, and beyond it, several leagues away, were the mountains. Snowdrop knew they were mountains but felt tempted to ask Arley to confirm it. They had stark gray slopes, sheer and rocky, poking up at the sky with pointed tops. Even though they blocked the view, they somehow made the view more grand and open with their dramatic peaks. No more trees dotted the landscape, and on the right side was nothing but flat, knee-high fields. Near to the road, patches of bare rock jutted out of the ground.

Snowdrop couldn't get enough of the wide view. She'd never seen so much space. Being out here felt entirely different from being in the forest—scary because the land was so open, but at the same time, safe, like nothing could sneak up on you out here. And the land felt honest with nothing to hide. She inhaled deeply to fill herself with the fresh air, closed her eyes, and turned her face to the hot sunshine.

A few minutes later, Arley grunted and she opened her eyes. Something tall loomed at the roadside ahead, but she couldn't make out what the shape was. She squinted.

"That's a sign," Arley said. "Is that what you're trying to see?"

"It's big. What's it say?"

Arley closed his eyes and exhaled. "It's an advertisement."

"For what?"

"For the village."

"You have to advertise the village?"

He shook his head slowly. "For some reason, the people who built Woods End put the village off the main road. Maybe they didn't like the noise of the one horse that clops past each quarter-moon. Merchants and travelers would pass by and not even stop, not realizin' they'd reached the village. So the villagers decided to advertise. And they came up with these signs. They're darn silly."

The sign was closer. It was a giant board on two tall legs. Snowdrop made out the letters.

"You're out of the woods," she read aloud. "Are you out of supplies? RESUPPLY IN WOODS END." She looked at Arley. "That's supposed to convince people to stop?"

"It's awful, right?"

Another sign appeared behind it. As they rolled past the first one, Snowdrop peered ahead. "The woods have stopped, and you should too. RELAX IN WOODS END." She shook her head. "Do the ads work?"

"No idea. I left for the King's Guard a moon later."

They passed another drive on the right, and back from the road, a cluster of trees sheltered a large cottage. No one was in sight and nothing moved. A third sign neared and this one stretched across the road. It flapped in the breeze—it was a long banner that covered the regular sign on the right and was strung across to a pole driven into the ground on the left.

"Ah, no," Arley muttered.

Snowdrop leaned forward. "WELCOME HOME ARLEY." She smiled at him. "That's nice!"

But he shook his head again and hunched down on the seat. The horses trotted along, the wagon rolled under the banner, and a new banner appeared ahead.

"THE SHEEP MISSED YOU," Snowdrop read.

"Bastards," Arley muttered. Edna laughed behind them.

"What does that mean?" Snowdrop asked.

"Never mind, princess."

"It means he was a dedicated shepherd," Edna said. That didn't seem like the whole story. It was probably some weird human joke.

A shack stood ahead along with one final sign pointing west to Woods End. They were upon the crossroad before Snowdrop had seen it, but Arley deftly turned the horses into the sun. It hung in the sky above the mountains, which were washed out of color in the glaring light.

"Almost there," Arley murmured. Snowdrop's nerves tingled. She was about to meet Arley's family—his parents and brothers. Human families were important, not like the fairies with their large community and loose family ties. And not like *her* family with her obsessive mother and terrible history. What would his parents think of her? Would his brothers be as bad as he said? Had they ever met a fairy before? She should have asked Arley but she didn't want to bother him with questions now when he was already nervous about returning home.

A few buildings clustered around the road ahead. Unlike at the forest crossroads, out here she could see them half a league off. The grasses ended at a cultivated field—the remnants of cornstalks littered the dirt, tilled under to make way for more planting. On the other side was pale gold grain. Someone walked along the road toward them carrying a hoe, but the farmer turned into the field before the wagon reached them. The field stretched on and on. How did anyone care for all of it?

"Are those oats?" Snowdrop asked.

"Yeah. Good eye."

"I always liked how oats look. Wheat looks violent."

Arley raised an eyebrow.

"Wheat is too spiky. Oats look like tiny bells."

"They look a bit like snowdrops, don't they?"

For some reason, she couldn't think how to reply. "What are the buildings?" she asked instead as they neared.

"On the right is the general store, and on the left is the smith's forge."

"No grange hall?" Larkspur asked.

"Nah. There's always talk of buildin' something but no one ever has time."

As they drew near, various wooden sheds and structures appeared tucked behind the main buildings. A wagon parked beside one was loaded with baskets of butternut squashes. Another open-sided shed was packed with crates of cabbages. Snowdrop smiled, remembering Arley calling her cabbage and how he liked it pickled in salt.

The smithy had a forge in a covered area outside and the chimney smoked slightly but no one was there. Empty chairs lined the porch at the general store.

As they rolled up to the buildings, the wooden door of the general store banged open and three children flew out. "Arley!" they shrieked, cascading off the porch and into the road. He slowed the horses. The children looked about twelve to fifteen winters old and had tawny skin and brown hair. Two adults older than Snowdrop came out the door, heading toward the wagon, big smiles on their faces, and someone else appeared under the awning at the forge.

The horses stopped and Arley secured the reins and hopped down from his seat as the three children swarmed him, all talking at once. He patted the youngest's head and exclaimed over how they'd grown. Snowdrop carefully climbed down from her seat. Her bottom was half numb and her legs were stiff. She stretched and twisted. Edna, Nem, and Larkspur climbed out the back of the wagon.

"Your mother said you'd be coming," the woman from the store said, stepping around Lady and Bird to hug Arley as the children continued chattering. She wore a loose cotton dress and had the same tan skin and dark hair as the children. The man—her partner?—stepped forward to hug Arley next. A burly-armed woman in a leather apron had come from the forge and now waited her turn for a hug. One of the children eyed Snowdrop and hid behind their father.

Someone else moved on the porch at the store. A woman about Snowdrop's age with long brown curls stood at the top of the steps. She wore a simple dress that hugged her waist and chest tightly. As Arley finished his hugging, he turned to her.

"Agatha," he said, tipping his head.

"Hi Arley," she said, gazing down.

She seemed shy, like Snowdrop. Maybe living out here—

"You look so strong," she said as her gaze lifted up, revealing a coy smile as she descended the porch steps and reached to pet Bird. "You must've trained hard in the King's Guard." She gazed across Bird's neck with wide eyes as Arley's smile faltered.

"Are these your horses?" Agatha continued. She batted her lashes twice.

"No, love, we borrowed 'em to get us to Mountain Rest."

"They're pretty," she cooed. "Maybe you could take me riding later."

Snowdrop stared. She'd seen fairies flirting with each other but it never went like this. How did Agatha get from pretty horses to "you could take me riding" in one heartbeat?

"They'll need to rest," Arley said. "They've been pullin' us along for three whole days. And you know we're here only two nights."

"On the way back then," she said. She gave Bird one final stroke and turned, smiling sweetly at Edna and Larkspur as they stepped up alongside Snowdrop. She saw Snowdrop and Nem last and the smile hardened. Snowdrop nodded at all the humans as Arley introduced them. The blacksmith was called Gracie, and the shopkeepers were Marta and George.

After a few questions about their travel, the blacksmith turned back to her shop. "I need to finish mending Cyril's plow but I'll be by tomorrow night."

"What's tomorrow night?" Arley asked.

"Your mother didn't tell you?" Marta said as Gracie sauntered away. "She told us to be ready whenever you arrived. She's planned a welcome home party."

"A party?"

"A dinner and dance. It's about time for the harvest celebration and she said they'd host it whatever night you were here so everyone could say hello."

Arley forced a smile. It must have fooled Marta and George because they said goodbye and herded their children back into the store. Agatha trailed after them, peeking back a few times as Snowdrop and the ladies climbed back into the wagon.

Arley muttered as he took the driver's seat, and the horses resumed their trot toward the blue ridge of mountains. A few clouds hung over the peaks, blocking the sun.

The fields of grain continued. Far out in the rows, a team moved with sickles and a cart, cutting the tall stalks and bundling them. The wagon slowly passed a farmhouse and matching white barn set back from the road on their left. The road climbed up a low ridge and another house appeared on the right as they crested the hill.

Arley jutted his chin out. "That's my parents' place." The house stood tall on a high plateau, facing the north–south road across the fields. It was also painted white and had a large barn and various outbuildings down the hill behind it and a few broad trees surrounding it. As Arley turned in at the driveway and they drew nearer, a wide, level lawn stretched out on the back side of the house. Punched tin lanterns hung on a wire strung along the boundary. The lawn ended abruptly at the top of a stone wall as tall as a person, and the ground at the base sloped gradually away.

A dog perked up on the front porch of the house and came down the steps, tail wagging. But the driveway split and Arley veered left onto a lower drive that curved down behind the back of the house and the lawn terrace. The dog trotted across the grass and came down the hillside after them. A dinging sound came over the whistle of the wind and a whiff of cooking smoke drifted in the air.

"I'm goin' straight to the barn to get the poor horses settled," Arley said. "Otherwise we'll be talkin' to my ma for an hour while the poor things stand waitin'."

The driveway passed the stone wall supporting the back yard— the lanterns swung high over their heads and one banged into a pole, the source of the endless dinging. All around, hillsides sloped away and fields spread with different colors and patterns, and far out, people moved about in one field, while another field was dotted with white animals.

"Are those the sheep?" Snowdrop asked, pointing.

"Yes." Arley's shoulders stiffened but then he slumped and gave her a tired smile. He directed the horses under the eaves of the barn before calling out, "Whoa." The driveway continued and curved right to circle the house and head back toward the road.

Everyone clambered out of the wagon and stretched. Arley directed them to follow the driveway to the front of the house and let themselves in. "Although if she's home, my ma will appear before you get that far," he added.

As Nem reached to lift their bags out of the wagon, first Edna's and Larkspur's and then her own, Snowdrop stepped closer to Arley, who had begun to unhitch the horses. He didn't react.

"Does your family manage all this land?" Snowdrop asked.

"Each farm is a quarter-league square of land."

"Isn't that a lot?"

"The families plan the annual crop rotation all together so the harvests don't coincide and we can all help each other."

The others trudged up the driveway. Did Arley want her to go, too? But a moment later he handed her Bird's lead. He had Lady's and he led the horse to a door alongside the wagon and opened it into the main barn. Snowdrop followed him in.

Inside was cooler and dark, and the air was still after the rushing of the wind. A bird flapped up to the rafters. Thick beams arched overhead to brace a high, vaulted roof. A musty smell of hay and horses filled her nostrils. As her eyes adjusted to the dim lighting, slits of daylight showed between the long vertical boards of the walls, but the roof was solid and dark. Under her feet were wide boards perfectly aligned to form a smooth floor.

A whuffling drew her attention toward stalls along one side. A large horse peered out over its stall door. Arley walked to it and it brushed noses with Lady.

"Hey, Thunder," Arley said fondly, giving his hand to the horse to sniff. He petted its broad head. It towered over him and over Lady and grew taller the closer Snowdrop got. Bird wanted to say hello, too, and pushed her way in, squashing Snowdrop beside Arley. They stood as close as when they'd been dancing, and in the quiet of the barn she could hear him breathing.

"This is Thunder," Arley said. "I don't know why he's in today. I hope he's all right."

"He's old?" Snowdrop asked. He looked sturdy but his eyelids drooped a little and his tall back was bowed.

"'Bout as old as me. He's the first horse I ever rode."

Arley showed her which stall to put Bird in and set her to filling the stall floors with straw. He lugged over a sack of grain and filled buckets for each horse, and after they had bedding and food and water, Arley retrieved two brushes so they could work at the same time.

They'd about finished tending to the horses when a voice from outside pierced the quiet. Snowdrop couldn't make out the words but the voice sounded commanding and enthusiastic at the same time. Arley patted Lady and walked over to Bird's stall. "Here comes my ma."

A figure appeared in the doorway. She was broad like Arley and about the same height and from her silhouette, she wore trousers.

"Young man, what's takin' ya so long?"

"I had to put up the horses, Ma," Arley said, heading toward her. "You know that."

Snowdrop followed him, glad the darkness hid her. What if Arley's mother didn't like her?

"Without even introducing your guests?" his mother went on.

"They can introduce themselves. They're adults."

They reached Mrs. Farnwell. Her face resembled Arley's very much, with creases that showed how much she smiled. Her canvas trousers were like his but extended up in front, covering her chest, and the bottoms were coated in dirt. She and Arley faced each other for one brief moment.

"Well give me a hug, love," his mother said and a grin broke across her face the same way it did on him, and he smiled back and hugged her.

"This is Snowdrop," he said as he stepped away, "from the forest near Woodglen."

Snowdrop smiled awkwardly. Mrs. Farnwell extended her hand and pumped Snowdrop's up and down. "I'm Letty Farnwell. Welcome to Woods End."

Chapter 14

Mrs. Farnwell led them up the drive with the dog trotting beside her. Snowdrop couldn't think of her as "Letty"—she seemed so formal, even in her mud-streaked trousers.

"I wasn't sure if you'd be at the house," Arley said.

"I was out in the fields all morning," she replied, "but I had a feelin' you'd be in today and I wanted someone to be here to greet ya and get everyone settled."

They rounded the bend and trudged along to the front steps. The house was made of wide boards—where had they come from? They must've been brought all the way from the forest. It had stone chimneys on either end and one had smoke drifting upward from the top. Purple asters and tall clusters of yellow wingstem lined the base of the porch, along with the remnants of zinnias and marigolds and other summer flowers. On the opposite side of the drive was a wooden gazebo-like structure with latticed walls and more flowerbeds around the base.

The front door was a heavy slab of wood, and it opened to reveal wooden floorboards, wooden walls, and a wooden ceiling. The space was so much taller and wider than Edna's cottage or even the human pubs she'd been in. There was so much bare wood showing—maybe here in the warmer north, the houses didn't need as much insulation. The hearth she glimpsed in the front room as they entered seemed to be the only part not made of wood. Being inside the large human house was like being inside a giant, square tree.

As they walked down a hallway, they passed room upon room. Each one had a rug on the floor and human decorations on the walls, and tables and shelves in the corners. Snowdrop saw both a spinning wheel and loom, and a table with sewing and a half-way-finished basket. She couldn't take it all in. Without the shops of a town like Woodglen, Arley's family and their neighbors must make a lot more items themselves.

When they came to the staircase she stopped to examine the structure. It was also made of wood and, unlike the compact one at the inn at the crossroads, this one climbed into the top of the house with open space beneath it.

"I'll show you your rooms," Mrs. Farnwell said and started up.

As the others followed, Arley's hand settled on Snowdrop's back and lightly nudged her forward. "Get settled in and I can explain how stairs work later."

"I know how st—"

He grinned and she snapped her mouth shut, and her traitorous cheeks tried to smile.

Upstairs, Mrs. Farnwell directed them to two bedrooms: Snowdrop with Nem and the two elder ladies together. She'd stacked towels on their beds and filled the wash jugs. She practically ordered them to have a rest before supper.

"Ma, come here a moment," Arley said, and he led her out of the room.

Snowdrop perched on the edge of the bed as Nem shut the door. The fairies talked a lot about the humans' gigantic beds, elevated off the floor on wooden frames and cushioned with extravagant mattresses. Usually the talk was related to how great the beds were for tumbling, so she'd discounted it, but as she shifted backward, her bottom sank into the soft quilt. Maybe there was something to all the praise.

Nem bounced onto the bed beside her. "It's a feather bed!" She rose to her knees and bounced a few more times.

"What's that mean?"

"The mattress is stuffed with feathers from geese or— Oh, will that bother you?"

Snowdrop bounced a few times. "No. I know humans eat birds so I guess it's better they use the feathers."

"Are you tired?" Nem asked. She crawled across the bed to the top and yanked up the pillows, propping them against the wooden headboard.

Snowdrop crawled beside her and they settled back, sitting side by side and leaning on the pillows. "Not really."

"What did you think of that woman at the store—Agatha?" Nem asked.

Snowdrop's face heated. "She was . . . I don't know."

"She came on to Arley kind of strong."

"Aye."

"But she looked like she's as young as me," Nem continued. "She was probably only a youngster the last time she saw him."

Snowdrop hadn't considered that. Agatha had seemed ready to pounce on Arley and tumble him in the fields after her horse ride, but maybe she'd nursed a childhood crush on him and wasn't so experienced.

"Nem," Snowdrop began, licking her lips, "when Trillium taught you about love and . . . and lust and all that . . . do you . . ." Her hands shook and her heartbeat picked up.

Nem waited.

Nem wouldn't laugh at her ignorance. Snowdrop steadied her breathing. "I never had those lessons," she said finally.

"Oh."

"Oleander told me about taking bitter herbs to avoid pregnancy but she never explained anything else."

"Have you ever been with anyone?" Nem asked. "Kissing or anything?"

"A few times. I didn't like it much. I mean, it was kind of strange and boring."

"How did it happen?"

"Both times, the fairy approached me and was talking and flirting and we went somewhere alone and it . . . kind of just happened? I don't think I liked *him* either time. But I liked that someone was paying attention to me. I went along with it."

"Was it consensual?"

"Yes. I wanted to try it. And both of them were nice about it—they hung around after and said sweet things. But I think they knew it hadn't really, um, worked for me? And they didn't ask again."

"You don't have to answer," Nem said, "but when you say 'worked for you' do you mean reaching a climax?"

"I mean that, but also I mean feeling anything at all? He was obviously into it, which made me glad, but I felt only this mildly uncomfortable scraping."

Nem winced.

"Like my body didn't work right."

"Does it ever 'work right' on your own?"

"Oh, um . . ." Snowdrop blushed. "Yes. That's no trouble at all. Doing it on my own."

"So it wasn't like that?"

"No. When it's just me, it's easy to imagine things. And I get turned on by the things I imagine, and it's easy to reach the finish. But being with someone else wasn't the same at all. We were touching without any of the good sensations. And it seemed rude to daydream about something else, but I'm not even sure it would have worked since everything he did was different than what I would imagine."

Nem frowned. "When Trillium explained things, she talked

about different types of attraction. She said some people feel all of them and lump them together, but some people don't feel them all the same."

Snowdrop waited, barely breathing.

"There's one kind of attraction when you like looking at someone."

Snowdrop pictured Arley sitting on the wagon seat. His tan skin, his curling hair. Or even his bulging muscles when she'd seen him washing up at the pump behind the inn. She shook her head. Looking at him felt no different than looking at Nem or Edna.

"Then there's one kind where you want to talk to someone and you connect with them by sharing your feelings."

This time when she imagined Arley, her chest heated. His talking had annoyed her at first, but the past few days she'd practically craved their time together and felt disappointed when she didn't get to ride beside him. She nodded.

"Then there's romance," Nem continued. "You want to have a relationship, sometimes exclusively, and do things together like going on walks or stargazing. Or like the humans go on 'dates' and have dinner at a tavern."

Snowdrop's face flushed. She nodded again.

"Then sometimes you get the urge to tumble someone, and that's one thing, but you can also like touching without sex. You might want to hug or hold hands."

Snowdrop remembered Arley holding her as they waltzed. She'd liked his hand on her back. But she hadn't wanted to kiss him. She'd *maybe* wanted to press herself against him. But not to fall to the ground and ravish him.

"The other thing," Nem continued, "is some people can feel all these attractions with someone they barely know, but other people won't feel anything for a stranger but start to be attracted once they know and like the other person."

"Oh . . ." Nem's words resonated. "I never understood when

the fairies would switch partners, like one day Petunia was with Magnolia and the next day she was with Coralbell, and she'd be humping someone new in the supply closet practically every day. But it makes sense if some people feel attraction right away."

Nem stayed quiet as Snowdrop pondered everything she'd said.

"Your friend Burne," Snowdrop asked, "he might be someone who needs to get to know the other person."

"I think so."

"Have you . . . have you met anyone you like?"

Nem smiled and shook her head. "I never had much chance until we left the Haven last spring. And Cliffside is pretty small. I like the people my age and I find some of them attractive to look at but not in the way that I'd want to touch them."

"Thanks for explaining all this."

"I'm sorry you had to wait so long to hear it." Nem took her hand. "There's nothing wrong with you, Snowdrop. So many people talk about tumbling it can seem like everyone shares their view. And some people don't talk about such personal things so you don't hear all the perspectives. But not everyone is like Petunia."

"Thanks, Nem."

Nem yawned. "I might need a nap."

Snowdrop reached for the quilt folded at the foot of the bed and shook it open as Nem pulled her pillow down and lay her head on it. Snowdrop covered her. How many times had she done this with a younger Nem? A lump of sadness and fondness and other unknown things welled up inside. She tucked the edges of the quilt as she used to.

Snowdrop sat back against her pillow. All the things Nem had said repeated in her head. Nem's breathing evened out and she lay still.

Snowdrop tried closing her eyes but her mind churned. She would never sleep. She slipped off the bed and left the room.

The house was silent. Everyone must be napping or outside.

Snowdrop quietly climbed down the steps. As she neared the bottom and turned into the hallway, the front door swung open and Mrs. Farnwell came in.

"Oh, love," she said, "since you're up—Arley has something to show you outside." She held the door open.

Snowdrop stepped outside. The wind across the plains hit her, blowing her hair into her face. Arley crouched on the ground out by the gazebo across the driveway, his back to her. What did he want to show her? As she walked over he looked up. He stood with something in his hands. A trowel lay on the ground beside a patch of recently dug earth.

"Here," he said as she neared. "These are for you."

She held out her hands and as his opened into hers, something passed between them. As if the clearest spring breeze rushed into her palms and tingled up her arms. She gasped and stared at him and he stared back, wide-eyed. He slowly pulled his hands away.

She held a dozen dirt-coated bulbs, small like coins but white under the dirt. They were dormant—no roots or green—but she didn't need to see a bloom to recognize them. Tears pricked her eyes.

"They're snowdrops," she whispered.

Arley rubbed the back of his neck and studied the ground. "I thought they might help with your magic lessons."

She held the bulbs to her chest. Sensations emanated from them, like they were calling to her. "How did you find them?"

"I asked my ma. She always has flowers bloomin' first thing in the spring, and I asked her if any of 'em was snowdrops. She knew where they were so I could dig some up."

Snowdrop started to cry.

"Aw, princess . . ." Arley began, stepping toward her, but he stopped himself and didn't reach for her. For once she wished he would. He stepped back, his brow crinkling.

"So nice— of you—" she managed between sobs. "No one— else ever—"

He lifted a hand to her face and wiped one cheek with his thumb before abruptly drawing away. "Come on now. It's no big deal."

"It is to me."

"We'll find a sack for 'em, and you can take 'em home and plant 'em in the forest."

She nodded and kept hanging on to the bulbs.

"Do ya want to sit?" he asked, gesturing into the gazebo. "Go on in and I'll patch up my ma's flower bed." He turned away and knelt beside the place he'd dug up.

Snowdrop staggered to the wooden structure, clutching the bulbs and blinking away her tears. She stepped up and in. The latticed sides blocked the wind and shadowed the interior from the bright sun. A bench ran around the perimeter and she sank onto it. For a moment she simply held the bulbs and sighed away the tears. Slowly she lowered them and made a bowl of the bottom of her tunic to hold them safely. She picked up one and ran her thumb over it. Warm friendliness seeped out.

What if she killed it?

The bulb sent a pulse of magic through her, good clean magic like the feeling she'd had from the wind two days ago, but clearer and stronger. As if it knew her worries and didn't share them.

Arley came in and sat beside her.

"They feel amazing," she said. "I can feel how alive they are."

"When I put 'em in your hands I felt somethin', too."

"Maybe that's normal—we'd have to ask Larkspur."

"Do ya know what to do with 'em?"

"Not exactly. Using them can make some magic easier, and sometimes they help beginners learn. It's different for everyone." She rubbed her thumb over the bulb. "I guess I could try the things Larkspur's been having me do. I can . . . it feels like the snowdrops are encouraging me to try."

"Do ya want to?" To his credit, he didn't move away.

She wouldn't kill the bulbs. But what if she tried and failed? If she failed at magic even with her name plant, she'd have no hope of learning.

But each time she thought of her fear, another wave of encouragement washed over her. She wanted to try. "If you wouldn't mind," she said.

"Go ahead. Turn your hair blue."

Snowdrop took a deep breath and exhaled through her mouth. "Okay. You stay here. I want to look at the sky." And if she accidentally called a flock of birds again, she didn't want them crashing into the side of the gazebo.

Snowdrop gathered her hem against her body with one hand and held the single bulb with the other. She went to the entrance of the gazebo and scanned the wide blue sky—wider than ever over the fields spreading to the horizon. This time when she closed her eyes and imagined the color flowing down to her, the entire sky responded in a jolt of blue. She didn't need a falling leaf or a bird—the color itself swirled and came straight to her, ruffling her hair and wrapping around her skin with barely a thought.

She opened her eyes and turned to Arley. He gaped at her.

"Did it work?" she asked. She shook her head so her long bangs fell in front of her face. They were blue.

She pushed her bangs aside. Her hand was blue.

Snowdrop looked down. Her tunic was blue. And her pants. The bulbs were blue, and her legs. Everything was blue, even the floor beneath her bare blue feet.

"Oh, bluebird," Arley said and he began to laugh.

Snowdrop let go of the illusion and the blue drained away. Her hands became their usual pinkish-peach color and her tunic faded to off-white.

"Don't laugh at me!" Snowdrop said, but the bulb in her hand beamed at her and her heart soared.

"I'm not!" Arley said, even though he clearly was. "Ya did it. Ya did it so well you turned everythin' blue. You can do magic, princess."

Chapter 15

Snowdrop and Arley sat in the gazebo all afternoon. She practiced turning blue until she could direct the color to her hair. She no longer needed to see the sky to do it. Then she took Arley's hand and turned him blue. And she tried carefully reaching out to the nearby birds and was able to interest several in flying into the gazebo to perch in the rafters, although they mostly seemed confused about why she'd invited them, hopping back and forth and chirping at each other. She'd been trying to ask them to sing to Arley.

When the noise of a wagon and horses arriving up the drive filtered into the gazebo, they went inside the house. Mrs. Farnwell had a bin where she stored extra sacks from the general store and she found a small one for the snowdrop bulbs, which Snowdrop packed away in her room. She kept the one bulb in her pocket, though, where she could reach in and wrap her hand around it. Knowing it was there filled her with happiness.

Mrs. Farnwell had a giant pot of stew on the hearth in the kitchen with a smaller pot beside it without any animal meat in it, for her fairy guests. She sent Snowdrop and Arley to the adjacent dining room to set the long table. As they set out napkins and utensils, loud voices sounded, growing abruptly louder as the door at the back of the house opened into the kitchen. She couldn't see Arley's brothers yet, but she already she knew she wouldn't be drawn to them. They were too loud.

"Here we go," Arley muttered and moved around her to the doorway.

Two men crowded into view, grinning. They were both a little taller than Arley but not as broad, and had similar features. One knocked aside the other to enter the dining room, where he grabbed Arley with an arm around his neck and pulled his head down, lifting his other fist.

Snowdrop froze, her mind racing through the ways she could defend Arley from the unexpected attack—break a dish over his brother's head, or go for his hair and yank? But Arley tucked his chin before the arm was tight and slipped out underneath. He pushed his brother back and stood with his hands on his hips.

"Aw, Rolf," Arley said, grinning back, "you'll have to try harder than that."

Mrs. Farnwell nudged the other brother into the room. "Stop behaving like children," she said, depositing a dish of butter on the table, "and get washed up for supper. We have guests and we're not waitin' on ya."

"I'm only teasin' him, Ma," Rolf said, and he leaned in to hug Arley. As he looked over Arley's shoulder, his eyes fell on Snowdrop. "An' who's this?" he asked, and she worried he might notice her shiver of repulsion at his tone.

Rolf tried to move forward past Arley, but Arley turned enough to block him. But he did it so subtly that it seemed unintentional. Arley held out an arm to her and ushered her forward, beside him and on the far side from Rolf.

"This is Snowdrop, one of the fairies I'm drivin' to the council meeting. My brothers, Rolf and Peter." Snowdrop dipped her chin in greeting. "They're assholes," Arley whispered loudly as Mrs. Farnwell left the room.

"Sod off, Arley," Rolf said, and Peter turned as if he might tell on Arley to their mother.

"Peter," she called from the kitchen, "come help me lift the pot, please, dear."

Peter's shoulders slumped and he trudged out of the room.

"So," Rolf said, once again trying to step toward Snowdrop even though Arley had wedged her between his body and the sideboard, "what's it like bein' a fairy?"

Snowdrop squinted. "Um, it, uh—"

"Is that supposed to be charmin'?" Arley asked. He continued in a mocking deep voice: "What's it like being a human?"

"Shut up." Rolf shoved him.

"Don't be an idiot."

Rolf was turning red. The situation might escalate if she didn't intervene. "It's okay," she said, touching Arley's arm. She turned to Rolf. "Have you ever met a fairy before?"

"No." Rolf's gaze dropped briefly before returning to her face. He lowered his voice and smirked. "And I can see what I've been missing."

"Skies," Arley muttered.

Snowdrop faced Rolf. Rolf was a dolt, like Wells in Woods Rest, but she didn't have anything to feel bad about. She wasn't attracted to him—it didn't mean she was doing something wrong or her body didn't work right.

She straightened up, feeling warmth off Arley at her elbow and the smooth snowdrop bulb in her pocket. "The fairies are all different, the same as humans. And I'm not interested in tumbling you or your brother so please don't flirt with me. It would be nice if we could get along while I'm here."

In the ensuing silence, Snowdrop realized what she'd said. She'd meant Peter, but Arley was Rolf's brother too. Would he think she meant him? She peeked over.

Arley had a smug grin on his face. Rolf's mouth hung open.

"Okay?" she asked Rolf.

"I don't flirt with my mother's guests," he snapped.

Right. Pretending he hadn't just done so—same as Wells had.

"How's the harvest going?" Arley asked, thankfully, and the tension leaked away.

As Rolf answered, the stairs creaked at the front of the house and Larkspur came down the hall, followed by Edna and Nem. Arley made introductions and Snowdrop was relieved when Rolf merely waved at Nem. The backdoor banged and Mr. Farnwell entered, and Mrs. Farnwell and Peter began carrying bowls of stew into the room.

Soon everyone was seated around the table, with Mrs. Farnwell at the end closest to the kitchen and Arley opposite her. Snowdrop was beside him with his father on her other side. Mr. Farnwell was stout like Arley and had the same twinkle in his eye. He asked about her life in the woods until Arley said, "Let her eat, Pops."

"Right, love, don't let your stew get cold." Mr. Farnwell winked. "While you eat, I can tell you all about Arley's childhood."

Arley groaned as his father launched into a story that began "When Arley was eight winters . . ." Snowdrop couldn't stop smiling as she ate. Arley hadn't done anything more scandalous than sneaking a whole batch of buns out to the barn for Thunder, but the way Mr. Farnwell built up the story and added voices made it entertaining. The stew had a hearty tomato-based sauce thickened with flour, and was full of potatoes, carrots, and beans. As she scraped the last bit onto her spoon, Mr. Farnwell rested his elbows on the table.

"Arley's a good lad," he said.

"Aw, Pops, don't—"

"He was always the first one up, never complainin'. When the boys played, he'd give up his turn to stop a fight. You'll hear how they tease him and call him a weakling but he has a different kind of strength."

Arley's face was red like a sunburn and tilted down. Snowdrop poked him until he looked up.

"That's enough, Pops," Arley said, pleading. "Besides, since my guard trainin' I can run circles around both of them."

His father shook his head, smiling, but he stopped talking and they turned to the other conversations around the table.

After dinner, Snowdrop showed Larkspur the bulbs Arley had given her and how she could turn her hair blue without even looking at the sky. Larkspur praised her and promised they'd resume her lessons, with the help of her snowdrop bulbs, as soon as they had a chance.

Lying beside Nem that night, Snowdrop could barely sleep. So much had happened that day, things she'd never imagined when she'd agreed to go on this trip. What if she'd refused when Dustan and Rose asked? She'd still be in the caverns at home, sweeping and sad, always alone. She'd be lying on her cot in the dark right now. She'd never have seen the plains or the mountains, or slept in a human bed or smelled Norlian coffee.

She'd never have met Arley.

Mrs. Farnwell had mentioned the party at dinner. It was the village's annual harvest celebration, with a communal meal provided by all the guests, followed by dancing as the sun set. They already had bales of hay set around the yard behind the house for seating, and tomorrow they'd create makeshift tables for the food with boards they kept in the barn for such events. She and her companions would help decorate the yard, and Mrs. Farnwell had a secret dessert she wouldn't tell them about, but she glowed each time she said "secret dessert" until her sons told her to quit bringing it up if she wouldn't tell them what it was.

Everything about the party sounded incredible: the decorations, the food, the mysterious dessert—even though the dessert was probably loaded with sugar. But Snowdrop was most excited for the dancing. Dancing outdoors under the stars and the full moon like at a fairy dance, but this time she wouldn't be shunned because no one would know she had a dangerous, vengeful mother. No one would be scared to ask her to dance. And maybe she'd get to dance with Arley again, like they had at the wayside the previous night.

Finally she slept, and in the morning they were immediately given tasks. Snowdrop reluctantly left her snowdrop bulbs in her room, promising them she'd use them soon. She kept the one in her pocket, though. She never wanted to be without one.

Arley's whole family stayed in from the fields, and by the time they stopped working to have a late lunch, the back yard had been turned into an enchanting wonderland. They'd woven garlands of long grasses, which dipped gracefully between the tall poles lining the perimeter, punctuated by wreathes of woven grain, each like a sunshine of wheat stalks. The lanterns hung from the poles, waiting to be lit at dusk. Clusters of pinecones brought in from the forest, surrounded by branches of holly and other leaves, graced the tables, while giant pumpkins and squashes lined the edge of the yard between bales of hay. Barrels filled one side of the lawn to act as tables for guests to stand beside while eating, and more haybales had been spread on the grass below the driveway, where guests could sit if they wanted to escape the crowd.

They spent the afternoon preparing food, both in the farmhouse kitchen and at an outdoor oven. By the time the sun was heading down the sky in the west, wagons began appearing on the road from the village. Snowdrop and Nem sat on the front porch to watch them approach, each dressed in her nicest outfit. Snowdrop's dress was pale green with short sleeves and a skirt that swished when she turned. She didn't wear it often but she was glad she had brought it to wear in Mountain Rest, so she had it for tonight. And Nem had used some clips to pin up Snowdrop's hair, leaving only her bangs sweeping down beside her face. She felt elegant.

The wagons turned in and rattled up the driveway carrying people of all ages, circled the house to unload their passengers, and drove out to park along the drive. Several people spotted them and waved. When the wagons tapered off as if most everyone had arrived, Nem insisted they join the party.

The table for food had filled with dishes, and Mrs. Farnwell was carrying out a platter of some kind of meat. Arley was surrounded by guests at one edge of the lawn. Everyone would want to visit with him since he'd been gone so long. He had a new plaid shirt on and he'd shaved since that morning. Snowdrop turned away from the crowd. Hopefully she'd get to talk to him soon.

As she ate beside her companions, sitting on bales of hay, neighbors came over to introduce themselves. Most of them had never met a fairy and a few asked what kinds of magic they could do. After consulting with Mrs. Farnwell, Larkspur gave a brief demonstration of basic illusions on herself, and she called a flock of field sparrows to fly in and perch atop the lantern poles and sing. The crowd stared as the birds gave volley after volley of their twittering call, the tweets overlapping into a chorus. When the birds swooped off, the humans clapped and cheered.

Villagers swarmed Larkspur with questions and Edna mingled with the crowd. The younger folks started a ball game on the grass below the party area and invited Nem to join them. Snowdrop stayed on her bale of hay, watching.

Before the sun set, Mrs. Farnwell revealed her surprise dessert, a gigantic cake covered in sugary frosting. The cake had multiple layers stacked one on top of another, like a snowy mountain with steps to the top, and had to be carried out on a board held by both of Arley's brothers. She'd made enough cake for everyone to have a piece, plus one to take home, and the guests gathered around to admire it. Across the front, Mrs. Farnwell had used icing dyed purple with blackberry powder to write on the frosting: WELCOME HOME ARLEY.

The cake would be served later in the evening. First would come dancing.

Snowdrop could barely keep her breathing steady as the guests cleared the lawn of seats and dishes. Her hands shook until she clasped them together. A group of musicians set up their instruments on one side. The late sunlight was tinted pink, and Peter carried a glowing lantern from one pole to the next, lifting each lantern down to open the small glass door and light it from his before rehanging it. They beamed in a row as the sun set and twilight descended.

Larkspur caught Snowdrop's gaze across the grass and winked. A moment later, several dozen fireflies, the last of the season, rose from the edge of the pond below the barn and blinked their way up to the lawn, where they hovered over the guests like warm little stars. The guests gasped and exclaimed.

In the east, behind the farmhouse, a full golden moon rose over the plains.

The musicians launched into a warm-up tune and the guests moved onto the grass, taking hands with their partners. From the edge of the grass, Snowdrop located Arley—still surrounded by guests and they were mostly young women now. Agatha was there, with her hand clamped onto his arm. When the tune ended and the band called for the dance to begin, Agatha led Arley onto the grass.

The dances were done in sets of eight dancers. Some of the moves were familiar, even if the formation differed from the lines the fairies danced in. Snowdrop scanned the guests, wondering who might dance with her. But while the Woods End residents had been friendly, none of them approached her for a dance. Maybe she made them nervous because she was a fairy or simply because she didn't make conversation easily.

And each time she spotted Arley out on the lawn, he was either dancing or surrounded by a flock of women begging for a dance.

Rolf and Peter were dancing, but after the way she'd treated Rolf, she didn't expect him to ask her to dance. Maybe she shouldn't have spoken to him the way she had. But if dancing with him meant being subjected to his leering and suggestive comments, she'd rather not dance.

Still, it would have been nice if they could have been friendly. How did other women handle such a situation? She watched Rolf with his partner. Was he flirting with her? She wasn't pressing herself against him or batting her lashes. But she also wasn't slapping him across the face or shouting. Everyone here was acquainted—

maybe he didn't bother to flirt because he knew she wasn't inter-ested.

Snowdrop exhaled. Nem was off with the youngsters, and Larkspur and Edna were seated amid the elder Farnwells and other neighbors. Other guests lined the edges of the dance area, but she couldn't bring herself to approach anyone and ask them to dance.

Stars pricked the dark sky as the last of the sunset's orange glow drained away over the mountains. A gentle breeze came from the fields, tempering the noise of the music and laughter. As one dance after another passed, the moon rose over the house until it shone down on them, and the lantern light was warm on smiling faces. The fireflies had drifted back to the pond where they blinked at their mates. The night was perfect, and she was alone, just as she'd always been at the fairy dances. It didn't matter that no one here knew about Oleander or her past. No one wanted to dance with her.

Finally the band took a break, and Arley was immediately swarmed with a crowd of friends, all talking excitedly. She watched until finally, finally he looked up and scanned the lawn. When his gaze reached her, he waited a moment. She smiled and he tipped his head and turned back to the woman talking in front of him.

"It's quite a party."

Snowdrop turned. A hunched man with bushy gray eyebrows stood beside her. He wore trousers with a bib like Mrs. Farn-well's—overalls, they were called—with a plaid shirt beneath it in colors different than Arley's. The man surveyed the crowd rather than staring at her. He'd introduced himself earlier, she realized, although she couldn't remember his name.

"Is this what it's like every autumn?" Snowdrop asked. The answer didn't matter but she wanted to keep him talking. At least someone was talking to her.

"Pretty much, although it's exciting to have special guests this time." He indicated her with a tilt of his head. "Have ya met my daughter?" He gestured at three women in simple dresses, standing in a group at the edge of the lawn. They all wore their long hair down their backs.

"I don't think so."

"Come on," he said, hobbling away. "She and her friends look about your age."

Snowdrop walked alongside him, her face already heating. They weren't going to want to talk to her.

They reached the young women, and he introduced her before wandering away. His daughter was called Fina and her friends were Constance and Helewise.

When Fina smiled it seemed genuine—warm, friendly, and it reached her eyes. They were much better at making conversation than she was—they asked questions about fairy life and Snowdrop answered. But with all three of them watching her, she couldn't think of things to say to keep the conversation going. When they began to gossip about other things, she quietly sighed.

She could stand beside them and pretend to be part of their group. At least she wasn't standing alone. But standing and not being able to participate was kind of boring. She tried to follow what they were saying but she didn't know the people they were talking about.

Only then they brought up Arley.

"Are you an item?" Constance asked. "Everyone's been wondering."

"I don't think so," Snowdrop said.

Constance squinted.

"I mean no." Hopefully the darkness hid her blush. "We've spent a lot of time talking this quarter-moon because we're stuck in a wagon together. I think we've become friends."

"That's probably for the best," Helewise said, and Snowdrop's heart sank a little. But she continued: "The way Agatha's got her fingernails dug into his arm, she might cause damage if he tried to get away." She didn't exactly snicker, but the way she said it cheered Snowdrop—as if it weren't only her who thought Agatha's behavior was a bit much.

"Were they an item once?" Snowdrop asked.

"Nah, she's only eighteen. She was in a younger crowd when we were teens. But all the gals had crushes on him. She's been talkin' nonstop about seeing him since Mrs. Farnwell said he was visiting."

"Did he date a lot when he lived here?" Hopefully she had used the human term correctly.

Helewise smirked. "Depends how you define 'date.' What do you think, Constance?"

Her friend grinned. "If you define 'date' as 'tumble in the hay,' I'd say he did it a lot."

"Everyone was sweet on him," Fina added. "Sometimes I got the feeling he didn't like to tell anyone no."

"And he was a lot of fun," Constance went on. "He'd always make me laugh harder than anyone."

"Yes!" Helewise said. "Sometimes I'd try not to laugh to tease him and he'd resort to tickling me."

"He loved it when you laughed while he was inside ya."

"And he loved doin' it in the hay."

"And tickling you with hay."

Fina cringed but the other two went right on talking about Arley's tactics all the times they'd been with him.

Skies, Snowdrop did not want to hear about this. Her insides squeezed and her chest ached. She'd known Arley must've had lovers but she'd never had to hear about it. And hearing people talk about their sexual exploits always made her sad—even knowing nothing was wrong with her, hearing about things she never did made her think she was missing something, somehow. And if Arley liked all these things Constance and Helewise remembered, he'd never want someone like her.

Had she hoped he would?

She'd been annoyed with him when they met. She'd convinced

herself she still was. But she'd been fooling herself. She hadn't been annoyed with him in a while. She'd wanted to ride on the driver's seat beside him two mornings ago and had longed to sleep out by the fire beside him the night before that.

When he'd shown her attention in the beginning, she hadn't liked it at all. She'd only liked him once he'd stopped being interested in her. She'd missed her chance.

She regarded Fina. "Did you . . . ?" She couldn't ask.

Fina smiled. "I'm afraid not. I'm attracted only to women. And my options are rather limited in Woods End."

"Hey!" Constance said.

Fina frowned. "You're no longer a prospect."

"We didn't work at all," Constance explained to Snowdrop.

"I'm glad you stayed friends," Snowdrop said. "Is it really that remote here?"

"The mail carrier is about the most excitement we get."

"And they've all been men lately."

"She has a plan, though," Constance said.

Fina grinned. "I do. I'm training my brothers to do all my chores. And as soon as the first of them turns sixteen, I'm going to get a job in Mountain Rest."

"Will you return?" Snowdrop asked.

"I guess it depends on if I fall in love. And if she finds farming on a wind-swept plain to be romantic or dreadful."

"Do you have a beau?" Constance asked Snowdrop.

"Me?"

"Don't sound so surprised. You have to know how pretty you are."

"But I'm awkward around other people," Snowdrop said, and they laughed, but not in a mean way. "You three are the first people I've been able to talk to all evening."

"So have you never been with anyone?"

"I have—"

"What's it like tumbling a fairy?" Constance's eyes gleamed with mischief.

"Don't ask her that!" Fina said.

But Snowdrop shrugged. "It's about the same as a human, I think. Most of the fairies my age turned, um, amorous when they reached their teens. And some of them paired off with life-mates while others just like to tumble whoever."

"But not you?"

"I . . . take things slower," Snowdrop said, and it didn't sound strange when she put it in words. "But not everyone's interested in that."

"But some people are." Fina smiled gently.

As they'd talked, the dance had resumed. Arley was already out on the lawn with another partner and this time the band was playing a waltz—one with the fiddle singing in a heart-tugging way. He and his partner gazed into each other's eyes as they swept across the grass. Snowdrop looked away.

"What kinds of magic do you do?" Constance asked.

Snowdrop paused. After confessing she had no beau, it would be the ultimate failure to add that she barely knew how to use magic. They'd wonder why she had never learned, and she'd have to admit to being the daughter of the former queen, and even the humans had heard about Oleander. Fina and her friends might even know someone who'd been hurt by her. They were the only people she'd connected with all night, and she didn't want them turning away in disgust.

"Well, um . . ." She scrambled to think of words that would be more or less true. "I grew up underground and I had a hard time learning magic. Being in nature makes it a lot easier. I've been catching up now that the fairies have their freedom. I can change my appearance and I can listen to animals and communicate with them a little. But I'm still learning." In her pocket, her hand closed around her snowdrop bulb, and it responded with a friendly little pulse.

"Will ya show us something?"

Snowdrop smiled. She had practiced changing her hair color so many times yesterday. With her hand holding the bulb, she closed her eyes and imagined the sky, only now the sky she imagined was dark with pinprick stars. The other women gasped.

"Your hair went all dark!" Constance said.

"And it has lights in it like stars!" Helewise reached a finger out to touch a strand.

Snowdrop grinned and let go of the illusion.

"That's fantastic," Helewise whispered.

Fina squinted up at the lantern over their heads. Something fluttered into the light, spraying dust as it collided with the glass door.

"What a large moth," Fina said. "Have you ever seen one so big?"

The poor thing tried again to reach the light. It was as big as her hand. "It's an emperor moth," Snowdrop said. It was going to hurt itself if it kept flapping against the hot lantern. She closed her eyes and calmed her mind, listening. The frantic thoughts of the moth reached her, drawn to the flame and desperate to be near it.

She closed her hand around the bulb in her pocket and tried to connect with the moth. She sent calming thoughts, asking her to leave the lantern light and come down by the women. With the magic from the snowdrop bulb, channeling her thoughts at the moth was easy and not a hint of darkness appeared.

Snowdrop opened her eyes. The moth had landed on the pole beneath the lantern. She was fluffy white with gray-brown stripes and four dark spots, one on each wing. Her beautiful wings were a tiny bit battered.

Snowdrop's new friends were glancing between her and the moth. She smiled.

She reached out again, asking the moth to join them. She held up a hand to make a flat perch in front of her face.

The moth flapped off the pole and fluttered down. She landed on Snowdrop's hand, her tiny legs prickling on Snowdrop's fingers. Up close, her wings had speckles of pink and yellow amid the white and gray, and her stripes had a beautiful scalloped pattern. The dark wing spots were rimmed in yellow, white, and black rings, and her wing tips had red highlights. Delicate feathered white antennae curled off her head. Snowdrop smiled again, telling the moth how beautiful she was.

"That's amazing," Helewise murmured. All three women gathered around the moth on Snowdrop's hand. The moth peered up at them as Snowdrop conveyed that they were friendly.

Nearby partygoers looked their way.

"I loved that trick your friend did with the fireflies," Fina said.

Using magic was easy with the snowdrop bulb to help her. She could probably invite the fireflies back, although this late in the evening they might be settled down for the night. She reached out with her senses to see if she heard them.

Something responded but not from the direction of the pond. Something was fluttering overhead—it must be another moth. Snowdrop listened. Was anyone else there? More moths replied, lots more. The one on her hand must be the only one drawn in by the lanterns. The rest were up in the sky, enjoying the night air and searching for mates.

Snowdrop grinned. "Watch this." She reached out to all the moths, asking them to flutter down to the party. She sent an image of the moth resting on her hand and of how ecstatic the humans would be to see the beautiful moths.

An enthusiastic response came back to her. No one had ever invited them to a party before! Faster than she'd imagined, the moths' motion shifted, heading down toward the lawn filled with people. They were no longer fluttering—they were swooping downward, and there seemed to be hundreds of them.

Misgivings stirred in Snowdrop's chest. But the flock of moths was rocketing toward the party. And—

A bat swooped through the crowd.

The moth on her hand took off, flapping into the darkness as more bats arrived. Snowdrop covered her mouth, staring in horror.

Dozens of bats descended on the party, diving at guests and weaving among the dancers as the music faltered. A bat landed on Agatha's hair and she screamed, waving her arms to brush it off. Snowdrop tried to reach the bats again, to send them off, but they were having too much fun. They thought the party with the humans was a game, and they darted among the people and landed on them amid their flailing hands and arms.

More bats arrived, so many the air was thick with them. Some of the party guests hunkered down on the grass, covering their heads, but others fled the lawn. People shrieked and stumbled, and in the fog of bats, a hefty man in overalls staggered sideways—right into Mrs. Farnwell's beautiful frosted cake. He rolled sideways, covering himself in frosting, and landed on the table, bringing the whole thing down. The cake smashed onto the grass.

Through the chaos, Larkspur stared at Snowdrop. Their gazes locked for a moment. Tears welled in Snowdrop's eyes and shame filled her. She had been reckless, showing off with her magic. And while she hadn't called anything dark or dangerous, she'd caused a mess and ruined the party.

She turned and ran, away from the people and the bats and the lantern light and into the darkness.

Chapter 16

❧✳❧

SNOWDROP HUDDLED AGAINST LADY'S STALL in the barn. She hugged her knees to her chest and rested her chin on them as her tears slowed. She sniffled. From outside, the shrieking had stopped. The bats must have flown off.

She couldn't stop seeing the swarm of bats, the panicked guests, and the towering white cake crashing to the ground. How had she not known the creatures in the air were bats? Emperor moths didn't gather by the hundreds in the night sky. She'd been so eager to impress Fina and the others, to draw attention, to have fun at the party and maybe even get asked to dance that she'd become careless and used magic when she shouldn't have. And while she hadn't summoned any truly dark magic, she had wrecked the party. The worst part was seeing Larkspur's disappointment.

Had Arley seen her? She hadn't noticed him amid the chaos. But even if he didn't guess what had happened, he would eventually find out the mess was her fault. By tomorrow morning, everyone in Woods End would know her faulty magic had summoned a flock of bats and destroyed their harvest celebration.

Voices murmured in the distance and a fiddle began a slow tune. Lady snuffled behind her. She would have gone into the stall to hug Lady for comfort, but the horses were sleeping and she didn't want to disturb them. The barn was dark and quiet, filled with the smell of hay and dirt. The floorboards were cold, and she shifted her bottom to stop it from going numb. Somewhere nearby, a small creature rustled.

The barn door creaked open, letting in a shaft of moonlight and the glow of a lantern as the faint noises of the party became clearer. Someone stepped inside, and she recognized his familiar silhouette before he spoke. "Snowdrop?"

She held still and watched Arley, waiting for him to back out and shut the door. He peered into the darkness. He stepped inside and shut the door behind him, and the music faded.

Snowdrop hid her face. She should have used an illusion to hide before he spotted her.

Arley's footsteps padded across to her and the light shifted as he set down the lantern. Pinpricks of light shone through the holes in the tin and speckled the floor. He stood a few paces away and said nothing.

"I destroyed the party," Snowdrop whispered.

"Ya did cause a bit of panic. But no one was injured."

"I destroyed your mother's beautiful cake . . ."

"Aw, don't worry about it, bluebird. The kids were eatin' hunks of it off the grass. It was so big—plenty of it didn't even hit the ground."

"Will she be angry with me?"

"She'll get over it. She prob'ly doesn't even know it was your fault. So, ah, was it your fault? What happened out there?"

Snowdrop forced her chin up, wiping the tearstains from her cheeks. "I tried to use magic."

The lantern light flickered on Arley's features. His face was serious but his voice was soft. "I guessed that much."

"I thought I was inviting some moths to the party. But they were bats. I couldn't tell the difference."

He squinted. "You were invitin' moths to the party?"

"There was an emperor moth by the lantern, and I didn't want her to burn herself, so I called her away. And it worked."

"Okay."

"And Fina and her friends were paying attention to me, and everyone loved the fireflies earlier, and I thought I could do something like that. Something to captivate people. I listened and I heard lots more creatures swooping in the night."

"And ya thought they were moths."

"Yes."

"But they were bats."

She nodded, staring at his feet.

"And you said 'Hey, we're havin' a party, want to come?'"

Snowdrop lowered her head and mumbled, "I asked if they'd come and land on people."

He waited.

"It was enchanting when the one moth landed on my hand. And I thought if I asked more to come, I might impress people."

"So you were showin' off?"

Snowdrop jerked her head up. Arley was smiling, his eyes crinkled at the corners. He crossed his arms over his chest.

"I . . . I guess?"

"Why were you showin' off?"

"I wanted to feel better. No one was asking me to dance." A flicker of jealousy leapt inside her. "You were dancing with everyone but me."

"Aw, bluebird, I would have danced with ya."

"Maybe two days ago," she said, morose. "But as soon as you had other options, you forgot about me. And don't call me bluebird."

"I didn't forget ya. I didn't know you wanted to dance. And the others kept asking me."

She would sound petulant but she couldn't stop herself. "I thought this time would be different than the fairy dances. But it was the same. No one wanted to dance with me."

"I bet they did but they found you intimidatin'. They've never met a fairy. Or anyone as pretty as you."

He was trying to flatter her. She ignored him. "And you flirted with everyone but me."

"You don't like it when I flirt with ya."

"It doesn't mean I don't like you though."

"You like me?"

"I didn't like the flirting. It felt fake—you didn't even know me."

"And do I know you well enough now?"

"Maybe," she squeaked.

Arley moved his hands to his hips and leaned back. "What do you want, princess?"

Snowdrop's heartbeat thrummed and she swallowed, trying to keep her breathing steady. She studied Arley's hands, the barn floor, the door, anything but his face.

"Calm down, love. Tell me what you want."

"I, um . . ." She swallowed hard.

"If you tell me," he said, his voice now dangerously low, "I can give it to you."

"I don't know," she yelped.

He exhaled. "How about a dance?"

Snowdrop peeked up. He held out his arms. With only the light of the one lantern, his face was shadowed but familiar, his eyes kind. He'd always been kind, but she hadn't realized how much she enjoyed his attention until it was gone. Her hands shook as she held them out. He stepped forward to take them and pulled her to her feet.

She placed her left hand on his shoulder and her right in his, the way they'd done it two nights ago. He held her and swayed gently, not moving her the way they had when waltzing but only rocking slowly, back and forth. "This okay?" he asked.

"You can come closer," she whispered.

He smiled and drew her in. "Like this?"

"This is good."

He'd left a sliver of space between them. She was glad her

bangs hid her face because his face was so close. Being this close to him was almost too much—his eyes watching her face, his smooth cheeks. And a straight nose. Noses were weird, pointing out the front of the face like that.

She'd gotten used to the stale, earthy air of the barn and she inhaled and caught warm Arley smell, the cedar of his clean shirt and rocky scent of his skin.

His hand rubbed on her back. "Okay?"

She nodded, trained her eyes on the cleft in his chin, and focused on his hand on her back as they danced.

"I'm a little scared to move," he said after a moment. "I don't want to do anything ya don't like."

She swallowed. "You can move," she whispered.

"You'll tell me if you don't like it? Or ya know, if you do." His lips settled in the slightest smirk.

"Okay."

He brought their joined hands to his chest and held hers there, wrapped in his. His rough fingers smoothed over hers, stroking them as he left them on his chest. The dark plaid shirt was soft, like a cotton blanket for wrapping a baby, and she skimmed her fingertips over it. He took her face in his hand and brushed his thumb across her cheek and down, his fingers combing into her hair until he held her head, cradling her.

She met his gaze. He smiled across at her. "Do ya like that?"

She nodded and the movement tugged his fingers against her hair.

She stepped closer, ducking her head to avoid bumping their faces together—and to avoid him trying to kiss her. His hand on her back pulled her in as she came but he didn't try anything else. He held her cheek to cheek, and she turned so her nose scraped his jaw—still a little scratchy even when he'd recently shaved, like being scoured with sand. She caught a whiff of his shaving soap.

She pulled her left hand down his shoulder and onto his shirt with her right. Under the soft fabric was hard muscle, a ridge that ended as her hands smoothed downward. She stepped toward him, slid her hands around his wide torso, and pressed her body into his with a sigh.

"Oh, princess," he murmured, and his fingers quivered in her hair.

"This feels safe," she whispered into his shoulder.

"Yeah, 'cause ya haven't left me any room to make a move on ya." But when she tried to move back, he held her tight and added, "I'm teasin'."

She relaxed back into him. His chest pressed against hers, her hips tilted against his, and—

"Oh!" She froze. He had a bump in his trousers and she'd rubbed up on it.

He stepped back, loosening his hold. "I'm sorry."

"No, it's okay."

"Ya feel so good. But it doesn't mean anythin'."

She studied his face, a hand's breadth from hers. He held her but gingerly, his fingers on her hips.

"Do you want me to touch you down there?" she asked.

His eyes widened. "Ah, uh—"

"I could, you know, um, I could hold your . . ."

"Uh . . ."

"Your . . ."

"My . . . corncob?"

"Your what?" Snowdrop said.

"My eggplant?"

She smiled.

"My big zucchini?"

She huffed. "It's probably not that big."

He stepped in, frowning. "Do ya *want* to touch me?"

She felt nervous. But touching him wouldn't be difficult—it wouldn't be uncomfortable the way being with a partner had been in the past. Arley wouldn't be touching *her* body or trying to make her feel good. That was the part that hadn't worked in the past.

And he'd probably like it if she touched him. Fairies did, any-way. She wanted to see what happened. She wanted to share some-thing with him more than dancing.

"I think so." She fidgeted with his shirt until she accidentally pulled the edge out from his trousers. She tried to tuck it back in but it wouldn't go and she was going to need it untucked anyway. He was waiting and she wasn't sure how to begin. He lifted one hand and touched her lips.

"You're sure? Ya don't have to."

"I want to. I just don't know what I'm doing."

He grinned. "It's not hard. I mean, what to do isn't hard. *It* is hard, obviously. Here—" He took her hands in one of his and brought them lower, onto the buttons of his trousers.

She undid the buttons, one by one, and as she did he took her face in his hands. Her fingertips bumped against him as she reached the last button. His cotton underclothes were stretched taut by his erection. She pushed his trousers out of the way and peeled down the hem of his shorts, careful as she released him.

"Maybe a young zucchini," she said, and he laughed but it sounded breathless. Like the time for joking was past. His eyes were closed.

She slipped her fingers around him and tentatively stroked from the bottom toward the tip. His breathing came faster and his hands curled around the back of her neck. He rested his forehead on hers, framing the space between them.

"Like that?" she asked.

"Just like that, princess," he said, gasping a little.

She stroked again, back and forth, and his erection grew hard-er, filling her hand. His foreskin slid up and back, and the hitch in his breathing showed her when to squeeze harder as it slid over the head of his penis.

She moved her hand faster. A sheen of sweat broke on his fore-head against hers, and his lips parted as he panted. She wanted him like this, losing control and consumed by his hunger, gasping in air and her able to satiate him. She almost wanted to kiss his mouth closed.

He moaned a quick "Oh" and his fingers fisted in the back of her hair. She kept stroking him as he jerked and came hot on her fingers.

He pressed his forehead to hers, his eyes closed, and she watched as he caught his breath. When he opened his eyes, his expression was open, vulnerable.

He gazed into her eyes, so close she had to glance back and forth between his.

"Was that okay?" she asked.

"Skies," he said, his voice scratchy, "that was more than okay." He rubbed the back of her neck. "Are you all right?"

She nodded.

"What do you need?" he asked, emphasizing each word.

"Wipe my hand?"

He smiled gently and let her go. Standing before her, he leaned back and pulled a handkerchief from his back pocket, shook it open, and took her hand. When he'd wiped her fingers dry, one by one, he kept holding her hand as he cleaned himself, tossed aside the kerchief, and pulled his trousers back up with his other hand. He fastened the top button.

"Do ya want me to touch you?" he asked, squeezing her hand in his broad one.

Her body felt light, tingling, and she wanted to stay near him. But if he touched her—if he *tried* to make her feel good by touching her between her legs—all the sensations would evaporate. That's how it had gone before. No matter how much she imagined it feeling good, once the attention was on her, she lost all her longing and wanted it to stop. She shook her head, studying his chin.

His head tilted. "Why did ya want to touch me?"

"I wanted you to feel good. And I like what it does to you."

"Do you feel anythin'?"

She bit her lip. "I do. But I don't think I feel what you feel. I don't think attraction works the same for me as it does for you. If you touch me . . . it won't work."

He rubbed her fingers, considering. "Do ya want to touch yourself?"

She looked up.

"'Cause if you did," he said, arching an eyebrow, "I would love to watch." Her body heated, from her chest up to her face. She stared at him. "Or," he added, "I could leave and sit outside the door and make sure no one disturbs ya."

She hung onto his hand so he wouldn't leave.

"Eh?" he prodded. "You're thinking about it. What's the holdup?"

"I've never done anything like that."

"We don't have to. It was just an idea."

"I don't know if it will work. I might not be able to . . . focus enough to do it."

"I'd want to hold ya in my arms whether you were writhing around or still as a statue."

Warmth filled her from her shoulders to her toes. "Okay," she whispered.

He smiled and squeezed her hand.

"Um, here?" she asked.

"Wherever is comfortable for you. We could lie in the hayloft."

"Like you used to?" Her face flushed hotter. She hadn't meant to bring it up but the words had slipped out.

But Arley smiled and wiped a hand over his face, somewhat abashed. "Aw darn, Constance and Helewise were talkin' about me, weren't they?"

"They, um, they said you were nice. And that you liked tickling them."

"I was sixteen. I didn't know what in the ten seas I was doin' back then."

"But it seems like people are interested in tumbling wherever there's hay, so if you—"

"No no no," Arley said. "I don't want ya thinkin' about all the things ya heard about me. Besides, it bein' autumn we might have mice up there. Wouldn't want to disturb them in the middle of the night. I'd feel terrible if they went out in the dark and an owl got them."

Snowdrop stared at him, speechless.

He pulled her in closer with the hand he held and slipped his free arm around her back. "Where would you be most comfortable?"

She glanced around the barn. The corners were dark but the space was large, with the lantern illuminating them. "Someone might come in."

"How about this," he said. He reached for the lantern and led her to the end of the barn under the hayloft. They stepped through a doorway into a narrow room with a lower ceiling. A sturdy wooden table was at the far end, and bales of hay were stacked along the back wall, blocking a small door to the outside. He hung the lantern on a hook on the wall.

The room was close and warmer than the open barn, and the sounds from the party had disappeared. Snowdrop let go of his hand and drifted toward the table. "This is better." She trailed her fingers along the old wood of the tabletop. It had deep ridges at one corner. Someone had carved letters into the wood. RF, PF, AF.

Arley came behind her—not touching her but his presence prickled the back of her neck and his body heat warmed her.

"Can I sit here?" she asked.

"Wherever ya want."

She dusted off the table with her hand. The wood in the center was smoother, sleeker, and it shone in the dim light. Snowdrop rubbed her fingers back and forth.

"Arley?"

"Hmm?"

"Is the table worn smooth because of all the people who've sat here?"

"Uh, sure."

She glanced back at him.

He grinned sheepishly. "I suppose technically it's not the sittin' that rubs it smooth."

She arched an eyebrow.

"It's the friction."

Earlier, thinking of Arley's past had depressed her. But now, she was the one in the barn with him. The past didn't matter. "Is there anywhere in this barn you *haven't* tumbled someone?" she asked.

He scratched the back of his neck.

"Was the barn your favorite place to bring girls?"

"Princess, the girls brought *me* to the barn."

For no reason at all, her face broke into a wide smile. She turned and slid her bottom onto the table and Arley stilled, like seeing her on the table was doing something to him. She reached for his hands, pulled him between her legs, and placed his hands on her hips. "Was it like this?"

He swallowed. "Yeah."

She tried to imagine it—her and Arley both without clothes and her sitting on the table, her body at the right height for his. But it didn't work to think about it happening while she sat there.

"I hope they didn't get splinters in their bottoms," she said.

He burst out laughing. "They kept their skirts on, princess."

And something clicked in her mind, a picture of a farmer pushing up the skirts of his lover, both of them all impatience to move together, and the place between her legs twisted with desire.

She pinched folds in Arley's shirt and tugged. "Come closer."

"Want me to put out the light?"

"But you won't be able to see."

He laughed again. "That's not important. Besides, I'll hear ya. I can imagine your face. Do you want the light out?"

"Yes, please."

He stepped away, reached to open the lantern door, and pinched out the candle flame. Everything went dark but a heartbeat later, his trousers brushed inside her thighs and his warmth touched her face. He stepped in close like she'd asked.

She leaned into him. "Would you put your arms around me?" she murmured, suddenly embarrassed, but he did it without hesitation. She rubbed her cheek on his soft shirt.

"Let me know if ya need more space," he said and his voice rumbled in his chest.

She'd lost the sharp ache between her legs but she had only to imagine the scene again—the nameless farm couple sneaking into the barn, her sliding onto the table as he pushed up her skirt and she fumbled to undo his trousers in her rush to have him. Him gripping her hips and pulling her to the edge so he could thrust into her. The desire rushed back in.

Snowdrop slid her hand down to hike up her dress and rubbed between her thighs. Her body was waiting for it.

She replayed the daydream on a loop and eased the ache between her legs. Without thinking, she snaked her free arm around Arley and pulled herself against him, knowing he wouldn't let her fall off the table. She rubbed her face on his shoulder and caught the scent of him before focusing again: bare thighs on the table, fingers digging in and pulling them forward, holding them steady as he thrust. The woman lying back on the table, leaving all the work to her lover, but undoing her ties so he could see her breasts.

The tension built easily inside her. Her dream farmer was coming close, unable to stop himself with his lover laid bare in front of him. The moment he finished, he drew himself out, went to his knees, and took her in his mouth.

Snowdrop's chest heated and the tension between her legs expanded. She rubbed harder to meet it, knowing she was close. One last thought of his mouth hot between her legs, giving what she needed, and the tension overflowed. She jerked in Arley's arms, hanging on to his shirt with one hand while her other stayed under her dress, continuing to rub herself as her body shuddered.

When she went still, she panted quietly, not wanting to move. Arley kissed her temple.

She opened her eyes. Through the darkness, moonlight filtered in through a small, smudged window beside the door. Arley's heart beat slowly against hers. She leaned back and met his gaze, the slim shine of his eyes in the faint light.

"You're so beautiful," he whispered. He smiled. "Especially when you go over the edge."

"I've never done that with someone else nearby."

"So I'm your first?" he said, and the flirting tone was back in his voice.

She pushed against his chest but he didn't move far, and she immediately took his shirt, pulled him back in, and leaned her head on his shoulder. His arms tightened around her.

"Thank you for sharin' that with me," he said.

He stood by her in the dark. The night had gone silent outside the barn. Maybe the party had finally wound down, with the children finished scavenging cake off the ground and the adults recovered enough from the bat invasion to drive home. Or maybe without Arley to dance with, the guests had gotten bored.

She didn't want to leave the barn but she couldn't stifle a yawn.

"You should go to bed," he said. "We have to leave early tomorrow to reach Mountain Rest."

She didn't move off him. "Are you going to bed?"

"In a little bit."

"Do you have to clean up from the party? Can I help?"

"The only thing I have to do is get myself off again because being with you when ya came made me hard as a post all over again."

Snowdrop smiled into his shirt. "Do you want me to help?"

"Princess, if I let you help, we might end up doing this back and forth all night. Besides, I might utter some filthy things while I'm goin' at it."

She sat up and laughed. "Filthy things about me?"

"Would ya like that?"

"I don't know."

"Next time I'll try it. Come on now. Straighten yourself up and I'll walk ya to the house."

Chapter 17

SNOWDROP WOKE THE MORNING AFTER the party as the sun rose over the plains and lit up the guest room. Nem slept on beside her, so she lay still. Staying in bed wasn't hard when she had so much to think about.

Last night had been wonderful. But also . . . unexpected? After she'd recalled all her favorite parts a dozen times and all the sweet things Arley had said, she wondered how it had happened at all. She'd never imagined tumbling Arley, even as she talked to Fina and her friends and realized she might have a crush on him. But their tryst had happened so fast. And every moment of it had been wonderful. And it hadn't led to the thrusting form of sex she'd experienced in the past. And Arley had seemed okay with it . . . hadn't he?

Back in the forest, when she was around couples like Dustan and Rose, sex always seemed to be one of the main things couples shared together. And since she didn't know what she could offer in that regard, she'd given up on the idea of finding someone to partner with. She'd told herself she didn't need or want a partner. But maybe she *had* wanted someone and simply hadn't seen it as possible.

All these days on the road, she'd gotten to know Arley and he didn't make her uncomfortable anymore. She was so used to him—so comfortable around him that she'd been able to have an orgasm in his arms! She'd never thought she'd be so comfortable with anyone.

But what would he want now? Would he want to continue something between them? Or was last night a one-time thing and they'd go back to being friends?

What if he wanted her and she couldn't give more than she already had?

And what was she going to say when she saw him today? She could tell she was blushing just thinking about it.

Was he awake yet?

The sun climbed higher and brightness filled the room. Someone walked past their door and thumped down the stairs, and a moment later the kitchen door banged shut from the back of the house. Nem stirred and half-opened her eyes. "Is it time to get up?" she mumbled.

"I think so. Arley wanted to get an early start."

Nem let out a giant yawn. "How far is it to Mountain Rest?"

"Twenty leagues. Arley thinks we can do it in one day if we start early."

Nem rubbed her eyes as they both pushed themselves up to sitting. Snowdrop pulled the top quilt around her shoulders and offered half to Nem. They huddled together in the chilly room. Someone spoke downstairs and more footsteps passed their door.

"Did you have fun last night?" Snowdrop asked.

"I liked the food. The ball game was fun."

"The young people weren't interested in dancing?"

"Not much. Did, um, did you have anything to do with the bats?"

Snowdrop nodded. "I invited them by accident." She hadn't gotten a close look at the empty lawn as Arley walked her in the previous night. The lanterns had been dark and clouds had covered the moon. But the white wreckage of the cake had been visible.

"Their arrival was pretty funny," Nem said. "The kids were laughing hysterically."

"But I destroyed the party."

"The party recovered. People kept drinking and dancing."

"I destroyed the cake."

"It tasted fine. They served the top part off the ground."

Snowdrop hung her head.

"I wondered if you wanted to dance," Nem said.

Emotions welled up as she remembered how badly she had wanted to dance, and how disappointed she'd been. How she'd felt crushed, like she was fourteen again and back by Oleander's side, watching all the young people get to know each other while she was left out.

"I did want to but I didn't know how to get a partner. And then I met some nice women and tried to show off my magic, and I summoned all those bats and I was so embarrassed I just . . ."

"You left," Nem said, squinting, "and Arley disappeared . . ." She turned her gaze onto Snowdrop.

Snowdrop blushed and couldn't stop her smile. "He came to find me."

When Snowdrop didn't continue, Nem put her arm around Snowdrop's shoulders and squeezed. "Let's go downstairs."

Nem smiled the whole time they were dressing and packing their things. From the landing, the noise of many voices rose up from the dining room. A booming laugh made Snowdrop's pulse race as they descended the stairs but she couldn't be sure it was Arley and not his father.

Snowdrop kept her head down as they entered the dining room amid boisterous talking. She swallowed hard, expecting everyone to notice her arrival, but the conversations continued. Nem nudged her toward the two empty chairs along one side of the table. She held the back of the chair and glanced around: Mrs. Farnwell sitting in the head seat motioned them to sit, beside her Larkspur held a cup of tea and smiled, Edna, the brothers . . . She forced herself to turn toward Arley at the end. Her heartbeat hammered as their eyes locked. Had he been waiting for her to look his way?

He smiled. Her face warmed. His father said something beside him and Arley winked before turning to answer.

Snowdrop took her seat. Dishes filled the table, loaded with scrambled eggs, slices of bread, and a fruit salad with apple wedges and raisins in yogurt, plus one dish of meat down at the end. Mrs. Farnwell had placed it far away from Larkspur. Snowdrop focused on filling her plate and then on eating the food, one bite after another, until she couldn't resist peeking at Arley. And he was again waiting for it, this time with a wide grin that made her blush down her neck to her toes. She stared at her plate. She was *not* going to look at him again. She was not.

As soon as Arley finished eating he went outside to hitch up the horses, and through the windows the wagon appeared as he drove around to the front door. When they had finished breakfast, everyone in her party got their bags and headed onto the front porch. Mr. Farnwell and Arley's brothers were at the wagon saying goodbyes.

No one had said anything about the bats or the cake. Did no one realize it had been her fault?

"Oh, one moment dear." Mrs. Farnwell approached her as Edna and Larkspur headed down the steps. Snowdrop froze and her stomach dropped. Mrs. Farnwell dug into her apron pocket and came out with a scrap of parchment. "Fina Jorgenson asked me to give ya her address in case you want to keep in touch. She said how much she enjoyed talkin' and she couldn't find ya to say goodbye."

Snowdrop took the piece of parchment and scanned the neat letters written across it: Fina Jorgenson, Post Box 16, Woods End. Fina wanted to keep in touch with her? Like they were friends? Even after she'd messed up her magic and destroyed the party?

"Thank you," Snowdrop said, her voice hoarse. "Thank you for hosting us, and for the snowdrop bulbs. They mean so much to me. And the party was wonderful. I'm, um, I'm sorry about the bats."

Mrs. Farnwell waved her off. "It worked out in the end." She followed the others off the steps and to the wagon.

Snowdrop's brow furrowed and she turned to Nem beside her. "What did she mean 'worked out in the end'?" she whispered.

Nem grinned. "Once they realized they were scaring people, the bats organized and did an aerial show."

Snowdrop's mouth fell open. "They *what*?"

"First they flew in a big circle, and they split off into different formations—they did a giant wave, and a sunburst . . . Everyone forgot all about being scared."

"Was it Larkspur's doing?"

"It certainly wasn't mine." Nem grinned at Snowdrop and followed the others off the porch.

Arley was checking the horses. She started toward him and he looked up.

"Snowdrop," Larkspur called. "How about another magic lesson now you have the snowdrop bulbs?"

Arley gave a grim smile and nod, and Snowdrop turned away.

They waved goodbye to the Farnwells and drove out the drive and back through Woods End toward the north–south road—the villagers here didn't call it the forest road, which made sense since the forest was far off across the plain to the south. Gracie waved from the forge but the rest of the village was quiet. As they turned north and trotted away, they passed another sign. Staring out the back of the wagon, Snowdrop read aloud, "Tired of seeing plains? It's plain to see you need a break. WOODS END NEXT RIGHT." She groaned.

Edna was knitting and Nem had her whittling out. Larkspur watched the fields.

Snowdrop cleared her throat to get Larkspur's attention. "I made a mistake last night," she said. "I shouldn't have tried something new like that."

Larkspur smiled. "We've all done some stunt when learning

in the beginning. Although usually not with so many humans around."

"Thanks for helping with the bats. Was everyone okay? No one got hurt?"

"Everyone was fine."

"And the humans?"

Larkspur stifled a laugh. "Everyone was fine," she repeated, "human and bat. Now, let's see what else you can do."

As Woods End disappeared behind them, Snowdrop sighed and focused on Larkspur. At least she wasn't leaving Arley behind in the village. He was right here in the wagon with her, and before the end of the day she'd get to be near him. She had to be patient.

She showed Larkspur how she could change her hair color to sky blue or to any other color. Larkspur instructed Snowdrop to focus on how the magic felt when she used it successfully and to try the illusion again without the snowdrop bulb in her hand. It took a few tries but eventually she was able to make it work. They tried more difficult magic, like putting an illusion of a hat on her head. Once she did anything with the help of her name plant, it became easier to see the way to do it on her own. And she sensed no hint of the dark magic, as if the snowdrops kept it at bay.

The plowed fields finally ended and grassy plains took their place, stretching endlessly on both sides of the road. The wind gusted down from the mountains, a relentless force that sometimes shook the wagon's frame. Eventually they rolled the cover all the way down on the western side to get relief. The sun was hot and the air dry. As the morning passed, the ground sloped upward slightly and the mountains to the left loomed closer. Patches of jagged rock poked through the grass in places and sometimes the road curved to pass around a taller outcrop.

The leagueposts continued, and six leagues out of Woods End, the road split for a wayside. The wayside had the same rough wooden table with benches attached, but out here on the plains, a simple shelter covered the table to block the gusting wind. A wide ring of rocks surrounded the firepit and a border of smaller gravel circled that, to separate the fire from the fields.

After they'd stopped for lunch, Larkspur suggested Snowdrop learn to cast an illusion on someone else and Edna eagerly volunteered. So when they set off, she climbed wearily into the back of the wagon. Not being able to sit by Arley and talk with him was torture! Did he feel it the way she did? She gazed longingly at her empty spot on the driver's seat before looking over to him. And he was watching her—and smirking. His smile widened.

She closed her eyes and exhaled, turning away.

"All right," Larkspur said as Arley called to the horses and the wagon jolted into motion. "Let's see if you can do this one without using your snowdrop bulb even the first time. Take Edna's sleeve and don't even think about it. Whatever color comes into your head first, send it onto Edna's shirt."

Snowdrop touched Edna's clothing. Her thoughts were a swirling mess of frustration. But she could do this. She was projecting a color, and the color was only an illusion. She wouldn't harm Edna with a simple illusion. She noted the outlines of the shirt, closed her eyes, and thought of the barn and the horses and the grasses, maybe the color of the grasses, and imagined it onto Edna's shirt.

Nem snickered.

Snowdrop's eyelids blinked open. Edna's shirt was plaid. It was the same plaid as the shirt Arley was wearing, up on the driver's seat.

Edna fingered the hem, staring at the color. "Why, it's just like—"

Snowdrop coughed loudly and let go of the illusion. She darted a look to the front. Arley's back was to them.

"Very good, Snowdrop," Larkspur said. "You got the color onto the shirt without any bleeding off the edges. And you even had a pattern." She pursed her lips. "Did you mean to do that pattern?"

"No," Snowdrop mumbled, and Nem tittered again. Some friend.

They practiced as the afternoon passed until, hours later, Larkspur said they'd done enough for the day. She praised Snowdrop's progress. In spite of her earlier frustration with having to focus on lessons when she was impatient to be near Arley, Snowdrop glowed with pride. She could use magic! If she kept learning each day, she'd be ready when she returned to the forest—ready for a job on one of the work crews, and ready to show the other fairies she was not a danger to them.

She had worked hard all day. She was so tired she wasn't even sure she wanted to talk to Arley anymore. She could lie down beside Edna and doze off.

"If you're all done with lessons," Arley called over his shoulder, "there's a nice view comin' up. If someone wanted to ride up front."

And just like that, he pulled her back in. She turned to the others.

Edna scoffed. "Don't look at me. I'm not leaving my pillows."

"I'll watch from back here," Larkspur said.

Snowdrop looked at Nem. "I think we know who he wants up there."

Snowdrop grinned like a fool as she climbed up over their things and onto the driver's seat. She was shaking suddenly and had to focus on not falling out of the wagon. Once she sat and was watching the horses trot ahead of her, she had no idea what to say.

"How was your lesson?" Arley asked.

"Good."

"Yeah?"

"I'm glad it's over." She stared at her hands in her lap.

"Me too. So . . . the first thing that pops into your head is my shirt?" He said it with a straight face, his eyebrows raised.

"Oh shut up." She shoved at his arm, knowing she wouldn't

budge him and wanting an excuse to touch him. He broke into a smile. She slid closer so her arm was beside his.

"Ya want to drive, princess?"

If she took the reins, his hands would be free. It gave her an idea. "Okay."

As he handed them over, she remembered her driving lesson and sat up, pulling her elbows in and wrapping the reins under and over her hands. The horses knew to follow the road, so she didn't have much to do.

Arley settled back.

"Um, I'm cold," Snowdrop said.

He sat up. "Shall I fetch your sweater from the back?"

"Not that cold."

His brow furrowed.

"Just a little cold. My shoulders, mostly." She scooched over so the sliver of space between their hips disappeared.

A smile unfurled across his face. He leaned against her, knocking into her shoulder. "Are you flirtin' with me?"

"No! I just thought maybe you could, you know . . ."

"What?" He hunched forward and slid his arms between his knees, stretching his back as he grinned.

". . . warm me up?"

"You want me to warm ya up?" He kept grinning as he sat up and stretched out his neck.

"Never mind." She risked saying it because she bet he wouldn't let it go.

"I'd be happy to warm ya up, princess. You didn't even need to take the reins. Here." He settled down with his arm across her back and his hand on her shoulder. "How's this?"

"That's good."

"Want me to take the reins back?" He waved his free hand.

"No."

"Are you actually cold? 'Cause I could get a blanket."

"I'm fine. Just be quiet." And she couldn't stop herself: She turned into him, pressing her face into his side and her nose against his shirt, close and full of the warmth and smell of him. His hand closed around both of hers, keeping the reins steady, and where he held on to her shoulder he squeezed. Something inside her settled.

She turned back to the horses and he let go of her hands. He kissed her temple and stayed quiet.

Snowdrop drove the horses with Arley's arm around her as the sun sank down in the sky. The ladies in back rolled up the wagon cover to let the sunlight in as the wind died for the evening. Arley never took his arm off her. He was quieter than she'd ever seen him. But his breathing was slow and deep, his arm was relaxed, and every once in a while his thumb would move, rubbing her shoulder.

She'd never had someone touch her for so long. Normally she shied away from touches—all that hugging most people did, or even a touch like Dustan placing a hand on her back. Touching made her squirm. And when others stood too close to her, she took a step back. But something had changed with Arley and she wanted him pressed up against her. She liked his arm around her and the slow swirl of his thumb on her bare shoulder under her sleeve. She liked how he smelled and how solid he felt in the space beside her.

The ground rose more steeply, winding left and then right around a rocky patch. It straightened and ahead it dropped off with nothing beyond it but sky.

"Let me have the reins, princess."

"Why?"

"Trust me. You'll need your hands in a moment to hang on."

She passed him the reins, and he took them in both hands. The imprint of his touch lingered on her shoulder. He called to the horses to slow their gait.

She watched ahead, swallowing as they climbed higher and higher and the edge of the land didn't change—no new hill appeared as they climbed toward the top. A squarish boulder on each side of the road towered like a gate and they rolled toward the opening at a slow walk.

They passed through and came out above a valley as wide as the sea, with pink sunlight streaming across hillsides of waving grass sloping down to a massive sprawl of buildings that could only be Mountain Rest.

Arley stopped the horses. A gentle breeze hit them, set free from the hillside that had sheltered them as they climbed. It stirred her bangs off her face and the reins swayed against the horses' sides. Ahead, more boulders lined the road as it curved sharply to the right.

"Look at that," Edna said. She and the others stood in the back, gazing over the driver's seat at the view. Arley slid away from Snowdrop to clear the way.

"It's bigger than I imagined," Larkspur said.

"All the girls say that," Arley said.

She lightly smacked his shoulder. "The city."

Tiny dots of people moved below, barely visible in the sunset light. The city had a wall around much of it, but cottages spread outside the wall, too, with a network of roads among them. Inside the wall was dense with buildings, and in the center a few towers rose up, with pennants flapping. It was like the castle in Woodglen but smaller. One of the humans' provincial lords had ruled from Mountain Rest before their revolution; that must have been his manor house.

Traffic came and went from a gate on the south side of the city, the gate their road would eventually reach. On the east and west sides, a straight road led away from the wall. To the west, the road headed out of sight on the plain, and beyond, the mountains towered up with the sun hanging behind them. To the east, nothing but the plains appeared, with no sign of the ocean, even from their height. Carts and wagons of all sizes moved along the roads.

"I'm thinkin' we should camp up here, at the wayside that's just a little farther on," Arley said. "We could get down the hill before dark but we'd be in that mess, and I don't know my way around the city streets."

"That's fine," Larkspur said. "We have food and it's better to arrive in a new place in the morning when you're fresh."

Anticipation welled up in Snowdrop's chest. They had one more night of camping and she had one more chance to sleep outside the wagon with Arley.

He tapped the reins on the horses, and they started down the incline and turned right at the wall of boulders. The boulders were positioned to stop travelers from barreling off the edge of the hillside. He guided the wagon down from the top of the pass, back and forth around turns barely wide enough. When the road flattened a bit, they reached another wayside, this one off to the west as the road made another turn.

The drive into the wayside led to a flat area and curved in a large loop, with the table and firepit in the center. Arley drove around the entire loop before stopping. He leaned in and squeezed her leg, giving her a smile before he climbed out and began to un-hitch the horses.

Snowdrop climbed down from the seat and joined the other women, stretching the kinks out of their necks and backs. The sloping hillside they'd descended sheltered the wayside from any breeze on the south side and another low mound to the west did the same. To the north was open air with the spectacular view of the city gleaming in sunlight—she could watch the tiny movements and the wagons coming and going all evening.

Everyone took a moment getting organized. Snowdrop tucked the snowdrop bulbs safely among her things in the wagon. As shadows slipped over the wayside, Snowdrop and Nem trudged up the western ridge and back into the sunlight to watch the sun descend over the mountains. As it sank, the tip of each strand of grass in front of them lit up like a taper. The light glowed deeper and deeper orange until the fields below shone like they were on fire before the light slipped away.

They returned to the wayside table, where Edna had spread out Mrs. Farnwell's provisions for dinner: a new loaf of a wheat-rye bread with a packet of butter to spread on the thick dark slices, a jar of pickled cucumbers and another of preserved beets (but none of the fermented cabbage Arley loved, Snowdrop noted with disappointment), two kinds of cheese, one soft and one hard, and some sort of dried meat for the humans. Arley carried an armful of wood from a small shed to the firepit and joined them. The tethered horses grazed on a patch of tall grass.

Where was Larkspur? Snowdrop scanned the shadows until she spotted her motionless figure near the road. She walked over.

Larkspur blinked at her but didn't move or speak. What was she hearing? Snowdrop waited, too tired from the long day to try to listen in herself.

Larkspur frowned and shook her head.

"What's wrong?"

"Nothing. I just . . . I can't tell. There're so few creatures out here on the plains and some have never communicated with a fairy before. I found a herd of antelope—remember we saw some at the edge of the forest? Those deer-like animals with straight antlers? But they were startled and ran. Occasionally I think I hear a horse, but we haven't passed a driveway in leagues so they must be wild. And since we came over the top of the pass, the messages are all mixed with the ones from the city." She smiled a tired smile and turned back to the table.

Now that the sun was down, a chill seeped into the air. The wind had abated with evening but they had climbed up so high from the plains that the air frosted in Snowdrop's nostrils each time she inhaled. Arley lit the fire and they gathered around it with their food.

"We can put down the sides of the wagon to keep ya warm," Arley said as they finished their meal. He already had his bedroll out. If she wanted to sleep near him, she needed to speak up.

"Thank you, Arley," Larkspur said with a yawn.

Snowdrop's heart thrummed so she could barely speak. She had to do it. She had to say something.

The silence stretched out. In another moment Larkspur would direct all of them to the wagon and she'd lose her chance to sleep outside with Arley. She opened her mouth.

"IthoughtImightsleepoutsidethewagontoo."

Everyone looked at her. Arley caught himself before he smiled and turned his face to the ground to hide his smirk.

Her body heated and her face flushed. She swallowed. "It's crowded with four of us in the wagon," she continued, trying to sound like this was no big deal, "and I think I'd like it better outside. On my own. With space to think."

"I'll get ya a bedroll," Arley said before anyone else could answer. He stood and walked over to the wagon.

Nem smiled at her and Edna squinted with her head tilted. Larkspur frowned at her lap as if she hadn't even heard Snowdrop's outburst. Maybe she was still trying to communicate with any animals who were nearby.

Across the wayside, Arley opened one of the storage crates and took out a bedroll. Snowdrop swallowed and her pulse raced harder as nervousness overcame her. She had a whole night ahead of her. Sleeping beside Arley. What had she been thinking?

Chapter 18

SNOWDROP STOOD QUIETLY AS ARLEY returned to the fireside and handed her a bedroll without a glance. "You lot all set?" he asked the others. "Do you want the sides down on the wagon?"

"We're fine," Edna said, rising and stretching. "We can untie them."

Snowdrop picked up her sleeping things and stood awkwardly beside Arley as the others shook their crumbs into the fire, gathered their things, and trooped back to the wagon. It was parked several paces away in the dark and only the light-colored canvas cover revealed its location. Low flames flickered on the last of the logs and cast shadows on Arley's face.

He ran a hand through his hair and caught her gaze. "So, ah, we could sleep here?" He glanced at the flat area by the firepit.

She hugged her bedroll against her chest. "What do you think?"

"It won't be any warmer than anywhere else once the fire is out. And it's . . ."

"What?"

He exhaled and looked in her eyes. "It's kind of close to the wagon. If we were to stay up talking, we might bother the others."

"Talking?" she repeated, at a loss for words.

"Or whatever." His cheeks were orange from the firelight but they darkened. "I don't want ya to think I'm expectin' anything. But if we *did* get up to anything, we might want to be off a bit farther."

Snowdrop's throat went dry. "That makes sense," she rasped out. He was thinking of things. Things they might get up to. Nerves and excitement and a tiny bit of dread swirled inside her. But she didn't want to back out.

Arley took up his bedroll and led her away from the fire, across the driveway, and up the ridge on the west end of the wayside. The air cooled instantly. A faint stain of paler blue lined the top of the mountains where the sun had gone down, but otherwise the sky was dark and a few stars had appeared.

Heat radiated from the stone under her feet as she climbed down the far side of the ridge, and the wind truly had stopped because all was silent and still, even the thin strands of grass. Behind her, the orange of the dying fire disappeared behind the ridge, and she could barely see the top of the wagon cover.

The ground flattened, giving them an area to spread their bedrolls. A few scraggly bushes formed a border, and beyond, the land sloped downward all the way to the bottom of the basin. The moon wasn't up yet and when it did rise it would need to clear the hillside to the east before it shone on them.

"How's this?" Only starlight illuminated Arley's face.

"This is fine," she said, clutching her bedroll tightly.

He held his bedroll in one broad hand by his side. He gave a lopsided smile. "Relax, princess. I'm as nervous as you."

"You are?"

"Sure."

"Why are you nervous?"

"We started somethin' last night. And we haven't gotten to talk about it or anything, and I don't know what you're thinking. It's scary, right?"

"Yes."

He knelt and tossed out his bedroll over the grass. It unrolled halfway and he leaned and spread it flat. She copied him. The bedroll was a thick blanket but once it was flat on the ground she realized it had two layers, like a blanket folded over to make a pocket with one side open. The open side of hers faced the open side of Arley's.

"I, uh, I assumed you wanted to be near me," he said.

"I do."

"You need to use the facilities?" He gestured into the darkness.

"I'm good."

"Be right back." He ambled off past the bushes and downhill until she could barely see his head in the darkness.

After glancing in Arley's direction to be sure he was gone, she quickly pulled off her clothes and donned her long sleeping shirt, along with a clean pair of underwear. She peeled open the top blanket of her bedroll and shimmied her bare legs in. The blankets were softer on the inside than she'd expected from the rough texture of the outside, and the bottom layer felt cushier than the top.

Sitting, she couldn't see over the ridge on one side or the bushes on the other. The taller grasses stirred gently and overhead the stars were coming out and shining brightly. While she waited for Arley to appear in the darkness, she folded her clothes and tucked them inside the bedroll, down by her feet.

Without her sweater, the hairs on her bare arms stood and pebbled her skin. She lay down, slid farther into the bedroll, and pulled it to her chin. Her back stretched out against the ground, hard even with the padding of the bedroll.

The bushes rustled and Arley towered over her. He hesitated. "Close your eyes."

"Why?"

"So I can take my trousers off."

She closed them. "I wouldn't think you'd mind being seen in your underclothes."

"I don't, but I thought you might not like it and asking you to close your eyes was the least awkward way to get around it. Why, do ya want to watch me undress?"

"No," she said, but she couldn't stop her face from curving into a smile. Scuffling sounded beside her.

"Admit it, princess," he said, his voice moving down toward the ground. "You would totally watch if you thought I couldn't see ya."

"That's creepy! I wouldn't spy on you if you didn't—" She remembered being behind the inn and seeing him washing up with his shirt off. "—if you didn't know . . . I was . . . I mean . . ."

He shifted on the ground and his warm exhale tickled her ear. "I knew you were watchin'," he whispered.

Her eyelids flew open.

Arley shifted back onto his own bedding, laughing. He leaned on one elbow on his side. He'd taken off his shirt. His top blanket wrapped around his chest but his arms and shoulders were bare. "It wasn't your fault," he said. "I knew ya were sleepin' in the wagon and might wake up if I started splashin' around at the pump. Maybe I even hoped ya would."

"You're awful," she said, but even she could hear the fondness in her voice.

He laughed more.

He hadn't shaved since morning and stubble covered his jaw and chin. "Do you ever grow a beard?" she asked to change the subject. She tried to imagine a beard where the dark shadow showed on his face.

"Why, ya like beards?"

A beard on him wouldn't cover half his head like some men's beards. The stubble made a neat line along his jaw and around his mouth but didn't creep up his cheeks or down his neck. But it would still be a bunch of hair growing on his face. "I don't think so."

"I tried to grow one when I was fourteen and wanted to be a man but it didn't do much. And when I was older and it did start to grow, I was over it." His hand came up and he ran it over his jaw. "Sometimes I let it get a bit scratchy though. A lady once told me it felt good to have it scratching against her thighs."

"That's a strange—" His meaning became clear and she imagined his face down between her legs—not rubbing on the outside of her leg like a cat, like she'd first pictured, but nestled between them and breathing on her, and the thought of his stubble scratching her there gave her a pleasant twist inside. As if the next time she was imagining things, the man was going to have a beard.

He was smiling at her. "What are ya thinkin' about, princess?"

She looked away from him and up at the stars. "You know what I'm thinking."

"With you, I really don't. But I want to."

His smile retreated but he gazed at her, waiting. He might be a human, but he was asking her to communicate with him. She took a deep breath.

"I haven't been with many people, fairy or human. The way we are now, I mean. But the times I have, I didn't like some of it."

His face changed, his eyes hardening and his jaw clenching. He'd misunderstood.

"I wasn't hurt or anything like that," she said quickly. "I wanted to try it. But it didn't feel like I expected from what I'd always heard the other fairies saying."

"What did it feel like?"

"Kind of like nothing? I kept waiting for it to get good and it never did—even though my partner seemed to like it. It made me think I'd rather do it by myself."

"Was it that way with men and women?"

"Fairy men. I tried to imagine being with a woman a few times, thinking I might be more attracted that way, but she kept turning into a man in my daydream. I don't think I'm interested in romance with women."

"Last night," he said, "were you okay with what we did?"

She opened her mouth and nothing came out. She couldn't find adequate words for how she'd felt, but Arley's brow furrowed. She hurried to reassure him. "Yes. A lot."

"You were a lot okay with it."

"Yes."

"You'd do it again."

"Yes."

"You'd tell me if you ever wanted to stop."

She squinted at him.

"I mean, if we got busy doing somethin' and you didn't like it as much as you thought, or you changed your mind about wantin' to do it, you would stop me—right?"

"Oh. Okay."

"Because I never want to make ya feel uncomfortable. Or like you're— What was it you said? Like you're 'waitin' for it to get good.'"

She pursed her lips, thinking. "I liked watching you come."

He choked out an embarrassed laugh.

"I mean I liked making you feel good—it made me happy to see it. I think I'd like doing more things with you. But I might want to try only a little bit at a time."

"You want to go slow."

"Yes. It's just, with the others, it always felt like they were grabbing me everywhere at once and assuming it was working on me," she said.

"That sounds unpleasant."

"It wasn't just the touching. I got sad. We weren't friends or anything—we weren't in a relationship. It was just about the act of sex. I knew that and I thought it might be fun. But even during the act, we had no connection and they didn't even realize it, or maybe they didn't need a connection to enjoy it. And I didn't want them to be disappointed but I couldn't make myself pretend to like it, so when it was over things were awkward and I just felt more lonely."

"Aww, princess." His hand resting on the edge of his bedroll twitched but he didn't reach for her.

"I hate that it's so complicated. Probably none of your other ladies were like this."

"Maybe not. But none of them were you."

Warmth spread inside her. When he said things like that, it

made her feel like she mattered. Even if it didn't make sense that he wanted her. Last night he could have gone with any of those women at the party but he came after her instead. And now here he was, letting her lie beside him and he seemed perfectly willing to . . . do things with her. But at the same time, he wasn't leaning into her space and trying to make it happen as quickly as he could.

"I don't know if I'm ready for your face between my thighs," she said at last.

He cracked up laughing. "That's all right," he said, his sides heaving. "I'm not sure I'm ready for that, either."

"You're not? But you've done it before."

"But the times I did it before, it didn't matter the same as it does this time. Those times, we both wanted a tumble so we had one. That's all it was."

"And this is different?"

"Is that all *you* want, princess? 'Cause if all you want is a roll in the fields, well, I'd prob'ly not be able to say no to it. But I'd be disappointed."

She tried to imagine it—being intimate with him and walking away after—but it wasn't how she worked. It never had been. "That's not what I want."

He pulled his arms in under his blanket. He had placed his rolled-up trousers beside him and he rested his head on them, facing her. Snowdrop fished around with her feet and nudged her own clothes up until she could reach them. She rolled on her side and copied him, using her clothes as a pillow. His eyes were dark in the shadows of his face.

"What should we do?" she asked.

"Could I hug you?"

"Okay."

He hitched himself across the space between them, taking his bedding with him, until she could smell the campfire smoke on his skin and the cool air between them disappeared, replaced by the heat of his body. He slid one arm out from his blanket and over her and pulled her, bedding and all, in against him. Her face was tucked against his neck, and his arm was warm but the rest was bedding.

She settled against him. His arm was heavy but not like a paperweight pinning her to a table, more like the twine around a bundle of broom corn, holding her pieces together. The bedrolls between their bodies irked her. She kicked her legs around, trying to free them.

"Could we—"

"Here—"

He reached down and pulled on the bedding and her bare legs came free and tangled in his. She found his chest with her hands and pulled herself against his bare skin. He had kept his undershorts on.

He arranged the bedding so the top of his bedroll covered them both, on top of hers.

"This okay?" he asked as he held her again.

She nodded, rubbing her cheek against his chest as she did. He was smooth and warm, a few curls of chest hair tickling her nose. His skin here smelled not like the fire's smoke but like smooth stones baked in the hot sun. If her own shirt were off, she could press herself against him—but she couldn't do that! It would be too forward.

But the longer he was silent the more the idea pestered her.

"What are ya thinkin' about now?" he asked above her head, his voice rumbling under her fingers.

"Taking my shirt off."

He did the choking-while-laughing thing again and his arms tightened around her. "Oh princess, you kill me."

"It's dark and you can't see me under the blankets. And it might feel nice. But it seems too bold. What do you think?"

"Me? What do I think? Uh, yes please."

"But will it, I don't know . . . will it make you want more? Will it be too much if I'm not . . . ?"

"It doesn't have to lead to anythin' else." He paused. "I mean, ya might feel me poking into ya down there, but we've got our underthings on. I'm okay with it if you are."

"Okay." She hugged him again. All the talking had distracted her and she no longer felt the pull to take her shirt off. But after a moment of silence his warmth soaked through her shirt and it chafed between them. She still wanted to take it off.

"And," he started again, and she smiled, "I've got a kerchief in my trouser pocket in case we need one. Whatever ya feel like doin', you go ahead. But no pressure. We could talk more too. Or sleep."

"Okay," she said again. She pulled away enough to tug her shirt up and over her head. Her arms got caught in it, but Arley pulled it off for her, letting cool night air swirl into their nest and brush her skin. She shivered and pulled him close again, now with all of their skin pressed together except for the few hand's widths where they wore undershorts. Where he was indeed poking her with an erection.

"Do ya think," he began after they'd settled, "that if the other person wasn't all grabby, you might like being touched?"

"Maybe?"

"With the others, did you want him before things got started—before he was touching you? Or was it 'nothing' the whole time?"

Snowdrop frowned. Had she wanted either of them?

All the fairies her age had been pairing off and talking about tumbling. She'd wanted to try it. She'd wanted someone to notice her. She hadn't had many friends—she'd missed out on lessons and games with others as a child. Maybe this pursuit—which all four of her brothers were pursuing with abandon—would help her get to know her peers and connect with someone.

She'd been both nervous and excited to try tumbling. But what had she felt? Nothing the first time. The second time, after seeing how it went the first time, she'd asked him to give her a minute. She'd closed her eyes and imagined a scene the way she did when she was alone. So when they started kissing and touching, she felt ready for it. But as it went on her arousal faded. And her feelings hadn't actually been about her partner, had they? She'd been aroused only because she'd daydreamed herself into it.

"I'm not sure I felt anything for him."

His hand lightly touched her shoulder and she tilted her head back to see his face. His brow was furrowed.

"It was okay though," she added, worried about how long she'd been silent. What would he think?

His brow relaxed. "Ya mean you didn't look at his body and think, 'Wow, I want to ride that zucchini all night'?"

"What? No!" As she broke into a smile, Arley smiled with her.

"Is that what it's like for you?" she asked.

"When I was fifteen it was." He hesitated so she lifted her eyebrows. "If the sun shined through a girl's skirt and showed off her legs or if I'd see her bottom when she bent over in the fields, I'd get hard and wonder if she'd be willin'. And when they were willin', I could barely get myself inside her before I lost it. I had to learn how to please girls using my fingers or I'd have disappointed many a maid. The first time one of them opened her shirt and I saw her breasts, I came before she even touched me, I wanted her so bad."

"Is that what most people are like?"

"I don't think so. When I was fifteen, I thought so but I mostly heard about it from my brothers and they're horny as rabbits. I learned to control myself better as I got older."

"I don't think I'm like that. I never notice other people and get turned on. And I never understood when I'd hear fairies say someone had a nice ass. What does that mean? A certain size? Or not hairy?"

He shook with laughter. "If my brothers said it, it would mean, 'I want to do her' and 'Maybe she'll let me do her in that ass.'"

"What about when women say it?"

"Ah, maybe, 'I want to be grabbin' that ass while we get it on'?"

"I'm definitely not thinking that. I always figured my strange upbringing warped me somehow and made me not feel things the way others do. But Nem told me what she learned about sex and romance and how there are different types of attraction. She said I might feel some types and not others."

"Mm-hm."

"Do you feel them all?"

"I think I might. I don't think about what I'm feeling specifically but . . . well, I like lookin' at women, and talking to them, and touching them. Seems like I might feel all of it."

A moment of silence passed. Her chest was starting to stick to his skin, and all the talking must have undone his erection because it no longer poked into her. She pulled away and turned onto her back but kept her hand on his waist so he stayed close. His arm hovered over her and he lowered it. It pressed into her hip but he kept his hand in a fist instead of gripping her.

"So, gettin' back to touchin'," he said, "what I'm hearin' you say is you're not totally against it but ya want to take it slow, and ya don't want one touch to turn automatically into a bunch of grabbing, and ya might need to fantasize in your head a bit."

"That sounds right. Only the trouble with imagining something is it never matches what's actually happening. Last time I kept thinking of things and he'd do something different and it would distract me so much I'd lose any good feelings I had."

"You could give me directions."

"Directions?"

"You could tell me where to touch ya."

"I could?"

"Why not?"

"You wouldn't feel, I don't know, like your skills are being insulted?"

"My 'skills'?"

"When Constance and Helewise were talking, they said you—"

"Whoa whoa whoa, stop right there. Even if these rumors from Woods End are true and I am in fact an amazin' specimen in the hay, it doesn't mean I know what *you* like. How am I going to know what's in your head if you don't tell me? You have to tell me. It would be like . . . like I'm your tumbling apprentice."

A smile unfurled across her face. "My *tumbling apprentice*? But how would it work?"

"Oh, I dunno," he said, and he pulled her tightly against him and leaned his face in beside her neck. "Maybe you'd say, 'Arley'"—his voice was soft and it shot up into falsetto, presumably imitating her—"'put your fingers on my right breast and rub them in slow circles until my nipple hardens and then—' Why are ya laughin'?"

She held onto his body, trying to stop shaking. "Skies, I couldn't tell you to do that."

"Why not?"

"What if you didn't want to?" She wiggled her left hand up to wipe the tears from her eyes without letting go of him with her right.

"If I didn't like it, I would say so. But that's prob'ly never goin' to be a problem."

"I'd be embarrassed to say that," she admitted.

"I bet you'd get over it. Want to try?"

She peeked up at him. Pale white starlight lined his nose and left cheek, but even in the dark his eyes were gentle. She trusted him like she hadn't trusted anyone before. He wasn't going to laugh at her or get upset if she made a mistake. Well, he might laugh but it wouldn't be mean. And he wouldn't be annoyed if she told him she didn't like something.

"Okay," she whispered.

He kissed her ear. "Ready when you are."

"Um," she said, licking her upper lip before mimicking the high-pitched voice he had used, "Arley, touch your fingers to my breast but only gently." She watched his face as his arm left her hip. Under the blanket, his fingertips tapped her side, over her arm and up a little farther to find her breast. They settled on it like a feather waiting for the wind to take it away. His lips parted slightly.

"You like touching me."

One of his fingers stroked lightly over her nipple. "You feel amazin'."

"My breasts are kind of small."

"They're perfect. Like a teacup that fits in your palm." He half-way grinned at her and his breathing hitched.

"They're softer than teacups."

"Are they?"

"Arley," she whispered, "cup your hand around my breast and . . . and rub your thumb over me."

His eyes drifted closed as his hand settled on her, curving to one side until he had it cupped around her. His thumb stroked her nipple. "Like this?" he asked with a gasp.

"Just like that."

"How does it feel?"

"Nice."

"Nice?" He gave a shaky laugh. "Would you rather be touchin' yourself?"

"No. I like what this is doing to you."

"But—"

"I don't need to have an orgasm every time we're together."

"Neither do I, but—"

"I want to watch you come again."

He cursed softly.

"Please, Arley? Unless it makes you embarrassed. Would you stroke yourself?"

"I'm not embarrassed with you." His hand on her breast stilled and he lifted it off.

"Wait," she said. "Could you, um, could you use your other hand? And keep touching me?"

He shifted under the blankets and settled again, returning his palm to her breast. His shoulder on the ground pressed against hers, and as he stroked himself under the blankets, the motion of it rocked against her. He sighed and closed his eyes.

His hand squeezed her gently. "That okay?" he whispered. "Not too grabby?"

"It's fine."

He kept squeezing, massaging her in time with the shaking of his body. It did feel nice, warm and tingling across her chest, and she could imagine his touch making her hard between her legs. The motion was repetitive, steady and even, not jarring. She didn't want to look away from his face but she left for a moment, closing her eyes to imagine lying on the table in the barn—the scene that had worked for her last night. When the lover put his mouth to her, his beard scratched inside her thighs. She didn't picture a clear face but the image of him kneeling between her legs and the thought of his tongue on her made her squirm with desire.

She came back to reality to find Arley sweating beside her with his eyes closed and his hand still on her, but it was no longer nice. She took his hand off her breast and squeezed it in her hands. His motion broke.

"Keep going," she said and kissed his damp forehead. She reached down and nudged her undershorts off and down her legs as far as she could. She held his hand in both of hers against her chest and slid her hips toward him until his hand on his erection was knocking into her. "Keep going and get it all over me."

He cursed again and his eyes opened, pleading at her as he sped up and jerked against her. His hand in hers clenched as he gasped once, then again. Heat warmed the skin on her thigh as he came, and a drop of it tickled as it rolled into the dip of her hipbone, and another went down the inside of her leg. She broke into a wide smile as he gulped in air and went still. She clung to his hand.

He slumped against her, pressing his face on her shoulder. "Black skies, princess," he murmured, "you make me feel like I'm fifteen again when you talk like that."

"Next time, maybe you can get up on your knees over me."

He laughed once. "Skies. That would do it for ya?"

She flattened his hand against her skin in the hollow between her breasts, holding it with her left hand so he wouldn't move it. She brought her other hand down and trailed it through the seed he'd left on her skin. She smiled. "I think so."

His eyes were closed and his voice was fading. "You want anythin'?" he mumbled.

"No—not right now." Answering no twisted inside her like a lie. With Arley beside her, his hand in hers, the wetness he'd left, she felt tempted to chase her own climax, regardless of what she'd said before about not needing to. But she didn't need him for that.

She'd liked when he'd teased her breast. Could she find a way for his touches to be what brought her pleasure instead of her own hand? Was there a reason to try? She didn't need it to be him who made her climax. But he would like it—she knew he would. He would like to see himself giving her pleasure just as she loved watching it on his face.

His breathing was steady. "Arley?" She barely whispered and got no response. His hand was lifeless in hers. She moved it back to her breast and closed both their hands around herself. Down deeper under the blankets, she wet her fingers with his seed and rubbed it into her center, slowly at first but with the slickness, her fingers sank right in. She took the rest, rubbing her thigh dry with the side of her hand and coating herself with the moisture. She wanted to push farther, pushing it inside herself, but she hadn't been drinking bitter tea to avoid pregnancy and it might be risky to push it too far in.

Still she teased the edges around her entrance and it took only a few swipes before her body spasmed. She rode through it, rubbing herself with what he'd given her until she was spent.

She fell asleep with his hand on her breast.

The sunlight woke Snowdrop—not direct light but the glow of the dawn over the ridge to the east. Arley lay beside her, flat on his belly on the bedroll but with his arm looped over her hip.

The blanket hid most of his face but his brown hair stirred in the breeze. The gentle rise and fall of his body echoed through the spot where his arm rested on her.

The blankets were warm from their bodies and realizing her top was bare reminded her of how they'd spoken and acted last night, how she'd watched him come apart with his hand over her heart. He had wanted to be with her even after they had talked, and she brimmed with happiness.

Everything was silent this morning except for a gentle shushing from the wind through the nearby grasses. She could check on the others but she'd wake Arley and he probably needed rest after all the driving yesterday. He hadn't gotten a moment to himself at his family's house. But he didn't seem to need time to himself the way she did. Something as dull as riding in the wagon all day with the three other women exhausted her, but Arley grew more and more enthusiastic the longer he talked with people. Still, he might need to rest.

And besides, from the silence, the others were sleeping in as well.

The shadows faded as the daylight brightened. Arley stirred, mumbling in his sleep. Finally a noise came from the road—the jangling of a horse and creak of a cart as it slowed—and Arley rolled back slightly. The traveler passed by and silence returned, but surely their passing must've woken Nem and the others.

Arley stretched like a backward cat, legs first and then his back and arms. He took his arm off her and rubbed his eyes. He blinked at her.

"Morning, princess." His voice was rough with sleep.

"Morning."

"It's past sunrise."

"I didn't want to wake you."

"Thanks, love." He leaned in and kissed her cheek. "You all right this mornin'?" She grinned and he broke into a smile. "Best get dressed and we'll get down to the city."

He sat up, careful to keep the blankets over her, and turned his back as he hunted around for his clothes. Snowdrop smiled at how he kept his face averted as she sat up, unrolled her clothing, and slipped on her tunic. She pulled her undershorts and trousers on and clambered to her feet to pull them up. "All set," she said as she donned her sweater.

He turned and smiled again as he hefted himself to his feet. He wore only his undershorts, with his arms and chest bare and all those muscles showing, and then he winked at her and she realized he'd stood up mostly naked on purpose—she'd fallen for it and ogled him. She closed her eyes and shook her head, and his laugh sounded in the silent morning. She kept seeing his warm brown eyes smiling at her even with her eyes closed.

"Are you dressed yet?" she asked, pretending she cared.

"One moment." The blankets rustled. "Just another moment."

Now he was messing with her, but she didn't dare open her eyes. Something blocked the wind. He was standing close.

"Now?" she murmured.

"Yeah." He stood in front of her, fully clothed, and the growing light glinted on the top of his curls. His voice was low and earnest. "I wanted to look at ya for a moment."

She stared back like a ninny, the two of them standing and staring at each other and she didn't know what to say but she didn't want it to end.

He glanced past her and frowned. Snowdrop turned. The top of the wagon showed over the ridge and the sunlight gleamed on the white canvas. Nothing moved. Arley snagged his bedroll off the ground and rolled it as he walked forward. Snowdrop copied him.

The shaded rocks were cool from the night as she climbed up the ridge. She squinted as the sun beamed over the horizon. The wagon was silent—and empty. The table was empty.

"They're gone," Arley said.

"But where—?" The horses were gone too.

They hurried to the wagon. The water barrel was on its side

on the ground and the crates in the wagon were open. Her heart pounded and panic rose in her chest. She scrambled into the wagon and pushed aside the empty crates. Her satchel was there, hidden under the edge of the rug. She hugged it to her chest and tendrils of calm curled around her. Her snowdrop bulbs were inside. But Larkspur, Edna, and Nem were all gone. What was going on?

Arley peered down the hillside, scanning the road. Far below, early rising travelers left the city's south gate.

"Maybe they had an emergency," Arley said, "and they didn't have time to hitch the wagon so they went on the horses."

"And didn't wake us?"

"Maybe they were embarrassed to come near us."

"But look." Snowdrop pushed aside a pillow. "Larkspur's bag is here. She'd have taken it with her."

"What do ya think happened?"

"I don't know but I have an idea how to find out." Snowdrop sat on the bed of the wagon and opened her bag. She took one of her bulbs out. "Give me one moment."

She closed her eyes and tried to relax. It was hard with the panic swirling around her but holding the bulb in her fist helped. Larkspur had said there weren't many animals out here on the plains. That might be a lucky thing if it helped her find Lady and Bird.

The response was immediate. The horses were upset. They knew they weren't supposed to be away from Arley but they couldn't help it. Someone was leading them away. Lady's fear drifted over Snowdrop and settled in her stomach.

Snowdrop leaned forward, blocking the light from her eyelids and focusing. Horses might not think of people in terms of a name. She tried a gentle thought, picturing Larkspur standing beside the wagon.

Yes, Lady replied. The nice fairy was on her back.

Who else? But all she could get in reply was the image of two more horses, with a lead from each tugging Lady and Bird forward. Sunlight shown from the left and all around was grass.

Arley stood before her with his arms crossed, his shoulders tense.

Snowdrop swallowed. "I think they've been kidnapped."

Chapter 19

ARLEY STARED. "THEY'VE BEEN *KIDNAPPED*?"

"Someone on horses is leading Lady and Bird."

"Where?"

"They're heading . . . southeast? They're not on a road. They're crossing fields with the sun rising off here." She lifted her left hand to the sun and turned her body to demonstrate the direction Lady had faced.

"And the others are with 'em?"

"Yes. At least Larkspur is. It was hard to understand but I pictured Larkspur and Lady seemed to say yes."

"But why would anyone kidnap Larkspur?"

"I don't know. But we'll go after them, right?"

"Of course we'll go after 'em! I'm supposed to be keepin' 'em safe and . . ." He kicked the wagon's wheel and cursed.

Snowdrop climbed out of the wagon and touched his arm. His eyes were wide and he inhaled and exhaled harshly through his mouth. "We'll figure it out," she said. "Something strange is going on. But it's not your fault." She squeezed, hoping he'd stay calm. She needed him to stay calm or she'd start to panic too.

He ran a hand through his hair and rubbed his forehead, cursing again. "You're right."

"We'll have to go on foot."

"Yeah." He glanced down the hillside toward the city. "We could get horses but by the time we got down there and figured it out, we'd lose too much time. The horses were walking, right? Not galloping away?"

"Right."

"Do you have coins?"

"Larkspur had our funds." Snowdrop silently apologized to her elder and hunted through her bag. Under her shawl and a stack of papers was a small purse that clanged with coins. "I wonder if she hid her bag under the pillows. Mine was under the rug and I didn't leave it that way."

"Edna's and Nem's things are gone?"

"Yes."

"We don't have food or water. The water barrel was emptied. If we can't catch up with 'em quickly, we'll have to find food."

"Should we take anything else?" she asked.

"You carry your bag and I'll take Larkspur's. We'll be faster if we don't carry the bedrolls. But we might have to sleep on the ground."

"I don't mind."

They tossed the bedrolls into a crate, and Arley hefted the empty water barrel in and shut the back end of the wagon. They did a quick search of the front storage area and the campsite, but anything else they might use had disappeared.

"South?" Arley asked.

"Yes."

They climbed back up the stretch of road they'd descended the previous evening. Arley's pace was quick, and Snowdrop hurried to keep up. Poor Larkspur and Edna . . . and Nem. Dread filled her. Was Nem frightened? She'd spent her early winters trapped by Oleander. She'd finally found a home where she was safe, and to have this happen . . . They had to reach her as quickly as possible.

Arley stopped at the top of the pass. Snowdrop squinted in the bright light, following his gaze. Far ahead on the road to the south was a wagon.

"A wagon passed the campsite before you woke," she said. "That must be it."

"It didn't stop?"

"I heard it slow but it passed on. I didn't hear any noises like a scuffle or anything. I think the others had already . . . gone." She scanned toward the southeast, shielding her eyes. Empty fields of grass stretched as far as she could see. She searched for Lady again and heard nothing.

They passed through the boulder gate and started down the incline, winding around the rocks until the road straightened. "Can you figure out where they left the road?" Arley asked.

"I don't think so. I can't reach Lady anymore but if I can find her and calm her, I might be able to ask her to ask Larkspur for directions, although . . ." She shook her head. Communicating clearly via a horse seemed fraught with failure.

"We'll have to watch for signs," Arley said. "Let me know if ya need to stop for any reason." He quickened his pace, and Snowdrop matched her strides to his.

Had the kidnappers known she and Arley were there, sleeping at a distance from the wagon? She shuddered to think they might have been seen. Hopefully whoever had done this didn't know they had missed two of the party and didn't know that they were being followed.

They hastened along the road as the sun crept up the sky. Both of them watched the field on their left, searching for any sign of their companions: trampled grass, or turned up clods of dirt where the horses had trodden, or anything amiss. Snowdrop continually reached out, searching for Lady or Bird, and when that failed, she tried simply listening to any creatures within range, the way she'd seen Larkspur doing. All she could pick up was a continuous, low jumble of mild feelings—brief joy over a tasty seed, a moment of fear at a shadow moving. Even with a snowdrop bulb in her fist she couldn't be sure she was doing it right.

The wagon on the road ahead disappeared in a haze. Far far

away, a dark smudge lined the horizon—it must be the hillside where the road dropped from the woods, south of Woods End. She was thirsty but nothing could be done about that. If they followed the kidnappers all the way to Woods End, they could get supplies and, hopefully, horses. But from what she'd seen that morning, with the horses headed toward the sun with nothing but fields ahead, they must have left the road long before Woods End.

She reached out again and heard something. Not the horses, more of a nonstop excited chattering. "Arley. Something's up ahead."

He slowed.

"Birds I think. I don't know what they're saying but it's different."

They proceeded more cautiously, and a few minutes later something fluttered in the road. Snowdrop's fear spiked at the sight of the bird. Was it injured? It flapped in the dust. But as they neared, it startled at their approach and swooped up into the air, along with three birds from the grass. They had brown speckled wings and bright yellow breasts and didn't resemble any of the birds she knew from the forest.

This close, and clutching a snowdrop bulb, she could make out details of their thoughts. The dusty one felt a soothing relief—flapping in the dirt of the road kept it clean. And they were all eager . . . to see Snowdrop.

She and Arley stopped as the birds coasted back to land on the road. They stood in a line and chirped and hopped, all facing the east.

"I think they were waiting for us," Snowdrop said.

Arley nodded. As if birds acting this way was normal. He'd gotten used to fairy ways.

Why had the birds waited here? Perhaps Larkspur had asked them to. Perhaps . . .

Arley waded into the grass as the birds bounced on the dirt, fluttering and trilling sweetly. "Snowdrop!"

She went after him and the birds launched into the air and cir-cled them. Arley bent to pick up an object from the ground. It was Edna's knitting, the needles sticking out of a malformed purple . . . hat? Arley slid the loops of yarn along the needles to the knobby ends to avoid them falling off. A lone strand of yarn trailed away through the grass.

"Skies above, Edna," Arley muttered. "Well done." He bent to-ward the ground and pointed. "Hoofprint." He wound the strand of yarn around the lump of knitting and followed it into the grass.

Snowdrop turned back to the road. The four birds had landed in a line and watched her quietly. She sent out thoughts of grati-tude, and they bobbed and chirped before hopping into the grass.

She caught up to Arley as he marched away, winding up the yarn and watching the ground. She turned her eyes down, too, and immediately spotted another hoofprint. They were hidden among the grass but occasionally one showed in the path of the yarn.

They walked and walked until her brow began to sweat and the swish of grass against her knees grew tiresome. Birds flitted across their path, snatching insects from the air, but none showed interest in her and she still couldn't reach Lady.

Arley wound up the end of the yarn and stopped.

They stood in the middle of the plains, the road nowhere in sight. The sun was high and the sky was empty blue, and the wind across the fields tossed the grass in waves. The rush of air was the only sound.

He frowned. "We could try to keep finding hoofprints, but it'd be slow."

"The yarn has led us straight. Maybe they continued straight awhile longer."

"It's the best guess."

"If we hurry, maybe we can get closer so I can reach Lady."

He scanned the horizon. "Do ya see the dark trees ahead?"

"I guess?" The dark smudge was larger than it had been earlier but was still only a smudge of color.

"They stretch from here to here," he said, indicating the endpoints with his hands. "If we stay on this path, we'll intersect them about a quarter of the way from the right end."

"Okay."

"It's not a precise method of navigatin', but if ya don't have a better idea, we can keep goin' toward that point on the horizon."

Arley stuffed the knitting and yarn into his bag and they resumed walking, with Arley in front. His head swiveled up and down, first watching the point on the horizon and then checking the ground. They spotted a few more hoofprints but then no more. Her chest filled with a dull dread the longer they went with no sign of the horses. Each time she reached out and listened, she heard nothing.

Her stomach rumbled as the sun neared its zenith. She ignored the discomfort and tried again to hear any nearby creatures. A group of birds burst from the grass to their right but they flew away so fast it seemed unlikely they had been asked to stay by Larkspur.

After another hour, she scanned the fields and something responded—something on the ground and close enough that she could feel it was nearby. She detected relief from the small creature—relief to hear from her?

"Arley. This way." She led him slowly as they neared the creature so she could watch where she stepped. Beneath the tall grasses, thick tufts of shorter grass dotted the ground.

Something squeaked. She stopped and Arley walked straight into her. He held onto her arms to steady them.

"Hello?" she said quietly.

A field mouse scrambled from under a clump of grass. It checked all around and overhead before blinking up at her. Its tiny furry body trembled and its whiskers shook.

"It's okay," Snowdrop said gently, kneeling before it. She wet her dry lips, squeezed the snowdrop bulb in her pocket, and focused.

She pictured the horses passing through the field. A shiver of fear came back, along with an image of the mouse cowering under the grasses as the hooves thundered down around him. She thought instead of the horses moving away through the field, and the mouse squeaked and scampered toward her, then away, and disappeared into the grass. He emerged a few paces away and squeaked again. He thought of Larkspur with delight—he'd never met a fairy before and wanted to help, since she'd asked so nicely.

Snowdrop stood and took a step toward him and he scurried onward, once again tunneling through the knots of grass and emerging farther on, stopping to look back.

"I think we should follow him," Snowdrop said and Arley fell into step behind her.

The edge of the forest was clearer. The trees weren't thick the way they had been farther west, where they'd descended the steep, forested incline and emerged onto the plains so suddenly. Here, the taller grasses disappeared and the low tufts that shielded the mouse thinned until they reached a place where arid, rocky land spread in front of them and pine trees grew in clusters, breaking up the flat landscape. A dark line of trees crowded the horizon ahead, where the trees grew more dense.

The mouse paused, hunching over with his tail tucked in. He washed his ears a few times before peering around, his nose twitching.

Snowdrop waited. She didn't want the mouse to put himself in danger, but without him, she didn't know how they could go on.

He squeaked and darted forward, then back, following a straight path along the ground. He picked up a tiny granule, a seed or grain. He regarded her and lifted the seed. More seeds littered the rocks around him—and they formed a line of granules continuing across the ground.

"Look, Arley—there's a trail of seeds. One of them must have pulled seed heads off the tall grasses as they passed and dropped them here."

Snowdrop knelt again beside the mouse. He didn't dare continue any farther out in the open, since he'd have to return to the cover of grass by himself.

But he didn't need to lead them farther—he'd brought them to the edge of the field where the trail of seeds began. How could she help him, beyond giving thanks and praising his bravery? She could offer him the seeds but they were the same ones he gathered at his home.

A mouse had no use for snowdrop bulbs or fire powder. Or coins or—

Granola! Snowdrop hunted down to the bottom of her bag for the packet of granola Dustan had given her. She opened it and placed it on the ground, inviting the mouse to help himself. He peeked inside, sniffing, before venturing in, picking up a pecan, and nibbling. A wave of delight flowed over Snowdrop as he wedged it into his mouth and scampered out.

"Go on," she said, "back into the grass where it's safe. Thank you."

He scanned the sky, and she checked too and was relieved to find it empty of hawks. With a final glance, the mouse darted away, a brown blur across the rocks and into the grasses.

Arley gave her a hand and pulled her to her feet. Dust coated his forehead and bits of chaff speckled his trousers. He stood tall but without smiling, and when she studied him, she thought his shoulders bowed in.

"They have to stop sometime," she said.

"So do we."

"But they don't know we're following. They'll stop at dark. They might even light a fire. We'll catch them. And look, I have this human food I forgot all about. It's filled with sugar." She showed him the granola.

That earned her a smile.

"Let's have a bite and we can follow this trail before the sun gets too low. Arley," she said as he took a handful of the caramelized oats and nuts.

"What's up?"

"I was thinking . . ."

"Yeah?"

"It might be useful if we could turn invisible."

His eyes widened. "I forgot about that type of magic."

"But I didn't practice with Larkspur."

"I bet ya can do it. Do you have any idea how to begin?"

"It might help to use the air or the wind. You don't mind if I try as we walk?"

"Of course not. I can't wait to see you invisible. Or, you know, to not see you."

In spite of her worry for their companions, she smiled. He always had faith in her magical ability, even knowing how her magic might go wrong.

At her smile, his body relaxed and he gave her a cheeky grin. "And once you learn to do it, you can turn invisible and run your hands over me . . ."

She scrunched her face up. "Why?"

He shrugged. "I think it would be sexy."

Snowdrop burst out laughing.

"Hey, don't laugh. People can like what they like."

"I'm not laughing at what you like," she said. "I was imagining you with your . . . zucchini bobbing around on its own."

He grinned. "Come on, princess. We'd better keep going."

"You go first," she said. "You can focus on the trail of seeds while I keep trying to find the horses. And trying to turn invisible. I'll stay back in case anything goes awry."

"You can do it." He squeezed her hand before turning away and starting across the rocky ground, head down.

She'd gotten used to scanning with her thoughts for the horses as they walked. Trying to summon the magic to turn invisible would be harder. Usually she closed her eyes to focus but she couldn't do that and keep walking. This time she focused ahead, following Arley but staring into the sky. She curled her hand around the bulb in her pocket. Thank the stars Arley had given her the bulbs—they made everything possible.

How would one turn invisible? She'd never tried this magic at all, even when she'd been younger and using magic the way Oleander had taught her. Invisibility wasn't much use when one lived among fairies because like the illusions, invisibility worked only on humans. Another fairy would be able to see her.

She told herself, I'm going to be like the air, and a shiver tingled from the bulb in her pocket and up her arm. She pictured herself fading and the rocky ground passing by underneath her without her feet visible. She pictured the wind wrapping around and hiding her.

"Can you see me?"

He glanced back and his eyes widened. "You're faded. I can see the ground through you."

"I'll keep practicing."

The afternoon dragged by. Her throat grew parched. She might not even be able to swallow granola at this point, if they'd had any left. With the sun beating down for hours, her tunic was stuck to her armpits. Would her skin burn like a human's? She'd stuffed her sweater into her bag hours ago.

The trees began to grow thicker around them until they rambled through a pine woodland with rocky spaces between the trees. At least they had snatches of shade. The trail of seeds ended, but after a pause to scan the surroundings, Arley noticed a pattern of broken pine branches on the ground, as if someone kept snapping the ends off the trees as they rode past.

And soon after, Snowdrop reached out with her thoughts and found Lady. She called to Arley to stop so she could focus.

Lady had stopped moving, finally. She and Bird didn't like the other two horses—brutish stallions who kept giving them the side-eye. A jumble of thoughts came through: a camp at the edge of dense forest, longing for Arley to be driving them, memories of the wagon. Snowdrop wanted to ask about their three companions, but Lady's thoughts were confused, as if she were tired.

How could she navigate toward the horses? She wasn't getting any sense of direction yet. Snowdrop and Arley continued forward, guessing at which branches on the ground had most likely been dropped by a person. And Snowdrop kept checking for Lady, making sure they hadn't moved away from her.

The sun sank low and shadows covered the ground. They needed water but at least they had some relief now that the heat of the sunlight wasn't on them any longer. But the ground and the branches were harder to see. The waning moon wouldn't be up for a few hours. Snowdrop exhaled. She wanted to sit down and cry.

"Wait." Arley took her arm to stop her. "Do ya see somethin' ahead—sort of bluish and glowin'?"

She peered past the nearest trees, blinking. She'd have thought she was imagining the color if Arley hadn't seen it too.

Slowly they walked toward the dim light. It emanated from something on the ground.

"It's a branch—why's it glowin'?"

Snowdrop sagged in relief. "Larkspur did it. To show us the way. Look." She pointed southeast. Several trees away, another glow illuminated the forest floor.

"Larkspur can make things light up?"

"It looks like sun magic. Certain fairies can gather the energy of the sun and put it into objects to produce light or heat. We use it for lamps and to make heated blankets. But I didn't think Larkspur had any sun magic. I wonder if she's been able to learn to do it somehow, or if she's made up something new."

"She's tricky like that, isn't she?"

"She's been using magic a long time."

"Can ya tell if we're close? We should be careful until we know who we're dealing with."

"I can't tell. I can reach Lady but can't figure out where she is."

They quietly followed the trail of glowing branches. Sometimes a stretch passed with none but a new one would always appear. And then, after a dark stretch, a group of fireflies blinking in the trees swirled into the air all together and danced in a circle. Once the insects had their attention, they floated along through the forest, blinking rapidly as Snowdrop and Arley stumbled behind them. She could sense Lady's presence but didn't get a response—as if the horse was dozing.

The fireflies' lights went out and they hovered away, back into the branches. Snowdrop and Arley stopped. An orange light glowed ahead. The color was different than the bluish lights of the trail Larkspur had created.

Snowdrop's stomach turned over and her palms were sweaty. All day they'd been walking, hoping to catch up with whoever had taken their companions. Now that they'd arrived, a sick sense of dread crept up her center.

Hours had passed since sunset and the white, uneven moon had risen, casting a gleam across the woodland. Only the shadows of the trees were deeply dark.

"If we stay in the shadows, we can stay hidden," Arley whispered.

"Okay. But how are we going to get them back? What if—"

Arley's hand curled around her upper arm and squeezed. "All we're going to do is gather information. Once we know what we're dealin' with, we'll make a plan."

"Are you skilled at fighting? What if we have to fight?"

"I hope we won't. But if we do, I might do okay."

"But what if they have knives? Or—"

"Let's not panic, love. We'll rescue them. We'll think of somethin'."

They crept forward. Snowdrop was silent—all fairies learned to walk through the forest without disturbing the other creatures, even if they'd spent only a little time in the forest during Oleander's reign. She heard every crackle and rustle Arley made but he wasn't as bad as most humans. Maybe he'd learned to be stealthy in the guard.

The orange glow brightened and flickered. "I think it's a campfire," Arley whispered, coming close to her ear. "See over that way?" He pointed. "The cluster of trees? If we went over there, we could stay in the shadows and try to see what's goin' on."

"Okay."

She followed him toward the trees and into the darkness. A pine bough brushed against her face and she jerked back. She had to keep calm or she'd give them away. She crept after him to the far side of the trees and peered through the branches.

A small fire crackled on the ground with a pile of branches beside it. Three bedrolls lay side by side with figures in them—Edna's short gray hair gleamed in the firelight. The other two were probably Larkspur and Nem, although their faces were covered. Were they asleep? Were their hands or feet bound? Given how they'd been dropping yarn and seeds and branches all day, it seemed unlikely. A fourth person lay on the opposite side of the fire. Snowdrop couldn't see much, but that person was larger than her friends.

Something moved to her right and she slowly turned. It was a horse, standing with its head down. The other horses stood nearby, all of them dozing. In the darkness she could not tell who was who, but two were larger and Lady had said their captors rode stallions.

Where was the other captor? The moment she had that thought, he passed by their tree with slow steps. He was pacing around the fire, maybe to keep himself awake. He was tall and broad—two people his size could easily have overpowered Larkspur, Edna, and Nem, even without weapons. The shadows shifted across him as he continued his slow circle. Fear drifted through Snowdrop's body. He was familiar—his height, the way he paced like a predator. The firelight hit his face and she gasped.

His head twitched up at the sound. She and Arley froze. She

held her breath and stared back at the figure, hoping the shadows were dark enough to hide them from her brother.

Chapter 20

SNOWDROP STOOD FROZEN BESIDE ARLEY and took slow, silent breaths. Across the makeshift campsite, her brother Beech peered into the darkness. He scanned the trees but kept returning to the place where they stood—as if he'd heard her gasp and suspected someone was near. Finally he turned to the fire. He reached for a branch on the ground and poked it into the flames until it flared up and he tossed it in.

Arley hadn't moved and Snowdrop kept still beside him. Beech kept poking at the fire but he also stayed still and quiet. He was listening. After a stretch he exhaled and resumed his slow pacing, moving away from them. Arley turned and led her away, keeping to thc shadows.

They stayed silent until they were some distance from the camp, with the fire once again an orange glow through the trees. Arley led her into another patch of darkness and touched her arm, pulling her to crouch beside him.

"You know him?" Arley asked.

"It's my brother Beech. And his twin Sycamore is probably the one sleeping by the fire—they do everything together. We haven't seen them since Oleander was removed as queen. Dustan thought they were down south."

"Are these the two who can't do magic?"

"That's what Larkspur said—they might have a human father. But we can't be sure."

"So the rumors about the south were wrong."

"Or they set Dustan up. I wouldn't have thought they were smart enough to plan something like that." Had she underestimated them?

"If they planned it, have they been followin' us this whole time?" Arley wondered aloud.

Snowdrop shuddered. All these days they'd been traveling through the woods and across the plains, and she'd felt safe and free, and to think they'd been tracked like prey. Could her brothers have caused the strange messages Larkspur had heard from the animals?

"If they'd been watchin' us," Arley continued, "they'd know about you an' me. But they took only three people—and you joined the party late and Nem wasn't officially part of it."

"That carelessness sounds more like them," Snowdrop said. "Acting without paying attention to details—kidnapping three people and not even questioning that one is only sixteen winters old and happens to be one of their mother's former servants. Although they probably don't recognize Nem—I hope not. She was only eight when she left the fairy caverns."

"Do you have any idea what they're up to?"

Snowdrop shook her head. "They might want Larkspur to do something for them. Some spell or potion. They know her magic is powerful."

"Fairy magic—can it be used as a weapon?" In the darkness, Arley cringed as he said it, as if he were embarrassed to ask. "I mean, from what I've seen, it doesn't seem like it can do much harm—the illusions and things. But I know you worried about using it wrong and hurting someone. Could they make Larkspur hurt someone for 'em?"

Snowdrop frowned. "I don't think Larkspur would use magic if it hurt a living thing. I don't know if she can do it that way but I'm sure she could learn. But most fairies would regard that use of magic as so wrong they would never try to learn it. I learned it only because Oleander led me down that path and I didn't know any better."

"What about fairy spells? Could your brothers use any spells to hurt us?"

"It's possible but I doubt it. Even if Larkspur is wrong and they are capable of magic, they were never skilled enough to make anything as complex as a spell. I only ever saw them use simple illusions or potions. But they might have human weapons. Dustan mentioned that. I could see them finding that option attractive once Oleander wasn't around to help them."

Arley ran his hands through his hair. "Okay. So we have to get three people away from 'em. We don't know if they have weapons or if they can see through illusions. We can't ride double on Lady and Bird for long but we could do it long enough to get some distance—only your brothers have their own horses. Could we steal those?"

"Maybe . . . if my brothers truly can't communicate with them. Although they've had them a long time. And I don't know how they were trained."

"If your brothers don't see us leave," Arley said, "they won't know which direction we go. It would be hard for them to find us in the dark. We could head straight for the road and we'd come out somewhere near Woods End."

"So we need to lure them away from the campsite."

"Right."

A flame of hope shot through Snowdrop. "How about another fire?" She rummaged in her bag. "Dustan gave me fire powder for emergencies. We'd need only a branch to light and we could make it bright. And the color's a little different than human fires—they'd surely investigate." She withdrew the packet Dustan had given her.

"Even if only one of them left, I could hold off the other while the rest of ya get on the horses and ride into the dark. And then I'd run. It's not the best plan but I can't think of another."

"Unless I try to talk to them."

"You think they'd listen?"

"No."

"Then I'd rather not lose you, too."

Snowdrop stood and stretched her legs, and Arley followed. They stood a moment in silence.

"This isn't what you signed up for," Snowdrop said. "You shouldn't have to deal with my awful family."

"You had to deal with mine."

"Yours was nice! And not dangerous."

"How bad are your brothers? I mean, back when Oleander was in charge—were they killin' fairies left and right? Murderin' villagers in their sleep?"

"They're not killers," Snowdrop said, considering, "but I think they could be. They're mean. They bully others."

"Did they hurt animals like Oleander did?"

Snowdrop thought back over all the seasons she'd spent with them. She shook her head. "Not that I ever saw."

"Anyway, it doesn't matter what I signed on for. You're my friends and I wouldn't leave a friend in trouble no matter what."

Even in the shadows she could see him watching her. "Thank you."

He nodded. "Let's get goin' before dawn comes."

The moon was high overhead. They crept away to the left of the campsite, opposite the side where the horses were tethered. They stopped when the fire was a faint glow. Snowdrop found a large dry branch—it would flare up brightly, and the magic of the fire powder would maintain that initial brightness. They moved to a rocky place where the fire could burn without igniting any nearby trees.

"Let's walk through the plan," she said.

"I'll go across first to get a head start. You count 200 heartbeats, light the fire, and come after me, going wide around the campsite to avoid passing your brothers. Once we're on the far side, we'll wait for them to leave if we need to. I'll untie the horses while you wake the others."

"I'll ask Lady and Bird to stay still."

"And if Beech leaves alone, we'll move in together so I can keep the other one quiet while you wake the ladies."

Snowdrop forced down her rising panic with a deep inhale. They didn't have any choice. They had to do this.

"Ready, princess?"

Her heart stuttered and she reached for his hand before she'd realized it. The night had gotten colder but his hand was warm and held hers tightly. She stepped forward and into his embrace.

"We can do this," she murmured to herself, hiding her face against his shoulder. But so many things could go wrong. He didn't reply but his hand rubbed her back. She stepped away reluctantly.

Arley set off in the direction they'd come from and a moment later he disappeared in the darkness. She waited, counting, and he reappeared in the moonlight farther on and disappeared again. When she reached 200, she knelt beside the branch on the ground and opened the packet of fire powder. She took a pinch, leaned back, and sprinkled it on. The branch burst into flame.

Quickly she tucked the packet into her bag and stole away, not looking back until she'd reached the nearest shadow. The flame was tall and bright with a yellow sparkle. This batch of fire powder had been made by either Rowan or Elle, but she would guess Elle, given the color and sparkles. Elle had nicknamed her dragon partner Sunshine. And Rowan seemed less likely to add decorative sparkles to a batch of fire powder, but who knew. Maybe he liked sparkles too.

Snowdrop circled the campsite to the far side and moved in. No figures moved by the campfire—Beech was gone. As she neared she scanned over Sycamore's bedroll: empty. All three ladies lay asleep. She darted toward the horses and found Arley untying their leads. Quickly, she placed her hand on Lady's flank, conveyed a calm thought of waiting for them to be ready to leave, and hoped Lady understood.

"Beech spotted the fire the moment ya lit it," Arley whispered. "He woke his brother and they left. We have to hurry."

Snowdrop moved into the light of the camp and dropped by Nem's side. Gently she shook her friend, hoping she'd wake quietly. But she didn't wake at all. Snowdrop shook harder and Nem rolled back and forth like a ragdoll.

Snowdrop's heart lurched and her hands shook. Nem was warm; she wasn't dead. Snowdrop put fingers to Nem's neck and her pulse beat steadily. She was alive. What had her brothers done?

She shook Edna next, then Larkspur, and they were the same: breathing, heart beating, but unresponsive. Was it a sleeping spell? Or a potion? Dustan could use both. But her older brothers wouldn't be able to use a spell without their own magic. It must be a potion—an effective one anyone could use, even a human. Maybe Beech and Syc had taken the potion when they left the fairy enclave. The usual sleeping potion kept someone asleep forever but its magic was easily broken if anyone tried to wake the person. So it must be some other potion.

Arley glanced over. "We need to go," he hissed.

"They won't wake. I don't know why."

Arley cursed and strode to her side. "Is it safe to move 'em?"

"I guess?" Her voice spiraled higher. They didn't have time to figure it out.

Arley pulled open Nem's bedroll and lifted her in his arms. "We can ride slowly with them in front and—"

"Black stars."

Beech's voice sent chills down Snowdrop's back. She turned and slowly stood.

Beech and Syc stood at the edge of the campsite. Their dark hair had gotten long in the seasons since she'd last seen them and they wore it tied back. They had the same heavy brow and large nose, but Beech glowered while Syc smirked. They each held a short dagger and the blades glinted in the firelight.

"It's little Snowdrop," Syc said, as if Beech couldn't see for himself.

She could turn invisible. She could take Arley's hand and hide them both and they'd sneak off. Air, she was like the air. She gasped for breath and pictured herself fading out but she had too much fear. And then the awful dark magic curled up, siphoning the life off the nearby trees, off insects in the wood, off Arley beside her. She cut off the magic, panting.

Syc's eyes narrowed. "Little sister, what are *you* doing all the way out here?"

Snowdrop tried to steady herself. Fearing them was probably smart but she didn't have to cower. They were the same stupid pair they had always been. "I was traveling with Larkspur," she managed. "Why did you take her?"

Syc opened his mouth but Beech growled. "Where were you last night?"

Snowdrop froze. Syc's eyes darted to Arley and back, and a nasty grin spread across his face. "I think I know," he said. "Little sister was off in the bushes tumbling the human."

Snowdrop's face heated and Arley tensed beside her. Beech squinted at Arley and Snowdrop braced herself for anger, but Syc laughed.

"This'll be fun," he said. "Where'd you meet this guy? You never had much luck with fairies, did you? So now you're slumming with the humans. Good for you."

Snowdrop tried not to shake. She would *not* let them upset her. They were idiots and they didn't know what they were talking about. "You had plenty of human lovers," she said.

"But not because we couldn't get anyone better," Syc said, sneering. "So who is this guy? Aren't you going to introduce us?"

They both focused on Arley, standing frozen with Nem in his arms.

"Put down the girl," Beech said, and he lifted his knife hand slightly. Arley slowly knelt and lay Nem on the ground.

"This is Arley," Snowdrop said. "He's driving us to the council meeting in Mountain Rest."

"Well unfortunately, we need Larkspur's help with something else," Syc said.

"What are you going to do to them?"

"Don't worry, we won't hurt them—as long as she cooperates."

"What are you going to do?"

"We're—"

Beech smacked Syc's arm and he stopped speaking. Beech glared at her. "You always were a tricky little bitch. You should have stayed away."

"Beech," Syc said with a note of warning. "We can't hurt her. You know Mother would kill us."

Beech turned to Arley and Snowdrop stepped in front of him.

"We can tie them up so they can't follow," Syc said.

"They'll starve to death," Beech replied, and Syc's face fell. "I've got a better idea." He slipped a hand into his pocket.

Snowdrop backed into Arley. He held her elbow, but when he tried to tug her behind him she held her ground in front.

"Don't worry, little sister," Beech said, stalking forward. Syc followed. "If you don't try to stop us, we won't hurt your little tumble buddy—I swear."

Snowdrop's chest thudded as she stared up at Beech. He was a head taller than her or Arley and he cast a shadow over them. Syc moved around behind them and Arley held her against him.

Beech cracked a smile. He lowered the dagger and his other hand came up, fisted in front of him. "This'll be fun. You even have a nice big moon overhead. That makes it extra potent."

Snowdrop's stomach dropped and her eyes widened. She sucked in a deep breath and held it as Beech's fist opened and he blew a shower of moonflower dust in her face. It hung in the air, sparkling in the moonlight. She had to warn Arley—but she couldn't hold her breath and speak. And she was too late—Syc shoved them from behind and Arley gasped and the dust swirled in the night air. Arley's hands went slack on her arms and his body stepped away. "Skies," he slurred as he staggered sideways. Syc caught him and lowered him to the ground.

Beech dropped his dagger and gripped Snowdrop's arm, holding her in place. She shook her head, trying to clear the air of the moonflower dust. She needed to breathe.

"You hate her," Beech said in a low growl. "You rejected her magic, you cozied up to Dustan and his human, you're out here pretending you're important." He shook her arm and stepped in closer. "But you can't escape your family." His heavy breaths hit her face. "The fairies don't like you. You can't do their magic. A human is the best you can do for a mate." He grunted and shook her again, whispering. "You hate her, but you're just like her."

Snowdrop gasped and Beech opened his hand again and blew the rest of the dust right into her face. It tingled up her nose and into her lungs.

"I'm not like her!" she said.

"Of course not," Syc said. "You wouldn't give us magic to use. But she will." Syc came around and lifted Nem's limp body. The firelight and shadows were pitching about, and Syc swayed back and forth but held Nem steadily.

"That's where you're going," Snowdrop said. Horror crept up her chest. "You're going to free her."

Syc grinned. Her legs were going weak and Beech dropped her to the ground and let go of her arm. It smarted where he'd held her but the pain was dimming.

"You can't," she said. "The prison won't open for you."

"That's why we need Larkspur."

"Larkspur won't do it."

"She will if we start breaking her old lady friend's fingers. Or if we harm this young thing—a half fairy. Interesting."

"Dustan and Rose will stop you," Snowdrop panted.

Beech huffed and turned away, gathering up Nem's empty bed-roll and turning to Edna. Syc towered over Snowdrop, blocking her view. "Too bad Dustan's off on a desperate mission to Tidal Creek to stop rogue fairies from hurting the humans. And Rose can't do shit. She better stay away. All of this is her fault to begin with."

"Enough, Syc," Beech called. "Let's go."

Syc put his foot on her chest and slowly pushed until she fell backward. "Have a nice ride, little sister," he said and stepped away.

She tried to focus, to hear what they were doing, but the stars overhead were swirling into patterns, colorful patterns, and a dull roaring had begun, like an ocean crashing with no end. Moon dust. They'd given her moon dust. It wouldn't hurt her. But she had to stay calm or—

Calm. Stay calm. She watched the moon and slowed her breathing. The stars reached for her and she floated up to meet them. She was a bird, soaring through the sky. She could turn invisible. She could turn into a rainbow. The roar quieted into perfect silence and everything around was still. Fires sparkled around her as the stars fell into them.

Someone groaned.

Arley, she remembered. Arley was here and he didn't know about moonflower dust.

She fought off the stars and rolled to her side. Arley lay in a heap. He groaned again. The fire leapt and flickered, and the darkness was motionless. Larkspur was gone. Edna too. The ground was bare except for Arley.

Snowdrop crawled across the dirt. She pulled Arley into her arms and fell back with him.

"Calm," she whispered. "You have to stay calm."

He struggled against her and moaned.

She stroked his face. "It's just moonflower dust," she said. "It can't really hurt you. It's just moon dust, Arley. Look at the stars. Watch the stars."

His eyes turned upward and moonlight fell on his face.

She snuggled into him. "It'll be all right."

Chapter 21

⁕

THE WHOLE SKY WAS BLUE, wide wide blue everywhere. How long had she been staring at it? Snowdrop tried to swallow but her throat was parched. She was lying flat on the hard ground, dirty with dried sweat and dust. She twitched her fingers. They came to life and stroked soft hair. Arley's hair. He lay halfway on top of her.

She closed her eyes, not yet ready to move. Arley's head rested on her chest and his body pinned her right leg to the ground. His chest rose and fell against her thigh.

Why were they here? And *where* were they? She tried again, opening her eyes and twisting her stiff neck. Pine boughs blocked the sky on one side. Scattered trees surrounded a clearing. She inhaled a dirt smell and lingering smoke. She flopped her head to the other side, where a stack of branches sat by the ashes of a fire. No one else was here. What had happened?

She closed her eyes again and rotated her neck, wiggled her shoulders, then her arms, moving each muscle down to her toes. Everything worked. She was just stiff and so thirsty.

They'd almost made it to Mountain Rest, up on the hillside overlooking the city, but this was not that place. Focus. What could she remember? She'd awoken at the wayside, cozied up with Arley, and then in the morning, the others were gone. They'd been taken. By her brothers.

Beech and Sycamore were going to free Oleander from the fairy prison. Dread crept up her body as she remembered. What would Oleander do if freed? What would she expect from Snowdrop? Snowdrop had disliked visiting the prison but at least she'd been free of Oleander's demands—she literally couldn't do anything to help her. If Oleander were free and Snowdrop resisted her, or tried to change her mind, would Oleander turn on her? Surely she wouldn't hurt her own daughter . . . would she? Snowdrop couldn't find the confidence to believe Oleander would value her daughter over her own goals.

Snowdrop scrunched her face and blinked her eyes open as the rest of last night returned to her. Her brothers had used a potion or some other means to subdue their hostages and then used moonflower dust to stop her and Arley from following them. Maybe they'd given the others the same treatment earlier in the evening and they'd already passed out.

What time was it? The sun was halfway up the sky.

The fear had roused her, and moving her muscles helped. Her body was coming back. She fisted her fingers in Arley's hair and released them, petting him. "Arley?" Her voice rasped in her dry throat.

She pushed her thigh into him, nudging his body sideways. His arm came to rest across her legs. He made a noise like a creaky iron gate and his arm twitched.

She tugged on his hair again. "Arley."

His head shifted and she slid her fingers down both sides of his neck and kneaded his shoulders. He moaned.

"Wake up," she ordered, losing her voice on the second word.

His arm moved again and his hand landed on her thigh, squeezing. He squeezed lower, moaned, and twisted his neck to scan around himself. His hand dropped off her body. "Sorry," he murmured. "I . . . Black skies. What happened?"

She kneaded his shoulders again, working outward. "Move your arms," she said and coughed. She lowered her voice and tried again, more carefully. "My brothers gave us moon dust," she said. "Made us sleep but it's wearing off."

Slowly his body stirred, still partly on top of her. She propped her left elbow and pushed herself up to see him better, holding him against her before gently lowering him to the ground. His body rolled away from hers and she sat up.

Arley muttered another curse but he flexed his fingers and rolled his neck. A moment later, he slowly pushed himself up beside her and rubbed his eyes open.

"Where the others?" he mumbled.

"My brothers took them. You remember any of it?"

"Iss foggy." He rubbed the back of his neck and yawned.

Snowdrop swallowed to clear the dust from her throat. "They're taking them to the fairy caverns," she managed without coughing. "They think Larkspur can use her magic to open the prison and free Oleander."

Arley stopped massaging his neck and regarded her. "Can she?"

Snowdrop exhaled. "Maybe?" She swallowed again. "The fairy prison isn't like a human prison. It doesn't have locks and keys." Her voice grew raspy and she cleared her throat. "It's imbued with ancient magic that knows when the person inside should be kept and when they should be freed. It knows if they're sorry for what they did and won't do it again."

Talking exhausted her. She closed her eyes and breathed a few times before continuing. "Someone created the prison's magic— some long-ago fairy. So a fairy who understands the magic should be able to undo it. But sometimes magic has a way of . . . I don't know. Of doing something unexpected. Of helping do what's right." She opened her eyes.

Arley's brow furrowed.

"Like one time when Rose needed help, a nearby flock of birds came to help her. But she's never been able to communicate with the birds otherwise."

"Okay." His voice sounded stronger.

"So there's no telling what will happen if Larkspur tries to override that old magic."

"Why would Larkspur even try?"

"Because they'll hurt Edna and Nem if she doesn't."

Arley cursed again.

Snowdrop slowly crouched, wobbled, and sat back down. She needed another minute.

"What was it they gave us—'noon . . . dust . . .'?"

"Moon dust—powdered moonflower seeds. It gives you hallucinations until you sleep it off. Some fairies think it's fun. It's not harmful as long as you don't do anything stupid like walk off a cliff thinking you can fly."

He rotated his shoulders. "I saw . . . this flaming monster. I thought it was going to burn me up. But ya drove it away."

"You were panicking. The hallucinations can be bad if you don't stay calm."

"Skies."

She pushed herself up again and this time she was steady. She slowly stood and stretched, and her stomach immediately growled. They had to find food.

She scanned their surroundings. She pictured the map in the fairies' library. They were near the edge of the forest, east of the forest road. Had her brothers taken the others to the road? No, if they had meant to use the road they never would have left it in the first place.

"I think they're making a beeline back to the fairy enclave," she said as Arley raised himself to his knees.

"The road would be faster with horses."

"Maybe they worried they'd be stopped on the road. The forest has trails the animals use. And my brothers spent more time out of the caverns than most fairies. They might know a route."

Arley traced a finger through the air. "The forest road heads straight south to the crossroads and then curves east toward the coast," he said. "We could walk west to reach it and hope for a ride. Or we could continue southeast into the forest and we'll eventually cross a road."

"I don't think I can go much farther without water. Especially in this sun."

Arley stood. "I might have some." He took a wobbly step and another. "I found a gourd last night and I dropped it." He walked more steadily after a few steps, crossing to the place where the horses had been tethered. He crouched, reached under the nearest branches, and came out with a small gourd, which he handed her.

She carefully opened it and sipped. The water was cool from the chilly night air and cleared her dry throat. She had a few swallows and handed it back.

"Do you know how far they are?" he asked quietly.

She met his gaze, considering. Regardless of how far ahead her brothers were, she and Arley had no hope of catching them on foot. He must know that. And her brothers might travel faster now they knew someone was following. Unless she could send the fairies a message to warn them, she and Arley would need to find a ride.

Her brothers must have considered the possibility of a message getting through. As far as they knew, she was unskilled at normal fairy magic. But Larkspur could easily send her own message once she was in range. Maybe they planned to keep her drugged on moonflower dust, or whatever they'd given her. Snowdrop's stomach turned. Or, they might have extracted a promise from her not to give their plan away, a promise she'd have to keep. That would be easier on everyone, if her brothers were smart enough to think to do it.

But how far ahead were they?

"Give me a moment." She reached for her satchel but it was no longer around her body. She scanned the ground and her hopes sank.

"They took my snowdrop bulbs," she whispered. Her satchel

was gone, and Larkspur's as well. She patted her trousers pocket. "They even took the one from my pocket." Tears pricked her eyes.

Arley stepped in front of her and held her arms. "You'll get 'em back or we can get you more."

"But I won't be able to reach Lady. I won't be able to do anything!"

Arley frowned. "The bulbs helped but you were learning to do the magic. You can do it without them."

"I don't know. I never felt any of Oleander's dark magic when I had them. I think they kept it away."

He rubbed her arm. "You were doing well. Don't let her magic scare you. You're not a mean person. You don't want to hurt others. You won't let yourself do any harm."

She focused on his fingers, smoothing over her skin. If only she believed in herself the way he did. But she had to give it a try. "I'll try to reach the horses."

She closed her eyes, and Arley stayed right beside her with his hands holding her. She should tell him to move away, to keep him safe, but she couldn't bring herself to.

She imagined Lady the way she had over and over yesterday and she might have felt a tingle of recognition. But no response came. She tried listening and heard a dull version of the usual chatter of birds and mice and snakes moving in the branches and the grass. But without her bulb, she couldn't make sense of any of it. Something different curled around the bottom of the sounds, something familiar in the woods to the south. She couldn't read it.

She opened her eyes. "I can't find anything useful."

"Which direction should we go?"

"I think we should go southeast to stay on their trail. Maybe something will hold them up and we can catch them. And if not, we'll end up near the forest crossroads, right? We can look for a ride there." But by then, it would probably be too late to stop her brothers.

He nodded. "The forest is mostly pine all the way south to the crossroads and the forest floor down that way is flat and open. It's as easy to walk in as it would be to walk on the road."

"And there's shade."

"And we're likely to find a stream. We'll have to cross those creeks that ran under the road."

Once they'd decided, Arley scoured the campsite for anything useful while Snowdrop checked the fire she'd lit the previous night to make sure it was out. She found only ashes. The air was silent except for the droning of insects and an occasional flutter of wings.

They headed southeast at a fast pace, and the remaining stiffness from sleeping on the bare ground and the other effects of the moonflower dust wore off. The longer they walked, the thicker the trees became until the ground was dappled in shade. As she walked, Snowdrop kept trying to listen to the sounds of the forest creatures. She never recognized Lady but couldn't be sure what she heard in the cacophony of jumbled thoughts. She kept getting an eerie sense of a large creature in the direction they were headed, but it didn't seem like a horse. Without her name plant, she didn't know how to learn more.

The sun had been high when they left the campsite and now it passed overhead. Arley refused to drink again so Snowdrop finished the last drops of water from the gourd. The forest opened and ahead, the trees seemed to rise in a less dramatic version of the ridge south of Woods End.

The trees closed in again. They were passing through a shadowed glade when the rush of water registered in her mind. It had to be water—what else could the sound be out here?

Arley glanced back. "D'ya hear that?"

She hurried to his side. "Yes."

"Let's hope it's not a hundred paces down a sheer cliff."

Snowdrop's face fell.

"I'm teasin', princess. I hope."

The noise grew and with it the worry—surely a little creek couldn't be making that much noise? What if they couldn't get a drink, much less cross safely? The trees cleared ahead and a cool, damp breeze swept through the forest. Moss covered the rocky ground and ferns appeared at the bases of the trees. They hurried through the final stretch and came out on the edge of a wide, flat stream. Upstream it burbled over rocks, creating the noise echoing nonstop around them. Arley stepped to the rocky edge and knelt, scooping water to his lips.

The bottom of the stream bed was visible for several paces out. It should be shallow enough to wade across, but they'd have to be careful not to slip. Pine trees lined the other side. And . . . it couldn't be. Snowdrop stepped onto the rocks and wobbled, reaching out and catching Arley's shoulder.

"Steady, love," he said, giving her a hand to squat beside him.

"Look." She pointed. "Blackberries."

"Blessed skies." The leafy bushes lined the water upstream, thorny branches arcing over the water. The leaves were red-tinged this late in the season but berries as big as pecans hung in clusters. Maybe the damp location helped the bushes keep producing berries this late in the summer.

Snowdrop was so hungry she could barely make herself drink. But she squatted beside Arley and sipped a few handfuls of cold water. And when he splashed water over his face she copied him, scrubbing the grime off her skin. He filled the gourd he'd taken from the campsite.

Arley stood and rolled up the cuffs of his trousers. He took off his shoes and tucked them inside his shirt.

"Ya want a hand gettin' across?"

"I'd feel safer," she said, taking his hand. "We can't risk an injury."

"We can hold each other up."

He slowly stepped out in the stream, rocking sideways as his foot slipped but found a footing. She hung on and followed. The water chilled her hot feet until they felt like blocks of ice clunking across the streambed. The rocks were slick but she could wedge her feet between two or stand flat in the spaces between. The water never became deep enough to wet the hem of her pants.

They stepped onto the bank on the far side and hurried upstream to the berry bushes. The first plump berry slid off the bush into her hand and dissolved with tangy sweetness on her tongue. They began gobbling berries like a flock of drunk cedar waxwings in the springtime.

They ate every berry they could find, following the bushes along the shore. Arley had a purple streak across one cheek and her lips were probably stained with the juice as well. Her hands certainly were. Arley rubbed his forehead and left another smudge.

"We should get going," she said.

"Yeah. Now that we've had a drink I can make another league before sundown."

They took one final drink and continued southeast. The forest grew thicker as they left the stream and the forest floor was soft with pine needles. Eventually they reached the second creek, also wide, shallow, and easy to cross. They walked as long as they could see. Finally the daylight faded enough that they couldn't make their way over roots and around branches, and they stopped for the night. A chill permeated the air as darkness came.

Without their supplies, they didn't have much to do to prepare for sleep. They scooped pine needles across the ground into a pile to give them warmth and softness.

"I feel awkward saying this," Arley began, staring down at their makeshift bedding, "but we should huddle for warmth."

Snowdrop's face heated. Why was she embarrassed, after the times they'd spent together? "That makes sense." She studied the ground too.

"I feel guilty, ya know."

"Why?"

"Seems wrong to feel happy about anything when the others are in trouble."

She warmed everywhere at his words. "I feel that way too."

"Well, ah, let's get to it. We'll be up at dawn."

They knelt in the pine needles and lay down side by side. The bedding smelled sweet and gave an illusion of being clean, although she'd probably have pine sap all over her by morning.

Snowdrop nudged Arley. "It seems like you should put your arms around me if we want to stay warm."

"Right." Arley rolled toward her and pulled her in against him with his purple-stained hands. He kissed her hair and settled behind her.

How far had her brothers gotten with their hostages? They couldn't be at the fairy enclave already, but it was only a matter of time. She hadn't been able to reach any animals or send a message. Her fledgling magic was useless without her name plant to help her.

She and Arley had walked far but if they'd gone to the road, surely they'd have gotten a ride.

"I think I made a mistake bringing us southeast," she whispered.

Arley's arms snugged tighter around her. "Don't worry about that now. Get some sleep."

She woke in the night to an owl hooting and the rustle of a creature passing nearby. She was too tired to try using magic to see who it was, and Arley's arms were warm and she slipped back into sleep.

A wet nose snuffled her cheek, tickled her ear, and moved to her hair.

The air was cold on her wet face. Snowdrop swiped her shoulder across her ear to dry it. She found Arley's arm and tugged his body more tightly around her.

Leaves rustled and something sniffed loudly. Arley was as still as a log behind her, snoring faintly. The rustling moved closer and the wet nose touched her face again.

Snowdrop opened her eyes. A huge black snout filled her vision, with bristly dark fur on the top. And a pair of brown eyes watched her. She gasped and the animal stepped back.

Slowly she sat up, sliding out of Arley's embrace. In the pre-dawn light, animals hunkered all around them, sleeping on the ground. The one watching her stepped forward and snorted a few short blasts.

"You're a boar," she whispered.

He was gigantic, with white tusks curving out of his mouth. Did he want to eat her? He'd had a chance and hadn't done any harm.

Snowdrop took a deep breath and let it out slowly. She could do this.

She closed her eyes and imagined friendliness, passiveness, and calm, sending her intentions out to the boar. She filled herself up with so many positive feelings she left no room for anything malevolent to find a way in.

A warm swirl came around her. Was that the boar's response? It felt familiar. And then—

Sticky buns. Thoughts of sticky buns.

Snowdrop opened her eyes and smiled. "You're my friend from days ago."

He exhaled and pawed the ground.

She held out her empty hands. "I don't have any food, much less sticky buns."

He snuffled over her hands and a wave of sympathy washed over her—sympathy for her, for being hungry. The boar's size was scary but now that she'd communicated with him, face to face, his eyes seemed intelligent and friendly.

A strange thought came to her from the boar, and she again closed her eyes to concentrate. Understanding him was hard without the snowdrop bulb to help her. She had to tune out her surroundings—the sea of boars sleeping around them and the feel of Arley behind her. Tentatively, she reached out a hand to touch the boar, hoping the direct contact would make communicating easier.

Another fairy—the boar had spoken with another fairy. Who could it be if not Larkspur? Snowdrop tamped down her hope and excitement. She imagined Larkspur up on a horse and the boar agreed—yes, that was her. She'd called to him as she rode through the forest and asked for help. He hadn't understood why but he'd roused his herd and gone to her. And he'd found her being carried away by the men from the forest—men who'd startled his herd into a stampede days ago.

What happened next? Snowdrop sent him the question. Had they helped?

A scene came to her—all of the boars milling about in the forest. Not stampeding, just sort of standing there or slowly trodding about among the undergrowth, and in the midst of the herd were four horses with riders. Snowdrop's mouth hung open in delight as the boar recounted the anger of the two male riders, but they hadn't been armed with guns so the boars had felt safe enough. They'd held up the riders for hours, constantly moving to stay in their path, even after one of the men approached the fairy woman and she slumped unconscious on her horse.

Snowdrop wished she had sticky buns for him, or anything. She sent him her thanks for helping her friends. Those angry men—they were bad and they'd taken her friends away. She was trying to catch them.

His ear flicked. They were far behind.

She slumped. She should have led Arley out to the road—

The boar nudged her shoulder with his snout. He could help her catch up with the riders. He could get her there in no time.

She sat up.

He was faster than a horse when running through the woods. And he could give her a ride.

She had to be misreading him. She imagined climbing onto his bristly back and hanging on as he ran through the trees, leaning forward to avoid whacking into low branches.

The boar grunted and stepped from one hoof to the other. He wouldn't whack her into any branches. He knew where the trails were.

Light was seeping into the forest as dawn neared. Snowdrop's body tingled with the chill of the night air and with hope coursing through her. Could the boar really carry her? What about Arley?

She leaned aside and contemplated him, sleeping with pine needles sticking from his hair. He truly could sleep through anything. The boar watched her. She pointed at Arley and at herself.

The boar turned and trod over to one of the bodies sleeping nearby. From a distance, he somehow appeared even bigger than he did close up—his stocky legs firm on the ground and his body stout and solid like a giant wheelbarrow piled high with cabbages. He pushed at the other boar—one as large as him—and the other snorted, woke, and scrambled to his feet. Together they returned. He'd found a ride for Arley.

Snowdrop calmed her racing heart and took a moment to share her gratitude with the boars. When this adventure was over, she would try her hardest to bring them sticky buns. Hopefully Nem's mother could help.

Snowdrop turned to Arley and gently shook his shoulder. He mumbled a few times before coming awake, blinking up at her with groggy eyes.

"Wake up," she said, grinning. "We have a ride."

Chapter 22

RLEY STARED AT THE TWO boars. "That's our ride?"

Snowdrop failed to suppress her smile. "What's the matter, don't think you can manage?"

He swiveled toward her, his incredulity growing. "Are you really teasin' me right now?"

"You were awfully confident about your horse-riding skills," she tossed off. "I guess you didn't learn anything about pig riding in the King's Guard."

Arley's eyes narrowed as he stood and his fists landed on his hips. "I'm fine at pig riding. Or I will be once I've done it."

"We'll see." She made herself stop there. It wasn't like she had pig-riding experience either.

His face softened as she stood too. "So, ah, do they have names?"

The first boar's ears twitched and he scanned back and forth between them. His friend rooted around in the dirt.

"Probably? I'm not sure how to convey that question."

Arley placed his hands on his chest and turned to the boar. "Arr-lee," he said loudly.

The boar snorted. Snowdrop almost snorted along with him. "I meant," she said, "that I'd have to send him a mental image to ask about names, and to share ours. The trouble with human names is they don't mean anything. I don't know what picture to send him to share your name."

"What do ya mean, human names don't mean anythin'? They mean things."

"What's an 'arley'?"

"An arley's not a thing. But the name means 'from the meadow' in archaic Sylvanian. And in the historical language of the eastern isles it means 'promise.'"

Snowdrop's gaze fell. "Oh. I didn't know." Why had she assumed human names had no significance?

"That's okay, princess."

She shifted on her feet. "Now that I know the meaning of 'Arley,' being named after a flower doesn't seem like much."

"But flowers are beautiful. Everyone loves them."

"Still. That kind of beauty is on the surface."

"Not really, not if ya think about it. Snowdrops make people happy not because they're tiny and delicate but because they're among the first flowers to bloom each spring. In some places they bloom right on the edge of the snow as it melts. They symbolize the transition from the cold and dead of winter to the new life of spring. People see them and think of new beginnings and feel hope for the future."

Snowdrop stared at him. In one breath he'd turned her name into the most meaningful word she knew.

He turned away. "We should figure out how to ride the boars."

Snowdrop shook her head and focused. "Let me try to find out their names."

She rolled her shoulders and relaxed. The boar stepped closer and bumped his head against her hand. She patted his bristly fur and kept her hand on him. She pictured tiny white snowdrops on the forest floor and thought, This is me. Had he ever seen a snowdrop? Did they truly grow in the woods here, the way Larkspur had said?

The thought, little flower, came back to her. She patted him. The name was close enough.

Another image came of a wide, solid tree trunk.

"Trunk? Your name is Trunk?"

He grunted a few times. Then he pointed his snout at Arley.

"Okay." She imagined a wide meadow like the ones around Woods Rest. Maybe the boar herd had wandered through a meadow at some point and would know what she meant.

This time the reply was Stone Wall.

She frowned, trying again.

Fence?

She peeked up at Arley. "How do you feel about them thinking your name is Fence?"

"Fence?"

"Or Stone Wall?"

He brightened. "Sure. I'll take that one."

It fit him—solid, dependable. "So, uh, this is Trunk. And that is . . . ?"

Dirt.

". . . and that's Dirt."

"Trunk and Dirt. Perfect."

Dirt perked up at his name and lumbered over to sniff Arley.

Snowdrop placed both hands on Trunk's back and he froze. What if she tried to get on and he bolted? Hopefully they'd correctly understood each other about the ride. She tried to convey an apology if she hurt him with her weight but nothing came back. She pushed herself up onto her hands and swung a leg across his back. His stiff fur poked through her pants and scratched her bare calves. But he stayed still. She listed to the side and Arley held out a hand. She used it to lever herself to the center of the giant boar's back.

When Arley let go, Trunk took a few steps and Snowdrop wobbled with each movement. She would never manage to stay on if she sat upright. She leaned forward the way she had to stay on Lady in Woods Rest and her body stabilized. Trunk moved forward. Her instinct was to grab onto his ears but that might hurt him. Instead, she curled her hands over his shoulders, scrunching his thick skin to hang on. He didn't react.

"I think this works. I'd like to try a test run."

She communicated her wish to Trunk. They were surrounded on most sides by the sleeping herd, bachelor boars who traveled together and who'd settled down for their daytime rest. Trunk jogged down a clear path among the bodies. His motion jostled her but not badly. She let go of his skin and instead draped her arms around him and hugged him. At the edge of the herd, he sped up until he galloped between tree trunks, dodging to avoid branches and the occasional boulder. An immense happiness welled up from him—running made him feel powerful and free.

He slowed and stopped. Snowdrop hugged him, gasping. Pig riding wasn't too hard, at least not for the first minute.

Branches rustled behind them and a moment later, Dirt jogged up with Arley sprawled on his back, clinging to the boar.

"Okay?" Snowdrop asked, sitting up.

"Ah, sure. Fine." He wasn't smiling but he'd stayed on his boar, as far as she could tell.

"So we're going to do this?"

"We are." Arley had a bewildered look on his face, as if he couldn't believe what he'd gotten himself into.

"Shout if you need to stop, okay?"

"Okay."

Snowdrop leaned forward again and as she tightened her hold, Trunk took off.

They raced through the forest. It quickly became uncomfortable with the endless jostling, the rubbing of her legs and seat, but they were covering ground much faster than she and Arley ever could on foot. They might catch up with the others . . . assuming they traveled in the right direction. She wasn't sure how the boars were navigating, but they occasionally slowed to sniff the ground and survey the surroundings. That gave her hope they were tracking her brothers. They weren't following a trail she could see.

The forest was open with a cushy layer of pine needles that increased the farther south they went. As the morning grew later, the boars slowed. Light filtered in ahead. They trotted out of the trees and came to the edge of a road. It ran straight with two parallel sandy tracks, east to west.

"This must be the road to Cliffside," Arley said.

"Should we go to the crossroads and try to find a different ride?"

He adjusted his trousers, wincing. "This one is a bit uncomfortable but we're making good time. I can stick with it if you can."

"Yes."

The boars continued across the road and into the trees on the far side. The pine trees grew more and more densely, and they passed a few oaks and other hardwoods. Undergrowth began to fill the ground, although their path stayed clear.

Her stomach growled as the day passed. They'd filled the one canteen at the stream the previous day, so when Trunk finally slowed and the two boars stopped, they had a drink. Trunk grunted and rubbed on the sturdy trunk of the nearest tree, calling Snowdrop's attention.

"Arley." She tapped his arm and pointed. "It's a pecan tree!"

"Thank the skies." Arley scratched behind Dirt's ears. "I can climb up and get some nuts."

"Wait. Let me try something."

Snowdrop sat beside Trunk and closed her eyes. She'd seen a few squirrels overhead, although they'd hidden when the boars neared. She reached out until she caught the chittering thoughts of one. She tried to communicate that they were hungry and asked if it would be all right to have pecans from the tree. The squirrel's thoughts shifted.

Snowdrop glanced up. A small squirrel crept out from behind a branch and peered down at her. Its nose quivered and it surveyed her companions.

She repeated her request. The squirrel darted out and snipped off a pecan with its teeth, and the greenish pod fell to the ground. It moved to another and another. When a few dozen nuts were on the ground, it scampered down the trunk and onto Snowdrop's leg.

"Thank you. I wish I had something to offer you. What's your name?"

The image that came back was hard to interpret—lots of branches and dry leaves swirling. Snowdrop's brow furrowed. She didn't know much about squirrel names, or any creatures' names for that matter. She'd have to guess. "Um, Fall Wind?"

The squirrel beamed. She was small even this close. She crept closer and reached out a paw to Snowdrop's sweater.

"You like my sweater?"

The squirrel rubbed her face against the wool.

"Here." Snowdrop pulled the pocket forward and stretched it out, exposing the threads that secured it to the rest of the sweater. "Bite through there." With the squirrel's help, she removed the pocket. She handed the knitted woolen square to the squirrel, who took it in her mouth and darted up the tree and into the leaves.

Arley gathered the pecans from the ground and they pried the pods off and cracked the shells open using a rock. Arley held a nut out to Dirt, and the boar gingerly took it from his fingers, but the boars wandered away after that. Maybe they thought Snowdrop and Arley needed the sustenance more. Once they'd eaten all the nuts, they stood and stretched, and the boars eagerly returned. They remounted the boars and continued southeast.

They traveled until the light began to fade. They couldn't be more than a day from home at the pace they'd been going. When they had to stop, they made a bed of leaves and fell into it, exhausted and sore. The boars settled down beside them.

Snowdrop resisted the pull of sleep. She focused on the night sounds—the late summer chirps of insects and the hoots of an owl. Were the others still in the forest? She searched for the presence of Lady, the animal she'd be most able to recognize. She caught a hint of the horse's familiar thoughts but couldn't be sure.

They were up at dawn and continued on the trail—the forest had grown dense and she could easily see the path the boars followed. Before the sun had reached its peak they came to the forest road. The boars trotted across the hard dirt, sniffed at the bushes on the far side, and delved into the undergrowth with their riders clinging on.

The forest looked familiar, with trees and bushes Snowdrop had seen her whole life. The ground rose and fell with boulders that the cold winters had driven to the surface over the decades, and with narrow channels where water ran down from the mountains in the spring but that were dry after the hot summer. A few times they had to dismount and scramble across an obstruction, but the boars trod confidently along their path. Once they turned right into a wide, flat depression running uphill with no undergrowth for several minutes before they climbed up the far side and continued southeast.

Snowdrop checked again for Lady's presence and found her. The horse was moving through forest. She was tired and wanted a stable with hay. Her captors smiled and spoke gleefully and it made her apprehensive. Snowdrop's hopes sank. Her brothers must be nearing the enclave.

All they could do was continue following. Larkspur would need time to overcome the magic of the fairy prison, wouldn't she? And her brothers would have to wait for Larkspur to wake if they'd given her moon dust. She and Arley might get a chance to stop them.

Snowdrop tried to find anyone else she could reach—Marshmallow or any of the other birds her brother Dustan had befriended—but she didn't recognize anyone in the mishmash of forest communication.

Trunk picked up his pace and she hung on. What would her brothers do? Go straight to the prison or cause some other trouble? Rose popped into her head and she swallowed with difficulty. Rose was clever but she wasn't a fighter. She wouldn't be able to fend off two large people with daggers. With Dustan away from home, Rose would be an easy target, especially if she had no idea an attack was coming.

They passed a bulging gray beech tree with a dozen trunks and it sparked a memory. She'd seen that tree over the summer when she'd accompanied Dustan on a search for wintergreen for a spell he was working on.

She reached out to Lady again and couldn't find her. Some *other* horse heard her, but not Lady. Snowdrop cursed.

"All right?" Arley called from behind her.

"I called out to Lady. I think she's fallen asleep." And if Lady were asleep, she must have stopped walking. The others must have arrived at the enclave.

The boars raced through the trees, stirring up fall leaves with their pounding hooves. They startled a few deer and a flock of turkeys fled from their path as the trees opened into a small meadow. On and on they went, around a pond Snowdrop recognized and plunging through a shallow creek and up the bank into more forest.

They burst from the trees into the fairies' wide meadow. Goats startled up from their grazing as the boars thundered across the grass toward the far side, where the barn rested between the trees. Two unfamiliar brown horses darted away from the barn door and into the shelter of the edge of the forest. She didn't remember her brothers' stallions looking like those.

Trunk and Dirt carried her and Arley right up to the large open side of the barn. None of the resident fairies' horses were about. They must be with Dustan in Tidal Creek. Where were Lady and Bird? Where were her brothers?

The boars slammed to a halt. Snowdrop practically fell off Trunk's back and stumbled with the effort of standing after the hours of riding. Trunk grunted, urging her to keep going. Arley dismounted beside her.

"Come on," she said. "There's an entrance just outside." She found her legs and lurched through the barn to the side door.

Outside, the enclave looked the same as it had the day she'd left—peaceful gardens surrounded by trees. No one was about though. Not a single gardener. No one walking along the trail into the trees. It was midday—were they hiding? Maybe Larkspur had been awake when she arrived and able to warn everyone. Was someone else trying to stop her brothers?

Snowdrop frowned. She could search for help but that would take time and endanger more fairies. Arley waited on her. What should they do?

"I think we should go to the prison," she said slowly. "If they expect Larkspur to use magic, they'll have to let her be awake. With three of us, we could stop them. As long as Oleander is still contained in her cell."

"I'll follow you."

"This way." She led him toward the trees that encircled the northeast entrance to the caverns, the one she'd walked out of just a quarter-moon ago, before she'd ever met Arley. At the top of the steps, she remembered: Arley was human. All he could see on the ground was grass and rocks. "Close your eyes and give me your hand."

He obeyed and she directed him down into the darkness and through the lower barrier. The familiar, cool air and scent of the caverns enveloped her. She hadn't expected to be back so soon, nor to return under such conditions. Leaving home had felt perilous and now returning felt the same—not that she feared Oleander harming her. But Arley, or Rose, or so many others might not be safe. Her mother was so unpredictable.

Arley's warm hand clung to hers. She squeezed. "You can open your eyes."

He let go as he looked around, taking in the rocky walls and ceiling.

"Try to stay with me—the caverns don't have a plan like human villages." Her voice rang out against the stone walls and she lowered it. "There's only one level but many corridors."

"But you know the way?"

"Yes. Come on." She began a brisk walk along the passage. When they reached the first intersection, she slowed to peek around the corner before continuing. The caverns were as empty and silent as they'd been all summer. After two turns, she scanned the deserted hallway with the entrance to the prison. All was still.

"It's just ahead." She hurried down the last stretch, imagining Beech or Syc appearing from the entrance or worse, Oleander. But nothing changed. She slowed, panting slightly, just beside the doorway to the prison and motioned Arley behind her. She held her breath and listened: silence. She peeked around the corner.

The center space of the prison was empty. Across from her was an empty apartment behind bars, and the bars of two additional living spaces lined the left and right sides. Oleander lived on the left side.

Had her brothers already been here? Had Larkspur opened the door to Oleander's cell? Or were they on the way now and Oleander was still in there?

Where *was* everyone?

Snowdrop took a deep breath and walked in. A figure—figures—sat on the sofa in Oleander's quarters. Edna sat in the middle. Her right arm hugged Nem, and her left arm was around Larkspur, who slumped against her.

Chapter 23

❧✳❧

OLEANDER WAS FREE. SNOWDROP'S CHEST tightened as she approached the bars of the prison cell. "Edna!" she hissed.

Edna and Nem jerked upright and Larkspur's eyelids fluttered.

"What happened? Are you all right?" Snowdrop shook the bars of the door, but it was firmly shut. "I don't understand why it won't open." She knew better than to try to force it. Magic kept it shut, not a metal lock, and it didn't wiggle the slightest bit at her shaking. For some reason, it didn't want to open.

"Larkspur did it," Edna said. "She did something with the magic. She locked us in to keep us safe after those twins made her open the door to let Oleander out."

What in the skies had Larkspur done? She looked unwell—worn out, with her eyes barely open and unable to sit up. She must have drained herself using her magic to open the cell, followed by whatever protection spells she had created.

Nem's face was pale but she seemed uninjured. Had Oleander recognized her? Thank the stars Nem was safe, and Edna too.

"Where's Oleander now?" Snowdrop asked Edna. "Where are my brothers?"

"When she couldn't get at us, they left."

"Did you see which way?"

"No."

Arley stood silently, waiting on her. Snowdrop rubbed at her forehead, picturing the fairies' entire enclave. The caverns had three exits: The one by the barn, but she and Arley had come in that way. The one to the south by the treehouses, on the edge of the gardens. If her brothers wanted to avoid meeting any fairies, though, they would avoid that area, and the barn as well.

The one to the north. That exit was in the woods and was the most secluded. They'd be able to hide their horses among the trees. That must be the way they'd gone. No one would be up there to stop them. Except—

Snowdrop inhaled sharply.

The north exit came out near the forge. Rowan, Jane, and Elle were there with the two dragons. The dragons would keep them safe . . . but what about the dragons themselves?

Dragons had magical power, a life force greater than that of the woodland birds and creatures. If Oleander got ahold of a dragon, she might try to use her magic to take that power. Sucking the life from a dragon was exactly the kind of thing she wouldn't be able to resist. If she sneaked up on them before they could fly away . . .

Snowdrop's heart thudded. She had to go, she had to—

Larkspur stirred and drew in a labored wheeze. Her eyes half-opened. "Let your mother go, Snowdrop," she rasped. "Let her leave."

"But she'll hurt things wherever she goes."

"We'll find her again."

"The dragons are at the forge," Snowdrop said. "What if she sees them?"

Larkspur eyes opened wider and she inhaled, holding her breath.

"Jane and Elle are there. I can't let her see them."

Larkspur exhaled and rested her head back onto Edna's shoulder. Her eyes drifted shut. "If anyone can stop her, you can," she whispered. "And not only because you're her daughter."

"Be careful," Nem whispered. Snowdrop caught her gaze and nodded.

She and Arley left the cells and retreated back to the corridor.

In spite of the cool stone, she felt flushed and shaky as fear for Jane and her family swirled through her veins. Standing still was impossible. She turned left and began to walk toward the northern exit with Arley beside her. As they hurried along, she kept trying and failing to think of any sort of plan. She didn't let herself run. She couldn't be out of breath when she found Oleander.

"You should stay back," she said.

"Not a chance." Arley took her hand.

"When the prison cell opens, Larkspur will need help getting to the healer."

"Then I'll go back to help her when it opens. Which will be . . . ?"

"I have no idea," Snowdrop muttered.

"Other than Jane and the dragons, is anyone in danger?"

"I don't know. Oleander might simply leave. But she might . . ."

"What?"

"She hasn't used magic in many seasons. She couldn't draw life from anything in the prison. I think she'll immediately take the life from something. And once she feels her power again . . ." The dread in her chest surged at the thought. She shook her head. "She can make spells with only a few ingredients. Some take time but others she can do instantly."

"What can her spells do?"

Snowdrop made herself answer. "So many things—put people to sleep indefinitely, make them think they're someone else, stop their sight."

"And the living creature—what could she use?"

"Anything. A tree or one of the horses." She quickened her pace when she thought of Lady.

"Could she use us?"

Snowdrop felt sick, as if worms were crawling through her gut. Oleander had never used another fairy to power her magic, as far as she knew. But she could.

And a human? She'd never had one to use. But she hated the humans.

"Arley." Snowdrop pulled him to a stop, her heart pounding. She had to make him understand the danger. "If you insist on coming, don't let her touch you. If she gets her hands on you . . ." She shook her head.

He squeezed her fingers. "Noted."

They continued and the end of the passage came into sight, with light filtering down the stone steps. Arley faltered. Oh right, she remembered. He saw a dead end. She considered leaving him trapped in the caverns to keep him safe but she couldn't make that decision for him. "Close your eyes."

She led him through the illusion of a dead-end wall into the final stone passageway. She released him and they crept up the steps.

They emerged into the familiar copse of oak trees, the musty sent of autumn on the breeze that stirred her hair. More leaves had turned in the quarter-moon or so since she'd last come out this way, and late afternoon sun shone in from her left. And across the clearing, some ten paces away, stood Oleander.

Snowdrop grabbed Arley's elbow to keep him beside her.

Oleander stood in her brown prison dress with her back against a trunk and her eyes slitted. She had a hand on the bark. Dead leaves drifted down in a continuous stream and settled at her feet in drifts like dirty snow. At least the horses were nowhere in sight—where were they, and her brothers?

Oleander opened her eyes and regarded Snowdrop without speaking. Her gaze flicked over to Arley and back. Oleander was taller than most fairies and her height made her always peer down her nose at others, whether she meant to or not. After so many seasons inside, her skin was pale, and her dark green eyes were hard in her sharp face. Her long dark hair hung limply over her shoulders.

She moved a step out from the tree, letting go of her connection, and relief washed over Snowdrop for the tree, even as she longed to step in front of Arley. But it was safer not to move, not to draw attention to him. Of course Oleander could see him plain as anything but she didn't know he and Snowdrop were involved. Oleander was unpredictable, and guessing what might upset her—and avoiding it—was a long-ingrained habit. And tumbling a human seemed a sure way to trigger her anger.

"Where have you been?" Oleander asked. "You haven't been to visit me in *ages*."

Snowdrop cringed. Oleander was always dramatic. But at least she sounded calm. Better that she be merely pretentious, not pretentious and angry. Maybe she *would* simply leave with Snowdrop's brothers.

Snowdrop inhaled deeply and straightened. "I was on a trip to Mountain Rest with Larkspur until Beech and Syc kidnapped her."

"A trip? You?"

Snowdrop bristled. Yes, her traveling was unusual. But Oleander asked as if she couldn't conceive of it.

"And what did you think of the world outside the forest?" Oleander asked, pursing her lips. Her question was probably a trap. Snowdrop should say she hated it, take her mother's arm, and lead her toward the barn, away from the forge. And Arley could stand still and maybe Oleander would forget she had seen him. Maybe if they found her brothers, Oleander would just *go*.

But distant memories of the wide plains drifted into Snowdrop's mind and she heard her voice say softly, "It was lovely."

Oleander sniffed. She examined a fingernail. "I suppose you hate me for keeping it from you."

"I don't—" Snowdrop's guts churned and she bit off her words. She couldn't say she didn't hate Oleander because it was a lie.

Oleander smirked but something about her eyes didn't fit the rest of her aloof expression. Or maybe Snowdrop imagined the hint of pain now that she knew more of Oleander's past.

"I'm not surprised you hate me," Oleander continued. "I should have let you have more freedom, like your brothers."

"That's not what—" Snowdrop stopped and tried again. "I

wanted that. But that's not why I . . . why I . . ." Telling Oleander flat out that she hated her felt too difficult. She stared at the ground. Arley's muddy shoe was beside her foot and in the moment of silence she heard his breathing. She was grateful he'd stayed quiet so far.

"No matter," Oleander said. "Your brothers freed me." She held out her hand, examining all her fingernails, but Snowdrop wasn't fooled. Feigning indifference was one of Oleander's most common acts. She was about to make a move.

"What are you planning to do?" Snowdrop asked. "I don't want you to hurt anyone."

"Who are you worried about? You don't have any friends. Your traitor of a brother is away, I'm told. Although his little trollop is here . . ."

Snowdrop stepped forward. "Leave her alone."

Oleander sniffed and her gaze darted to Arley, now a long step away from Snowdrop's side. Snowdrop froze. Of course Oleander wouldn't simply leave without asking about him. She still couldn't reach him without getting past Snowdrop and she was several paces away. If she took even a step toward Arley, Snowdrop would intercept her and shove her to the ground.

"Who's this?" Oleander said. "What's a human doing in the forest?" She tilted her head. "He's awfully quiet for a human man. He hasn't interrupted us once. Can't he speak?"

Arley's clothing rustled but before he could answer, Snowdrop said, "Arley was traveling with us. He came with me to rescue Larkspur."

"Larkspur also had a human with her. And a half fairy."

Snowdrop's pulse spiked at the mention of Nem, but Nem was safe below ground.

Oleander's eyes narrowed. "The half fairy was one of mine, wasn't she? They implied my servants died. Tricky liars."

Snowdrop's patience nearly slipped. Keep calm, she told herself. Keep Oleander calm. But the nerve! As if the crime committed had been Larkspur and her helpers lying about the children. She clamped her mouth shut.

"Did any of them truly die?" Oleander asked.

Snowdrop didn't answer. Those children had suffered enough without Oleander going after them now. And Elle was nearby, just through the trees and inside the stone basin at the forge. As if on cue, the ring of Jane's hammer at the forge began.

Oleander tilted her head. "Someone's working late. The sun's almost down."

Snowdrop couldn't think what to say.

"What are they making at the forge?"

"Someone new is learning the process." Snowdrop's eyes dropped. Only for a beat and she forced herself to meet Oleander's stare, but Oleander's eyes narrowed. Snowdrop flushed.

Oleander watched her another few beats and turned to Arley. "Human. Ar-ley." His name was harsh on her tongue. "You accompanied my daughter all this way. You must like her."

Skies, now she was just embarrassing. But Arley stepped up beside Snowdrop. His familiar voice warmed her. "I care about her very much."

"Do you? You may think so. But how long will it last?" She frowned at Snowdrop. "I warned you about humans. They don't know how to love. He will betray you."

Heated anger rushed up Snowdrop's neck. "I know a human hurt you. But that man is not Arley." Oleander's eyes widened. "And maybe your human didn't mean to betray you," she plowed on, suddenly wanting Oleander to see the truth. "Maybe he misunderstood what you wanted. It's no reason to blame all the humans."

Oleander's shock passed and her nostrils flared. Her hands curled into fists. "You don't know what you're talking about—"

"I do!" Snowdrop couldn't help herself. She knew she was angering Oleander but she couldn't keep the words in. "Larkspur told me what happened to you. And you've hated humans ever since. You've let it control your whole life."

Oleander's head jerked up as footsteps rustled in the trees. Beech appeared, leading his stallion, followed by Syc with his own horse. And Lady. And Bird.

Arley started. "Snowdrop," he murmured.

She stepped forward. "You can't take Lady or Bird. You can ride double on one of the stallions."

Oleander frowned but Snowdrop didn't step away. "And you'd rather ride with one of your brothers?" Oleander said.

"Me?"

"You didn't think I'd leave you?" Oleander smiled a poisonously sweet smile.

Dread pooled in Snowdrop's chest.

"Besides," Oleander continued, and her tone had shifted back to her theatrical lilt, with an underlayer of menace. Her brothers' arrival hadn't deflected her anger. "I'm not *taking* anyone. The horse *wants* to come." She turned to Lady and Lady stepped away, but Syc held her lead. "Don't you?" she asked Lady.

Snowdrop's heart hammered but she closed her eyes and breathed slowly. She reached out to Lady. Dark magic swirled around the horse but this time the magic wasn't coming from her. Lady was scared and thought she had to go to Oleander, even though she didn't like how the fairy was ordering her to approach.

It's okay, Snowdrop told her. You don't have to go to her. Pull yourself free and come to me and Arley.

Snowdrop opened her eyes. Lady took a step toward Oleander, jerked her head to yank the lead rope from Syc's hand, and pranced over to Arley's side.

Oleander's nostrils flared again with her loud exhale. "That's enough." She strode forward and grabbed Snowdrop's wrist, twisting, and pulled her across the clearing.

Snowdrop struggled but she was too late. As Beech and Syc moved, she yanked and clawed at the fingers around her, crying out like a trapped animal. Arley should be fleeing but he was trying to push through her brothers to reach her. He slammed Syc aside but Beech caught him around the neck and Syc recovered. Her vision blurred and fear closed in as Arley struggled.

Oleander screeched and shook her silent. Arley went still, panting, his eyes focused on hers.

In the sudden stillness, Lady dropped her head and stepped once, twice, around the men to Oleander. Oleander took a fistful of her mane.

"Incapacitate him," Oleander said, "and follow us to the barn. We'll leave from there."

Arley heaved his body against Beech, then Syc, shouting Snowdrop's name as he resumed his struggle, and Snowdrop pulled back toward him. Oleander's grip tightened and Lady whinnied a pitiful whimpering sound. Snowdrop froze. Where Oleander held her, her wrist was cold, and a force touched her beyond the press of Oleander's fingers. As if Oleander's magic were in her fingertips and waiting to leach power from her, held in check for the moment.

"Come quietly or the horse will suffer," Oleander said and dragged her down the track into the trees. Behind them, her brothers laughed.

Snowdrop tripped over roots as she stumbled after Oleander on the narrow track. She had to help Arley—but how? Could she use her magic? If she could focus, she might be able to ask the birds in the trees to swoop down and peck at her brothers. But her skills weren't that advanced.

She could use the other kind of magic. It came so easily to her. She didn't even need to touch another living thing to take power from it. But what could she *do* with that kind of magic? She'd never wanted to use it, once she understood how it worked, so she'd never advanced in her ability to use the magic for anything practical.

Unless she used the magic itself as a weapon. Oleander was

holding her wrist. She could drain power from Oleander. And Oleander could do the same to her. Who would be stronger?

But the thought of using dark magic against any creature, especially another fairy, made her feel sick.

"You're better off without him," Oleander said.

Oleander was talking. Maybe Snowdrop could reason with her. She would do anything to protect Arley. "I'll leave him if you stop Beech and Syc."

Oleander's pace faltered. She shook her head and dragged Snowdrop and Lady on. "They won't kill him. I said 'incapacitate.'"

"They'll beat him." Her voice cracked.

"He'll live."

"You're wrong about humans," Snowdrop pressed on. What could she say to make Oleander stop and go back? "Fairies visit the village all the time now. Some have bonded with humans."

"Your youngest brother is an aberration. He's been warped by that mate of his. And she's only half human."

"It's not only Dustan. Larch's friend Rowan loves a human and she's devoted to—"

Oleander stopped, pulling Snowdrop against her. Dread flowed into Snowdrop's chest. What had she done?

"Rowan," Oleander whispered, eyes staring ahead at the forest, but unseeing.

Snowdrop shrank beside her. She should have gone quietly—now she'd made everything worse. If Oleander connected Rowan with dragons, if she suspected what was happening at the forge . . .

Maybe Snowdrop couldn't help Arley. But if she could keep Oleander walking away from the forge and toward the barn, they could leave the enclave before Oleander hurt anyone else—before she learned about the dragons. The fairies would help Arley. He would recover. And she'd figure something out once they were away. She'd send a message to Larkspur and ask her advice and make a plan—

"Where is Rowan?" Oleander asked quietly.

Snowdrop grasped about for a half-truth she could use to mislead Oleander. "They live in Woods Rest."

"And what does he do among the humans to pay his way?" Her voice was so quiet it barely sounded above the rustling leaves overhead, like the ominous hush before a violent storm.

"He was working as a blacksmith," Snowdrop said, trying to speak normally.

Oleander's brow lifted. "A blacksmith? Rowan?"

"Why is that a surprise?"

"I've known Rowan since he was a boy. He hates fire."

What did Oleander know about Rowan? Snowdrop didn't trust herself to speak.

Oleander shook her. "Don't trick me. Where is Rowan *right now*?"

Snowdrop tried to lie. She'd never done it before. Her insides squirmed and her face contorted. "I don't know," she gasped out.

Oleander closed her eyes, shaking her head. "Where is he right now?" she repeated softly, and Lady began to whimper again.

Snowdrop couldn't bear to have Lady suffer. "He's working at the forge." Tears escaped her eyes. No matter what she did, someone would get hurt—Lady or Arley or Jane's family at the forge. But Lady was the most defenseless.

"I knew it," Oleander said, breathless. "I knew something powerful was nearby. He's working with a dragon, isn't he?"

Snowdrop didn't answer but Oleander's eyes were glassy, as if she'd forgotten she was dragging Snowdrop and Lady through the forest. She turned off the track and pulled them in among the trees, striding forward as Snowdrop scurried to keep up.

"A dragon," Oleander murmured. The distant clink of a hammer on iron sounded again. If Jane was still at work, Elle and Rowan must be, too. All of them were at the forge. What was Oleander planning to do? Would the dragons be able to stop her or protect their charges? If Oleander planned to use Snowdrop and Lady as hostages, the dragons likely wouldn't care—they would escape.

But if Elle saw Oleander, she'd be terrified. She'd been free of Oleander only a few seasons. After Snowdrop had avoided the forge all summer, little Elle would see Snowdrop *and* Oleander and remember her seasons in captivity.

The trees broke for a wide surface of exposed bedrock, worn smooth over time. The low sun shone brightly at the treetops, staining the rocks orange with its late-day light. The hammer rang more clearly from the other side of a rocky wall ahead, occasionally pausing before resuming. And another sound reached them, a roar like a tree on fire, building and snuffing out. Elle's childish voice babbled and the roar came again. A dragon exhaling fire.

The courtyard with the forge was encircled by rocky outcrops and boulders, with an entrance at the south side and another at the north. Elle's voice echoed inside. Oleander pulled them toward the south entrance across the slanting rock. Snowdrop's feet slipped on soft moss and pebbles stung her bare soles. Lady's hooves clopped unevenly and her eyes were wide and frightened with the uneven footing. A tall boulder marked the entrance to the forge.

Snowdrop hated Oleander's magic. She hated that she'd learned to use it, sucking the life from plants and trees. She'd vowed never to use it again, hoping she could regain the trust of the other fairies if she went long enough without causing harm.

But if using dark magic was the only way to stop Oleander from showing herself to Jane and Elle, from causing more harm to the child, from possibly getting her hands on a dragon and the immense power one could give her . . . let the fairies hate her. Let them shun her or banish her from their community. Stopping Oleander was the right thing to do however she made it happen.

Oleander was used to everyone obeying her without question. She was used to Snowdrop obeying her. But that time was over.

Snowdrop found Lady's frantic mind. In a moment, she thought to Lady, you will run. She sent calm, loving thoughts to the horse she'd traveled with. She would give Lady a chance to escape, too.

Snowdrop twisted her arm, brought her fingers up and over Oleander's wrist, and grabbed on. She clung like a viper and summoned the darkness she'd kept in check for thirteen winters. She felt Lady's fear and Oleander's triumphant confidence and the moss cowering under her toes. The sway of the nearest trees. And distantly, the powerful attention of the two dragons beyond the stone barrier. They had noticed something was coming. She let go of thoughts of Lady and the moss and the trees, and focused on her grip on Oleander. And she pulled into herself.

Oleander cried out, letting go of her own grip on Snowdrop. Her fist on Lady opened and the horse bolted before Snowdrop had finished shouting "Run!" Oleander struggled against Snowdrop's fingers, her eyes wide, but Snowdrop held tight and pulled with her magic as Oleander's skin drained of blood. Magic like sparks tingled into her hand, a heady sense of magical ability, extreme control, abundant energy, the very meaning of power. Oleander's eyes bugged out, but Snowdrop felt no sense of any pain.

"Run!" she shouted again, this time toward the entrance to the forge.

Metal clanged from beyond the rocks and a woosh of air sounded as a dragon rose over the wall—the bright green scales of the dragon Sunshine, with the child held safe in her claws. Sunshine's wings beat the air and lifted her clear of the walls of the forge. She turned toward the sky and soared away even as the other dragon rose up carrying two figures wrapped in its talons and following Sunshine. The dragons disappeared over the trees.

Everyone was safe. Snowdrop's grip loosened as she turned away from the sky.

Oleander yanked her arm free. She staggered back a step and sucked in a breath, straightening to her full height. Her brow lowered, like roiling storm clouds, and lightning flashed in her eyes.

"How dare you," Oleander snarled. "You're supposed to be my daughter, loyal to me."

"And you're supposed to be my mother." Snowdrop lifted her chin and stepped closer. "Go ahead," she said. "The only one left for you to hurt is me."

Oleander's fingers slid around Snowdrop's neck, icy and smooth, her nails like a hawk's talons on a mouse. She clamped her hands shut and Snowdrop struggled to draw breath as her arms and legs went weak. Her head spun, the orange sunlight and rocks tilting and fading as darkness descended. Was it her vision, or was Oleander blacking out the sky? Pain lanced through her head. Someone was screaming.

She was screaming.

She stopped herself and through the stabbing in her mind, she trained her gaze into Oleander's eyes. She saw a monster. But Oleander had been young once. She hadn't started out this way. She'd been lonely and hurt. Snowdrop tried to see all of her, the past experiences that had turned her into the horrible fairy she'd become. Oleander flinched and her fingers loosened.

A figure flashed out from the tree line and staggered toward them, and Oleander jerked away in surprise. Through her haze, Snowdrop saw brown curls matted with blood, a torn shirt, familiar hands. How had Arley gotten away from her brothers?

Arley shoved at the tall fairy, and she stumbled backward, her hands wrenched away from Snowdrop. Oleander stared at him in disbelief. Snowdrop sagged into his arms as he dragged her away from Oleander and toward the trees. Her vision began clearing now that her mother's magic was gone but her limbs wouldn't work and the pain in her head was like an explosion. Arley stumbled and halfway dropped her onto a bed of moss, collapsing beside her and panting.

Oleander stood across the rocky ground, leaning forward and coughing with her hands on her knees. Black fog swirled about her. Snowdrop's head pounded. The fog faded, pierced by orange sunlight into a murky veil.

Oleander straightened and turned. Her face was in shadow as she glared down at them. Snowdrop tried to sit up but her arms were too weak to support her.

"Why did you follow us, human?" Oleander growled. "Didn't you get enough of a beating from my sons?"

Behind her, Arley's jagged breathing hitched as if he tried to speak and couldn't.

"You shouldn't have interfered."

"Mother," Snowdrop rasped, and Oleander turned to her.

"Is this what it takes to win your love?" Oleander asked, gesturing at Arley. "Letting you make the same mistakes I made, now that you're old enough?"

Snowdrop tried to shake her head and the pain spiked. "You didn't have to win my love," she murmured. "I loved you. I just wanted you to stop hurting things."

Oleander's gaze pierced into her.

Snowdrop winced with the effort of speaking. "It's not too late."

Oleander laughed, short and harsh. "Not too late for what?"

Snowdrop gasped in another breath. "Not too late to change."

Oleander shook her head and stepped forward, and Arley pushed himself up, groaning. He leaned forward over Snowdrop's body, shaking, as if to shield her from Oleander.

Oleander stopped a pace away and studied him. "Let me have my daughter and I'll leave you alone," she said calmly.

Arley only leaned farther, crouching low as his body pressed onto hers. The moment stretched on with Oleander frozen above them. Arley's arm shook and tremors ran through him with each breath but he didn't move.

"Let her go," Oleander said. "I won't hurt her. I'll heal her."

He swallowed.

"I could kill you in a heartbeat."

He didn't budge.

Oleander exhaled, long and resigned. She came near and knelt beside them, reaching out with both hands. Arley feebly tried to block her but she caught his arm.

"Quiet, human," she said. "Let me help."

Her fingers found Snowdrop's arm and a soothing warmth flowed from her. Snowdrop's fingertips tingled and she twitched them as movement returned.

Snowdrop's vision cleared and her legs and toes lost their numbness. The fog in the air evaporated to reveal a bright pink sunset sky over the rocks and trees. The pain faded from her head. Oleander watched her face and when Snowdrop blinked and met her gaze, Oleander let go of her arm and focused on Arley. Oleander had Arley by the wrist.

"Mother . . ."

"Hush," Oleander said. "I will not hurt him. Given a chance, maybe he will love you longer than mine loved me."

Snowdrop sank into the moss. The worst effects of Oleander's magic had faded, as if she had reversed her magic somehow, giving instead of taking. Instead of sucking the life from Snowdrop, she had healed her, even as she was now healing Arley. How could she do that?

Arley shifted beside Snowdrop and sighed in relief.

"Thank you," Snowdrop whispered. "I'm sorry your human hurt you."

Overhead, Oleander's arm still reached across her to Arley. "I'm more sorry that I lost your love," Oleander said, and her voice was weak.

As if the healing process were weakening her. Oleander's magic took the life from other living things to power her spells. If she were using her magic to heal others, she must be using her own resources. Her own life.

"Mother . . . ?"

Oleander met her eyes briefly and nodded. And she slumped to the ground. Snowdrop's eyes drifted closed.

Chapter 24

⁕

OICES DRIFTED INTO SNOWDROP'S CONSCIOUSNESS. She was lying somewhere comfortable, in soft pajamas and covered with a soft woven sheet under a warm blanket. Muted daylight filled the room. She blinked her eyes open.

Through a doorway stood Rose, talking with someone slight with white hair—Thistle, the fairies' most experienced healer.

A breeze stirred Rose's hair. She was out on a porch and this was a treehouse. The room was small. This must be one of the fairies' simple guesthouses. It had a lone window beside the door with a wash basin under it, and the rest of the space was filled by the mattress, which was wide enough for her and the person lying beside her, a lump under the sheet. Arley's curly hair poked out the top on the pillow. He breathed steadily with the slightest snore. He must be all right or Thistle wouldn't leave him here. What had happened to him?

Outside, Thistle departed and Rose turned toward the doorway. Her eyes met Snowdrop's. She came forward quietly and knelt beside the mattress.

"Larkspur?" Snowdrop whispered.

"She's fine. They're all fine."

"How did you get them out?"

"Apparently the cell door opened on its own."

Snowdrop's brow crinkled. "I wonder why . . ."

Rose sat back on her heels and her voice quieted. "It opened when it was safe for them to come out. Because . . ."

"Because Oleander died." The words felt strange on Snowdrop's tongue.

Did she feel anything inside? After all the harm Oleander had caused in the world, Snowdrop had long thought the world was better with her locked away. She hadn't been a very good mother. Snowdrop hadn't depended on her for affection or guidance or resources. She'd hated visiting her in the prison. Losing Oleander shouldn't be that much different than when she was living in prison the past turn of the seasons, should it?

But as long as Oleander had been alive, a sliver of hope had remained that she might change. And she had changed—she'd died to help Snowdrop and Arley. Although they'd only needed help in the first place because of Oleander's actions. But still, her final act had been one of kindness, and that made Snowdrop sadder than anything. Sad that Oleander had gone down such a bleak path in life, that she hadn't had anyone to guide her, and that she hadn't found it in herself to change until almost her very last breath.

Rose's big green eyes watched Snowdrop. "I don't know if I'm supposed to feel sad she's dead," Snowdrop said slowly. "I have a weird feeling. I don't know what it is. Maybe relief."

"Do you want to talk about how she died?" Rose asked gently.

Snowdrop shook her head. She would tell Rose and Dustan eventually. She wanted them to know Oleander had done something right, something good, for once. But she wanted to consider it more. For now, she felt relieved knowing Oleander wouldn't hurt anyone again. But—

"What about my brothers?" Snowdrop gasped. "Beech and Syc? They beat Arley. And, and they were waiting by the barn, but Oleander was distracted by the dragons."

"I wondered how you ended up at the forge," Rose said. "Unfortunately your oldest brothers must have realized their plan had gone awry. They disappeared with their horses, but Aster and her team are tracking them. Once Dustan and Larch get back, we can decide what to do about them."

"And Nem and Edna? They're okay?"

Rose smiled. "Nem came out of the caverns once the prison opened. She remembered the way to the clearing, and when Marshmallow alerted me, I went down to see her. We had to carry Larkspur out, but she'll be fine. She was drained from the magic she had to perform."

"What did she do to open the prison? I didn't think it was possible to trick it."

"Neither did I. Your brothers threatened to hurt Edna and Nem if she couldn't do it, though. She had to lie to it, a really big lie, telling it Oleander was no longer a threat. And you know how hard lying is on a fairy."

"How did she get the door to shut and protect them from Oleander?"

"Apparently the magic used to create the prison came from swallowtail butterfly cocoons. The cocoon keeps the caterpillar contained until it has changed into a butterfly, so whoever built the prison used the empty cocoons to create cells that keep their occupants contained until they've changed into a better person."

"I never knew that."

"I don't think anyone did. Larkspur figured it out."

Larkspur must truly be okay if she was already discussing the workings of magic with Rose.

"Larkspur knew they'd be in danger once Oleander was free," Rose continued. "So she used the magic from the cocoons and formed it into something new. Cocoons also protect the caterpillar, so she re-formed that cell's magic into a protection spell. As Oleander came out, Larkspur pushed Edna and Nem into the cell and pulled the door shut behind her, and the door locked again. Oleander couldn't open it to reach them."

"Wow." Snowdrop had never heard of magic that complex.

"Anyway, Thistle took care of Larkspur. She's weak but she'll be fine. And the others were unharmed, just frightened. Well, your friend Edna might have been more indignant than frightened, but she's okay is the point."

"Nem was the oldest of Oleander's servants. She was rescued before you came. I didn't want her to have to see this place."

"She told me her history. She wanted to stay to see you but she was anxious about visiting her brother in Mountain Rest and letting her family know she's all right. She and Edna departed at sunrise."

"Oh!" Snowdrop sat up. "What about Lady and Bird? My brothers had Bird, and Lady ran from Oleander."

"They were in the barn. Lady must've found her way back. Clover brushed them and got them oats and apples last night. They were the only manageable horses we had, so Clover hitched them to a wagon this morning to take the ladies back to Woods Rest, and Edna said she'd get them back to their owner."

"We left the wagon from Woods Rest all the way at the edge of the hills," Snowdrop lamented. "I hope Arley doesn't get in trouble for losing it."

"I'm sure it will be fine. You rest now."

"Wait. What about the boars? Was there a pair of boars in the meadow?"

"Oh, yes. They asked about you."

"They carried us all the way here from north of the crossroads. We'd never have made it without them."

"Clover said they were lying in the barn with the horses, and they asked if you were all right. They wanted to get back to their herd. Clover gave them apples, too, before they left."

"I hope I can find them someday to thank them."

Something clattered outside and Rose glanced over. "I had food brought. I'll bring it in." She stood and retrieved a tray from outside the door. Snowdrop scooched back and leaned on the wall.

Rose set the tray on the floor beside the bed. It had a covered tureen, bowls, and spoons, along with bread and a steaming mug.

Rose pointed at the mug. "It's bitter tea. I wasn't sure if you'd want it but just in case."

"Oh." Snowdrop wasn't sure if Rose bringing the tea was more embarrassing or thoughtful. "I, um, I'm not sure either."

Of course it was thoughtful of Rose. But she didn't need Rose poking into her business and gossiping with Jane about it. Or worse, with her brother. She didn't need Rose striking up a conversation about her use of bitter tea. "I mean, thanks, that's fine, you can leave it, I might have some."

"And here's some other things you might need," Rose said, placing down a satchel. "Toiletries and things. You know, like toothpaste. And the wash basin is filled." Rose was blushing. But toothpaste wasn't embarrassing . . . ?

"So," Rose concluded, "if you wanted to freshen up, you could. Um, is there anything else you need?"

"You can go," Snowdrop squeaked. "Thank you."

Her brother's mate dipped her chin once, and as she turned away her face broke into a smile. She hustled out of the room and closed the door behind her.

Snowdrop waited until the creaking of the porch stopped. Rose had either gone down the ladder or climbed down the tree. Cautiously, she reached for the satchel. She opened the top and peeked inside.

Toothbrushes. A packet of toothpaste and another of soap. And a pot of—

"Whatcha got in there?"

Snowdrop jolted.

"Sorry, love." Arley leaned up behind her. "I thought you'd heard me."

She turned toward him. In the morning light coming through the leaves outside, his clear brown eyes were bright and wide open. Someone must've washed his face because the dirt and grime of the road and sleeping on the ground were gone. She herself felt far cleaner than she should have after their trek through the forest.

"How long have you been awake?"

"Since around the part about Oleander passing. Are you all right, princess?"

"I think so. Why did you pretend to be asleep?"

"I was kind of panickin' about being in the same room as Rose. And in my PJs. Or someone's PJs." He examined his blue top. It matched hers.

"Panicking over *Rose*?" Snowdrop asked. "Why?"

"She's a celebrity! She was the royal princess for nineteen winters. I wasn't sure if I'm supposed to kiss the hem of her dress or whatnot."

Snowdrop rolled her eyes. "Skies. That would be a weird thing to do."

"See?"

"She's just a person."

"Says the daughter of a former queen."

Snowdrop humphed.

"Speakin' of weird, I feel weird," Arley said.

"Weird how?"

"I was all beat up. I could barely walk they pummeled me so bad. And now I'm sort of sore but I'm all full of energy or somethin'."

"Do you remember what Oleander did?" Snowdrop asked, and her voice wobbled.

Arley nudged his hand close to hers on top of the blanket and she took it. They sat side by side, and he pulled their pillows up to cushion them as they leaned back. "After your brothers finished with me, they dropped me on the ground and left. I didn't think I could move. But I heard you shoutin' so I dragged myself up to find you. She had her hands on your neck when I got to you. She was hurting you."

"She got angry. And she used her magic against me. I don't think she meant to—she was out of control. I thought she'd kill me. And then you came."

"I got you away but I was too weak to carry you. And she came toward us. It's fuzzy. Did you fight back?"

"I could barely move. But I didn't have to fight. She . . . I think she used her magic in reverse somehow. I think she used it to heal the harm she had caused. But she drained her own life to do it."

"Why would she do that?"

Snowdrop paused. Who knew why Oleander did anything. But the expression on her face when Arley appeared by the forge . . . "I think she saw you cared for me. You came after me even though you were hurt. I think she realized you weren't like the human who hurt her all those winters ago. I think she was sorry."

Arley rubbed her hand and leaned his shoulder against hers and they sat in silence for a moment.

"So what's in the satchel that's got you all secretive?"

"I'm not secretive." Snowdrop studied the floorboards. "It's toothpaste and things, but Rose acted funny when she gave it to me."

"And you're bein' funny now. It's just toothpaste?"

"There's something else."

Snowdrop reached in and withdrew the lidded pottery dish. She leaned back against the wall and Arley leaned beside her, watching. She opened it.

He snickered. "Is that—"

"Yes."

"In case we—"

"Yes."

"Aww, princess, ya know we don't have to."

"I know. It's just embarrassing that my brother's annoying mate knows we're tumbling! And assumes we're doing it the way she does and would need this. Why does everyone assume everyone else is doing it too?"

"People have no imagination, that's all. So how do the fairies make their, ah, sex goo?"

"Sex goo? Is that what humans call lubricant?"

"No, we call it lubricant. But ours is kind of oily. That stuff looks . . ." He swallowed. "Rather nice."

"The fairies make it with this cactus plant from the north. We can grow it in pots if we keep it out of the cold. The goop is useful on burns, too."

"What's it called?"

"Aloe."

"How do they get it all gooey like that?"

"It comes out of the plant that way."

"No kidding." He studied the pot of goo. "They don't use magic or anything?"

"Sometimes. But Rose wouldn't have brought one of those without warning me."

"Wait a minute. The fairies have magical lubricant?"

Snowdrop couldn't help grinning at him.

"What does it do?"

She shrugged as she placed the jar on the floor.

"Come *on*, princess, ya can't tease me like this."

"If you stick around, maybe I'll get you some."

"If I *stick around*?" Arley reached for her, catching her sides with his warm hands. She hesitated but his hands felt nice and she leaned in to his touch.

His fingers twitched, tickling her.

She shrieked, pulling away, but he held on, tickling her down onto the mattress.

"Come on," he said as she laughed and pushed futilely at his hands. "Tell me."

"Okay," she said. "Stop."

He let go and flopped onto the mattress beside her, leaning on his elbow.

"Um, there was one that glowed in the dark."

Arley cringed. "What's the point of that?"

"You're asking me?"

"I guess if you're at some after-dark orgy it might be fun?"

Snowdrop squinted up at him.

"Right. I've never been to one of those either. How do they make things glow in the dark?"

"Sometimes sun magic. Usually fireflies."

"The fairies kill fireflies to make glow-in-the-dark lubricant?"

"They don't *kill* them. Of course not. They . . . have them fly around or something? I don't know exactly."

"Well I can skip that one."

"Okay." Snowdrop fingered the hem of the sheet. It was smooth white linen.

"Do ya want me to stick around?" Arley asked cautiously.

"Do you want to?"

"I'd like to. If ya want me to."

"I do."

He leaned in and kissed her bare arm below her sleeve. "Then I will."

Silence settled around them. The forest sounds were muted. "What do you want to do right now?" she asked. "Do you feel well enough to get up?"

"I do." He leaned in and lowered his voice. "But I really want to smear that cactus goo on ya."

She grinned. "Where?"

"Anywhere you'll let me."

"Okay." She straightened on the mattress, resting her arms by her sides, and closed her eyes.

"'Okay'? Just like that?"

She nodded. Giving him free rein to touch her was a risk. But it was Arley. When had he ever done anything to make her uncomfortable? And if he ever did, he wouldn't mind if she stopped him.

"Are these pajamas meant to indicate places I *shouldn't* put it?"

She wiggled out of her top and tossed it off the mattress, pushed the shorts down, and kicked them to the bottom of the bed along with the covers. The room was surprisingly warm for morning. She couldn't resist a peek at Arley. He was staring at her breasts with his jaw hanging open and longing in his eyes.

She closed her eyes again. "Better?"

"Much better." His voice was breathy. The mattress dipped as he leaned over her and the pot of aloe clinked. He sat back.

His fingers brushed her left breast, the pads of them rough but leaving a silky dab of aloe at the center. A moment later his thumb slid over her other breast. In the warm room, she could barely feel the substance on her. He shifted again and a breeze hit her, cooling the one wet spot. Her nipple tightened and ached. He repeated it on her other side, blowing across her skin. She could imagine him smirking at her body's reaction.

"All right, love?"

"Yes." Now she was the one panting out her words.

A cool finger landed at the top of her belly and painted a line down her center, over the divot of her bellybutton and down the slope of her body until it ran out of paint. Another line followed from her left hip and along the crease of her leg, and a third line from the right.

"I see where this is heading," she whispered.

"That be all right?"

She hesitated only a beat of her jittery heart and nodded.

His body moved in alongside hers, hotter than the air in the room. He kissed her temple and his bicep nestled against the top of her head, pillowing her. The pads of his fingers smoothed over her between her legs, wet and soft, and settled on her. He gave a tentative rub. It was about the spot where she'd have done it, if she were wanting to work herself up to a release.

"This okay?"

"Mm-hm."

He circled again, settling into a slow rhythm. The touching was . . . fine. Having someone else touching her was strange.

"Will you be disappointed if it doesn't work?" she murmured.

"It's workin' pretty well for me." He nudged against her hip with a hard lump in his shorts.

She smiled. "Can you keep it up? The way you're doing, slow and steady. I want to try to stop thinking so much."

"I can keep it up *all morning*," he replied.

"Will you blow on me again?"

In answer, a cool breeze drifted across her chest and her breasts again responded. She reached for them, working the sensation, rubbing her nipples under the drying stickiness of the aloe and pinching each between her thumb and finger. The ache came between her legs as it usually did, only this time, she didn't need to let go of her breasts to attend to it.

She pressed up against Arley's fingers. "More."

He pushed harder, rubbing deeper against her. She opened her legs for him.

"Ya want it there?"

"Yes."

His touch left her for a moment and returned, bringing a dollop of coolness that he quickly warmed with his fingers, spreading it over her and down between her legs. He'd used enough to slather his whole hand with it. She wanted pressure on her front again. She wanted it everywhere.

She reached down and trapped his hand in hers, holding the knuckle of his thumb against the place he'd first touched her and rubbing herself against him. His wet fingers slipped in and out of her skin. She pushed them against her, losing control as she rutted against his hand, thrusting with her whole body. She whimpered out a cry as she came.

She clung to his hand, keeping it against her as the aftershocks passed. She squeezed it between her thighs. Her panting slowed. She had to give his hand back but she didn't want to. Skies, what if she'd twisted his arm?

"Is your hand okay?" she whispered. She loosened her legs and patted his wrist.

Arley nuzzled her ear. "My hand is the luckiest hand in the world right now," he murmured.

"I didn't hurt you?"

"I long for the day when you grind on me hard enough to injure me."

She smiled and tucked her chin down, opening her eyes. Sunlight had found the window and lit a patch on her bare stomach. Arley's shorts pressed against her hip, his erection poking out above her.

"I made a bit of a mess on ya," Arley said. He swiped one of his fingers a smidge in all the aloe goo between her legs.

"Be a waste not to use it."

"Oh, are ya ready for another round?"

She turned her face to his. His warm eyes twinkled in the morning light.

"I meant we could try, um, you know, putting you in me."

His breath caught. "You want that?"

She wanted his weight pressing on her and to watch his face as he found pleasure in her body. "I want to try."

"What about bitter tea?"

"Rose brought some. I'll drink all of it."

"Uh, how do ya want to do this? What would be comfortable?"

"Um, I thought you could lie on top of me." She reached for his shoulder and tugged him forward. He whisked off his pajama top and shorts and rolled onto her. She spread her legs wider to fit his hips.

He leaned on his elbows above her. "Like this?"

She nodded as her fingertips skimmed his ribs. "Just don't forget I'm here."

He gazed into her eyes. "How do ya mean?"

"Before when I did this, I hated feeling like . . . like I was just a body underneath him."

Arley's hands came in to cradle her head. His thumbs brushed her hair to the side and he kissed the tip of her nose. "You want me to look at you like this?"

She smiled.

"Want me to say dirty things to ya?"

"Like what?"

He adopted his falsetto. "Oh baby, you're as tight as a cantaloupe!"

She laughed. He was always making her laugh right when she needed it, right when she might start to get nervous. "I'm starting to worry about the young people in Woods End," she said. "And about the produce."

He grinned.

"You can say things," she said.

His thumbs stroked her cheeks as he gazed down at her, his grin fading. He hesitated, his lips parted, and ran his thumbs along her cheekbones again.

"I think I love you, Snowdrop."

Tears pricked her eyes. "You do?" she whispered.

"I think so," he whispered back.

Someone loved her. *Arley* loved her. Nothing had ever meant so much to her.

She smoothed her hands around his sides and nudged him down onto her. His erection bumped against her thigh, and she shifted her hips to line it up with her body.

"Try lifting your knees," he said.

She did it and he fit into the space. His erection pushed against the wetness of her body but slid up and over her.

"A lady once told me it was more comfortable with her knees up."

"I think it is."

"I should prob'ly not talk about other ladies."

"I don't care as long as they're not here anymore. Are you nervous?" she asked.

"A little."

"Go on. I'm ready."

He took one hand off her head and reached down, guiding himself into her as he leaned on one elbow. With all the lubricant he'd smeared on her, his shaft slid right in. He gasped and turned away. His hand found the back of her thigh, stroking up from her bottom and holding her leg up. He pulled out and slowly pushed in again.

His thumb brushed her forehead and he turned back to face her. "Okay?"

"Yes. I like having you there."

He began to move, gently thrusting out and in. "Still okay?"

"Yes."

"You want me to touch ya or anything?"

Snowdrop smiled. He could do both at once? But she shook her head. "I just want to feel what you're doing now."

His eyes closed and sweat sheened his forehead. As he kept going, his breathing changed as if he were losing control, but his pace stayed steady. His fingers stroked her hair and his hand on her thigh squeezed, and every few heartbeats he opened his eyes and forced a smile between his panting, watching her until she nodded.

He shook slightly, the barest tremor in his hand on her head. She pulled his body closer until his elbow slid away and his chest covered hers with all his weight, and their cheeks met. Now when he thrust into her, his body pressed her into the mattress. She had to suck in her breaths but she could handle the weight. She liked the sounds he was making, the barest moan, broken each time he pulled back.

"Ya feel so good," he whispered in her ear. And then, "Can I go a little faster?"

"Yes."

His fingers tightened in her hair, reminding her he knew she was there. His thrusting accelerated so she dug her fingernails into his back and held on, tilting her hips even farther and letting him rock into her until he gasped and jerked in her arms.

As he stilled, he panted and kissed her temple before sinking down on her.

"Am I squashin' ya?" he whispered.

"I like it." She wrapped her legs around him and held him against her with her legs and her arms.

"You want me to—"

"Shh. Just stay there."

She hugged him tight, feeling his shaft still inside her and all the places their bodies stuck together. He wanted to stay with her. And he wanted her the way she was. He *loved* her, the way she was. Tears leaked from her eyes.

Hours later, after they'd untangled themselves and eaten the lukewarm soup and Arley had drifted off to sleep again, she had the last sip of bitter tea and nudged him awake.

"I can't stop thinking about the meeting," she said.

"The meeting?"

"The Council of Villages meeting. I've been counting. It's supposed to start in two days."

"Rose said Edna returned to Woods Rest," Arley said. "Do you think she planned to continue on to Mountain Rest?"

"I don't know. I bet after being kidnapped she just wants to go home to Ruth. And I got the sense Larkspur needs time to heal."

Arley rubbed his face awake. "Ya want to go find out what's happenin'?" She nodded.

They washed up and pulled their clothes on. Arley squinted out the window, where green and orange leaves flittered in the breeze.

"Are we in a tree?"

"Yes." She tilted her head. "Didn't you know?"

He peered out the window. "I heard the fairies had treehouses. I didn't realize it meant . . . this. How did we get up here?"

"Good question. Come on."

She led him out the door onto the small porch and showed him the ladder. "That's the usual way up but . . . oh, here." She pointed. "It's a platform for bringing things up. Some of the treehouses have them."

"They lifted me up here on that?"

"Apparently."

"Let's take the ladder down."

As Snowdrop descended, she surveyed the forest and experienced the enclave as Arley might for the first time: glimpses of other treehouses through the autumn leaves, the quiet murmurs of conversations, and the birds and squirrels using the trees with no fear of the fairies. Children darted along the trail as she neared the bottom and they slowed and smiled at her before hurrying on.

Once on the ground, Snowdrop led Arley toward her brother and Rose's home. The enclave was strangely quiet although a crew was out in the sunny gardens. Arley scanned all around. Marshmallow swooped by, and by the time they neared Dustan and Rose's tree, Rose was dropping to the ground at the base. Arley stepped halfway behind Snowdrop and didn't say a word.

Rose confirmed that neither Larkspur nor Edna would be attending the council meeting. Larkspur was sleeping and Thistle didn't want her disturbed. "Dustan's two days south of here," Rose added. "He'd never get to Mountain Rest in time, even if Redbud ran without stopping. It's the first ever meeting. I hate that neither of our villages will be represented."

Snowdrop licked her lips. "What if we went?"

Rose brightened. As if Snowdrop going was no big deal. "Would you?"

"We could."

Rose frowned. "How will you get there?"

"Aren't there any horses in the stable at all?"

"None that anyone can ride. Two wild horses came into the meadow a few days ago—just in time for the end of the apple harvest, which might not be a coincidence. They've been hanging around and begging Clover for handouts."

Snowdrop remembered their arrival and the brown horses she'd seen in the meadow. "Maybe I could ask them."

Rose lit up at that but she bit off her words—words that were sure to be her gushing over Snowdrop using magic. "That reminds me," Rose said. "There's one more thing." She pulled a bag from her pocket. "Oleander had these."

Rose handed her the sack of snowdrop bulbs. Snowdrop clutched them to her chest as their magic twined around her like a hug.

"Thank you, Rose."

"If you leave, send a message so we know where you are."

"Okay."

Rose remained standing in the path as they left her.

Snowdrop and Arley followed the forest path away from the treehouses, past the split where another trail headed to Woodglen, and around to the barn.

"Is this where we came through yesterday?" he asked.

"Yes. I saw two brown horses." As she said it, she spotted them out in the meadow. They looked up and trotted over, stopping a few paces away and sniffing the air as they stepped from one hoof to the other.

"You want to try mounting one?" Snowdrop asked.

"Not a chance."

Snowdrop stopped herself from reaching for the bulbs. They were there if she needed them but maybe she could do this without them. She reached out with her magic and found the two horses immediately—their curiosity about her and Arley, and wondering why she had come to see them since she hadn't brought any apples. They were grateful they could stay with the fairies after an encounter with coyotes at the edge of the mountains. They were young stallions and they were disappointed Lady and Bird had left so quickly.

Snowdrop smirked. Good thing Joe's horses had returned to Woods Rest.

She tried to communicate back to the stallions, asking how they'd feel about carrying a rider. The horses stepped closer, sniffing her and Arley from their ears to their hands.

"I think they might take us," Snowdrop said quietly.

"Yeah?"

"If we bring apples. Give me a boost."

She patted one horse's neck and smoothed her hands along his side, and he stilled. He felt calm to her. Arley bent to make a step with his hands and hoisted her up.

The horse had a moment of fear but calmed again. He stepped a few times and Snowdrop balanced on his back. "Okay?" she asked. He snorted and tossed his head.

After they tested out Arley sitting on the other horse, they went to the supply shed for blankets and basic supplies for the ride, and they filled a sack with apples. They walked back to the barn.

"Ya know," Arley said, "I think you've won."

"Won what?"

"Our bet."

"What bet?"

"Don't ya remember? The one where you bet me you could learn to ride a horse better than me, with or without magic."

"Oh, that bet." Snowdrop shook her head, smiling.

"So?" he asked.

"So what?"

"You never told me what you wanted if you won."

"Oh." Snowdrop stopped outside the barn. The breeze blew across the meadow, carrying with it the damp leafy scent of the coming autumn. In the quiet afternoon, the birds stayed in their trees. She squinted against the sun as she regarded Arley. His arms were full of the sack of apples.

"I think I'll take a kiss," she said.

Arley's eyes widened. Before he could speak, she stepped forward and pressed her lips to his. She stepped away just as fast.

He fumbled with the apples, catching the bag again before he dropped it.

"Now that I've had my prize," she said, "let's go for a ride."

Six Moons Later

SNOWDROP CRINGED. "THIS IS COFFEE?"

"I told ya it tastes like crap."

She inhaled deeply. How could it smell so divine and taste so bitter? She had another sip. "I think it's growing on me."

"Do ya *want* to like it?" Arley asked. "Why bother tryin' when it costs a fortune for a single cup?"

"It makes me feel sophisticated." Outside the tall window beside their table, the gray ocean frothed with whitecaps. Even in winter, the Inn at Cliffside was her favorite place to stay. "Besides, the price will go down once we have a steady supply of it."

"Do ya plan to smuggle it? We don't have any room in the cart."

"We'll get a different cart. We'll give up the mail route and run a coffee delivery service instead. Or we can drive two carts. I'm a much better driver now."

"You are. But I'd miss sitting beside ya."

Snowdrop melted. "Me too." She reached across the table for his hand. In six moons she'd become as sappy as her brother and Rose.

"We'd need our own horses if we became coffee merchants," Arley said—as if he actually would become a coffee trader simply so she could drink coffee.

"Do you think Farmer Joe would sell Lady and Bird yet?"

"He might. He's nearing time to retire."

Farmer Joe had promised he'd offer them to Arley first. All she had to do was be patient.

Nem glided into the dining room carrying a giant tray of dishes piled with food. They helped her unload one after another—fluffy scrambled chicken eggs filled with cream cheese and sprinkled with early spring chives, thick slices of fresh bread and a pot of plum jam, sautéed mushrooms with onions and hothouse peppers and tomatoes, strawberries with whipped cream. Breakfast at the inn truly was a culinary masterpiece.

Nem put aside the tray and slid into the seat beside Snowdrop. "What do you think of the coffee?"

"Undecided."

"Well Kate is ecstatic. Says the Inn at Cliffside will be the only establishment on this end of the continent serving authentic Norlian coffee. She's already sold a dozen cups this morning."

Around the dining room, the other guests enjoyed their breakfasts and a few sipped from porcelain cups, but Snowdrop couldn't tell if they had coffee or tea.

The dining room was the fanciest room she'd ever seen. Each table had a cloth covering it and trailing onto the parquet floor (the things humans liked were so strange!) and a candle in the center that had been lit for dinner last night, when it was dark. The room had floor-to-ceiling windows, with ironwork forming diamond-shaped panes for the glass, that faced out over a sprawling orchard with the sea beyond. If she came down early enough, she could watch the sun rise over the ocean. The panes of glass broke the pink and gold dawn into sparkling patterns.

The orchard had every fruit and nut imaginable. It was more impressive even than the orchard the fairies tended at their enclave. Of course, a fairy had planted all the trees—Grape Hyacinth's sister. Humans couldn't grow anything so well, although they did seem to be pruning the trees properly and keeping the deer away.

Snowdrop was glad she and Arley got to visit Cliffside. At the Council of Villages meeting last autumn, they'd met the person who ran the continent's mail service. The flourishing trade and greater freedoms that followed the end of the human monarchy had increased travel across the continent and as a consequence, the number of letters and packages needing delivery had increased. And without the king's taxes, the humans actually had disposable income—hence even more packages traveling across the land. When Snowdrop learned she could be paid to hang out with a team of horses and drive a mail cart up and down the forest road, she signed right up. Of course, she wouldn't have done it if Arley hadn't signed up too.

Since the winter solstice they'd driven the route three times. It took about a moon to do the loop: north from Woodglen all the way to Nor Bay, then south along the coast to Cliffside and west back to the forest road and Woodglen. She'd seen and learned so much. She'd had boiled peanuts (weird) and human fermented cabbage (much tangier than the fairies' version), and she was adept at driving the horses with human reins or her magic.

Between trips they stayed with the fairies in the woods. She'd pitched in with the kitchen crew several times, and she and Val had become friends. They'd begun planning an event to raise funds to go to the families Oleander had harmed. This summer they would host a human-style formal dinner in the fairies' clearing, with tablecloths and metal utensils and everything. They were researching the humans' favorite dishes and would make a grand meal served on plates, one per person, instead of in the fairies' usual communal style. So far they were calling the event The Human Banquet, but Rose cringed every time she heard it and Dustan said they needed a classier name.

And during one of their stays, she and Arley had been helping out with the stable chores, and Clover had asked him about the humans' use of verbal and touch commands with horses. Even though ey could communicate with all horses, ey was curious about the technique and if horses accustomed to being ridden by humans preferred the humans' method. So Arley had trained Snowdrop and Clover to use human commands to ride horses.

Arley had used Chipper and Knotly, the mail horses assigned to Snowdrop's route, to teach them. Once they could trot around the pasture without any fairy magic, Clover had asked the horses about it. Clover said they seemed to prefer the familiar method when they were working, although they liked fairy communication too. When ey was in the barn with them, they asked eir about apples and keeping flies off and many other topics.

Along the mail route, Snowdrop and Arley visited all their favorite people—Edna and Ruth in Woods Rest, the Farnvilles in Woods End, and Fina, now in Mountain Rest. The first time Snowdrop knocked on Fina's door to hand her a letter in person, Fina had hugged her so hard she might have cracked a rib. Fina had been living in Mountain Rest only a moon and had been homesick but determined not to give up on her plan to live in the city.

At the end of the mail loop, they saw Nem and her family in Cliffside on the journey south. They could stay with Nem's family at their house on the cliff, but Kate always offered a room at the inn. And Snowdrop loved the inn. The beds were as soft as Mrs. Farnville's.

Arley was going to finish the eggs if she didn't start eating.

"We'll see you this evening, right?" she asked Nem, pulling the plate of eggs out of his reach.

"Yes. Burne found the . . . the manka board?"

"Mancala."

"Where did you see this game again?"

"They have a board in the pub in Woods Rest. But we saw people playing in Nor Bay and learned the rules, and I've been wanting to play ever since."

"Well Burne and Gray are expecting us for game night. It'll be fun. I'd better get back to the kitchen." Nem paused and added, "I'm glad you're here every moon," before hurrying away.

Snowdrop piled her plate with breakfast and dug in.

"We haven't found Trunk and Dirt," she said between bites. She and Arley had hoped to thank the boars for helping them last fall but they'd seen no sign of them around the forest.

Arley leaned back in his seat, staring out the windows. "They might come around now spring is near. They were prob'ly lyin' low for the winter. Don't worry, love. We'll see them again."

She popped a strawberry in her mouth and studied him. He was staring out at the sea. He had a blue and green plaid shirt on today, echoing the colors of the ocean and forest. She wanted to crawl across the table and hug him but the food was in the way. He turned to her and she blushed.

"What's that about, princess?" he said with a grin.

"Nothing."

"Right." He smirked.

"Do you want to sign on for another trip with the mail?"

"Sure."

"Even if the farm wants you back?"

"What would you do in Woods Rest if I were farmin'?"

"I could find something."

Arley's chair tipped forward and landed on all four legs. "Doesn't much matter to me what I'm doin' as long as you're around."

She looked down and grinned. "Okay."

"You still like life on the road?"

"I like tumbling you in the back of the wagon."

Several heads turned toward them. Arley smothered a laugh. "Quiet, love. They'll start to wonder what their taxes are payin' us for."

"We deliver the mail," she whispered. "Why do they care what we do between times?"

But Arley only laughed harder.

"I like life on the road."

"You never think of stayin' in the forest with the fairies?"

"What would you do if we lived in the forest?"

He shrugged. "Lie about all day and let you pay the bills."

"Fairies don't pay bills."

"Lie about and let you dote on me and bring me breakfast in bed. Like your brother and Rose."

"Dustan is lazy as a cat in the sun. I think Rose likes him that way."

"You don't?"

She wrinkled her nose at him. "You wouldn't be content lazing about like my brother."

"Nah, prob'ly not. But if you wanted to live in the forest, we could make it work."

It was tempting. For so long all she had wanted was to fit in among the fairies and to have a position on one of the work crews and the respect of her peers. Since Oleander's passing, the fairies had been different toward her—or maybe she saw things differently. More of them smiled at her, and when she and Arley had been at the enclave on the full moon before the solstice, she'd taken him to the fairy dance and had no shortage of partners—although after a while she'd wanted the comfort of dancing in Arley's familiar arms. And once they were dancing together, Arley had whispered that she'd rescued him from Petunia's groping hands.

But even though she felt welcome in the enclave, she wanted to see more of the world. She had so many seasons to make up for. And she wanted to see her friends all around the continent. Nem was right—seeing her every moon felt right.

Oleander had been laid to rest. But her two older brothers had disappeared into the swamps near Tidal Creek. What were they doing? How did they get by without magic? Since last autumn, no reports had come of crops dying or animals disappearing. Hopefully they were making their way without hurting anyone else.

When they finished every bite of food, they stacked the empty dishes and left the table.

"I still feel bad leaving all our dirty dishes," Snowdrop said.

"That's just how humans do it."

"Humans are so weird."

He shook his head. "Let's go for a walk. Nem told me about something to see in the woods."

The dining room had a door out onto a wide terrace. In the warmer moons, patrons could eat outside, but the wind was blustery this early in the spring. Arley took her hand and hurried her down to the sheltered orchard where they set off across the grass. Forest surrounded the inn on three sides and Arley headed south toward the tree line.

As the breeze tossed her hair she absentmindedly turned it green like the grass, then purple like the plums that would ripen here in several moons' time. The buds were appearing on the boughs. Arley glanced over so she made herself invisible and he shook his head and squeezed her hand.

In the moons after the council meeting, she and Larkspur had met for a few more magic lessons. But once she began to succeed without her snowdrop bulbs, the magic had come more and more easily. Just before the solstice, she'd planted the last bulb with its fellows in the shade of the oak trees at the north entrance to the caverns. The bulbs had been dormant for the winter, but she'd felt them preparing to sprout roots and flowers and leaves in the coming spring. She wanted each one to have the soil and water it needed. She didn't need to keep one with her.

As they neared the forest, the tang of damp earth and new growth filled the air. Clumps of green fronds bordered the trees and Snowdrop smiled—someone had planted a whole lot of grape hyacinths in Cliffside for Gray to use, probably his sister.

Here at the edge of the orchard, though, in addition to the clumps of grape hyacinths, every other spring bulb she could think of waited beneath the grass. Green-yellow spears broke the soil, ready to shoot up and open into daffodils, and the tips of frosty green tulips were a hand's width tall. Starflowers and bloodroot dotted the grass around the roots.

A swirling breeze danced through the trees and wrapped

through her and she inhaled suddenly, scanning the forest floor and letting go of Arley's hand as she stepped further into the forest. Inside the first row of trees she spotted them.

Snowdrops.

She dropped to her knees and bent close. The tiny white blooms hung from their delicate green stems like drops of water, all clustered together. She ran her fingers lightly over the top of the greens and felt laughter and joy at spring coming again. Deeper in the forest were more blooms, some closed and others opening to expose the green, lacy inner petals. A few of the larger variety of snowdrop towered two hands tall. They had bell-like blossoms with pointed green tips.

Snowdrop sat on her heels and breathed in all the new life and hope. She met Arley's gaze.

"Do you think mine are blooming at home right now?"

"Don't worry, princess. Nem said the coastal climate stretches the warm season here. Everything blooms earlier."

"But mine will bloom soon."

"How about we leave tomorrow? That way you won't miss it."

She stood and jumped into his arms. He held her until she'd willed away her tears.

As they headed back to the inn, a seagull cried overhead. The cry went on, long enough that they both peered up. A few gulls circled in the sky over the cliffs and the sea.

"That one's carryin' something," Arley said, pointing.

Snowdrop groaned. Her brother and Rose and their little avian minions had a knack for finding her the moment she re-entered their home range.

Arley grinned. "What do you think they've sent this time? More sex nuts?"

"Hopefully not. Those were horrible."

"Aww, they weren't so bad if you held your breath when ya ate them. What were they called again?"

"Ginkgo. They're from the eastern isles."

"Well I didn't mind them. Although I'm not sure they did much to help things down below."

"You don't need help down below."

"Thanks, princess."

"Maybe it's cookies or more of that granola."

"Sent all the way here by bird?"

Snowdrop frowned. "I guess not."

"Maybe it's more of that magical tea that—"

The seagull swooped in and stumbled, landing on the grass by the terrace, dropping its cargo as it did. It squawked and began preening its feathers.

"Don't talk about that tea," Snowdrop mumbled.

He pecked a kiss behind her ear but stopped his teasing. "I'll go find our courier a biscuit."

As Arley headed inside, Snowdrop picked up the parcel and checked in with the bird. It was intent on its feathers, excited for the biscuit, and ready to sleep after the long flight up the coast. As soon as Arley returned, it took its reward and swooped up to the top of the inn to find a roost.

"You open it?" Arley asked.

"I was scared to open it in public."

"Good thinking. Let's go in."

Back in their room, they sat side by side on the bedspread. Morning sunlight shone in the tall windows through gauzy curtains and a patch of it landed in the center of the bed. From the third-floor room, they had a view over the patio to the ocean. Large oil paintings of landscapes and flowers in gilt frames hung on the walls over shiny blue wallpaper. Staying here was like being human royalty, as far as Snowdrop could tell.

Snowdrop untied the ribbon holding the parcel closed. She unwrapped the fabric and several tubes fell out onto the bed.

Arley picked up a tube. They were flattened cylinders of a flexible material with a spout on one end. "Are they toothpaste?" Arley asked, squeezing.

"Take the cap off the spout."

He plucked the cap off and squeezed and a ribbon of goo streamed onto his fingertips.

Snowdrop stared. "They sent a seagull all this way with lubricant?"

The squiggle of goo glowed blue. And then green.

Arley leaned in. "It changes colors."

"But that's pointless—"

"It's getting hot." It faded to yellow and warmed to orange before turning back to blue. "Aaaaand it's cold again." He pulled out a kerchief to wipe it off.

Snowdrop rubbed her forehead. She picked up another tube. "This one's labeled 'peppermint.'"

"Are we supposed to eat it?"

"I don't think so. Aloe's bitter." She squeezed a little onto her finger. "It kind of tingles." It lit up, sparkling with green lights.

She held out her finger and Arley swiped a bit off and sniffed it. "Huh."

The next tube let out a horrible wail when she opened it. Arley jumped back.

"Aaaaah-eeeeeee," moaned the tube.

"What in the skies is that?" he asked.

"Musical lubricant?"

"What did the music come from, a whale?"

Snowdrop considered. "My guess is it started as birdsong and it's gone bad. Imagine how it would sound if it were sped up."

Arley lifted his brow. "I can see that being nice. Adds some woodland atmosphere to your activities."

"You could just tumble in the woods."

"What if it's rainin'? Or if you're so loud you scare the birds away?"

"We're not *that* loud."

"Other folks might be." He squirted more of the heated rainbow lube on his hand. "I don't need lube that changes colors. But . . . I'm not against using it."

Snowdrop arched an eyebrow.

"I mean, that poor gull carried this package all the way here. Be a shame to take it all the way back to the enclave tomorrow without even trying it."

"You think?"

"And it seems like it would work just as well as the plain kind. Unless you're against sparkles and rainbows."

She smiled. "I'm fine with sparkles and rainbows."

"We've got a few hours until game night."

"And?"

"I have an idea." He held up his hand to show her. He had two blobs of lube on it, one blue and the other yellow. "It comes out of the tube blue. So if I time things right, I could have a few colors goin' at once."

She waited.

"So I could paint a picture on ya."

"On me?"

"Yeah. Take your clothes off."

"*You* take your clothes off."

Arley dropped the tube on the bed, wiped his hand, unbuttoned his top button, and whipped his shirt over his head in one smooth motion.

Snowdrop stared. "Did you practice doing that?"

"Maybe." He unbuttoned his trousers and stood to push them down until he stood in front of her completely naked. He didn't have an erection. Not yet, anyway. "You checkin' me out, princess?"

"Just seeing how things stand." She undid two buttons, crossed her arms, and pulled her own shirt over her head, tossing it away and leaving her topless. She pointedly looked at his penis again before meeting his gaze.

"No fair," Arley said with a mock frown, shielding himself with his hand. "You know seein' ya makes me hard. And you're the one who practiced, flingin' your shirt off like it's on fire."

She grinned coyly and slipped her pants off. "So," she said, leaning back on her hands until the sunlight fell on her chest. She shook back her hair so it glowed in the light. "Where do you want to do this painting?"

"Right there's fine," Arley rasped out.

"But what do you want to use as a canvas?" she said and batted her eyelashes innocently.

"Aww, princess, cut it out," he said and fell onto the bed, pulling her farther on until she lay beside him. "You know you're torturin' me with all that seduction stuff."

She smiled up at him as he leaned over her on his elbow. "I know," she said.

"You minx. I think ya better roll over to give me half a chance of actually paintin' something before I'm too distracted to function."

Snowdrop kept smiling as she rolled onto her belly, away from the sunlight. She rested her head on her arms and closed her eyes.

"Can I sit on you?" Arley asked, rustling beside her.

"Sure."

His skin brushed against her hip and he straddled her and sat lightly on her bottom with his knees hugging her. He brushed her hair to one side, clearing it off her back. A few beats later his fingers smeared the cold gel onto her skin. She shivered but it warmed quickly, although each new dab of it was as cold as the first. The cycles from cold to hot and back to cold were kind of entrancing. Maybe the fairy inventors were on to something. Arley smushed it around, first making broad strokes across her middle with several fingers and then using one finger to draw something.

"Okay," he said after a few minutes, and he climbed off.

She twisted her chin over her shoulder but couldn't see any of her back.

"Come by the mirror." Arley gave her a hand.

A full-length mirror in a gilt frame hung beside the wash basin.

Snowdrop turned and looked. Glowing colors covered her entire back: a broad swath of orange on top, a strip of purple below, and vertical blue strokes on the bottom. Between the purple and blue was a green smudge.

"Wait for it," Arley said as the colors transitioned. They changed again

Snowdrop gasped. "It's us!" Arley grinned. The bottom color had turned yellow like the wheat fields north of the forest, while the next layer had become the green hills and the top was the wide blue sky. The smudge in the middle was supposed to be their wagon.

Snowdrop pulled him into a hug but squealed a protest when his arm moved over the painting. He carefully placed one hand above her bottom and the other on her nape as she leaned on his chest and twisted to watch the painting cycle through its colors.

"I should've loaded the wagon up with coffee," Arley said after a minute.

She snaked her arms around him and held him tight. He didn't have an erection, as far as she could tell, and for some reason that made her blink back tears—they could hang around their bedroom naked and paint pictures with magical lubricant and he seemed content just being there with her.

"You don't have any brown color," she said into his neck.

"I do now—the whole thing's turnin' brown."

She glanced back and grimaced. "It must be drying out."

He let go of her. "I'll get you—"

"Wait." She took his hand and led him toward a window. "Watch this." Snowdrop turned her back into the sunlight. The smears across her back tightened and burned off with a tiny sizzle.

"Skies, what was that?" Arley asked, smoothing his hand down her newly bare skin. He leaned in and kissed her shoulder.

"It's self-cleaning," she said. "Sunlight makes it dry up and fall off."

"Huh. How do the fairies manage that?"

"Slug goo."

He winced. "Slug goo? But you put it inside your—"

"It's only a tiny bit," Snowdrop said. "And it's all natural."

"Well it's *your* vagina." He stroked along the curve of her spine and kissed her shoulder again.

"We've still got a few hours before game night," she said.

"Yeah?"

Her back was hot in the sun but she liked it, and she liked the rhythmic motion of his hand on her hot skin.

"And we've got a lot of lube."

His hand stilled.

She leaned back far enough to see his warm brown eyes. "I love you," she said quietly.

"Love you too."

"Want to use up some of those tubes Rose sent?"

He smiled. "Lead the way, princess."

A Note from the Author

DEAR READER,

Thank you so much for reading *The Magic Seeker*. I've been gravitating toward writing characters on the asexual spectrum, and with Snowdrop, I wanted to write a character who doesn't feel sexual attraction at all. This goal was largely because I was exploring my own identity and what I do and don't feel. I also wanted the book to be consistent with the rest of the series in terms of "steaminess." My reading on asexuality has led me to believe an ace person might have a libido, feel other types of attraction, and choose to have sex, so these were guidelines I used in developing Snowdrop and Arley's relationship. But the language and labels related to asexuality can seem complex and I never feel certain I'm using them correctly. I welcome other interpretations of my character's identity ("death of the author" and all that ☺).

I love writing stories in my cozy fantasy world, and I hope you enjoy reading them. I appreciate any online ratings and reviews to help other readers with similar interests find the book. And I extra appreciate the occasional email to tell me you like my stories (it's so encouraging) or to share fan art of my characters (so cool!), so thank you for those.

The Magic Seeker is a bit of a turning point as all three villains from *The Forest Bride* have now been dispatched with! Many times I have rued the haphazard plot I created in *The Forest Bride* with all its non-cozy elements that I had to rectify: from misogynistic guards to oppressed mermaids to grieving mothers to (supposedly) dead children. But *The Forest Bride* also gave me conflicts to solve, which was a huge help as I worked to improve my writing. I plan to continue writing novels in this world but start a new series. The next book is tentatively titled *Sourdough and Sweethearts* and features a human bread baker with impostor syndrome and a fairy cheesemaker who only wanted some starter for her crackers, not to start a village rivalry. I may miss my usual March equinox launch date but still hope to have the book out in 2027.

You can subscribe to my email list at https://janebuehler.com for an email when the new book is available. I send quarterly emails plus a few more when I have a new book. When you subscribe, I'll send a link to some bonus material! This now includes artwork, a recipe, a link to an explicit nature video (!), and, just added, a fairy safety brochure on magical lubricants.

Sincerely,

Emily Jane ♡

Acknowledgments

Thank you to all my readers. I appreciate you whether you've just now taken a chance on a new author or followed me along on this journey from the start.

I had three fabulous beta readers for *The Magic Seeker*: Angie M., as always your feedback was so insightful and helped me tackle the more difficult parts of the story instead of glossing them over. Thank you to Ashley G., who nudged me into rewriting my least favorite scene and helped me write a richer and more fulfilling story. And thank you to Autumn Brown at Write & Whimsy Book Editing (https://autumnbrownux.com), who offered helpful suggestions and as always was lovely to work with.

Thank you to Christy R., Grace C., and Erin C. for always being there with feedback on blurbs and ads.

And finally, as always, I'm grateful to have Kelly Urgan (https://www.editegrity.com) as my editor and Cory Podielski (https://podielski.com/) as my cover designer.

About the Author

EMILY JANE BUEHLER WAS ADRIFT for many years before real-izing she wanted to work with words. She published two non-fiction books—one on the science and craft of baking bread, the other a memoir of her bicycle trip from New Jersey to Oregon—before venturing into fiction. She now writes cozy fantasy romance: lighthearted stories that focus on a protagonist finding their courage and happiness, as opposed to plots with a lot of fighting and darkness. She also copyedits (mostly science material) and teaches bread-making classes.

Emily lives in Hillsborough, North Carolina, with a bossy cat named Coco. Her favorite things include letters sent through the mail, her fair-trade wool leg warmers, and chocolate cake with frosting. She is passionate about living waste free and supporting locally owned businesses.

Emily publishes fiction using her middle name, Jane.